Legacy of Dragons: Emergence

T.D. Raufson

Copyright © 2013 by T.D. Raufson
Cover Illustration Copyright © 2013 by Rio Sirah
Cover Photography by Bodhi Tree Photography
Makeup/Body Art by Lynn Cole Body Art with Rio Sirah
Cover Model Jessica Moss
Editing by Carrie Woods, Susan Basham, David Thurmond

All rights reserved. This book or any portion thereof may not be reproduced or used in any manner whatsoever without the express written permission of the publisher except for the use of brief quotations in a book review.

Printed in the United States of America
First Printing, 2013
ISBN 0-9888635-0-2
ISBN-13: 9780988863507

Twin Cedars Enterprises
twincedarsenterprises@gmail.com

DEDICATION

To Shirley Nelson who lit the fire, Karla Horner who fanned the flames and Susan who maintained the boiler for all these years.

CONTENTS

	Acknowledgments	i
1	Sunset on an Era	1
2	Dawn of a New Age	22
3	Chaos of Birth	58
4	An Unnatural Truce	81
5	Peace of Silence	95
6	The Conclave	114
7	Betrayal	148
8	Ambassador of the Dragons	185

ACKNOWLEDGMENTS

Although it is easy to see a novel as an individual effort, I can tell you that I could not have completed this one without the help of an extraordinary band of brothers. I use that phrase because I see them all in that way when it comes to my writing.

Above all others, my wife has listened to me go on for days about the characters, the plots, the ideas and the worries, probably so much that she could have written this book herself. She is in my dedication because she has manned a difficult station for many years and deserves much of the credit for this books completion. Susan, thank you for supporting the craziness that is my life as a writer.

No book ever comes together without the assistance of a cadre of readers, editors, confidants and coerced compatriots. This list is by no means complete but those listed here have been right beside me along this road. First, Mike and Jodie, you have to know that your initial reads and edits were the foundation of my work, without that support this would not be possible. Next, Chris, Lisa, Christopher and Courtney, you will never realize how important your sanctuary was to my sanity. Without those moments of peace in my crazy world I could not have reached this point. Joe, John, Steven, Amy, Mike, Angie, Eric, Deb, Grant, Bruce, Jeff and Jason, your support as initial readers and supportive friends and family cannot be over appreciated. To the staff of Rib N Loin where I spent over a year writing at lunch most days, thanks for understanding that I really just needed a quiet place to sit and write.

This story first saw the light of day in a friends living room among the members of my writer's group as an idea for a short story. Becky, Ryan and again my wife Susan, helped me dig into places I think we all would rather never visit again. In those enjoyable and sometimes difficult exercises you all helped me to find a voice for emotions I hope I have captured a little of here. Your opinions and ideas inspired me.

Thanks to Lynn Cole of Lynn Cole Body Art, Grace Moss of Bodhi Tree Photography, Rio Sirah and Jessica Moss for the fantastic cover art on this book. You all really helped to breathe life into this story. See you soon for the next cover.

It is easy as a writer to tell yourself that you don't need an editor. It is easy to believe that you have the right pacing and depth to every scene. But most often you are too close to the project to really see everything. That is why I must thank Carrie Woods, my editor, for helping me see the places where my scenes came short, or I needed more emotion. Thanks for bringing the best out of this novel so I can share it with everyone. Also, I must thank David Thurmond and Susan for their additional assistance with editing my final draft. They walked a difficult path and defended the heroic comma at all costs. All of the remaining errors in this text are because of my arrogance or ignorance.

I'm sure there are others who deserve mention. I know I am surrounded by people who have listened to me go on and on about my writing. I thank you all for your patience, advice and support. You may never have known the simple word or phrase you shared with me that gave me the idea or the strength to write it. This is not a lonely journey. I have walked this path with you all and you have molded this as much as I have. To you all I give a heartfelt,

Thank You!

CHAPTER 1 - SUNSET ON AN ERA

June 20, 2012 – 1940 EDT – Signal Mountain, Tennessee.

Melissa ran a finger over the disguised lock on the copper clad box that was the only thing holding the beast of change at bay. Ivory claws dug into the copper at the two front corners as if the intricate dragon hammered into the cover was going to rip the ancient box open. Hammered scale work ran up the forelegs of the embossed dragon to its wing roots. Wings opened behind the relief, creating the illusion of darkness plunging into the night's void behind the dragon. Mountains hammered on the front side of the box rose up from the valley on either side of a village situated at the cove of the valley in front of a small lake. The scene on the ground was peaceful, but Melissa couldn't decide if the dragon and the contents he protected in the box portended doom.

The intricately hammered neck of the dragon projected forward from the shoulders with sharp neck ridges jutting up from the metal cladding like a saw blade. The head crested the box's cover at the edge where ivory horns thrust into the air and emerald eyes stared down onto the village. The master metalwork disguised the hinge in the neck behind its horns and the keyhole in the nostril so that the latch and lock were lost in the intricate artwork. Yet again, for an uncounted number of times, her finger passed over the lock. She eyed the key she was holding in her left hand and rubbed the matching metalwork between her fingers. She had been holding the key so long that it was warm to the touch, and she wondered tangentially if she could melt the key from worry.

Her grandmother, who yet again drew her wandering attention back to the lock, the box, and her duty, seemed to be standing over her shoulder even now. Melissa glanced up to look out across the back lawn into the slowly dropping sun at the small headstone and mound of soil they had carefully placed that day. A full day's sorrow settled back into her soul. That the service was exactly what Helena had asked for did little to soothe her.

The mound of dirt was neither the beginning, nor the end of this very long day. The aged metal box that had come with the will, the deed to the estate, and the unimaginable responsibility for her 21 years, demanded her attention. It accused her of avoiding her promise to the overly nervous lawyer that had left it with her. Again, she fingered the key that he had squeezed into her hand as he had finished the reading.

She whined to the empty room. "Why me? Why did she leave all of this to me?"

The question was rhetorical. She knew there was no stability in her father. He would liquidate it all and pour the money into the same financial pit he had already *invested* their family fortune. But, that was still no reason to put all of this on her young shoulders. She couldn't even pick a major, how could she run an estate and whatever else the box demanded?

She pushed the accusing box away from her on the blotter and looked up at the sun that refused to set. Nothing would make this horrible day end. If everything remained the same, and this day was allowed to continue, it would be nothing less than catastrophic.

The large grandfather clock in the foyer began to chime the hour. She listened to the deep tones, counting. When it reached eight and stopped, she sighed. The old house was empty without her grandmother, and yet she could still feel her in every corner of the library and emanating from every book surrounding her. It was comforting, and Melissa would have been happy to spend the rest of her life in the room among her grandmother's legacy.

The door behind her swung open, chasing the peaceful moment away. Charles, her grandmother's butler, slipped into the room with a silver tray and the Royal Albert tea set. To say that Charles slipped anywhere was to be polite. He tried, but he was too large, at six feet four, to be very stealthy. He was an excellent butler, trained by his father and his entire family to carry on the ancient tradition of caring for nobility, but in Melissa's mind he did not fit the role. He sat the tea set down and poured the steaming liquid into a single cup. The delicate aroma of peaches surrounded her.

"Charles, what is this, the longest day in history?" she grumbled playfully at him.

"No, Miss, just the year."

She stared at him. The formality of his response stunned her a little. She could still see the little boy she had grown up with in the back garden and felt a little offended at his formal response. He looked back at her and motioned toward the tea.

"I knew you had some work to complete, and I thought you might like some tea. The guests have all left."

Melissa leaned back and looked at Charles again, and it was if she was seeing him for the first time in years. Her last real memory of him was when she watched him carry his high school football team to the championship. She could not deny that she had a crush on him back then, but she had left for Spain the next week, and he had left for boot camp the next summer. Their lives had not really intersected again until that moment.

She had been away, engrossed in school, when he unexpectedly came home from the war and took over for his father. She remembered being disappointed, in the passing way that high school girls are, because she always thought he was meant for more. She liked the image of Charles the warrior. As she looked at him in the passing moment between them, she still saw him that way.

The war, or more likely the drama that had forced him back into the duties he had run from originally, had carved a permanent frown into a face she remembered as gentle. The change did not conflict with his duties; in fact, it made him exactly the kind of butler she wanted at her door. But, she did miss his smile. No matter how hard he tried to live up to his father, though, he could never hide the fact that he just didn't fit serving tea among the antiques in the old manor. He looked like a puzzle piece forced into place because it should fit. With that last passing thought, she found herself smiling and allowed a quiet laugh to escape.

"Did I make a joke, Miss?"

"No, not intentionally." She paused. "Do you remember the last time we just talked?"

"Yes, Miss. It was the weekend you left for Spain."

She nodded. "It's been a while hasn't it?"

"A lifetime, Miss." His words verified how he saw the years he had spent serving her grandmother since coming back from Iraq.

Her grandmother had refused to talk about it, but Melissa knew there was more under the surface of that story. Melissa had not thought about it in years. Apparently, Charles still did.

"I've missed those conversations. Would you consider joining me for a little tea? I could use the company."

"I'm sorry, Miss, but I thought you had work to complete. It would not be appropriate anyway." He smiled professionally and stepped back into his place.

"Yes, of course."

She could not ignore the disappointment his answer had caused, but it was part of being the mistress of this house. She sat back down in the chair and pulled the box toward her. This relationship was not going to work for her if her new position was going to keep them from being friends. There were certain barriers one maintained no matter how lonely, confused, and in need of a friend one felt. Dismissed, he turned and left her alone with her duty. She scowled at the box.

Beyond the French doors, the sun refused to drop below the long green lawn that led down to the overlook, the valley that plunged away from the edge, and the new grave that surmounted it. She took the cup of tea Charles had poured for her and sipped the perfectly prepared enchanted peach white tea. The aroma and flavor stirred memories of her grandmother writing her novels at the desk. A few tears dripped from her cheeks as she stared into the setting sun. She sipped her tea.

The chime of the clock at the bottom of the hour forced her from the warmth of the tea and back to her duties. Melissa set the cup down on the tray and placed both hands on the top of the box. There were conditions to her inheritance. In the box, she would find one of her grandmother's journals with important instructions for her to follow. Like a test she had not studied for, Melissa braced for the contents of the box, inserting the key into the lock that held back what she had been avoiding. Why had she let the lawyer talk her into this? Why had she signed the man's forms? She wished she had just told him no. None of this would be her problem if she had just told him she was not interested. Was it even possible to turn down an inheritance?

She took a deep breath and pushed it back out before turning the key in the lock. A quiet, anticlimactic click filled the room as she lifted the lid.

Inside, among a stack of things that had belonged to her grandmother, was the small crystal encrusted claw on a heavy gold chain her grandmother had always worn around her neck. It was a little macabre, but Melissa could not remember a time it was not with her, and, because of its constant presence, she smiled at the memories the amulet unearthed. The crimson crystals seemed to grow from the black three-talon claw and shimmered in the sunlight reminding Melissa of the day she and Helena had walked together along the overlook just before Melissa had started college. Her grandmother had scolded her for considering not continuing her education. Mixed with the pleasure of that memory was a little anger that she had taken that advice now. The years she had lost with her grandmother seemed too large a price for what she had learned.

She picked up the amulet, clutching it in her left hand. A warm tingle ran up her arm, and the memory of her grandmother intensified. The stones throbbed in her palm. She blinked and looked at the talisman. Suppressed tears rushed down her cheeks, and it took her a moment to recover from the flood of emotions. When she had recovered a little, she set the amulet aside with trembling hands. If everything in the box had the same effect, she would never get through this.

Below the amulet was her grandmother's favorite pen. At the bottom of the box, she found the cause of her current turmoil. A small, leather-bound journal with no indication of what it contained waited for her. It was new compared to other journals filed on the shelves around her. Her grandmother was never without one, and by the time each journal was filed onto the shelves, it was worn and ragged. This one was so new that the cover was still stiff, and the binding popped as she opened it and turned to the first page.

Her grandmother's neat script filled the page. Melissa started to cry, again, but she forced the tears back and read.

Melissa,

You have always been a blessing to me, and I've told you more than once how very special you are. Remember when I told you there was something inside of you that made you that way? I wanted to explain what I meant before I died. I have run out of time to tell you everything. I thought I could handle it a bit longer and it was important that I be with you, to help you with what is about to happen. This sickness came upon me before I could finish my research.

I had to be sure about it. You see, it involves our true legacy, and it is far more serious than I once believed. I think I've collected everything here, but I'm afraid it may be too late. Please read this as soon as possible. I've lost track of the time.

You have to read this and follow the instructions before sunset on the solstice this year. If you do not, the consequences to this world will be dire. It is imperative that you take my place and complete the ritual.

Do not talk to anyone about this. Do not let them near this journal. Trust Charles. More than anything, do not trust anyone in our family, especially the males.

You asked me about Charles a few years ago, and I owe you an explanation. I can never explain completely, but I brought him back from the war to save him. I know that I cost him his career, but his life is far more important than that.

If you succeed, and I do hope that you do; I expect you will understand this all better. Good luck and do not be distracted by anyone.

Helena.

The next pages explained her family history. She started to read the very dry descriptions and found herself nodding off. If she were going to read it all that night, she would need more tea, and she was not going to waste a perfect cup of tea on that.

Melissa closed the journal, placed it back in the box and sat back in her chair. A long deep sigh exited her chest, and she closed her eyes. She was not sure she could take anything else today. She didn't have the energy to face it. In one day, she had gone from a simple college student to a landowner. Now her grandmother was leaving her secret instructions she had to deal with before the solstice. She certainly didn't feel up to this challenge.

She opened her eyes and glared through new tears at the chest and the journal hidden in it. She closed and locked the box and pushed it away from her. She could not take any more. She opened the top drawer of the desk and started to put the box away but paused to flip through the calendar on the desk when the door behind her flew open.

Nicklaus, her cousin, stepped through the doorway and into the library as if he owned the estate. A tremor of anger slipped across her face, but she quickly controlled it. Nicklaus had been roaming the estate with her for as long as she could remember. She was not in the mood to deal with him today and he seemed agitated. The aroma of cigars and bourbon hung around him like his attitude, and she knew he had been talking to her father.

"Mel, what is this that I hear about your father? Why was he excluded from his mother's will?"

The big family secret was now out.

"Nick, I'm not going over this with you right now. I have things to do and I'm tired. Thanks for coming to the funeral, but I have a great deal of things that remain to be done. Not everything was all wrapped up when she died."

Melissa caught herself before she gave away the secret her grandmother had just entrusted to her. The look in Nicklaus' eyes made her wonder if he already knew. The hairs all over her body seemed to stand up with his reaction, and she felt a little creepy.

The door swung open again, and Charles stepped past Nicklaus to take a position between them.

"Miss, I'm sorry. The staff is not sure how you want visitors handled tonight. I'll see Master Nicklaus back out. I'm sure he was not aware that you were busy. Master Nicklaus." The imposing figure motioned gently with his hand toward the front of the house. Nicklaus did not move but looked at Melissa.

"Show him to the Parlor, Charles." She visibly shrugged at the responsibility she knew was not leaving. "I need to see to this before I get back to what I was working on."

"Yes, Miss, but those items need to be dealt with."

"Know your place, Charles," Nicklaus snapped. "She is aware of her duties."

"Of course, sir, I meant no disrespect. This way please."

Nicklaus turned to head toward the parlor at the front of the house with a pious air.

"Charles."

"Yes, Miss?"

"Make sure he stays in the parlor. I'm going to change."

"You know, I can send him away if you're too busy." His eyes crossed to the box on the desk.

"No, I should see him, and I just can't face this right now." She pushed at the box again. "He was here for the funeral and was nice enough to leave then. He has heard the news and has been with my father since the meeting was over. He's all excited. If I don't see him tonight, he'll be back first thing in the morning, anyway. Give me a few minutes to prepare for my betrothed, won't you?"

"Miss, I believe the journal is far more important than meeting with Master Nicklaus."

She felt the anger cross her face and controlled her reaction. There was no reason to be angry; he was just doing his job. "Perhaps, but it can't be avoided." His common frown deepened for an instant, but he bowed as his training required and exited the library.

She unhooked the gold chain that held the amulet, slipped the key to the box onto it and put them both around her neck. She needed to get away from the stress she had inherited. She wanted this day to end more now than ever before. She needed a break already.

Over the next fifteen minutes she took her time changing from the little-black-dress she had worn to the funeral just to irritate her mother. It had worked. She would hear about that in the morning, but there was always something. Melissa could not be around her mother without somehow disappointing her; why should today be any different?

Melissa decided a pair of comfortable sweats would make the meeting easier. She wrapped a formal receiving robe around them just to avoid offending Nicklaus and checked her image in the full-length mirror. Her black hair fell along the back of the scarlet robe to her waist. Satisfied with her appearance, she started down the stairs as the clock announced the bottom quarter-hour. Behind her, the more horizontal rays of the sun were streaming in through the second floor windows of the library.

Nicklaus' raised voice assaulted her as she walked down the front stairs to the parlor.

Charles was standing in front of the one exit from the parlor with his arms crossed across his chest. Nicklaus stood beyond the door, blocked by tradition and honor more than by Charles.

"I have never been refused the right to use this house as if it were my own. The former owner afforded me the respect equal to my position."

He could consider the act an insult if he wanted, but Melissa didn't really care. It was her house now. She would decide who could roam its halls, and it was better to keep Nicklaus off balance, but Charles did deserve a break. She walked up behind him.

"What seems to be the problem, Charles?"

"No problem, Miss."

"Very well, you may go now," she said, walking past his bulk in the door and entering the parlor. "Okay Nick, What's on your mind?"

The young man's attitude changed immediately. He stood a bit straighter and pushed back his shoulders. "Well, you've settled in very nicely, Mel."

"Please don't call me that."

"I'm sorry, but I believe my relationship accords me some latitude. I am to be your husband, after all."

For a moment she gave him the smile he expected.

"By that awful arrangement, yes you are." She dropped her smile and replaced it with a face she had learned from her grandmother. "But I warn you, take no liberties. I'm doing all I can to void the Schwendemann-Kellmunz arrangement," she answered very matter-of-factly and walked past him to stand in front of her chair.

"Why fight it, cousin? It's the way of our ancestors. We must keep the line pure. We're royalty, and we'll soon return to the old country and free it from those who took it from us."

"Please. I've heard that from my father since I was a child. After millions of dollars and years, He's no closer to accomplishing it. What makes you think you will?"

Nicklaus smiled. Something in his smile gave Melissa a chill.

"I can feel it, Mel. It's time, and if you think about it you do too."

Melissa rolled her eyes at both the fascination that Nick shared with her father and grandfather and the honorific he had inherited from them.

"Two generations have fought that battle. Don't you think it's time to put it down?"

"You dare mock me! I'm the next in line." His voice rose with true royal indignation. The only thing missing from his reaction was the *woman* he wanted to add to punctuate it.

"After my father, yes, but he's still alive which keeps the royal line here for now. That's the whole reason you and I are betrothed, *cousin*."

"True, but that's no reason to give up on our ancestry."

"I've not given up on it. I remember it daily as my grandmother did."

Nicklaus recognized the dangerous ground he was on and took a moment before he continued.

"No one questions her contribution, Mel. Her books put our little country back on the map. I'm not sure publishing historical romances about dragons and kings in our dark history was the only way to do that, but her contribution is appreciated. I'm talking about getting the land back; recovering our birthright; taking back what has been stripped from us for centuries. What do you intend to do to help with that?"

Melisa felt a sudden surge of vertigo and stumbled into the wingback chair behind her.

Had his eyes flashed or was that some artifact of the charged encounter?

Recovering control by grabbing the armrest and slipping into the chair as smoothly as she could, Melissa hoped she had disguised her sudden weakness.

What was he talking about? It had been generations since their almost-country had been swallowed into the redrawn maps of Europe.

Swabia had fallen apart over centuries of dukes and counts who failed to bring it together to form a single unified nation. None of the powers, including the United Nations, had recognized their claims so far. He, along with every male of the royal line, was losing his mind. Her grandmother had told her about the plan that they passed from father to son, how much it had already cost all of the families and what she thought of it.

"I'm too tired to argue with you Nick. I know you didn't come here to talk about our history or wedding plans. What do you want?"

She punctuated her query by flopping against the chair back and looking up at him. She hoped the act covered her dizziness, which was not going away. Now, there was a buzzing in her ears.

He paused a moment before continuing, again smiling. He drew his hand over his face. For an instant, she thought she saw fatigue but she could not be sure.

"I wanted to ask you some questions, about your grandmother. Before she died, did she talk to you about any deadlines?"

"No, she was sick before she died. I hadn't seen her for a while. I was away, at school, so were you. When I did see her last, she talked about parties and people she remembered and went on about a particular ball when she was a child." The only deadline her grandmother had ever discussed with her had been in writing just before he had arrived, so to deny it was not a lie. Reminded of the deadline, she looked up at the calendar on the wall. It was too far away to make out.

"Odd, was she working on another book? You of all people would know what she was working on."

"I'm not sure... Why? She was always writing something."

The dizziness was making it hard to think. Her skin itched with a prickling irritation, and the fine hairs on her arm were standing up. She resisted scratching.

"She was asking a lot of questions about some very old texts my father kept in the library at home," he pressed. "She borrowed them and I wanted to make sure they made it back to the library. With all that's happened things can get lost, you know."

"I'll make sure you get them back as soon as I can finish a quick inventory. I have no idea what all is here. I expect most of the family will want to pick through it. Anyway, questions about what?"

"That's what I'm trying to figure out."

Nick sat down in the chair in front of hers. A deeper flash of vertigo rushed over her as he sat down. She looked away as her mind filled with an image of an ancient castle. She could see it as if she was hovering over it. Along the battlements, dragons stood with their wings folded back looking down into the valley around the castle. It reminded her of the painting on the ceiling in the library. Fire ran down her arms, legs, and spine. An uncontrollable shiver ran through her body. When she looked up at Nick, he was grinning back at her. The clock in the hall sang the hour with nine clear rings. Somehow, each chime made him look happier.

"Look, Nick, I'm really tired tonight. Can we talk about this tomorrow?"

"She seemed pretty insistent. She said it was important. If I could just look at what she was working on I think I could help."

Each sentence was an attack to her focus. Melissa resisted shaking her head at his request.

"I'm not even sure what she was working on yet. I need some time to review it. I'll know more in a few days, but not tonight."

She stood from the chair and walked toward the door leading out of the parlor, fighting vertigo with every step.

"I think it would be best if you left tonight. I need to get some rest. Today has really worn me down. Would you mind?"

"I can't leave now, Mel. I need to see the journal," he snapped.

A stronger wave of vertigo nearly dropped her to her knees. She could see that this wave affected Nicklaus as well. His eyes flashed red. This time his reaction was clear, and he did nothing to hide it. He bared his teeth at her and growled.

Fear slammed into her already shaken mind, and she could not help the look of surprise that crossed her face. How could he know about the journal?

"Charles, get in here! I need you!"

Her skin prickled and fire ran down her limbs again; it was all she could do to remain standing. The amulet around her neck seemed to vibrate, and Nicklaus fell away from her as if an invisible hand pushed him. He braced against the hearth and grinned.

Across the foyer behind her, a door leading to the dining room swung open and Charles rushed across the tiled floor. All hints of the gentle butler were gone as the fast-moving tackle rushed past her into the parlor.

"Holy—what the hell's going on?" Charles shouted as he crossed the last few steps to grab Nicklaus as he was stepping toward Melissa. He wrapped his arms around the smaller man and pulled him away from the door. "I've got this, miss. May I suggest you retire to the library or your room?"

"Yes, of course."

Even in her addled state, she knew the journal had to be protected.

"Make sure he is shown off the property and tell the gate no one is to be allowed in tonight. No exceptions."

"I can't let you do this Melissa. Your grandmother is wrong. What she's asking you to do will enslave us, again."

Nicklaus' eyes pleaded with her. He was not resisting Charles who was holding him in place in front of the fireplace, but something in Nicklaus' eyes scared her.

"Don't do what she's asked you to do. We have to be allowed to reclaim the power we've lost."

His face changed again. She saw it coming and opened her mouth to warn Charles, but never got the words out. He must have expected something because he turned his hip as Nicklaus drove his elbows into Charles' side. The power in his strike was unnatural and more than Melissa had ever seen in the small man. His eyes suddenly glowed brighter.

Distracted by the attack and Nicklaus' unexplained strength, Charles lost his grip and stumbled back against the hearth. Nicklaus pushed off and rushed at her. Vertigo enshrouded her and Melissa's feet twined together as she turned away from him. She stumbled into the doorframe, trying to escape. Against the wall, she gained some control and pushed off and around the doorframe into the foyer. The safety of the library was only a few feet down the hallway, but she could feel him behind her. She swore his hands were hovering above her shoulders. She risked a look back as she turned toward the back of the house.

Nicklaus, tripped up by Charles, slammed into the wall and doorframe, splintering the wood and spraying the hallway with chunks of plaster. The force of the strike spun him around into the front door barely missing her as she ran out of his reach. The impact with the wall should have stopped him, but he was pushing against the front door to come after her.

She couldn't stop the scream that escaped as he continued to chase after her. Watching over her shoulder, Melissa ran faster through the library door toward the back of the house. There was no way the two way door would hold up against his strength, but she had to secure the journal and figure out what was going on. Just as the door was closing behind her, she caught a glimpse of Charles slamming into Nicklaus in a classic football tackle and driving him across the foyer out of view.

The noise of their scuffle drove her past the desk where she grabbed the box and turned toward the French doors. Charles' cry of pain alarmed her and drove her to the doors. She hoped Charles could stop him, but knew in her heart that this was not the end of her flight.

The deadbolt stopped her, and she fumbled with it. Her fingers knotted, and she cried out in frustration before the lock yielded. Throwing open the doors, she raced out of the house and into the twilight of the back lawn. At the foot of the stairs, a crash of glass caused her to look back again as Nicklaus tore through the back doors. Distracted, she tripped on a root and sprawled across the rough ground.

As she fell, she released the locked box and brought her hands up to protect herself. Without looking, she sensed Nicklaus on top of her. She rolled over looking into his crazed eyes.

As he fell upon her, his chest felt jagged against her soft flesh. He was stronger than she ever remembered. His hands were reaching for her neck, and panic shot through her as she realized he intended to kill her. She closed her eyes.

Helpless in his grasp, she knew she could not surrender. Instinctively, she reached for the talisman at her neck. His rough hands closed around her throat. She opened her eyes to look into menacing, glowing orbs. Fire ran through her hand, and the stones in the pendant flashed.

Nicklaus stopped. Surprise filled his eyes as an invisible force slammed into his chest and threw him off of her and across the yard.

He crashed into the stone wall of the mansion and then dropped onto the steps with a loud thump, like a rag doll cast aside by an angry child. He stayed where he landed.

Fire raced up her arms, and a spike of pain exploded in her head. Her vision blurred with the pain and she clenched her eyes shut. A vision of a massive black dragon flashed into her mind as the pain blossomed in her skull. When her mind cleared, she could suddenly hear the katydids in the woods around her and the crunch of glass under Charles' feet.

Melissa opened her eyes, sat up, and stared at Nicklaus where he lay as Charles limped onto the porch. His left arm hung at his side, and blood streamed down his face from a bad gash on his head.

"Get to the overlook," he ordered, "I'm right behind you. Don't wait for me. Run. Stay on the path, it's safer."

Calm control emanated from him. He looked at the limp form on the steps and shook his head.

"This is about that box?" He pointed at it and looked at her.

She stood up and looked toward the overlook nodding her head.

"Go on, then. I'll be right behind you."

Melissa hesitated.

He looked up at her as he grabbed Nicklaus under the arm and hoisted him onto his shoulder. He pointed at the overlook and turned his back on her.

She collected the box and ran down the path to the overlook. When she was on the stone floor of the overlook, she turned back. Charles was on his way down the path. She looked at him with the question she wanted to ask on her face.

"Yes, he's still alive. I locked him in the pool shed. It won't hold him, but it will slow him down. He won't know where we are in a minute anyway."

Charles looked her over professionally as he reached the stone circle at the edge of the yard. She suddenly felt like a little girl who had fallen in the back yard. Charles reminded her of his father, and she took some comfort from that strength.

"Step back a bit."

With his right hand, he turned a stone near the center, exposing a handle. He pulled on the handle and a door, disguised in the cobblestone, opened, revealing stairs leading into the blackness and toward the house. He stepped down a step and leaned the door against his left shoulder with a grimace. With his only usable hand, he fumbled with a flashlight in his right coat pocket.

"Here, let me," Melissa said as she pulled the Maglite from his pocket and turned it on. "You don't have to be the hero all the time."

"I didn't stop Nicklaus with a piece of jewelry. I'm not sure why he's that strong or how you did that, but I knew things were getting weird when your grandmother sent me out here last week."

"What's out here?" Melissa asked as she led the way down the stairs. Charles closed the disguised door behind him and engaged a locking wheel on the center of it.

"You don't know? You'll have to see it, then. There's a large cave down here. It's safer than the house, and it has something to do with that journal."

He pointed at the box, and she looked at him as if he was going to explain something to her.

He shook his head. "No, I knew she was writing it before she died, and she left it in that box for you. She told me it was important. I just hope you have all you need down here because Nicklaus will have access to the house now. I can't keep him out, and I don't think we can go back up for anything until you figure this out."

"I have what he wants." She lifted the box up. "I'm not sure what else I'll need. I'm not even sure what you're talking about."

"You didn't read it?"

She frowned and kept walking. She didn't need his disappointment on top of her own. They followed the stairs until they leveled out in a room as large as the entire north wing of the house. They had been descending for a few minutes, but Melissa was not sure how far under the house they were or even how deep. Most of the cavern was rough and natural. The floor was level and covered with chests of different sizes.

"What's all of this?" Melissa asked, amazed that such a secret had been kept from her. She had been all over the house and property since she had been a baby. She was a little upset she didn't know about it.

"The foundation of your estate, literally. Your grandmother told me these were the crown jewels of your country."

"Who else knows about this?"

"Me and you, as far as I know. I was supposed to show you this when you asked. She expected you would be busy tonight."

"What do you mean?"

"She spent her last days writing in that journal. She told me she had little time and had to finish it. I was supposed to bring you here when you asked me to if she died before the solstice and she was unable to finish the preparations."

"What do you know about all of this?" She held the box up in front of her.

"Not much. I know she felt it was important that whatever she was preparing happen before sunset tonight. She was always asking me how much time she had left. I had to mark the solstice on my calendar and tell her how many days she had left every morning."

"*Today's* the solstice?" Melissa gulped.

She felt cold all over.

She could feel the color draining from her face.

Her stomach turned nearly over.

"What time is it?"

Charles lifted his left wrist and looked at his watch. "9:17."

Melissa bent down to put the box on the floor and settled beside it. Using the flashlight to locate the lock, she clutched at her chest to make sure she still had the pendant and the key. When she felt the comforting weight, she exhaled; but she could not escape the fear that she had failed her grandmother.

"Hold this," she ordered without thinking and handed him the flashlight.

Looking down at the box in front of her, she used the key on the chain to unlock it. Inside was everything she had left there before going to meet Nicklaus. She lifted out the journal and flipped to the first page. Her grandmother's writing appeared readable, as if she was sitting in the library.

"Help me, please. Do you have any idea what she wants me to do?"

"No. She never told me."

Melissa looked back at the journal and the first page she had not read. It was describing the history of her family going back over a thousand years. Melissa didn't have time to read it, so she skimmed the pages until she reached a section that seemed to be instructions. Those she slowly read and then set the book down in her lap.

"She wants me to cast a spell."

"What? What do you mean?" His face showed the conflict of a man who lived in a concrete world.

"She wants me to cast an ancient spell. If I can't cast it before sunset I won't stop what she's calling the emergence and then it'll be harder to correct..." She couldn't finish. She couldn't believe what the pages had told her.

"What are you going on about?"

"I'm not sure. What time is it?"

"9:24."

"I'll never make it. I can't get it right in that little time." A vision of a giant black scaly body passed before her in her mind. Its head turned to look at her. Nicklaus was with her for a moment and was urging her to stop.

"Okay, what is this emergence, and why do you have to stop it?"

"I'm not sure. I can't take time to read it all, but if she thought it was important, I'm not going to question it."

"What do you need?"

"Time, everything else is here." With that realization and the pressure in her mind from Nicklaus, she stood up.

"Shine the light around."

The beam of light exposed the floor in three-foot-wide slices, and she followed it until the outline on the floor matched the diagram in the journal.

"Stop," she shouted while comparing the mosaic on the ground with the drawing in the journal.

Convinced they matched, Melissa stepped into the central circle of what would be a giant pentagram mosaic in the floor of the cavern.

Vertigo, like she had felt facing Nicklaus in the parlor, rushed over her. Dropping to one knee and looking up at Charles, she swore she could feel wings protruding from her back. A different but familiar voice in her mind screamed, and she had a sudden sense she was about to do the wrong thing. An image of dragons surrounding the pentagram with their wings raised filled her mind. Nicklaus, in the form of a dragon, walked the outer edge looking in at her in the middle where she stood. Her hands trembled.

"I'm not sure I can do this."

"She believed in you, so do I," Charles urged from nearby. "You can do this."

Reassured, she opened the journal. She closed her eyes to clear the visions that continued and exhaled slowly. With effort, she forced Nicklaus' urgent arguments away and resisted the pressure from her own mind to stop. When she finally calmed herself, she began reading the words written out for her in the journal aloud. As the first sentence was completed, the text before her began glowing like a bad karaoke song. As the words passed her lips, they vanished on the page in a flash, turning to ash.

The pentagram on the floor began to glow.

Charles stepped to the outer edge and watched. The flashlight he was holding was no longer needed.

She read each line until she had finished the first page. Ash fell from the journal as she turned to the next page. She wanted to speed up, but the glow set a specific cadence and would not allow her to change it.

At the end of the second of three pages, she waited for the glow to go on, but it had not moved on from the last word. The glow of the pentagram vanished, and she stood in darkness waiting for what was next. A bell rang through the room, and she knew in her gut that she had failed. There was no need to go on.

"What was that?" Charles shined the flashlight around the cavern looking for the source of the bell. When he couldn't find it, he turned to look at her.

"I didn't make it in time. It's sunset."

"Go on, finish it then."

"I can't." The weight of her failure made her feel tired. She wanted to lay down and sleep.

Suddenly, Melissa's mind blurred with a whirlpool of images. Memories rushed through her head. Vertigo and excruciating pain overwhelmed her, and she fell to the floor. The individual tiles of the pentagram swam before her eyes. Images of her father, mother, and other relatives in a foreign place filled her mind. She saw Nicklaus changing from a dragon into the man she knew, only older by a few years. Melissa heard the a voice in her head.

Finally!

A feeling of relief filled Melissa's mind with the thought. It was as if something was suddenly resolved. A shiver ran down her spine.

"Charles, I don't know what's happening."

Melissa pushed away from the tiles and tried to stand but could not overcome the vertigo that held her there. She could feel minds, imprisoned for ages, celebrating their freedom.

There is no reason to resist. We are one, the stranger in her mind said to her.

Flashes of realization ripped through her mind. The spell was gone now.

They would emerge.

The dragons were coming.

They were already returning all around her.

"I'm not a dragon!"

"This is not me!"

"I can't allow it."

"I'll not be consumed," she cried into the stones beneath her hands.

She felt a rush of strength and power pour over her body. It felt good. She was euphoric in the sudden flow of energy.

Release me!

"No! Why should I?"

Focus on me and return to yourself. Why are you making this so hard?

Melissa struggled against the power surging through her body demanding to be released.

There's nothing wrong with being a dragon. Why should we be suppressed? Why were we? How long has it been?

Melissa felt a blast of pain in answer to the question. The power inside her fought back, and it felt so good to be strong.

Charles had stepped over to help her where she writhed on the floor, but he backed away as a guttural growl escaped her throat.

In her mind, images of her past formed and flashed by. Some brought joy with them. Others were cauldrons of sorrow. Her mind was a whirlwind of childhood thoughts. Her mother the dragon; the castle where she had lived; humans she had fought beside… Melissa fought the images by reaching out to recent memories of her relatively short life. It was insane to believe she was a dragon. She would not surrender. This demon would not take over her mind and body. She would not be lost to it.

She looked up from the ground to Charles and reached out a hand to him. He hesitated a moment. She could see fear in the eyes of a man who had witnessed war, but he recovered and stepped in to take it.

We will not be held back!

Power surged through her body.

We will be free.

She felt it fighting within her.

You will understand if you relax.

It suddenly tried to sooth her with a mellow crooning voice in her mind.

Melissa gripped Charles' hand and he winced as she squeezed.

"NO!" she screamed.

With Charles' help, she stood up and forced herself to breathe. She looked around the cave and realized she could see everything. The light they had used to find their way into the cavern glowed in Charles' injured hand but did nothing to aid her. She could read the text on the floor and see every crack in the distant wall.

You resist for no reason. I'm not taking you over. We are one. We are the same. We are Meliastrid.

In her mind, a red-scaled dragon stood on a frozen courtyard. It spun in the flakes falling from the grey sky, and Melissa could feel the childish joy of the moment. She loved the snow. She loved the castle. Melissa found herself spinning in the cavern as the dragon had in her memory. She could feel the event as if she had lived it.

You did. I did. We did.

As the joy enveloped her mind, Melissa relaxed a little. The crack in her defense was small, but it was enough. The power inside her surged, and coppery wings sprung from her back. Instead of pain, she shivered in a euphoric spasm. With the chill of the spasms, scales rippled over her skin and covered her body. Her clothes ripped and fell away from her as her armored form grew beyond their capacity.

Charles fell away from her and raised a hand to defend himself as if she might hurt him.

"Charles, I'm okay. Don't be afraid," she said with a little trill in her voice.

The feeling of emerging into this form was so overwhelming she could no longer resist it. Her own fear was suddenly lost in the uncontrollable spasms of growth and emergence. She was still afraid of what was happening, but the quiet cooing in her mind assured her it was safe.

She didn't want to believe it. She struggled again to remember. She fought to see if she was being deceived. As payment for her effort, pain ripped through her head and interrupted the transformation. She clamped her hands over her pointed ears, but it did nothing to stop the pain. She nearly dropped to the floor again when another surge of power fought against the pain.

With the pain suppressed and all of her resistance quelled, a long tail extended from her back and raised her into the air as her legs grew beneath her. The power turned into strength as her chest expanded and she grew to her full height. Stronger and stronger spasms wracked her. Large, triangular scales covered her chest as the tail consumed her. Her neck grew from the root of her chest, and wings carried her head away from her much larger body. Melissa could feel the crown of horns and spines grow from the back of her head. Fleshy, scaled whiskers extended from her chin. Thin wing flaps grew from below her ears.

Her nose expanded into a long snout. Her black hair vanished into bronze and black scales that covered her neck down to her wings. She could not suppress the grin on her newly emerged face.

A huge bronze and copper colored dragon replaced the short frail form of Melissa on the tiles where she had lain moments before resisting the transition. In her mind, the others that she had felt before were celebrating their freedom. However, the joy was quickly overwhelmed by a closer mind, a mind filled with rage.

"This is the emergence that she wanted to stop." Melissa spread her wings behind her and thrilled at the feeling of power that rushed through her.

That was a silly idea, I fear.

The thoughts and memories of the emerged dragon filled her mind, and she struggled not to disappear in the swirling memories and pain that still wracked the mind. It was not clear which thoughts she could trust.

"Emergence? That's exactly what Helena wanted you to stop! What are you doing?" Charles asked.

She could see the terror in his eyes, and Melissa was not sure what kept him in the cavern. The door was not blocked. He could leave if he wanted. The little girl inside wanted him to run and take her with him, but she couldn't go.

"You should not be here, Charles." Melissa could hear her own voice in the dragon's mouth. Charles stared at her and stayed where he was.

"I'm not leaving Melissa. Whoever *you* are, I'm here to help her."

Brave for a human. The voice in her mind seemed unimpressed and somewhat agitated by his presence. *He should not have seen this. We should kill him.*

Melissa reacted physically to the threat to Charles by turning the dragon's head away from him to look elsewhere. As she focused on a large opening on the other side of the cavern, the nearby rage turned into familiar agitation. Nicklaus was awake. He had emerged, and he was searching for her. His rage returned, and she could sense his desire to kill someone. He wanted to kill Charles. A final surge of Nicklaus' satisfaction filled her mind as he sensed his prey.

She turned back to look at Charles where he now stood. He had marshaled his fear and faced her. Flashes in her mind mingled his face with another's who was decked in a full suit of armor and sitting astride a charger. She grinned at him and realized in those images that there was no doubting his faithfulness.

Our mate will not see it that way. Are you prepared to deny him his retribution? This human has wronged him.

"This human has defended us. We were taking a stand, and he helped us."

But was it the right stand we were taking? Now that we are free, do you agree with what Heliantra wanted?

Melissa struggled with the massive memories that she had suddenly come to possess and tried to find an answer that she could rely on. Pain filled her mind as she tried to fight her way through memories and with a shake of her dragon head she surrendered and made a decision.

"In the absence of proof that she had reason for her directions tonight, I will still listen to my grandmother before I trust to Nicklaus."

Then you will face that decision soon. He will find you. Be prepared for it.

Melissa looked down at the small form of Charles in front of her. She slowly dropped her chest and forelegs toward him and tried to make soothing sounds to keep him from being threatened. It came out wrong, and she could see him tense in preparation for whatever she was doing. Unable to stop the reaction she carefully placed her foreclaw on his shoulder and stopped him before he could run. He looked down at it and up at her.

In her other claw, she handed the journal to him.

"My mate comes. He comes to kill you and perhaps me for defending you. I need your help. I don't know what tomorrow will bring, but the world we both knew has changed. Dragons have emerged. We will have to face it, and I need your help."

Charles wrestled with his fear and looked into her eyes. He studied them for a moment and then knelt on one knee, dropping his eyes to the floor.

"I swear, my lady. I have done the wishes of your kin and will continue to serve you."

A surge of excitement and pleasure filled her mind as Nicklaus found the cave entrance. They were out of time. She turned to face the direction in which he would appear as a blast of air rushed into the hall in front of his black shiny body. Nicklaus folded his wings back and landed in the middle of the floor to join the pair in the center of the hall. Melissa pushed Charles behind her and shifted her body between them. Their chests nearly touched when Nicklaus had stopped.

"Why," Nicklaus roared into the chamber, "do you protect this human?" His head leapt at the small form hiding behind her, and his teeth clashed in loud snaps. Fire flared in Nicklaus' otherwise dark eyes.

"Because, he has served me well. He was doing what he was charged to do. His courage saves him. You have no right to him." Her knee slammed into his eye and sent his head away from Charles.

"They have enslaved us." His foreclaw defended his injured eye as he withdrew his head from the sudden danger and looked at her, shocked by her physical attack. Only partially derailed by the assault, he continued his thought after a pause. "We will avenge this disrespect. You understand now, don't you?" He looked up at her, confused. His left eye blinked to recover.

Thoughts from her rebellious mind rushed forward to defend what Nicklaus was saying. Melissa could feel her resolve failing as her mate tried to convince her that humans deserved to be punished, starting with Charles. She paused as Nicklaus fought with his injured pride to think. There had to be some reason Helena wanted her to cast the spell that would have stopped this. Through the pain, she struggled for an answer that was just out of reach when the image sprang forward in a blast of excruciating realization. Like she had felt the joy of the dragon spinning in the snowy castle courtyard, she again could sense the fear and dread as her young mind chanted similar words into the crisp air of that same castle. Nicklaus paced beyond a magical boundary and a circle of dragons that protected her as she cast the spell. The pain of the memory exploded into her mind, eradicating the image in shards of agony. It was enough to stop the argument from her mind and strengthen her resolve.

Melissa extended her tail to point at Nicklaus' injured eye. She raised her wings above her head to balance herself for his attack and reached out with her foreclaws to protect her space from her one-time mate.

"We are free now. This is a different time, though, and we must be careful. You are wrong, my love, as you have been for generations before and since. I know how angry you are, but you must be cautious and not be overcome by emotions not supported by facts. Do not surrender to your rage, or it will be your end."

"Never again," he roared into the cavern. "Across the world we have all emerged, and we will never again be subjugated to them. The humans will pay for their insolence, and I will not be stopped by you and your love for them." Nicklaus raised his head level with hers, keeping his eyes on her. The flickers of hatred in his eyes warned her he was ready to fight. She puffed up her chest and thrust her wings forward, pointing the claws on each joint out to show him the fight he would be in if he chose to attack. She wanted to look like the porcupine she would be. He would pay dearly in this fight.

Her show of force worked, and Nicklaus turned his back on her to leap across the cave. As he retreated, he continued to threaten her.

"You will see you were wrong. Others will agree with me. Your father will stand beside me and end your love affair with humans. They have stood against us, and I will see that they pay for their arrogance."

Without looking back, he exited the cave, leaving only the aroma of his anger.

Melissa sighed the tension out of her body and relaxed her wings. Part of their history was becoming clearer in her mind accompanied by the pain that drained her strength. She believed her grandmother's decision had reason.

No! Do not return us to the prison of that weak form.

"It is the form I am comfortable with."

It is a prison.

"Then you shall be imprisoned."

We, you mean.

Melissa shrugged her mighty shoulders and refused to fight with the voice. She was in control of her body. She returned her thoughts to the problem of what to do about the ancient spell she had failed to cast. There had been a reason for it before. If her memory was correct, she had actually cast it before. What could the reason be? Fire rushed through her head at the attempt to recapture that memory, and she shook her head to clear it from the pain.

Suddenly triumphant against both her own confused mind and Nicklaus' anger, but otherwise a failure, exhaustion overwhelmed her. She took her last ounce of strength and focused on her human form. Melissa collapsed from her dragon form into her completely exhausted and naked human body. She felt Charles' strong, comforting, human arms catch her as the shroud closed over her eyes, and peaceful darkness swallowed her mind.

CHAPTER 2 - DAWN OF A NEW AGE

June 21 – 0700 CEST – North of Grendelwald, Switzerland

Renard awoke. He couldn't move, but he could open his eyes. As his lids drew slowly back, total blackness remained. He blinked a few times to assure himself that his lids were working. Darkness remained. Panic struggled at the edge of his mind, trying to break through the barrier wall of sanity and take over. A single agent of panic broke over the crest and succeeded in overwhelming him, but even the urge to flee had no effect. His legs refused to obey, and his arms were locked in place. Nothing obeyed the tyrant panic, and it died amongst his other thoughts.

As his panicked mind relaxed a little from the failed coup, Renard reviewed his situation. He was not able to move his body at all. Even if he could move, he still couldn't see. The army of panic rose at the edge again. He fought it back this time with the logic that there was nothing he could do, but that would not work much longer. He couldn't feel anything but his face.

Wait, that meant he could feel something. This was progress. He focused on the new tingling feeling in his cheeks and stabbed back at the encroaching panic army with it. He opened his mouth to take a deep calming breath. His lips parted but nothing happened. No air entered his lungs.

Again, the army surged forward. A single scout broke through his defensive line. With his mouth wide open, he screamed silently within his mind. No sound escaped his lips. No air entered or left his lungs, and again the panic agent died in his logical mind.

I'm alive!

The hammering strike to the invading panic threw them back where he could concentrate. Thoughts of slowly dying swirled into a whirlpool of questions.

Why can't I move?
That's my nose but why can't I feel my toes?
Why can't I see?
Why can't I breathe?

He latched onto the last question and used it to drag his tortured mind out of the grasps of the vanguard of panic.

His lungs were not screaming for air even though he was unable to breathe.

He was not drowning.

He was not buried alive.

Think, Renard, he commanded himself. *What is this?*

This is magic, he answered quickly.

It had to be a spell.

Sudden calm settled over his mind. Magic he could understand.

So, what kind of magic is it?

He could not move or breathe, but he was not trapped by a horrible weight, nor was he dying from lack of air.

I'm held.

That type of magic would not kill him. His mind relaxed further, and panic shook its fist at logic while sweeping the remaining pieces from the chessboard of Renard's mind. Logic had won. He was again in control of his mind.

Cracks, like rock splitting open in the darkness, began to appear over his open eyes. Light pursued panic into the back of his mind where it sniveled now like the spoiled child it was.

Petrified, turned to stone.

The spell was weakening, crumbling away, and he would be whole soon. He had never been turned to stone before. It was an odd feeling he would not like to repeat. He wanted to dust off his lap and move on to the next challenge since he had solved the problem, but he was still inconvenienced by the effects of the spell.

With no way to move, Renard focused on discovering why he might find himself turned to stone. He concentrated on his last memory, and a new challenger raced onto the freshly lit battlefield of his mind. The pieces reset, and this time the armored warrior on the other side was formidable and, as yet, had no name.

He raced through the opening moves trying to outsmart the guardian of his memory, but nothing he tried worked.

Who cast the spell that trapped me?

Pain answered harshly.

Where am I?

Again, nothing but pain.

What was I doing before?
He braced for pain, but instead there was nothing but an answer.
Waiting.
The first piece fell, and the formidable knight reeled backward at the assault. He had been in his own keep, waiting for a messenger. No, they had come, and he was so close to...

Pain ripped through his head like a blinding light as the knight's reinforcements swarmed the battlefield. He squeezed his still darkened eyes closed to it, but nothing stopped the bright flash and searing agony. He fought back against it and reached through the pain. His queen raced across the board with the bishops to protect the king.

What had it been?
What had he been reaching for?
What had he touched?
Yes, he had touched it, and then this.
Someone had trapped him.
Someone had fooled him.
Someone had tricked him in his own keep, how was that possible?
A talisman.

That had to be what it was. His quest was almost done, he had almost succeeded in—the knight raced his rooks to the front and forced a stalemate. His memories would not yield this day. Renard reviewed the easy memories he had freed from the knight as he conceded the game and the board reset. The past few years had been about collecting talismans. That was what he knew. That was probably why he was turned to stone and standing in the cold.

Yes, it was cold. He was outside.

Air flowed into his throat and lungs, but he was still not breathing freely. A new pressure in his chest made each breath shallow and difficult. His lungs were breaking free, but his body would not give to allow them room to expand.

If he had not realized everything would be back to normal in time, he would have been forced to play another round with a pouting panic. Instead, he focused on the problem.

Where was he? He could feel the wind blowing in his hair now, and the pain in his temples threatened to make him sick. He was changing. Flesh was replacing stone.

He blinked his eyes to focus the light, and the rest of the stone covering washed away. He could see, after a moment of refocus, that he was in the mountains; in fact, he was standing on an overlook. A snow-covered valley stretched out beyond his perch, and cold fingers of black rock surrounded him. He couldn't move his head yet, but he could feel the cold air on it. Slow tingles began working their way down his neck as if life were crawling its way back through his veins. He could feel the sun reaching for him, fingers of warmth stroking away the cold stone that had imprisoned him.

Attempting once again to ascertain his location, he shifted his eyes from side to side trying to seek a landmark he might know, a person, a sign of any kind. From where he stood, all he could see was stone and snow.

The bitter cold air tickled his cheeks and nose as suddenly the sun covered more of him. He wrinkled his eyebrows and felt the skin move over his forehead.

Who was he dealing with? Powerful magic had done this.

Dragons!

It had to be the cursed dragons. The knight that was receding from the edges of his mind turned and raised his metal-shod fist. Renard grimaced and declined a new battle. He couldn't remember why he hated them right now, but there was no denying the hatred that warmed his stone heart.

They were all that were left.

Yes, that was why it had to be them. There were no others left who could trap him. Their talisman had been the bait. The knight stomped his foot and shattered his mind with pain before he surrendered the pursuit deeper into his memory again.

Had dragons finally succeeded in taking over the whole world? Why had they not just destroyed him? Why was he still alive? Had his defeat secured their kingdoms? He wished he knew what was going on. The knight guardian stomped back onto the mental battlefield, driving his spurred heals into the soft flesh of Renard's mind with every step. Renard conceded the game before he reached the table and finally surrendered the search for the memory.

Back in the world Renard was returning to one limb at a time, he could feel all of his head, and his neck finally relaxed and responded to his attempt to look around. He glanced down toward his feet and found them perched on an icy platform. There were rough steps carved in the stone, covered in snow. A few small packages, long dead flowers and what looked like folded parchment letters laid about and stuck out of the snow. An ironic smile formed on his face.

This is one way to be worshiped, he thought.

"Oh, my God, it moved," a shocked female voice cried behind him. He was glad he was still unable to move his shoulders so she would not see him jump from the surprise. Her words were in a strange dialect that sounded familiar, but he could not understand them.

Is it a dragon?

Am I guarded?

He thought he heard alarm in her voice and the sound of rocks moving underfoot.

Is there a struggle? Is someone running for help?

"Where are you going?" another voice asked, male this time, incredulous and agitated. Renard still could not understand him, but the inflexion in his words gave away his attitude. Whoever was moving should not be.

"I'm leaving. That thing moved. No one said anything about it moving."

"It's just the light, Barb. At least wait till the sun is up."

"The light? Light didn't cause his head to move. The legend says the solstice sun makes it look alive, like a real man. No one ever said it would move." The female voice trembled. Was it fear or adulation?

Renard listened closely to the foreign tongue. She was not crying out in alarm or for help.

He remembered the gifts around his dais. She was afraid. She feared him… as she should. There were two of them, but they were not his captors. They were here to worship him. Renard grinned.

"That's unusual. I've never seen it move either." The fascinated voice of the man chased after the retreating footsteps of the female. Together they stopped on a dirt or gravel path that he could not see.

Renard focused on what the strange man said and worked the familiar sounds through his head. The language was foreign but could be a dialect he had never heard before. It sounded familiar. Maybe they would understand Renard. He swallowed to wet his dry tongue and tried to speak. His first attempt came out as a croak. He swallowed again as the saliva started to flow.

"Be faithful…" was all he could get out with the contents of the small cavity of his chest. He tried to inhale, but his chest would not expand. With another gulp of air he croaked out, "you will be rewarded."

The woman screamed, and Renard heard her turn away again and start walking quickly away. She was more determined to leave but the other one, the male, was not going with her. She stopped.

"Rich, come on. I'm not staying here." Again he could not understand her words, but he understood the context.

"Stay, and I will reward your faithfulness." He spewed the words out in a deeper gulp of air and immediately hated how he sounded. He would not beg to them again. He needed their help, but he would not grovel.

The man behind him chuckled, reinforcing Renard's chagrin at sounding weak; the watcher would suffer for that disrespect. Renard was son of a king. They should be kneeling before him.

"I think he believes we're here to worship him. I'm not sure what he said, but listen to his tone."

"Rich, you're talking to a statue."

"This has to be some kind of trick to take in the tourists."

"I don't care. This is not why I came out here. This is freaky, Rich. Come on, let's go. I don't like this—it's a long hike back and I'm cold."

The words were hard to translate, but Renard was beginning to find the patterns. He understood enough by context to figure out some of her words.

She wanted to leave, but she was walking back toward his pedestal. She would not leave without the male.

"Stay," he shouted in as clear and commanding a voice as he could produce.

"Let's go!" She stomped her foot and there was more shuffling of rock. The man was now walking away with her.

They were really of little concern to Renard. His upper arms were starting to tingle. When the spell's effects wore off he would catch up to his morning guard and find out why they were watching him. They were on foot in the mountains, which made them resourceful. Either they had shelter to return to nearby, or they were not far from a village. It would not be long before he would be free of his stone prison and he could catch up with them.

With the couple far enough away that he could think about other things, he again focused on his fight with the guardian of his memories. There had to be some way around the pain he felt when he tried to remember. Again, it was obvious magic was being used, but he should be able to find a way around magic.

Wherever this was, it was clear that he was in a foreign land. The dragons had exiled him in stone to a mountaintop. They did not want him to survive, yet the key to his survival was walking away from him. The dragons' plan would not succeed. Fate would see to that. It had in the past, and it seemed to continue to smile on him. He laughed with recently regained full breaths.

Have they figured out my plan?

He was not the master of his own mind yet and he couldn't remember the details of his plan, but he could never forget his hatred of dragons and his goal to rid the world of their meddling.

His review had taken enough time that the sun was now down to his waist and the long staff in his left hand was changing from stone back into metal-shod hardwood just above his hand. The silver hand that gripped a clear gem sphere at the top of the staff flashed in the sunlight. His chest was both cold from the air and warm from the sun. He was breathing freely now, and he could feel everything above his waist again.

He twisted his upper body as far as he could and leaned back to see what was behind him. The dais was sitting on a rocky ledge that led back to an opening in the wall of the mountain. He could not see beyond the opening, but it appeared that the ledge was accessible somehow or his observers would not have been able to reach him. He relaxed his torso and looked at his staff again. His fingers were tingling, and he could feel the metal and wood beneath them. He could command the staff, but it could not help him quite yet.

There was no magic infused in the staff that could speed up his transformation. The spell would have to follow its own course, but he wanted to know if the staff's magic still worked. In his mind, he formed the trigger word for the staff's power and called on something simple. A ball of intense light appeared a hand's width above the gem. It would appear that he was not completely unarmed or unprepared, he realized with a reassuring laugh, dismissing the orb of light with a mere thought.

For the first time, he wondered how many sunrises he had stood on this peak as a stone guardian. There was no easy way for him to tell, yet everything around him seemed to testify that it had been a very long time.

The rays of the sun had reached his waist. He could feel his cloak and shirt brush and move against his skin as they began to relax over his back. This last revelation verified that his backpack was missing, which meant that not even his traveling spell book was with him. This was disappointing. His fractured memory could not be trusted; the spells he normally had at his disposal were gone. He could only rely on his tools and the simple spells he could never forget.

He continued his inventory. He did have his travelling bag slung across his chest. Some of his preferred potions and elixirs rested on the strap that secured it to him. Items he never traveled without were in the bag. His favorite wand rested in a slot along the strap that crossed his chest and his rod seemed to be tucked into one of the long pockets of his cloak. He had not traveled here on his own. Someone, the dragons perhaps, had moved him to this location, but he had what he needed to get back to his keep.

The staff was still stuck to the stone base next to his foot, glued in place until it too could be graced by the sun's seeking rays. A single, powerful trigger word was all that was needed to send magic flowing through the staff again to shroud his still vulnerable form in a clear dome of protection. With the shield in place, he released the powerful wood to focus on other matters.

"Now, let's look around." Both hands were now free, so he pulled a small metal sphere from his travelling bag. Chanting at the sphere, he tossed it into the air above him. It climbed away from him in a straight line, faster than his toss could have propelled it.

Eyes closed so that he could see what the orb was showing him, he ignored the concentration-crushing tingling in his legs as the sun continued releasing the rest of his body. In his forcefully focused mind, an image formed of his perch from above. He was the small dot on the edge of a lower peak of the mountain. A trace vanished into the mountains behind him. When the sphere stopped its climb and hovered, he turned his head, directing the orb to twist and show him another view. On the edge of the sphere's vision, he found the signs of life he was looking for. The couple was walking quickly away from him, following the trace down the mountain. They were dressed in jester's attire and carried oddly shaped parcels on their back. The woman was still leading.

Beyond them, he could see what looked like buildings on the edges of the curved orb's image. It was a village. Someone there would be able to help him. Breaking the connection by opening his eyes, he released the orb from its orbit. The sphere dropped into his hand, and he slipped it back into his bag.

As the sun reached his feet, he flexed his knees and gingerly tested them to see how well they would perform on the walk out from his perch. His cloak billowed around him in the breeze, which he inhaled deeply into his lungs. The air, coated with the foul smell of dragons, agitated him. They had obviously extended their rule over the entire world, as they had wanted. Once they had figured out how to trap him and stop the Arcane Brotherhood, they had been free to do whatever they wanted. He should have known better than to try to deceive them. Lesson learned. That made his next step simple; he had to destroy them completely before they undid everything he had achieved. Renard again flexed his long frozen muscles, grabbed his staff as the sun released it from the stone and kicked snow off his boots. Turning away from the overlook he had watched for far too long, he faced the trace behind him. Down that path, he would find answers and his way back to his keep. Something he had wrested from the grasp of the knight guarding his memories told him what he wanted was still waiting for him there. Once he had it back in his hands, he could finally end his fateful dance with the dragons.

June 21 – 0750 CEST – Munich, Germany.

Rebekka was ready for her day, and this was going to be *her* day. In her mind, it had been a long time coming from her last year in college three years before, but it was finally here. She had used her skills, her wiles and a little bit of her grandmother's magic to earn this position, and nothing was going to stop her, not even the whispering simps she chose to ignore. Who cared if the slow movers around her said she slept her way to the top? What did that matter? She would still be on top. The fabric of reality would have to change to keep this from being *her* day.

Stepping out of the elevator, she walked past the receptionist who grinned and waved at her like the child she was. Rebekka returned the salutation; no reason to burn a bridge before the announcement. After the announcement, she wouldn't care what half the women in the office thought, and the other half only mattered because they were still above her. Things were changing, and Rebekka had to remember who had helped her get where she was and who had stood in her way. A wink and a thumbs-up punctuated the childish ritual. Rebekka wanted to be somewhere else. To avoid any further conversation, she ducked into the bathroom just beyond the receptionist's desk.

Inside the door, she paused to remind herself that tomorrow those international executives the young receptionist had been signing in would be Rebekka's clients. This was the last day of bouncing from project to project and helping overpaid accountants look good. All she had to do was keep Jaeger focused and everything on track.

She looked up and down the plum business suit and preened. She adjusted a few things, checked the white camisole for makeup, fluffed the blonde hair a bit and then stared herself in the eyes. She voiced the words her grandmother had both taught her and warned her about on her sixteenth birthday. At that point in her life, the words had helped her get through taunting and jests at school. Since then they had become a reliable tool whenever she needed a little extra confidence. The familiar tingle of assurance she felt from the spell straightened her spine.

Spell cast.

Appearance checked.

She turned to leave the bathroom, ready for whatever was beyond the door.

As her hand reached for the door, it sprang open. Gertrude, her friend from college and member of her mother's coven, stumbled through the opening and paused when their paths merged.

"Guten Tag, Gert," she said, just a little agitated that her friend couldn't look up from her own feet as she walked.

They had been friends for years. Rebekka had tried to help her stand up and take her place at the company, like she was helping the young receptionist, but Gertrude was weaker.

The glow of immediate recognition started to fill her friend's face as she looked up from the floor. The normal smile she always had for her coven sister began to form until their eyes met and a cloud descended over Gertrude's features. Her eyes sparked and became angry. Her fists clinched at her side, and she stood up for the first time in years. Neither moved. Rebekka braced for a slap that she was sure was coming.

Gertrude walked around her, as if she were a pole in her way and slammed a stall door. Rebekka didn't move as she recovered from the encounter. Although her friend had not slapped her, she was still reeling from it as if she had. What had she done to offend Gertrude? She hadn't, recently, stolen any men from her, that Gertrude knew of. From the stall, Gertrude mumbled something under her breath that Rebekka chose to believe she had misheard. There was no way her friend would have called her *that*.

Glancing at her watch, Rebekka decided to leave this problem where it was for now. As soon as the promotion was announced, she could tell Gertrude about her new job, and that would smooth over whatever she was angry about. At this moment she needed to be in Jaeger's office.

He didn't know he had a meeting with her this morning, but she intended to see him before he went to the meeting. He was going to let her present her plan today, and too many things could derail him. She had to shore up his resolve, and that might take a few private minutes in his office. She turned around just in time to confront the angry face of another woman entering the doorway. She snuck through the doorway without too much difficulty to nearly be run down by Jaeger's boss' wife. She stepped aside to avoid the imminent crash as the woman stiffened and rolled her shoulder down to drive it into her.

"Watch where you're walking, whore," the passer-by said more loudly than an office would allow.

Standing against the wall where the woman had forced her, Rebekka watched her walk away. She shook her head and looked down the hall. Had she forgotten the full moon? What was up today? Too much to do to worry about one angry woman, but that was weird. Jaeger had introduced them a few weeks before at a spring party when a new client had been secured. She had really liked Rebekka then, which made the encounter even more odd. They had talked for most of the party. She could not afford to have the boss' wife angry with her. Rebekka was all too aware of how much power the boss' wife wielded. That problem would have to be fixed, just not today.

She relaxed against the wall to regain her composure for a count of ten before deciding to go on. When she was confident there was nothing she could do about the situation, she pushed off the wall and focused on the door across the no-man's-land of cubicles.

She was glad she had cast that spell, otherwise she would be feeling overwhelmed already. On particularly difficult days, it bolstered her spirits so she could make it through. Today, she was going to need a maximum dose. All it did was polish her aura a bit and increase her allure. Past results had been mixed, but she liked the way it made her feel, so she used it whenever she needed a boost. As she walked across the floor toward Jaeger's office she wondered if, for the first time, her grandmother's warning about the spell had come true. According to the legend, the spell had the opposite effect on the same-sex observers of the caster. She discarded the random negative thought as she approached Jaeger's door. He would be glad to see her.

With the safety of Jaeger's door in sight, Rebekka started to feel like she could relax, when Wilhelm approached her like a sergeant major. He was a very Catholic, very married, man who worked with Jaeger . He had told her more than once that she needed to find God. As a joke, she had written a little hex for him last Halloween and stuck it in his desk drawer. It was supposed to make him a little more amorous toward his wife and maybe get him off her back. She had forgotten all about it until he stepped in front of her as she reached for the doorknob. The look of devotion and love in his eyes frightened her.

"Fulfill my greatest dreams and come away with me. I have a little time coming. We can go to the coast and explore each other." His hand was on hers before she could pull away. He looked into her eyes and the total submission made her shiver.

"Wilhelm, you're married. That would break several of your commandments. Think about what you're saying." She smiled at him as if she was continuing his joke and reached past him for the door.

The spirit in his eyes drained from his face, and he suddenly looked all of his sixty years. Taking the opportunity, she opened the door and continued into the room, closing the barrier behind her. She leaned against the door as if it were a bulkhead between her and the wild beasts. What a strange beginning for *her* day.

"What's wrong, Bekka?" Jaeger looked at her from over the top of his newspaper. He smiled his familiar smile, and she relaxed in it. She was safe here.

"Nothing." She shook off the morning's odd events and returned his smile. No time for trivialities, she had to possess this day. He set the paper aside. "I just wanted to check with you and make sure everything was still set."

He stood from the desk and approached her. He placed his hand on her face. The sign of affection had been reserved for private moments so it surprised her a little, but she leaned into his caress and smiled up at him. She couldn't afford to lose him now. Tomorrow, who cared, but today she had to maintain his interest.

As if on cue, the phone on his desk demanded his attention. He ignored it and leaned in to kiss her, but the incessant ring would not go away. Grudgingly, he released her with a growl before their lips could meet. He spun the base around and read the display to see who it was. Guilt and concern replaced passion on his face.

"What does he want?" He lifted the receiver before she could read the name. "Yes, sir?"

It was their boss. She knew by the way he said *sir*. It was not abnormal for the boss to call, but Jaeger was acting as if he had been caught doing something bad. Rebekka grinned at the realization of what he was feeling guilty about and watched her rather uncomfortable lover.

"I understand. Yes, sir. I'll make sure of it. Today?"

Jaeger refused to look at her, and an odd feeling filled her gut. She put on her most alluring smile and cleared her throat.

Jaeger looked up at her, grinned a guiltier smile and raised a finger for her to wait before looking back at the blotter on his desk.

"Are you sure that's a wise choice, sir?"

The question seemed to cost him all of the energy in his body. His shoulders slumped as the answer came across the wire. He looked up at her, and his eyes showed the conflict in his mind.

"I see. Yes. Of course. I'll let you know when it's done. Yes, of course."

He hung up the receiver and looked at her again. This time he looked like an animal that had just lost a fight with the alpha male. If he'd had a tail it would have been between his legs. He picked up the receiver and dialed another number. She watched the numbers and realized he was on the phone with personnel. He was calling the "Axe Man."

"You're busy, and I need to get to my desk." She tried to extract herself from the office. It was bad for her to be witnessing these events. Someone was about to be fired.

"No, wait. Have a seat. I need to talk to you." The look in his eyes had changed from desire to distress. He seemed to be begging her to stay while wishing she were in a different country. Rebekka felt a cold chill run up her spine.

What was going on?

What was happening to *her* day?

What had happened to *her* plan?

This man was supposed to be *her* hope for a future, and now he was acting like *her* executioner. No one knew about their relationship. No one knew how she had used him. Jaeger hung up the phone, and her mind returned to the office where *her* future was being decided.

"Rebekka," he said and sat down in his chair.

He shifted papers on his desk as if he was looking at something.

"There have been some complaints. I was going to talk to you about them, but they've gone too far. There is nothing I can do."

What?

Anger filled her mind. She wanted to melt her lover into his seat, but she couldn't remember the long and mostly useless incantation. So, this was the way they were going to do it. She smiled her most innocent smile, and his face seemed to shudder. He was not happy with this, but he was doing it. She hoped his guts would boil as he struggled with his cross-purposes.

"It seems that several people have complained. The company is going to have to separate you."

"What?" This time she said it. She had expected a warning. She would not get that promotion, and she would have to start over with someone else; but she never expected to lose her job. "How can you do that? There've been no warnings. My record here is clean. I have rights. What is this all about?"

"The complaints are quite serious, and we would rather not draw this out. We'll mail you your check. You will be paid until the end of next month, but you cannot come back here."

There was a knock at the door as if cued by his words, and two security guards stepped into the room.

Really, they even sent in security. What was she going to do, fight for her job?

"I'm going to need for you to go with these men."

She looked back at them and wanted to hurt them. She wanted to pay them all back for what they were doing. There were no complaints. When she woke that morning, everything had been in line for her to start a new life; the life she had built for herself over the past three years. She cocked her head to the right and looked at the door. It looked like she was going to start a new life, just not the one she had planned. She grinned at the two men and whispered the secret words she often played with when someone made her very angry. The little spell she had learned as a child from one of her mother's books had a nasty little ring when repeated aloud, and it took a few seconds to get the whole chain out. She had forgotten what the book said it did because it had never done anything but make her feel better. She loved the way it sounded as she spoke the last few words into the air of the small office. As usual, with a wicked flourish of her hands, she pointed at the two men as the book had said to. Unlike the other times she had cast the spell, this time she felt some of her anger rush from her gut to her hands and exit her fingertips. Her targets' eyes grew incredibly wide as blue, fiery bolts leapt from her fingers and struck them both in the chest. The force of the bolts threw both men back through the door. The frame, the glass windows on either side of it and the door shattered and fell back onto the nearest desk as each man created a hole in the wall. The cracking of bone accompanied the sound of each man striking the desks and rubble. Office drones rushed away from the crashing glass wall and stood off to the side of the now disturbed work area. The security officers lay in the rubble rolling on the floor. They were patting at the blue flames that were burning their uniforms with limbs that were not broken and groaning at the pain. Rebekka stared for a moment at what she had done and didn't move. That had never happened before. What would have happened if she had released all of her anger into the little curse? They were alive but not getting up from where they had landed.

She forced herself to recover from the surprise and realized she really needed to leave. Jaeger was staring at her from behind his desk where he was crouched on the floor. Good, the coward needed to be hiding behind his desk. He was lucky she didn't have time to send a present his way. She did look back at him and pointed with an evil grin. He ducked below the desk, and the comforting sound and aroma of his urine running out onto the floor satisfied her. She walked through the broken wall past the two men and a room full of shocked watchers.

Odd time for spells like that to start working, but it was *her* day after all. Maybe this was the direction she needed to be heading anyway. Something more was happening than what she had expected. First, her allure spell had caused women to hate her, and now bolts of energy were rushing from her fingers at her command. There was little doubt that she would need to find a new job, but before she could do that she would have to figure out why spells she had cast her whole life with no effect were suddenly twice as powerful and blowing people through walls. That might open several doors, literally.

She exited the shattered work area and walked toward the receptionist's desk on her way out. There was no other exit, and she was not hanging around. When she reached the front, the young receptionist was looking at her with her finger on the speaker in her ear. It was obvious from the look on her face that she didn't like Rebekka anymore either. Jaeger's boss was standing next to his wife with an unbelieving look on his face. His wife looked at her with a mixed expression of hatred and fear. Rebekka smiled and shook her finger at them all. The two women jumped, and the older man looked like he wanted to melt into the floor. With a giggle of excitement, she recited her favorite phrase again. This time she could feel the power build with each word. At the crucial moment, she was careful to hold back the power a little and pointed at his crotch. A little tickle coincided with the blue streak that struck him and bent him over next to his wife. She didn't wait to watch the reaction.

Rebekka turned her back on them and walked out the door into the foyer to wait for an elevator. So far, no one was coming after her, but that would not last. She had broken the law. She couldn't take it back now. How could she defend what she did? She couldn't just tell them she had cast that spell hundreds of times but today, it worked.

She giggled hysterically at that idea. How could she possibly explain what had just happened? How could anyone? Her hands started shaking, and her knees followed. She needed to get out of the building and find a safe place to sit down before she fell down. By now someone was calling the police. The next elevator to open on the floor could be full of security and then she would have to do something worse than she had already done. Could she escalate? Could she attack the police?

The elevator was taking too long. She looked toward the door to the stairs and cringed at the walk down, but felt it might be safer. She turned toward the stairs as the elevator dinged. It was too late to run now. She turned back and braced for a rush of security officers preparing the spell she had used twice already. A woman from a higher floor was standing in the car looking at her with an open look of disgust.

Great, Rebekka thought, *another angry woman.*

She hesitated a moment recovering from the absence of an attack, walked into the car and hit a button for the main floor. For a moment, she thought the woman had growled at her. She laughed aloud at the absurdity of the situation. At least the car was not full of security guards or police.

As they descended in silence, she thought about what to do now. She obviously had no job. They might have changed their mind about paying her to the end of the next month, too. She couldn't be sure it was safe to go home.

Her nerves didn't improve on the trip down. When the elevator stopped at the other woman's floor, Rebekka waited for her to exit, punched the first floor button and jumped back against the rail in the back of the elevator. She was alone and her shakes turned to tears. As they formed and she felt her emotions rising to overcome her she inhaled sharply, voiced her little confidence spell and fought them back. She was not going to be weak like those men and women wanted her to be.

She could hear her mother in her head telling her that using magic came with responsibility. She and her grandmother had lectured her about the power of magic and how important it was to respect it. They believed it had always existed and still worked in small ways. She remembered the lesson now; respect the power in its small form so when it returned she would be able to handle it. Obviously, she had failed to learn that lesson, but she was starting to understand it now.

The door opened again, and she held her place at the back of the car. She had no idea if security was waiting for her on the ground floor. As the doors parted, a cluster of men looked into the empty car at her. None of them were security, and they all looked like she was holding them up. One of them exhaled and shifted to enter the car. She released the rail and walked past them, trying to look as calm and confident as she could. The man who had started to enter gave her an angry scowl. She scowled back, refusing to give ground. She didn't stop once she was heading toward the front door. She cleared the entrance and walked with purpose down the street, but she refused to run, no matter how much her fear was screaming at her. She was two blocks away before she stopped to look at the first newspapers she had cared to see that day, *her* day.

Normally she would have read the paper on the way to work, but she had been caught up in what was going to happen. The picture on the front was impossible. It looked like a scene from a movie so much that she checked the banner on the paper again. She dropped change onto the stack, took one off the top and walked toward the metro where she could sit for a while and read.

As she skimmed the article, she understood why no one had called the police. If the seemingly impossible scene on the front of the paper and the other stories were true, or if everyone at work had read them, she would be just another impossible event that no one knew how to handle. Her grandmother's belief, that magic would return some day, was right. All of those spells she had told her about, the ones that filled the grimoire she had received when she had joined the coven as a teenager were real. Rebekka paused.

So, how could she use this to her advantage? She needed a job. She laughed at that idea, what she really needed was a kingdom. She needed a way to turn her abilities to her advantage. She needed a way to stop working so hard. She continued to giggle like the little girl she had been when she realized her mother and grandmother were witches. Their powers were weak, but she would be much stronger. The days of spells being gentle nudges to reality were over. The age of the witch was here again.

She looked up and noticed where she was on the metro map. She hadn't realized where she was subconsciously heading but it made sense. Powerful people congregated in a few places in every city. She wanted the internationally strong. The business centers where the conferences met would give her access to some of the most powerful people in the country. Once she was in that group, she could move up. Now, all she had to do was get that grimoire and get better at what she already knew. For a moment she wondered how long this would last, and then she shook off the doubt and waited for her transfer point. Today was *her* day. Tomorrow would take care of itself. She was taking advantage of what came her way. If everything changed back tomorrow, she would figure out what to do then, but that would be on someone else's day.

June 21 – 0550 EDT – Langley, Virginia

Silas keyed into his office with a rapid tattoo of numbers on the keypad. As his fingers flew across it, he glanced around, aware of any observers in the dimly lit basement hallway. Although the code had changed every week since he had moved into the office four years ago, he had no need to look at the keypad. He had not been born with the deep distrust of other human beings. That he had cultivated with the help of his father, grandfather, and several key members of the Milli Istihbarat Teskilati. Now, distrust was as close to him as a twin brother.

The buzz-click of the lock grated his nerves. To trust lock-work to electronics was a mistake. He had told them that when he first moved into his cell at Langley, and then proved his point by disabling the electronic lock with his pocketknife. To be fair, his pocketknife was special, but locks should not be that easy to defeat, especially at the main office of the Central Intelligence Agency.

He turned the handle and walked into the small office, which he used to comfort himself through his exile. The back wall was blank with only a picture of his parents' property in Maine. The wall on the left side of his desk contained a glass shelf filled with puzzle boxes collected from all over the world. Among them were a myriad of closed metal polyhedrons that looked alien among the other opened wooden and stone puzzles. Two, on the lowest shelf, had wicked looking blades sticking out in all directions, mocking his failure. He would solve those one day. He certainly had enough time on his hands each day waiting on *the* call that would never come. Although his new duties at the agency were consultation and training, he had done very little of either since his old college friend had won the election. Who would have ever guessed that knowing the President of the United States could damage a career?

Each day Silas had to remind himself of the secret truth about his reassignment. They had talked about it before the election. It made sense to have someone she could trust standing by to help with any sticky problems that may come up. Now all Silas had to do was live through the ninety-nine-percent of dull waiting for the one-percent excitement. It had been an amazingly quiet four years. In a few more months, once the election was over, either his sentence would continue or he would be released and allowed to return to Turkey or somewhere else that didn't have basements. Some days it was enough to make him consider changing his vote.

The rest of the agency could never know about the secret line to the White House. They could never suspect he was under cover. He had to look like a disgraced field agent, one put out to pasture in the early years of his career waiting on retirement and just holding on, somehow, against the merciless budget knife. It was tough to look like a failed agent while remaining ever vigilant, but that was what undercover work was all about.

Each day he scanned his office for any sign that he had been compromised. The most rudimentary of his signals was broken so whoever had entered his office was a novice. Silas felt his hackles rise as he quickly scanned the room. His eyes paused for a moment on the only award he felt he had ever really earned. The third place trophy from the International Snipers Competition, perched on a small glass shelf by the door, had earned a place of honor on his wall where he could see it all day. The event had been early in his career at the agency, and he would never forget the grueling training that led up to it. No other event or mission had challenged or taught him more. The award reminded him that he could accomplish anything. In a way, he was proving that with this mission every day. This was no weather-swept pinnacle where he watched secluded from view for his target, enduring days of solitude while waiting for the word. No, the weather here was a little nicer.

Silas finished his scan by returning to the most obvious evidence someone had been in his office. A single box sat on his desk that had not been there when he left the day before. The irritating box reminded him of the insanity of requiring locked doors then giving everyone keys. He took a moment longer to reassure himself that the box was all they had left and then stepped into the room. The door closed behind him with a reassuring click.

He took out his pocketknife and turned the box around gently with the unopened implement. The label on the box made him smile and relax a little. The address was handwritten in a very pretty Abjad that he recognized as the handwriting of a dark-haired angel in Istanbul who sat at the front desk of Akil's small import-export business. Silas opened the thin blade on the knife while enjoying memories of his friend and brother.

He had met the slender Arab in a musty storehouse full of stolen Persian artifacts. As he recalled, neither of them really cared about anything in the building. They were both looking for a secret passage that, according to a family legend, led to something far more important, something hidden by the Folkvardr, their shared ancient lineage. After several attempts to fool each other, they finally figured out, mostly by mistake, that they shared the lineage they were trying to track down. Together they found the first and most dangerous of the polyhedrons on Silas' wall. He stole a quick glance at the menacing little puzzle box on the bottom shelf with blades sticking out all around it and grinned at the shared memory.

He and Akil had designed the matching set of pocketknives after nearly killing themselves with that puzzle. There were only two in the world. They looked like any number of Swiss-style knives, but they had a full set of lock picks and other useful tools secreted among the blades.

The spicy aroma of the packaging and the handwriting on the label diverted Silas' thoughts from his clansman to the most perfect woman in his memories. He could never forget the smooth creamed-coffee color of her satiny skin and one hot night in June. It had been too long since he had seen Dalal and enjoyed a good cup of coffee that she made in the very old Turkish cezve. The memory of sitting among dusty exports in his friend's warehouse smoking a pipe and sipping a good Turkish coffee was starting to dim. He needed to visit his old friend and the only woman Silas could ever really consider as more than a challenging puzzle to figure out and then place on his shelf.

He ran his fingers around the taped edges feeling for wires or other indications of an explosive. It was not that he didn't trust Akil. In fact, he trusted him as much as he trusted anyone, but he could not afford to drop his guard. Silas still had enemies in the field, and being in a basement office in Langley, Virginia, made finding him too easy. He took a few more seconds to scan the box. Satisfied he was safe, he ran the blade under the tape that enclosed what had to be a new treasure from Akil.

The packaging, as always, was filled with crumpled newspaper, which he discarded into a drawer. He would read what Akil wanted him to know later. First, he had to see what the man had found. Nestled in the bottom, surrounded by packing foam, he found the prize—a dodecahedron with several interlocking metal plates on its surface. The metal of the puzzle box was tarnished but not rusted. It had aged well, but it was very old. With caution, he lifted it out by placing the creases of his fingers along the edge of two opposite sides. There was no way to know what would set off the trap mechanism in the package, but he had learned over time that the edges were usually safe to hold when carrying them. Uneven pressure on any one side could set off the trap and take the hand. He gingerly placed the new prize on the blotter on his desk and stepped back to look at it.

As always, there was no writing on the outside. There was never any indication there was anything inside of the puzzle box. Silas could not prove, even through years of trying to open the menacing little things, that there was anything in them. But he knew from stories that never should have existed that the Folkvardr had often hidden important treasures in this form of puzzle box. Ask anyone else, and neither the Folkvardr nor the treasures ever existed, and that was how Silas wanted to keep it.

He looked at his watch. Although the offices around him would all be filling up over the next few hours, it would be unlikely he would have any visitors before noon. If everything remained the same, he would not have a visitor at all today. Why not see if he could find the secret of his new puzzle?

Although the pocketknife was an acceptable tool in a pinch and was always his first choice, this work would require his full kit. From his key ring, he selected a small nickel-plated box. He opened the box and removed a delicate key that looked like three very thin toothpicks with fine hairs lining both sides of the blades. He inserted this key into the lock on his desk drawer and turned it. The reassuring click of real security thrilled him and with a fleeting thought of thanks, he put the gnome key back into its case. As a final show of respect, he ran his thumb across the raised rune on the lid of the key box.

From the side drawer he pulled a battered leather roll. The leather had been around for generations and had that warm beaten feeling he loved. It still smelled of leather and oil, which spoke to the respect the men who had owned the kit had for it. A combination rune that looked like thurisaz struck through with a long diagonal stroke was tooled into the corner of the roll. The tooling had almost vanished back into the leather, but the lesson and matching tattoo that marked Silas as a member of the ancient protective brotherhood would never leave him. He ran his thumb across the symbol on the roll.

He opened the case and rolled out the covers to expose a collection of tools ranging from very fine to more coarse. Each tool had a place in the rolled pocket, and they decreased in size from the top. The ones he wanted were at the very bottom and were almost hair thin. In a small pocket, masterfully added to the kit by a later generation, he found a delicate pair of levered lenses attached to a bar with a nosepiece in the center.

He set the lenses on his nose and turned his attention to the puzzle box on his desk. Satisfied the space was workable, he sat down in the chair to focus on his prize. He selected several lenses, changing the magnification until he had them set just right. When he could see the space between the joined plates, he started studying how the thing worked. It was very intricate, and he had no idea how it had been made. No one had yet matched this level of machine miniaturization in the modern world, not even the very old Swiss watch on his wrist. Computer chips and electronics had surpassed this miniaturization but not physical machines. Cautiously he inserted a thin blade selected from several probes in the kit. The magnifiers made the tool look almost too big to fit into the tiny slot.

Just as the probe entered the slot, a menacing warble issued from the phone. Silas pushed back from his desk and jumped up from his seat in case he had triggered the device. The tool hung between the plates where he had inserted it. He stared at it with his last breath trapped in his chest.

No blades shot out of the sides.
The ringing continued.
No deadly gas filled the room.
The ancient box sat on the blotter with a tool hanging from it.
The ringing continued.
He was okay.
He released his breath in a slow hiss.
The phone continued to demand attention.
He scowled at the irritating disturbance as if it had tried to kill him and did

nothing while he marshaled his pulse and breathing. The ringing ended.

A minute later, when he was ready to return his attention to the puzzle, a light on the phone's surface blinked, demanding he deal with business. Three things convinced him to abandon his new toy, his phone never rang, no one ever left a message, and it was the secret line to the White House.

"Not today apparently," he growled as he carefully lifted the dodecahedron from his desk and set in onto the glass shelf.

Even though the impossible had happened, there was no reason to take a chance and leave the landmine of a puzzle box out where he could mistakenly kill himself. He put the tool and lenses back into the case, rolled the case up, and placed it back in his drawer. With everything back in place, he jabbed at the button on the phone and waited for the irritating caller to tell him why they had disturbed and damn near killed him.

"Silas, this is Tara." The excited voice of his friend filled the room. "Look, I brought you close to me for those special situations I knew I would be facing. This is one of them. Have you seen the papers this morning? I know you don't read domestic news so you don't get pulled into it, but this isn't just domestic. Look, I know you know something about the occult. I've sent you a few links; give me a call when you've had a chance to review them. I need someone on this. My cabinet is all, hair-on-fire, right now. I need to know how to react to this. I need to know if this is real. Call me back when you get this."

Silas stared at the phone, three years of silence and now a call at dawn. He had to admit it was good to hear from her, but he would have preferred if she wanted to have drinks and talk over old times. Silas reviewed the call in his mind. The closest thing to occult he had ever done was make pledges cover themselves in goats blood and repeat the lyrics to Metallica songs in Latin. He had studied most secret societies, and his great-grandfather had made sure he knew the truth about them, but he wouldn't call that occult. The world believed far more about those societies than was ever true, thankfully. What was Tara going on about today?

He turned to his left and smacked the keyboard. The monitor sprang to life and a password challenge jumped onto it. He keyed in the twenty-four characters he had randomly selected and memorized for this month and waited. The screen appeared, and he quickly navigated to a not well-known e-mail account where the message was waiting. He clicked the first link, and his newsreader filled the screen.

The impossible picture on the front page made him check the source newspaper to make sure it was a real story and not something three guys in IT had slipped into the President's in-box to get her going; not the best way to end a career. Convinced, he turned back to the story. The picture was of a long snake-like creature that had several muscular arms along its body. It was wrapped in between cars stopped on a dark street in Egypt. The open mouth, forked tongue, and large teeth made it look very unhappy. The story said it had rushed into the street screaming in Arabic and trashing cars. When the police approached it, several of the men in the front fell over dead. The others opened fire as they retreated and although several of them hit the target there appeared to be no damage done to what some officials called a "basilisk".

Silas flipped to another link. This one was more his speed. Two very attractive Indian women were standing at the end of the street surrounded by lines of men who were handing them money, food, and several other parcels. They appeared to be naked from the waist up. The picture was altered from the original; the publisher of the story had blurred the inappropriate parts. Even ignoring the possible fake pictures, Silas was not sure what the news was here. Then, he looked at the blown up pictures and the highlighted regions that showed the women had no legs. From the waist down they were snakes.

"What is this, the Chinese Year of the Lizard?" Silas commented aloud as he flipped through several more stories.

In each one, the creatures at the forefront reminded him of some mythical lizard story. He had no idea what to tell his friend. Each story told the same tale. The creature was confused or disoriented. They had wandered into the street, mall, or other public place. They all seemed to be peaceful until they were pressed for information and then reacted violently, or in the case of the females, charmed their questioners. This had to be a joke.

He picked up the phone and dialed the number he knew but never called. It rang once, and Tara answered.

"What took you so long? I don't have time to be waiting on you."

"If you want to bust something, look in your own pants, Madame President."

"You're never going to respect me, are you?"

"Do I need to send the pictures out?"

"Funny—Now, seriously, what do you think? Crazy stuff, huh?"

"I think you're wasting tax payer money playing jokes on your old college lovers." It was a fact, and it was in the past, for her.

"No joke, Silas." She paused to make the point clear. "I've seen them, on video anyway. Secret Service won't let me get close to one of them."

"Someone's playing a joke on you then. Look, this kind of stuff can't happen. These creatures don't exist."

"I know. But, they're on every news channel. I have governors calling. They've called out the National Guard. Texas has a breakout of five giant lizard men who have taken over some kind of sports equipment plant. That one's been kept out of the news. I have to take a stance on this. I know those guys down there. They won't wait much longer."

Silas swallowed.

It wasn't a joke.

If it wasn't a joke, then what was it? Something his grandfather had told him as a child made him shift in his chair.

"Tara, listen. I'm not your guy on this. I'm out of my league."

"Bull, Silas, this is just up your alley. I want you on this. There's a plane waiting for you. Get to Texas. Find out what's going on. You have my backing on anything you need. I've already called your boss. Open the packet on the plane. It has everything you need. If it doesn't, call me on the cell in the packet."

"I'll see what I can find out then," Silas answered, surrendering to the insanity of it.

"Silas, I know you hate technology, but keep me in the loop on what you find. This could take a nasty turn."

"Or it could just go away," he reassured the woman at the top. "I've got your number."

The line clicked off, and Silas stared at the next story. It was a little different. The story said a young woman was being questioned about a fire in an apartment building in Bangkok. Apparently the fire started in her apartment but spread through the entire building in seconds. They found no evidence of accelerants, and the girl said she was asleep when the fire started. She was the only one to escape the building.

Silas closed the reader and sat back in his chair. For a moment, he thought about Tara and why he was willing to sit in a cell every day for her. He knew it was over, but something about the way he had been raised didn't allow him to abandon her when she needed him. He put the past aside and turned his mind toward the problem again.

He had been rubbing the rune on his key box as he thought about it. He had never really believed his grandfather's warning. Even if the old man had been on the level, what did this have to do with an ancient, long forgotten wizard king? Silas pushed his grandfather's tales out of his head and looked around his office. There was not much he could use here; he would grab what he needed on the way. As an afterthought he opened the locked drawer again and took his tools with him. Something was nagging at him, and it had little to do with June in Texas.

June 21 – About the same time – Kennesaw, Georgia.

A scream had forced Adrian out of his sleep. He couldn't tell at the moment if it had been his dream or if it was real. He couldn't remember dreaming. He didn't feel completely present.

He threw back the covers on his bed and slipped his feet to the floor. He was not fully awake because his head felt larger, and his hair felt funny. In fact, his whole body felt strange. As always when he first woke, he looked down at the floor and his feet. Green and blue scales covered his legs down to the four claws on what had been his feet. A fifth claw gripped at the wood floor from the back of his foot. He stifled a scream of his own and ran his hands over his eyes. He could feel his heart racing at the change in appearance. This had to be a dream.

A new scream from down the hall drug him from his stupor. There was something going on in his parents' room.

He threw the covers to the side and ran for the door. Adrian pushed his odd appearance out of his mind. His mother needed his help. Everything else would have to wait. He yanked the door handle to open the door, and the hinges in the wall ripped free from the wood frame. He stared at the reptilian hand that was holding the door for a second before tossing it onto his bed. This was a weird dream; too much pizza, had to be too much pizza.

He ran down the hallway and opened the door to his parents' room more carefully. He wanted to help her, not make it worse. He stepped into the room. His mother was crouching on the edge of the bed looking at a monster covered in scales standing on the other side of the bed. Out of its back, a tail twitched back and forth as its long-nosed and horned head looked around the room. Adrian lunged across the room at the back of the large lizard attacking his mother.

The monster must have seen him coming. It spun around using its tail and arms to catch Adrian and throw him into the corner of the room. His mother screamed louder as the lizard looked from him to her. It shook its head and raised its arms up to its waist. It turned clawed hands up and out to each side.

Adrian expected the monster to rip him open and eat his guts, but it just stood there and looked at him. Something that reminded Adrian of sadness passed over its eyes as it looked from him to his mother.

Adrian glanced at the bed where his father should be. Had the monster already feasted on him? Where was he? Why wasn't he helping? He couldn't see him.

"Mom," he shouted as he stood up. "Calm down. I'm going to help you."

Her scream stopped with a gurgle as if it caught in her throat. She stared at his face. Her eyes were wide, and she tilted her head to the left to look at him again. She stared at him like she would a troubling stain. Her eyes widened more than he thought possible, and the scream in her throat escaped as if shot from a cannon.

The monster turned to face him.

"Adrian?" His father's voice was coming out of the monster's mouth.

He felt himself mirror his mother's actions. The monster hadn't eaten his father; the monster was his father. Adrian slumped backward against the wall. It was too far away to hold him so he slid down onto the floor.

"It's me, your dad. Trust me, I know how hard this is. You have to listen to me. Your mom won't listen. She's freakin'. We need to calm her down." The permanent sadness in his father's eye was mirrored on the reptilian face of the monster.

Adrian looked down at his own hands. He still had no idea why he and his father were lizards, but it was important to calm his mother down.

"Mom, it's dad and me. Calm down." Adrian tried to help. "It's Adrian. We're not going to hurt you."

He stood up from the floor finally and placed his hands out in front of him to show her he was not going to hurt her. He looked just like his father had a few moments before.

She stopped screaming again but just shook her head and then started crying. His dad moved to comfort her, but she cringed and slid back further toward the corner of the bed.

"Dad, what's going on? What happened to us?"

"I don't know yet. We'll find out as soon as we can calm her down."

"Shut-up," she shouted from the corner. "I don't know what demons you are, but you're not my husband and son. What have you done to them? Why are you doing this to me? Get ye behind me, Satan." Spittle flew from her lips as she cried and yelled the last words. She clutched with trembling hands at a small cross at her neck and pointed it at each of them. Her eyes showed hatred. The fear was going away.

She self-consciously covered herself and the thin gown she was sleeping in with a robe she left at the foot of the bed. As she did, she watched each of them. Her eyes darted from corner to corner. She shifted her feet on the bed and then stepped down at the foot of the bed. When her feet were on solid ground she still shifted back and forth. She never dropped the cross and always kept it between her and them.

"Mom, listen to me." Adrian tried to use a comforting voice like his father used from time to time. "Don't I sound like myself? Can't you see it's me? I don't know what's happened to me, but I'm still Adrian. I'm your son."

He felt a sharp pain of worry that she might not believe him. What would he do if she didn't? Maybe he would wake up. Even as he thought the thought, he knew he would not be waking up from this. It was too real. His mother had always been there for him. How would he get through this if she didn't believe him? What would he do?

She looked at his face and his eyes. Her face softened a little but then terror filled her face.

"What's happened to you?"

He felt the thrill of her recognition. Maybe all of this would be alright.

She reached out to him for an instant, but then she pulled her arms back around her and hugged herself. She kissed the cross and pointed it at him. Tears streamed down her cheeks.

"My little boy. Why did you take my little boy?"

She dropped her face into her free hand and cried. As she broke down, she leaned back against the wall and slid down onto the floor next to the bed.

"Mom, it's still me. Nothing's happened to me. No one has taken me. I'm here with you." It was the truth as far as he was concerned. He couldn't deny that he didn't understand why he looked different, but he was still the same person he had been. He could feel the fear of her rejection grow with every word he spoke.

"Lies! I'll hear no lies of the devil."

She refused to listen and moved her hands from her face to her ears. With her eyes closed, she leaned from side to side in time to her sobbing moans. His father had turned away from them both and was staring at the mirror shaking his head at his strange appearance. Adrian stood from his corner and approached him.

"What's happened, dad? What caused this?"

He held his hands out in front of him. His father turned from the mirror and looked at him with a look Adrian had never seen before. His eyes looked tired and weak. Adrian thought he was going to faint, but his hand dived into the top drawer in the dresser. In a flash his father's hand was out and pointing a stainless revolver at his own temple.

"Dad, No!" His words came out just as the trigger clicked the double action revolver to life. The flash filled the space between the barrel and his father's head. Adrian had expected a slow motion explosion of events. He expected to see the bullet travel the short distance and burrow into his father's head. Instead, the whole sequence was over in the flash and bang of the revolver.

His father was leaning against the dresser. Adrian's ears were ringing and his mother was screaming again. She leapt up and ran past him through the door. Adrian felt like the only sane person in the room, and that was an awful feeling for an eighteen year old. Although he often said he was the only sane person in the house, he didn't like being right.

He reached out to catch his father, but he was still standing. Adrian looked for the wound and pulled clothing from the drawer to stop the inevitable bleeding, but there was none. His father stood there looking at him through disappointed eyes. He dropped the gun to the floor. Adrian wanted to scream, but it would serve him no better than it had his mother. He pulled his father's scale-covered shoulder toward him and looked at his head. The bullet hadn't even scratched him. The force of the shot had pushed him over. His eyes were vacant, and there was no reaction. The shot must have knocked him senseless.

"What the hell were you thinking?" he screamed at the vacant stare.

His father didn't say anything. Adrian released him and stood in the middle of the room. What the hell was going on?

June 21 – 1000 EDT – Signal Mountain, Tennessee

Clouds flowed over her long scarlet wings as Melissa descended from the malevolent sky. Cool wisps of fog flowed around her head and streaked across her body, leaving swirling eddies in her wake. As she broke through the darkness, tendrils of mist chased her toward her destiny in the slender valley below.

She scanned the approaches for the spy who would alert him she was coming. The blue-green water of the river and small lake reflected moonlight onto the valley, casting a chilling light over the land. The walls of the valley closed in on her like his fist. The single moraine, more ancient than she, ignored her as she dropped from the sky toward it. Turning away, she flew toward the menacing wall of the valley. On a flat outcropping along the cliff's edge, a tower, the only witness to her approach, scrutinized her with no malice. It convicted her with its single digit, pointing out the unobserved invader. He knew she was coming. She could not surprise him. What was she doing here?

Melissa bolted upright in her bed. Sunlight was pouring into the room through the slightly east facing window, which meant she was sleeping late, but that was normal for a summer visit with her grandmother. In fact, everything was exactly the way it should be, except she was naked. She released a breath she realized she was holding.

Had yesterday been a dream? She ran her hands across the sheets. The dull ache of loss locked in her chest seemed to tell at least part of the story. The funeral, the will, the journal: when did reality stop? She looked around the room. The journal sat accusingly on the nightstand beside her bed. She shivered a little as the pieces continued to fall into place. She didn't remember putting the journal there.

Had Nicklaus, the boy she had spent most of her life teasing, really attacked her? Had she run from him and fought him in the yard? Her hand came to her neck and the gold chain that had not been there the day before. Her fingers followed it to the gem-encrusted claw hanging at its end along with the key to the box. The claw pulsed warmly with her touch. Her shoulders slumped a little. That was real, too. There was very little left to question, but Melissa hesitated to face the one thought that filled her with fear and uncertainty. Did she really change into a dragon after failing to cast an ancient spell in time?

Yes, you did, traitor. Why are you struggling with this so? The voice in her head answered her with a growl.

Why did it insist on calling her a traitor? What had she done? She had tried to cast the spell. She had followed the directions but failed.

You failed – this time.

The accusation hissed at her. This time, the words convicted her of some greater crime. She suddenly saw herself again, standing on the pentagram with her wings spread wide voicing the words of the spell. The image shattered into a spike of pain that ripped into her head. She threw her hands across her eyes and cried out, but she couldn't block out the searing light that was still receding to pinpoints of pain in her eyes.

As it cleared, she tried to recapture part of the image. Anything that would help her understand what she did. The pain and brightness returned immediately like a warning. A tear ran down her cheek, and she retreated to a thought of something safe, her grandmother writing in the library.

She had failed this time, not before. She had failed to fulfill her grandmother's last request, but some time before she had not failed. Some ancient time ago, *she* had cast the spell. Was that such a crime?

You know the answer.

"How?" she asked the room.

Think. Use that ancient brain of ours.

"We're free now. The spell is broken."

Right.

"I cast the spell that trapped us." *She* had intentionally trapped dragons in their human form.

That's right, I did. The voice sounded both accusing and consoling.

But, why? She struggled to drag a memory out of her resistant mind and paid again with pain. She had no idea why she cast it the first time, but she knew why she had failed. She had ignored her grandmother's directions. She had wanted to go to bed. Maybe in her heart she had wanted to fail. Maybe she had made a mistake ages before. Maybe no one was ever supposed to cast it.

Maybe.

"Then why did she want me to cast it again? Why was it so important?"

The voice in her mind did not answer.

Melissa pounded her fists into the soft mattress.

Why had she forgotten?

Why was her memory such a mess?

Who was she?

Was she this frail girl in the bed?

No!

The command stopped the breakdown that was rushing into her mind, and halted the panic that was screaming from the resistant corner of her mind. For some reason, she remembered things she never could have done, but she couldn't be sure when and what she had done the night before.

I am Meliastrid. The voice in her mind shouted.

"Who's Melissa?"

I am.

Her eyes rolled to the ceiling and she flopped back into the soft pillows.

The comfortable and well-known memories of Melissa were floating on an ocean of memories she didn't have the day before. Which ones did she trust?

Both and neither.

She brought both hands to her face and pressed her palms into her eyes, wishing the horrible headache would subside.

Melissa sighed into the empty room and stopped resisting. She stopped trying to remember any one thing and just laid on the bed thinking about what she knew.

She was Melissa and Meliastrid. She was human and dragon.

No, I am one. They are just forms I take. I am Meliastrid.

Again, she sighed and accepted these points as fact, and the voice in her head sighed as well.

"Now I just have to figure out why this spell is so important."

It is important, why it was cast may not be important. The fact that it was is, however.

She rolled onto her side and stared at the leather bound journal on her nightstand, its mere presence seeming to accuse her of neglect and avoidance. In a single motion, she threw the covers back and was standing on the plush carpeting of her room. It was time to face this new day.

Dressed in blue jeans and a red sweatshirt, Melissa looked nothing like the mistress of the manor that she now was. She didn't feel like her, either. She walked down the empty hallway on the second floor of her new home and into the middle level of the library where she was always so relaxed. The overstuffed chairs and old carpet of the expansive room with the dark wood immediately comforted her. This was the heart of the house to her.

There were equally elegant rooms on the ground floor and throughout the house, but this was its soul. It was where her grandmother had written. It was where every book Melissa had ever read was stored. Old friends watched over her here. She felt bad that she might have abandoned them for a while, but she was back now.

She ran her hand along the warm wood of the rail surrounding the opening in the second floor that looked down onto the desk below. The sounds of work and the smell of sawdust and wood stain greeted her from the damaged doors where Nicklaus had smashed into the back yard. A cool breeze from the open doors wafted through the opening and she shivered.

In her mind, his hands closed around her throat in a final attempt to kill her. Rage filled his eyes. She wished she could forget that scene, erase the black mark of that encounter and what it meant about her childhood friend.

He's more than that.

She nodded to herself. He was, and that made the situation even more complicated. He was Nickliad, her mate.

The odd feeling of old memories of what seemed to be thousands of years blending with what had been her very short life made her a little dizzy. She gripped the railing and looked down at the new doors. The repairs were well on their way to completion. Charles had already been busy.

He would be down there somewhere among the work, seeing to the manor. The construction blocked her normal path to the ground floor, so she retreated back to the hallway and down the main stairs into the front landing. Another group of workers was repairing the damaged woodwork in the foyer. In a few hours, the scar of the fight that had ranged through this house the night before would be gone. Yet the wound Melissa carried within herself struck far deeper.

At the foot of the stairs, she turned left into the kitchen to get away from the noise and intrusion she felt from the workers. She stopped on the other side of the door to collect herself. It seemed wrong to wipe away the evidence this soon. There should be a period of mourning for her ancient relationship.

Why do you wish to leave your mate?

"He tried to kill me."

You still don't understand his side of this.

"He was going to kill Charles."

He was angry, and that is a human.

"He was wrong. Humans didn't trap him."

No, we did.

"And you think he should kill me?"

I think he would be angrier if he knew what I know.

"I had a good reason."

Share it with me when we find out.

Charles cleared his throat from deeper in the kitchen to let her know she was not alone. She stopped talking to herself and walked over to join him. The comforting sameness of the kitchen along with the rock-solid presence of Charles helped stabilize her. She had spent many of her years in the brightly lit, white pine and stainless steel of this room. For five years of her life, she had eaten her oatmeal at the long bar and watched the news with Charles before they each had gone to school. This morning was a little different but still brought back the comfortable memories of her childhood. New, deeper, memories swirled beneath those, threatening to dislodge what she knew of herself, but she clung to the familiar to keep the panic at bay.

You are more than that. If you accept those memories, we will not suffer so much.

She ignored the advice and sat down at the bar in front of a tray where Charles was pouring a glass of orange juice. His left arm seemed stiff as he set the carafe aside. There was no other sign he had been in a fight with a dragon the night before. A news story continued to play and hold his attention.

Throughout her years away at school and into college, she had stopped watching the news. It had never been important to what was going on around her, but this morning it was all about what she had failed to accomplish.

A video clip of two young men fighting filled the small screen above the bar. The clip was very short and changed quickly to a dark scene in a large city where a single man was running down the street screaming something at the camera. The scene changed again to a bad quality video of two women at the head of a traffic jam. They were mostly naked, and the video was appropriately digitized for television. Across the bottom of the screen, a ticker scrolled with short snippets of news to go with the quick intro scenes.

"Reptilian men fight to the death in the streets of Athens."

"Snake women stop traffic in India."

Charles pointed out the tray on the counter. Beneath his coat, she caught a quick glimpse of a pistol that had not been there the day before.

"Good Morning, Miss. I was bringing you some breakfast."

That will not be enough.

"Thanks, I thought I would come down and see what was real this morning." She ignored the sudden empty feeling in her stomach and the complaint about the size of the morning meal.

Grabbing the remote to the television, he turned the volume down as the reporter was talking over the image of a fifteen-foot-tall, blue-scaled basilisk that was crawling over cars in a scene out of the best Hollywood films. Smoke and fire flashed across the screen as rockets leaped toward the beast. The scene shifted back to the reporter before the rockets hit.

"What's that?"

"You should eat first." He switched the set off completely and motioned for her to sit down.

He's protecting you. How sweet of him.

A flash of fear crossed his face.

"Relax. I'm not going to hurt anyone."

"Of course not, Miss."

She sat down in the suddenly cold and foreign room. She would not be able to stand it if Charles was afraid of her.

But, he should be. That is where humans belong.

Melissa shook her head and looked down at the plate. The tray held a plate of eggs and ham with wheat toast. She had requested the same breakfast the day before, but this morning she was craving raw meat and lots of it. How did she tell Charles that when he was staring at her that way? She moved the eggs to one side of her plate and cut into the ham. The salty meat soothed the edges of hunger she had not realized she had. She would need more of that, lots more.

"Charles, I think we should talk about this."

"About what, Miss?"

"Well, to start, what's with the pistol?"

Charles never looked away from her face. He had been trained by the

Marines to deal with questions he didn't want to answer and by his father to control a delicate situation.

"I felt, with last night's events and this morning's news, that I should be prepared." There was no request for permission. There was no apology. There was just fact.

"Prepared for what?"

"This is a compromise. I didn't think you would like me walking around with a rifle and grenade launcher."

His humor, dipped in truth, took her off guard as it always did, and she grinned. He was as serious as he had been with his first answer. He had no intention of backing down, so she decided to pay attention even though he was being flippant to soften the impact.

"What makes you think you would need them?"

He sighed. "The news is not good this morning. Apparently whatever happened here last night was repeated all over the world." He refilled her juice. He was avoiding something. "There have been incidents. The news is reporting both outbreaks of lizard man violence and hunt teams scouring the woods and jungles for them. They've even killed a dragon."

Fear and dread she had never felt before filled her mind.

That's not possible.

Melissa realized it was wrong to think humans could not kill a dragon and asked the question that was troubling her.

"Where?" She ran through a list of dragons she knew were near her.

"Not around here." He seemed to realize her fear. "It was in France. That was the report you were just watching. It's been all over the news, and they won't stop showing that video."

Muscles she was not aware she was clenching relaxed, and for the first time that morning she had agreed with the voice in her head. "That's not a dragon. It's a basilisk."

Charles stared at her for a moment, and she realized suddenly why he was confused.

"It's an abomination. It's a merging of species that creates a rather vile creature that has no redeeming qualities at all. They were right to kill it. It has no mind but hate and rage." Melissa had no idea where the information had come from, but she knew all about the beast and why it was important to kill it.

Charles continued to stare at her until she stopped eating to think about why he was confused.

They are common to us, but he has never seen any of this. But, why are they here? How did they return?

Fear returned for a moment when she considered what it would take to create the creature that was supposed to be extinct. The fear was followed by a searing headache when she attempted to remember why it was extinct. She couldn't answer her own question.

Charles was waiting for some kind of answer to the unasked question on his face. She had the impression that if it had not been for his training his mouth would be open.

"What?"

"Nothing, it's just... strange, Miss. No disrespect meant."

"I know, don't you think I know? I have no idea why I suddenly knew that was a basilisk and not a dragon. I can't tell which of the thoughts in my head are mine and which ones belong to the dragon that I changed into last night."

They are one and the same, we are the same being.

Melissa shook her head at the intruding thought.

"What you can't hear is the argument I'm going through as I try to figure out all of this. What's real? What's fantasy? What will cause the pain." She threw her hands up. "I can't explain why that thing is here."

It really shouldn't be.

"I can't explain why I'm glad it's dead."

Because it's an abomination and should be destroyed.

"Ahh!" she screamed into the ceiling.

Charles watched her internal argument with concern. She shook her head at him.

"Don't think I'm not concerned. This is freaking me out. I'm trying to figure out what's going on, and every time I get close to an answer I get slammed in the head with this blinding, painful, bright light. The only thing keeping me sane is that I know I'm still Melissa. I'm still Mel."

Meliastrid.

He grinned at the use of the nickname he knew she protected. She felt a little better. A flash of pride crossed Charles' eyes as he nodded to her that he understood. They were not back to what they had been before he left for basic training, but their shared experience was breaking through his stony exterior. She smiled back at him from her plate.

"Could I have some more ham?" She had eaten all that was on her plate, and she was not going to be able to make it without more meat.

"Of course, Miss." He nodded and stood up to prepare it for her, and she felt a pang of guilt at continuing to treat him like a servant, but a gentle pressure at the back of her mind stopped her from saying anything about it. Her mother was reaching out to her. It was the first time she had felt another dragon's mind that morning, and it awakened a desire far more voracious than the hunger she still felt. She had not felt a deeper need in ages and to feel the suddenly warm feeling of her mother's presence soothed an absence she had not been aware was there. When it retreated, she felt disappointed in being alone again. She nearly cried out at the loss of the connection, but she controlled her emotions and looked up at Charles. He was watching her with a curious look on his face as he seared another ham steak.

"My parents are coming."

"In what form?" he asked.

Odd question, why would they not come in dragon form?

Melissa suddenly realized he would have no way of knowing the answer that seemed so natural to her.

"I expect father will be very unlikely to ever take human form again." She grimaced at how right he had been searching for their birthright and how disappointing it must have been to him for so long. Had he known all along that he was trying to get back this heritage? How many other dragons knew they were trapped? How many had suffered and for how long? He was the King of the European Dragons, and he was trapped in such a feeble form. That was not how she wanted to think of her father. "In fact, I expect this will be a very uncomfortable meeting."

"More so I expect, if he flies here."

"What are you talking about?"

"Melissa, I'm not the only one armed this morning. Didn't you hear what I said about hunt teams? They're out there, near here, scouring the woods for lizard men. This is the wrong time to be flying around exposing yourself. Do you want to draw attention to yourself right now and turn them into dragon hunters? Do you want to draw them here?"

How dare he try to tell us how we should act! Her inner voice growled, and she had to struggle to keep it in.

"It is wise to be cautious," she answered both Charles and herself.

Humans had not seen a dragon in… She struggled with a sharp pain to find the answer and finally gave up. Humans had not seen a dragon in a long time, and they would react to what they saw and believed. They would be fearful and react accordingly. Charles' fear was tempered some by what he had experienced with Helena. No other humans had his experience to lean on, so, what seemed like a normal thing, flying to meet her, was probably not safe or smart. That was what Charles had been telling her while she had focused on her ham. Instinctively Melissa reached out to her mother.

"You must not fly here. You must remain in human form and be discreet. You must make him understand."

Agitation returned to her in a wave; and although the presence was comforting, the emotion was not.

"I've warned them. When they arrive, please show them to the back patio. My father will need to stretch his wings." Charles nodded, placed the new pieces of ham on her plate, and left the room.

Her mother's presence, agitated or not, had been far too short, and Melissa found herself longing to reach out to her. It was not for several minutes, while she enjoyed the savory flavor and aroma of the meat, that

Melissa realized she had given an order to her parents. She would pay for that.

CHAPTER 3 - CHAOS OF BIRTH

June 21 – 1000 CDT – Outside of Dallas, Texas

The black Bell 204 Jet Ranger with "FBI" painted on each sliding door descended into a military staging area. If the colors had been slightly different, Silas would have thought he was flying into an LZ in Vietnam instead of a field in Texas. He closed up the packet he had been scanning since he left Washington and took in the scene.

Two National Guard Humvees were anchoring a containment ring at the entrance to the lone office building of the sports equipment manufacturing plant. There was nothing else around for several miles. Beyond the plant, Silas could see the other side of the containment anchored by two more Humvees. From this distance, it was hard to tell but he thought he could make out the .50 Caliber machine guns, affectionately known as "Ma Deuce" by their gunners, traversing the scrub in the no-man's-land between them. He borrowed a pair of Steiner 10x50's to verify the armaments.

Silas scanned the positions drawing the lines of interlocking fire as the pilot threaded through a pair of news choppers angling for the money shot. From a quick review there appeared to be no avenue of escape for the lizard men who had taken over this remote manufacturing plant.

Silas didn't need to read the packet again to recall the details. Though quickly thrown together, the report, now hours old, said the five "men" had entered the break room of the manufacturing plant, ripping open the secured doors and threatening anyone who tried to leave. "The Angry One" struck a man who tried to confront them. No one was aware of his condition. A few young women had escaped through the kitchen entrance and now provided the only perspective of the scene. Silas hoped this little war was not being staged because of that report.

The pilot pointed to a taped off square on the ground behind a cluster of vehicles including one Humvee, an old model Suburban, and a nondescript sedan with government tags. A small easy-up covered a quickly prepared command center. Silas gave the pilot a thumbs-up and with minor control motions, he executed a landing apropos to the scene into which they were descending.

Everybody lived for the action. They all wanted to perform their duty. They all wanted to get it right like they did in the exercises, but sometimes that desire got in the way of the control needed to keep something from getting crazy. There was so much commitment to the performance that it was almost too easy to start a war. Someone needed to back off the button a little before this powder keg became a petard. Silas was not interested in foisting himself on one today.

The skids touched down lightly on the dry soil, and a cloud of dust billowed around the helicopter. The sound of the engine changed as the pilot cut the power and the craft settled to the ground. Silas scanned his gear to make sure he still looked like the FBI agent he was supposed to be. He flipped the ID pocket of his new FBI vest out where his equally new ID could reflect the early morning sun into the eyes of the already too excited agents and soldiers. There was no way to avoid the immediate jurisdiction competition that was coming, and he had no authority to take over from the local incident commander. If he was facing the National Guard, then Silas had nothing in his packet big enough to help him. He would need to talk to Tara about that, but today he would have to use charm. Silas smiled at the familiar situation. One last adjustment of his go-bag and he was ready.

The pilot gave him a thumbs-up, and he was out the door, walking toward the taped off edge of the LZ. At the opening, a young corporal was waiting for him.

"Sir," his eyes darted to the ID and then back up to Silas' face, "If you will come with me, the colonel is about to start his briefing."

Keep the new guy moving to avoid the inevitable conflict; good tactic. Silas nodded and motioned for the corporal to lead the way with a smile. No need to take it out on the enlisted, he was just doing his job.

As they crossed the interestingly deserted highway, Silas got his first solid impression that something was not right about the staging. He reviewed what he had seen from the air again and suddenly felt much better. He nodded as they slipped into the 10x10 square of people looking at a situation board.

As soon as he saw the map, he knew what his gut had told him as he crossed the road was true. The cordon around the building was intentionally hard but it had one weakness. The incident commander wanted to push the subjects to run, but he did not trust their mental stability to do it. He was using subconscious clues in the staging of the cordon to lead the fight-or-flight response to flight. He was going to funnel them out of the fight. It was a risky move. Silas hoped it would work.

The incident commander, a colonel with "Holloway" embroidered on the tape above his left pocket, returned his nod as he entered the circle. A single shift of his eye told Silas that he had been wrong about his first impression of this man's operation. There was nothing haphazard or reactive in the way he set up this scene. It just looked that way. He had read the brief Silas had thrown together on the plane. Silas pulled his tablet from his go-bag and connected to the field network. Everything clicked into place like it had been planned for years; Tara had this organized for a long time and was pulling it all together like the puppet master that she was. Silas scanned the badges around him and realized that they all had that just printed look. None of these people were what they appeared to be, except the colonel. There was no way that Holloway was anything but what he said he was. The armored cavalry badge on his ACU told him he was dealing with the real deal there. Nothing worked this well out of the box; Holloway was following Silas' brief without even meeting him. Silas felt Tara's hand there too, but it was more comfortable than a forced détente.

Silas let the man lead his briefing and bring everyone up to speed on the plan. While the others listened, Silas measured the collected group. The major standing behind the colonel was not a problem. He was as authentic Army as the man he followed. They were hand and glove. To their right was the FBI HRT team scrambled from the local office. They would be the hammer of this scenario, highly visible and backed up by the heavy National Guard firepower. They would have no problem with their role; and if they were trained right, they would understand the benefit of the bluff as well as the hard hit. The real worry was the authentic regional director of the FBI standing with them. His badge and his body language presented all the signs of someone who had not been read-in and was not happy about it. Silas shifted toward him.

The locals were standing to the left of the briefing map. This was not the first time they had been part of something this big. The sheriff looked backwoods, but he carried an air and knowledge under the wide brimmed hat that could only come from experience. He was sitting back listening to the plan, happy that someone else would be on the hook if it went bad, but he was not showing any sign that he was worried it would fail.

Silas looked back toward the airspace around them. The helicopters that had been circling when they arrived were gone. Someone had sealed the airspace behind him. This event would have no play on the local news at all. A special agent back in town was probably writing the cover story even as they all planned this mission. That was the last piece of the puzzle; the news could not report that the FBI and National Guard had let hostage takers escape. The story on the news tonight would be a completely different story of peaceful surrender after tense negotiations.

With the briefing complete, each team started to break and move to their staging areas. Silas was standing next to the FBI regional director as they started to break up.

"You think this will work?" he asked conspiratorially.

The guy rolled his eyes. "I think we had better be careful that no one gets killed on our team when this idea falls apart. That's why my team will be ready to take the real shot." He even winked at Silas.

Silas grinned and nodded back to him. Convinced he was among friends, the director angled his head back toward the western horizon. Silas followed his glance looking for any tell-tale signs from the sniper team the director was hinting he had out there. Silas couldn't see them, but he knew where he would be.

There was nothing Silas could do now. The agent was in place, and it would create a disturbance in the otherwise clean plan if he tried. He would just hope none of the lizard men were interested in fighting instead of running, but that had always been his opinion. They were confused and agitated, but not violent unless trapped. Either way, they would know soon enough.

After the director was well on his way back to the FBI staging area to organize the HRT, Silas joined the colonel at the map. Holloway and Major Carson were carefully scanning over the terrain, looking for any holes or weaknesses in the plan. The eraser on Carson's yellow pencil was pointing toward a small rise to the west of the containment ring. Carson had worked with snipers before. When he realized Silas was walking up, the pencil nervously adjusted down to a completely unimportant location on the map.

"So, I told them they had better get those MRE's down here if they didn't want some hot-and-bothered soldiers in their barracks in the morning asking what happened."

"Relax Mike, this man's no more FBI than my boots. Ain't that right, Silas?"

Silas grinned at the older man. "How long have you known her?"

"Before you met her in College, I'll assure you. Can't say I'm sorry she wised up about you."

Silas nodded smiling at the protective jab from the older man. They both knew they were on the same team here. "If this works, that little nest will be no issue."

"I was just saying that same thing to Mike."

Mike nodded to Silas, accepting the relationship between the two men completely, but continued his argument. He was a good soldier, looking for all possible problems.

"Right, but all it takes is one move by one of the X-rays and that sniper's going to take a shot."

"And he will be correct to take it," Silas answered. Honesty in conflicts was the right option. "Look at the reports we have. We don't know exactly what we're dealing with here. Every scrap of intel we have comes from the foggy memories of a few scared witnesses. We have to assume they are more powerful than we think." Not for the first time that morning, Silas realized how absurd all of this was. If he stopped to think about it, he would not be able to do his job, so he ignored the feeling and went on.

Holloway listened and nodded. Carson paused a moment taking in what Silas had said.

"Right," Holloway said. "We leave him in place. We really don't know what they can do, and our lives are on the line here. The FBI has full control of the breach."

"Can we get ears on the FBI?" Carson asked a question he should have had the answer to.

"Nope," Holloway answered flatly, "didn't have time to get everything here."

With a simple slash of the pencil through the air, Carson marked the missing radio unit off his list and returned to the plan. Now neutral and waiting, his pencil bounced in the air between him and the map as he stared at nothing and focused on the problem.

"I might be able to help with that," Silas said.

"They trust you?" Carson asked, using his pencil to punctuate his question. With a little spin he slipped it behind his ear.

"They do now."

"Do it," Holloway decided and Silas moved to make his connection to the FBI's radio net.

After a few minutes of convincing and a little pulling rank, Silas had his radio set to the FBI's tactical net and a call sign assigned. The final pieces were falling into place. He could hear the National Guard talking to the FBI on the shared frequency in one ear and the FBI's private conversations as they set up their actions and covers in another. They were not taking chances. The order was shoot-to-kill at the first sign of trouble. Everyone was in place, command and control of the breach was in the FBI's hands. Silas scanned the tactical board to familiarize himself with the call signs in use. They had two moving teams, Bravo and Hotel. Bravo was the breaching team, and Hotel was the Humvees covering the entrances. Romeo and Tango were the primary command units. Romeo was the FBI team leading the assault. Tango was the National Guard Command Center. It looked like a standard setup. The doors were coded by the facing side of the building and numbered. There was only one floor so everything would be on the Alpha level. The lizard men were accounted for as five X-Rays. All the players were present except for one, and his call would not be on the board.

The radio crackled to life. "Bravo-One, Romeo-One advise when you are in position."

In a textbook demonstration of how to give your enemy too much time to react and time to think, the HRT, Bravo, was breaching as far away from the X-rays as they could without too much risk.

"Romeo-One, Bravo-One, in position at Green-One."

"Bravo-One. Clear to breach."

Silas grabbed a pair of binoculars from the table and stepped away from the tactical board to lean across the nearby FBI sedan's hood. From his position he could see the breach area and the exit point on the back of the building, Black-Four.

He heard the breaching charges go, and the quiet controlled voices of the agents carried none of the adrenaline charge that must be filling the air of the commissary kitchen. They were all pros. Motion at Black-Four drew Silas' eye. Four lizard men poured out of it into the parking area. Bravo-Five and Six, the HRT team covering the lot, herded them into the chute. Hotel-Five, a Humvee on the perimeter, raced toward the lot with the "Ma Duce" traversing onto target. One of the X-rays pointed at it and they all ran for the "weakness" in the perimeter to the west.

"Romeo-One, this is Overwatch. I have four on the move. Missing one." The FBI tactical net came to life as Overwatch, the only unaccounted call sign, reported in. The sniper team had eyes on the exit.

"Overwatch, stand by."

"Bravo-three, what's your situation?" the same voice requested on the operation net.

"Romeo-One, Bravo-Three, all hostages clearing through Green-One. One X-ray holding Black-Four. Clear to Fire?"

"Bravo-Three, negative. Hold fire. What is X-ray's stance?"

"He has a metal door held out like a shield. He's blocking Black-Four."

Defensive, Silas grinned. They were running, so far.

Silas keyed his mic. "Romeo-One, Tango-One, have Bravo-Three apply grazing fire."

"Bravo-Three, grazing fire now."

"Romeo-One, Bravo-Three wilco."

The staccato bursts of submachine gun fire echoed from the doorway as if it was on a movie playing in the building.

"Romeo-One, Bravo-Three, he's falling back."

"Bravo-Three, maintain pressure."

The fifth lizard man rushed from the door and raced after his companions. He was shaking his hand and seemed rattled. Silas zoomed in on his face and adjusted the focus dial. He was angry, not scared. Too much.

"Romeo-One, Tango-One, cease fire press with heavier cover fire."

"Hotel-Five, Romeo-One, close on X-ray-Five and press."

"Hotel-Five, Roger, oscar mike."

A cloud of dust appeared behind the Humvee that had pressed the others to run. Silas watched as the soldier racked the arming lever on the M2 and aimed near but not at the last X-ray.

The loud report from the heavy machine gun smacked at Silas as the gunner fired five rounds at the ground near the last lizard man. Silas zoomed in again and noted that the face showed the fear it needed to, but instead of pushing him to move faster, the lizard man stopped running to turn toward the advancing Humvee.

"Hotel-Two, Romeo-One, close in and support."

Tires near Silas ripped at the dirt and grass before another Humvee raced forward toward the runners. The smell of soil, gas, and oil settled around them as the soldiers raced to force the last runner into the funnel. Silas heard the arming lever slam home and the thump-thump of the "Ma Duce" opening up close by distracted him for just a moment. He refocused on the last X-ray. The new threat drove him further into a panic, and he looked at his departing companions. They were making their way, unmolested by the racing Humvee. Freedom was there if he would just turn and run.

Silas groaned as the decision filled the X-ray's eyes. The die was cast. Silas could sense the sniper tensing on the trigger. The X-ray stopped running and turned to face the new threat. He raised his hands in front of him and crossed them at the wrists as if they would protect him from the bullets he thought were coming at him. The gunner had been keeping his rounds too close for the wildly jumping firing platform so his last round clipped the X-ray's hip. As the pain registered, he uncrossed his wrists and an invisible force drove through the dust-filled air and struck the hood of the racing Humvee. Like a hammer striking a matchbox car, the hood of the Humvee creased in half as the forward suspension collapsed. The gunner slammed forward into his gun and then fell back against his restraints. A spray of blood haloed around his head as his nose shattered. He would survive. The Humvee and the gunner were disabled though, and the FBI would react to the attack.

"Overwatch, Romeo-One, take him." The order over the FBI tactical net came just as Silas was analyzing the event and before he could call them back. The X-ray's head jolted to the left with the impact just as the crack from the rifle reached them. The force of the shot threw the X-ray to the right as he fell to the ground, and the conflict was over as quickly as it had started.

Silas scanned the other four X-rays who were running now without looking back. He hoped he was right that they would be no threat if they could get away from this initial agitation. They would all know soon enough.

"Romeo-One, cease fire, all units." Silas called over the tactical net.

"All units, Romeo-One. Hold fire. Secure your positions. Bravo-Five, Close on X-ray and secure with caution."

Silas looked back over his shoulder at the colonel and the major. They both motioned him toward their Humvee. They would join Bravo-Five in the parking lot and mop up.

"He's getting up." The excited report on the radio came across the operational net, drawing Silas' attention to the spot in the parking lot where the X-ray had fallen.

"Romeo-One, Overwatch. I have movement on the ground. Clear to take it out?"

"Negative, Overwatch. This is Tango-One. Stand down." Silas took charge. He was surprised the lizard man was still alive, much less able to move. If the last shot had not killed him another one probably wouldn't either. Silas heard the FBI channel open as Romeo-One started to countermand the order, but then decided he liked his career.

Romeo-One's voice finally filled the open carrier. "All units, hold position."

The major stopped the Humvee. Silas and Colonel Holloway jumped out as the last of the lizard men stood up and ran after his companions.

"How the…" Holloway began to ask as the last X-ray was running away from him. He gave up on getting an answer and looked back at Silas. "You were right. They didn't really want this fight. They were just confused and angry."

"This time, but look at what one of them did without much effort. What are those things? Where did they come from? What do they want? These are the questions we have to answer. Hopefully before we're faced with a horde of pissed off lizards that can shake off a bullet to the head like it was a paper cut." He motioned to the Humvee with the crushed front end. The driver was checking on the gunner who was responding and holding a compress over his profusely bleeding nose.

"I'm sure that's exactly why you're here," Major Carson said over the hood of their Humvee.

Silas bent to the ground to pick up the flattened mushroom of the metal-jacketed slug that had struck the X-ray. It had been a thirty caliber, probably 7.62X51mm NATO. He dropped the quarter-sized disk of mangled lead into his pocket and shook his head.

"That's why we're here, major. Let's get this report out. We're not the only ones working outside the box today, and I'm thinking our other units could use this intel. I don't want to keep antagonizing them and speed up their desire to fight us. Don't forget to include that 7.62 is useless against them."

"What?" Carson asked.

"The sniper round hit and delivered quite a punch, but didn't penetrate. We don't want soldiers and LEO's thinking their standard ammo's going to work."

"The fifty worked," Holloway said pointing to the pool of blood from the round that clipped the last X-ray. He followed the last lizard man with his eyes as he ran to join the others. "Where are they going?" he asked.

"No idea," Silas answered.

"Romeo-One, Overwatch, first group is passing my position. They have slowed down to wait for their last member. They are no threat at this time. They look scared."

"Overwatch, Romeo-One, roger. Observe their retreat. Report as soon as they pick a direction so we can tag and follow."

So far, Silas was right. So far, they were just scared and upset. Silas needed to understand why. He needed to know, under what conditions they would turn their powers against them. He reached into the back seat of the Humvee and pulled out his tablet. It was a puzzle a lot like the ones on his wall, but it had a major difference. This puzzle had an intelligent brain behind it and could change its mind.

He opened the e-mail account and prepared the quick report to Tara. She would want to know the results as soon as possible. He liked the compacted chain of command, but it meant there was no breathing room between success and failure. Today he had avoided the failure, but the spark was still out there looking for a fuse.

June 21 – 1130 EDT – Signal Mountain, Tennessee

Melissa had finished the rest of her breakfast and retired to the library to wait for her parents. The small meal had helped cut the desire for meat a little, but she still felt like she had not eaten since the spell had first been cast. The television continued to show stories about half-dragons and other abominations appearing all over the world. There was a madness driving them into the streets. She couldn't watch anymore. She needed a quiet place to think and, as always, the comfortable chair on the second floor of the library became her sanctuary.

Her silent refuge had a view of the pool house that Charles had locked Nicklaus in the night before. A group of workers was removing the debris where he had emerged in his dragon form and broken out of the small building.

Dragons had never desired attention.

Melissa agreed with the voice as memories agreed with the statement. Dragons preferred to stay to their own lairs even if those had become castles and kingdoms ages before. Dragons had emerged around the world the night before, and the leading news stories were about half-bloods and abominations, as they should be. Melissa was proud that dragons had returned without much fanfare. Except for Nicklaus and his half-blood rage, dragons were living within their environment.

It is too soon to celebrate. Your mate is resourceful. A headache chased the warning.

Charles cleared his throat to get her attention. "Miss, your parents are here."

She stood from the chair and walked to the spiral stairs that would lead her down to the back patio. When she stepped out through the newly framed hole in the back wall, she had to stop to take in the couple before her. The day before, at the reading of the will, her father had seemed worn down. He had looked well over fifty to her, but this morning, standing in the cool morning shade of the patio, he looked almost her age.

Her mother, who shared her dark hair and olive complexion, looked more like her sister than her mother. Both of her parents looked at her with an angry scowl.

"Follow me," she said, aware that everything she said sounded like a command. She transformed into her dragon form for the second time since she had emerged. The thrill of taking the stronger form was dulled some by a wave of weakness that filled her as she leapt into the air from the top stair.

Her wings beat the air enough to get her above the ground and allow her to glide. A few more strokes and she was half way across the yard. She glided across the lawn and her grandmother's grave until she was above the ledge. When her tail cleared the edge, she dipped her wing to start the spiral down to the landing ledge. It felt good to fly. She wanted to soar into the morning air, but she forced herself to deal with the business following her. She instinctively found her footing and then leapt into the cavern beyond. In the large vaulting chamber where she had transformed the night before, a huge fire was burning in the hearth against the back wall. She smiled. Having the chamber prepared for her father's presence would relax the situation quite a bit. It appeared that Charles didn't miss much.

Melissa landed in the center of the room and drew her wings back behind her. Her father's blue form filled the opening as he landed with his wings wide and head high. In her mind, she greeted Valdiest, King of the European Dragons. He stepped forward enough to allow her mother's green form to settle behind him. Again, she greeted and welcomed Kaliastrid, her mother and Queen of the European Dragons. The three dragons shifted around in the cave to make room for each other, but Melissa held her place in the middle of the floor.

Her father was scanning the chests that covered the floor. The cave was a secret of the estate that had been kept from everyone along with all of the treasure in it. She could see the appreciation in his eyes as he turned to face her again with far less anger in his face. She could tell he was considering how he could use the vast treasures hoarded around the cavern.

"Father, Mother." She spoke her greeting and dipped her head in respect at each of them. Her mother, who had not seen her in dragon form before this moment, stared at her as if she was seeing something amazing. Her head tilted somewhat on her long neck and she dropped her torso onto her forward legs and claws. The position dropped her head below Melissa's eyes, and she settled into a deep, reverent bow. Melissa was confused by the stance.

It is a sign of reverence and respect. Normally the king and queen would bow to no other dragon, except... Fire filled her eyes and her mind exploded in pain as the comments approached some memory they could not recover.

In an equal conversation each dragon would choose whatever position is comfortable, like Valdiest. He is relaxing onto his hind legs. He is comfortable because it is difficult to get out of that position. You would never see him take that stance if he felt alert.

Melissa considered what she was learning and wondered why her mother was not relaxing.

Her bow shows that she believes that you are above her. She will not stand or relax unless we give her permission.

Melissa stared at her mother for a moment with no idea what to do.

Her father noted her mother's stance but held his position. Melissa cocked her head to a side in confusion. Her mother smiled at her and raised herself from the bow, but did not stand back up. Her father harrumphed and snorted at the show.

"Meliastrid, Nickliad told us how you're protecting these humans." He growled his greeting to his daughter. "It's wrong. It's abnormal. We've never needed them before, and we don't need them now." He paced on the floor a little, maintaining his standing position. "You know they are why we have been imprisoned?"

Melissa didn't answer.

He doesn't know the truth either. How is that possible?

"And these abominations that have returned, what's happened while we have been subjugated?"

Her mental shadow helped her answer her father's question. Although she refused to surrender completely to the voice, she allowed the answers to flow without check.

"If you will recall, father, we have used humans in our past. In fact, we have a long history of working with them."

Melissa struggled with the information and tried to reconcile what she was learning. She accepted the fact that dragons had worked with humans once.

Her father whirled around and scowled at her. She was beginning to wonder if he had another expression.

"I'm not saying we should attack them, not yet. But they're responsible for our imprisonment. I know it as well as I know my own name."

He agrees with Nickliad.

"There are many things that are different today; more so than they have been for a long time. We would do well to remember that these humans have not seen a dragon in a long time." Melissa started the response but her inner voice continued as her thoughts were becoming easier to merge in a complete statement. "As I recall it, father, even when we ruled, we were careful to work *with* humans and not against them. You're letting Nicklaus'—Nickliad's—emotions and your own human feelings cloud your judgment."

The last words were delivered with a confidence that she didn't feel. The child who had become mistress of the manor the day before wanted to drop her head lower and submit to her father, but an ancient instinct told her to hold her head high. Valdiest was not taking it well, either.

As he started to reposition and tower over her, she added, "I would have expected something like this from Nickliad, but not you."

"So his tales are correct. You have protected a human from him. You stood between him and his wrath?"

"Father, Nickliad was beside himself last night. He raged like some half-blood with no control of himself, not a dragon. I did what was right." Melissa pondered how much her father knew since he was angry with her about Charles but said nothing about her part in casting the spell. Nickliad could have told them she had failed to recast the spell, but he had kept that to himself. Why? "None of that matters, anyway. Nickliad came here last night and attacked me. Charles defended me, as he would have defended either of you. I'm doing what I think is right. Nickliad can stay wherever he is if he's not happy with me. The next time you see him, father, you can tell him I said that." There was no resistance from her inner voice when she decided to end the relationship. She took a moment to ask why.

We are working through these memories a little at a time. Your mother helped me understand a confusing memory. We cannot have a mate anymore.

Her mother's sudden intake of breath at her comment drew her back to the conversation immediately.

"Meliastrid, be careful what you say. Are you not aware of what power your words have?"

The fear in her message surprised Melissa. She looked at her mother's eyes again and she could see fear swimming in them.

She knew she hadn't tried to hold back, it had just felt like what she was supposed to say. She would have to consider why her mother was so concerned.

"How dare you! He is next in line, and I'm the accepted king of our kind. You have been his mate for longer than, well for a long time." His eyes dilated and his whiskers twitched as he tried to remember the details of how long she had been Nickliad's mate.

We are not the only dragon suffering from this pain. None of us can trust our memories. We must be careful. Something is not complete about our emergence.

"Yes, father, you are and he is, but I am the mistress of these grounds and these people. I'll not have them attacked, not by him or you." She reared back to her full height and extended her wings with her wingtip claws pointed at his head. The show of power was not lost on her mother who rose to her full height in support. The claw on Melissa's chest flashed at the end of her decree.

Valdiest looked around at each of them with surprise and hissed. Melissa could see the confusion in his eyes as he wanted to resist her but could not. Melissa wondered why she had such power but did not relax her stance.

"There will be a conclave," he said, "Nickliad is organizing it as soon as we can…" He paused as if searching for the word and his whiskers twitched once again. "…reach all of the heads of the clans." His words seemed odd. She struggled with pain to figure out what was wrong with what he said.

Dragons do not have problems communicating. Something is missing that would make this easier.

Melissa looked at her mother. She was the only one talking to her in her mind. Why was that connection only between them?

"Why are we the only ones who can speak like this?"

"We aren't. The males just don't remember. There is some kind of mental block. I can't explain it."

"There is much dissatisfaction with what has happened," her father continued, unaware of what was passing between Melissa and her mother, "we must stand up and take our place as dragons. Together we will decide what is to happen to the humans, especially considering their attack against us and their lingering disrespect."

Nickliad and her father had been busy since they had emerged. Melissa felt a surge of fear at what he was planning. He was planning to avenge their imprisonment.

"As meaningful as that may be. I recommend everyone be sure of their facts before we take any more steps. Our return has created chaos in their cities, more than I like. The reports are terrifying."

"That is not our doing. We cannot be held accountable for what half-bloods do. Humans don't know terrifying; I'll show them terrifying," he blurted out angrily before he continued more regally. "We will decide how to educate them about our new place as their rulers. It looks like we will have to terrify them into it. Besides, the chaos is caused by their continued pact with abominations and half-dragons."

His memories are badly misaligned, her own mind told her. *Some humans stood with half-bloods but most saw them as bad as we did.*

Valdiest continued, "Nicklaus is already looking into those strange events. I will assure you, no dragon has been involved in any violent activities. We have not lost our minds like the beasts the news is reporting. Partials have always been a blot on our existence. They will ruin it for us all. He's looking into it. Their return to this world must be another horrible use of foul human magic. We will handle the humans though, like we handled the partials and abominations before."

"Father, you can't be serious. You know how much the humans have advanced, and our magic..."

He turned his face away from her and refused to hear her arguments. "None of that matters. It will be decided in the conclave, child. Mind your place."

She adjusted her tone to be more respectful of her father's position and attempted a different approach. "If you would just stop and review your memories and stop letting the emotions of your human form drive you, you might save yourself from a mistake."

"I'll not be afraid of the humans, their magic, or their weapons, and just who are you to lecture me about my human leanings? I'm not the one sleeping in their buildings and turning back to my human form."

Melissa dropped her head at this statement. She could not argue with him in this state. There had to be another way. She couldn't fight the feeling that he was overstepping his authority, but she held her tongue.

"I don't believe dragons should return to their true form and risk conflict with the humans until more can be learned about what has happened. Dragons must, as always, be discreet." The claw talisman on her chest flashed again and drew her father's attention. Something in her mind clicked. Sharp pain filled her head. Her mother's intake of breath was nearly a hiss.

"Whatever your concerns, they will not stop us from returning to our grand place over this world. We will resume our place and finally wipe human magic from this world."

Melissa started to argue with him again when her mother joined her in her mind. The feeling was euphoric but fleeting. *"Let them have their conclave. They need to vent some anger. They can do it in that setting without hurting anyone. Once they've had a chance to release some of the rage they're feeling, it will be better. The males have always needed their meetings. Don't steal their power from them. There are others who may be able to speak reason in that conclave. You cannot imagine how much rage is among our kind. Something important is missing, and we need to find it before we lose control like the half-dragons. You are wise to require discretion. There is too much chaos in our minds. We must restore order to our memories."* Wisdom filled those words, and Melissa fought with childish anger from her human form.

Listen to what she says. Her advice is sound.

Her mother's color turned pale with an obvious shiver of pain. It was affecting all of them.

"I will await this conclave's findings," she said as she raised her tail from the floor and pointed at her father. "But don't act on anything, for your own good. I warn you to wait." Again the talisman flashed.

Her father looked at her with surprise. "You warn me? You should embrace your dragon form, child, and stop living among them. Perhaps, then you will understand better. We have forgotten what it was like to be the most powerful race on this world. We have forgotten how we ruled. We have been in human form, subjugated by them for centuries. We are letting that weakness control us. I, for one, will not continue to bow to them. I'm not sure how we ever let them overcome us like this, but I'll be damned if I will ever be a human's toy again. And, if I ever remember who was responsible for this, he will pay with his hide along with his entire lineage." He turned his head and body away from her and lunged toward the exit cave.

I am here father, take your retribution now. She thought to herself and dropped her head to stare at the pentagram on the floor.

In her mind she suddenly saw the painting on the ceiling of the library. The smaller female dragon in the painting sat higher than the male around the castle and only her tail touched the gem encrusted egg in the courtyard. The image was fleeting, surrounded by pain and disappeared quickly. Her mother was looking at her nodding, while struggling with her own pain.

She smiled and turned to follow him. *"I will encourage him to be discreet until the conclave has met and a course of action is decided. It has been spoken, it will be done."*

"I'm not sure we ever ruled the humans the way you seem to think we did," she said to the empty space where he had been.

Her mother looked over her shoulder and smiled at her. The green and black ridges on her back shimmered in the firelight. "Patience child, you're well equipped for this challenge. More than I ever knew. He will never make it as far as you have. They hardly ever do." Her mother's eyes seemed to swallow her for a moment and a tear appeared at the side of her face. Her tail swished behind her. "We will talk as soon as we can. Eat child, your color is off, and it is such a beautiful color you have acquired. Your grandmother would be proud."

Melissa cocked her head at her. What did she mean by that? The woman who had been her mother did not like her grandmother at all. That had been a serious part of her human anger. Her mother had never been happy with how much time she had spent with Helena.

Heliantra. Melissa nodded.

Her mother had been sour at the reading of the will because she and her father had both been left out of it. As her mother followed her father out of the cave, she kept her forelegs on the ground and kept her head below Melissa's. It was a ridiculous pose, and Melissa had no idea why she had not stood back up. Her mother hopped only a small height and glided to the entrance where she flapped to the landing and then disappeared.

"Thanks." It was a small gesture, but her mother deserved it. She had changed a lot overnight, and Melissa missed her presence both in the cave and in her mind.

"Mel." The calm and assured voice of her mate carried across the mosaic from behind her. The scales and whiskers behind and around her ears twitched and her tail shifted to point at where he was standing. There was no other dragon in the room with her so she dropped onto her forelegs and turned to face him where his human form stood in the doorway leading to the long staircase to the surface.

"How did you get in here?"

He raised his hands in a peaceful gesture and stepped away from the door; his face was anything but peaceful, and she felt agitation surround him. "That's not how I hoped our reunion would go. Why so nervous? I'm here to talk to you. You wouldn't listen to reason last night; I thought a calmer mind with more perspective might rule today."

"That is not an answer to my question."

"I guess I was wrong. Same mind is in charge today. Where is my Meliastrid? Where is my mate and the future queen of our kind?" He crossed his arms behind his back and stood defiantly in front of her. "Why don't you take the form you have forced me into so we can talk?"

The whiskers around her ears twitched again and a cold knot formed in her stomach. Two questions wrestled in her mind. *Does he know I cast the spell* and *Where is Charles* tormented her for a moment as she considered the man standing before her. With her memories askew, she didn't trust the fond thoughts of him, but she also knew how much he and her father had struggled for their homeland as humans. It was all part of the whole now, even the painful cauldron of memory she could not access, and it defined who she was just as it defined who he was now. Not wanting to appear out of control, she transformed into her human form. She chose the same relaxed jeans and sweatshirt she had started the day with in an attempt to relax him.

Just as she completed the transition, she realized it was a mistake. Nickliad was across the distance before she could react. His hand flew from his side and struck her across the right cheek with a resounding smacking sound. Fire enveloped her ear, cheek and eye and she nearly collapsed to the floor. An angry growl escaped her throat as she took a step back and raised her hands to defend against further attack. She had transitioned into a scaled partial human form and she stood before him covered in coppery scale armor with viscous claws extended to take his next attack.

"I see you have not lost all of your dragon instincts, but that human you love has polluted you. You never should have let your guard down. Not even for me, love."

The new honorific irritated her as much as the old one. "I'm still not sure how you came to be here, but you should leave." Her suddenly battered mind still spun; she was leaning on instinct until she could get her wits back.

Where is Charles? The fear that human question raised tormented her.

"First, I owed you that. The knee to the eye last night hurt, but that is not why I'm here. As I said, I came to appeal to the mate I once knew to join me. Take your place as the future queen of your kind. Form the future that is before us when we take vengeance on the humans who have done this to us."

"That covers why, now how?"

"Of course, you're worried about Charles."

Nickliad had stepped back from Melissa's reach but remained in his human form. Melissa still could not focus her mind well enough for this intellectual fight, and that was exactly where he wanted her. She didn't rise to his bait this time.

"I wanted to kill him. I've wanted to kill him all night. I stood up there on the lawn and ached to kill him, but no matter how much I wanted to kill him I couldn't. Why is that Mel? Why can't I kill one human that has wronged me so much?"

She shifted her weight to leap at him. She suddenly tasted his blood on the back of her tongue. She wanted to kill him. He raised a hand to ward her off as he saw her anger, and a smile filled his face.

"It is good to see that there is still a dragon in there. I came to talk, not fight, but we can fight if you want." A grin flashed across his face, and Melissa felt dirty.

She marshaled her anger somehow and transformed back into her fully human form. "Get to your point or get out. I have no time for you and I need to check on my butler."

"He's fine—well, he will be fine. It's just a bump and he will survive. I'm sure he's had worse."

She recognized his manipulation and forced herself to ignore Charles and focus on the immediate threat. Why was Nickliad here?

"The point?"

"Like I said, I came here to appeal to you to stand with me like you should. With your support I know we can rule this world."

A sudden coldness replaced the confusion and fear she had been fighting. With no pain from her ancient memories, she knew she could not accept his offer. She had no desire to rule this world.

"Then you should leave." The claw amulet around her neck suddenly warmed against her skin. "Do not return here Nickliad. I will have nothing more to do with you or your plots."

He growled at her and transitioned into his full dragon form. She transformed with him until they were facing off across the pentagram with their wings raised and claws extended. She prepared herself to defend against his attack, and the amulet flashed with her defiance.

He cocked his head and looked at the amulet for a moment. He sniffed the air around them and growled at her. His long nose and jaws shifted into a dragon scowl and his eyes danced with hatred.

"Why do you defend them so? Why do you protect the humans who deserve so much of our hatred?"

"Why do you hate them so much, Nickliad?"

He roared at the use of his name. "I do not have to explain myself to you. You will never again call me by that name. Forever more you shall refer to me as Nethliast. I shall lead our kind to their appropriate place. Never again will I allow you to subjugate us under them. When I find out how they were able to trap us, I will expose their true colors. Even you will have to surrender to the inevitable rule of the dragon."

"She said you should leave." Charles' small voice challenged Nickliad from the doorway at the base of the stairs. Melissa glanced toward the door while keeping her eye on Nickliad. Charles was leaning against the stone archway with a short tube extending from his fist. His voice carried defiance. He could never stand against a dragon, but he was willing.

Now we see why we respect humans and why you are right to stand the way you do. This is what infuriates Nickliad and what I had forgotten. We have stood beside humans for generations because their heart will always triumph over tyrants.

Nickliad roared at them both and staggered back a step. He inhaled sharply, and again Melissa was sure he was preparing to release fire into the cavern.

"Nickliad, you should leave here now." This last challenge came from her mother, who had landed in the outer chamber and was now shifting away from the only exit available to the enraged black dragon that was wavering between decisions. Melissa moved into the path of any attack he had and stared into the flashing eyes of her mate.

"Nethliast, you will leave here now. We will have no more of this here. I am the master of this cavern, and you will respect my words. Depart now before I must expel you." This time the flash from the amulet included a pulsing wave of force that pushed at Nethliast to back up her threat.

With a departing flash of anger, he turned away from her and charged out of the cavern.

Melissa relaxed her wings and settled onto her forelegs with a cleansing sigh of exasperation. She looked around her at those who had come to assist her against her mate. Charles was still leaning against the door, nearly unable to stand up and struggling to point the rifle stock with the short tube on its end at the cave entrance. She transitioned to her human form and rushed to catch him before he fell to the floor.

Kaliastrid was with her when they made it to the doorway. Melissa looked at her with concern.

"Your father is pursuing the wrong course. He will wander a bit until he realizes the truth. I'm going to let him wander alone, my alliance belongs with you, my daughter. Let's get this brave and foolish man up to the house where he can lie down."

Her mother's calmness under stress reminded her of Helena, or Heliantra as she would be known among dragons. Melissa felt the moral support bolster her as she gently lifted Charles with the talons of her foreclaw. Together they walk him out into the chamber where Kaliastrid lifted him from the ground and carried him out of the cavern on the short flight to the yard above them.

June 22 – 1230 EDT – Signal Mountain, Tennessee

They settled Charles in a chair in the library against his protest that he was all right. Melissa felt the irritating chills of an unknown emotion racing through her. Her mother was beside her and looking at the gash Nickliad, now Nethliast, had left on the back of his head. Charles, ever vigilant, had not been able to defend against Nethliast's assault and was lucky he had not been killed.

Melissa considered that for a moment. Nethliast had not killed him on purpose. He had told her that himself. He had wanted to kill him, but had not. Why not? Melissa was more confused now than she had been when she first woke.

Her mother, who had until that morning been her worst human enemy, was now standing in her newly acquired library helping tend to her injured butler. One night, out of all of the nights of stupid decisions in her life, none had caused as much chaos as this one. Anger at Helena's decisions to keep all of this to herself bubbled up inside Melissa. She had never been angry with her grandmother, but this mess was all her making. Why had she not just told Melissa about all of this?

Melissa paced the floor in front of the desk and looked at her mother and Charles helplessly. She could not help him. She could not help anyone. She had barely made it through college, if she finished the next semester and graduated. Why couldn't life just go back to being what it had been before her grandmother had died? Why did her childhood friend want to take over the world?

That question caused her to laugh a little as she paced a five-foot hole in the floor.

"What's so funny?" Her mother asked.

"What?"

"What are you laughing at? If you have a joke, share it. We could use a laugh."

Charles, who looked much better now, grinned at her with a worried look and nodded.

"I don't know. I'm losing my mind. I'm trying to figure out why this is all messed up and why Nethliast wants to take over the world. I realized out of everything that has changed, he is still honest to his goals. He has always wanted to take over the world."

That is true.

"Who?" Charles asked.

"Nethliast. Great Nickliad has changed his name to Nethliast. Until I referred to him that way he would not leave."

Kaliastrid laughed a gentle laugh that had been absent in her human mother. "He's been raised to be king."

"You make excuses for him?"

"No. Explanations."

Melissa launched into another round of pacing trying to figure out what that really meant.

"So what have I been trained for? It seems he thinks I am to be queen, but I have no such aspirations."

"No, you don't, do you?"

Her mother, who was so much not like her mother anymore, looked at her with concern and what seemed to be admiration.

"There is something different about you that I noticed when we arrived this morning. Since that moment, I have deferred to you out of habit, but I can't remember why and every time I try to remember, I get the most excruciating headache. There is something different about you. Something regal."

"Yesterday I was not a dragon."

"Oh, that is where you, Valdiest and Nickliad are wrong. Yesterday you were a dragon. Everything about Melissa is important to what Meliastrid is. Valdiest is angry because he lost years he cannot account for and his throne to humankind. Nickliad—I guess Nethliast now—is angry because he has always been young and impulsive. That is why the two of you were together. You will be surprised by this, but you calmed him and kept him stable."

Your mother speaks the truth as well. The two of us were a balanced pair. Without us, he could be unstable.

Memories she could reach agreed with that assessment, but she had not calmed him last night. Her mother and her own mind helped her fight back the emotion that was threatening to consume her, but she felt its tendrils at every corner.

"I don't know what to do."

Kaliastrid turned to face her now. "Are you sure?" Something in her piercing eyes made Melissa think.

"She wants me to cast the spell again." The words were out before she could pull them back. Something about her mother's actions made her think she could trust her; that and something deeper, in a pain-fringed corner of her mind, told her Kaliastrid was an ally.

"Again," Kaliastrid stood up straighter and brought her hand up to her mouth, "what are you saying? You cast the spell that trapped dragons in human form?"

"I don't know. My memories are a mess. For everything I remember, there is more detail that I can't reach. I feel like I want to run into the street and scream sometimes because of the voids I can't fill."

She paused, unwilling to admit what she knew to her mother.

"That's what's happening with the others, the ones on the news." Charles spoke for the first time and they both turned to look at him. Melissa felt a little relieved to have the attention drawn away from her admission.

"I was thinking about what was similar about all of the news stories and they all had a single thread that you just described. All of the lizard men and angry lizards on the news have acted the same way, as if they are desperate and confused. None of them are acting like the angry monsters the news is painting them as. They're acting like lost children."

Kaliastrid picked up the thread. "They were affected by the spell as well. Half-bloods have always been difficult to manage, but is seems they are worse off than dragons. We're confused, but we're not out in the streets going insane."

Charles nodded.

Melissa stared at them both. She agreed with them, but there was something else. When her inner voice answered the question, she repeated it to the room. "They're not supposed to be here. That's why they're acting weird."

Kaliastrid turned back to her and pointed at her nodding her head. "You're right."

"They were all killed in the purge," Charles added.

Again Melissa and Kaliastrid turned to face Charles and waited for him to explain how he knew what they had just figured out. How could Charles know about the purge?

He noticed how they were looking at him as he continued to consider the thought he had voiced and explained. "Helena told me. She told me several stories over the weeks before she died. She seemed to be dropping deeper and deeper into her own little world. When she wasn't writing in that journal, she was telling me stories. Some days she spent all day telling me some fantastic tale. Those were the best and worst days."

"What do you mean?" Kaliastrid asked.

"When she told me the stories she was very clear and precise. She seemed like she was present in the stories, as if she was remembering them instead of making them up. At the time, I thought she was telling me stories from her next book. Now, I'm not sure she wasn't telling me stories from her past."

"If she told you about the purge, she was telling you stories from our past," Melissa said and sat down on the corner of the desk.

Her grandmother was a famous author of, ironically, dragon romances. She wrote love stories about dragons and kings in a time similar to the dark ages but with more magic and magical creatures.

"She wrote our history in those books?" Kaliastrid looked up from pondering the same thought Melissa was working on.

"I read some of them. I was never a fan. I didn't like the way she wrote about women," Melissa admitted.

"I thought they were degrading to our family and never cracked a cover."

Melissa looked around her at the library her grandmother had amassed and all of the books that filled shelves across three floors of the manor house. Her grandmother had always been writing something. In the last years she seemed to be driven to get even more stories out instead of relaxing and enjoying her royalties from a very popular series. She looked around the room at all of the books her grandmother had collected. She remembered the times she would read to her on the back patio or up on the second floor while Melissa would sit in her lap in the big stuffed chair. Helena had left this to her for a reason. Melissa thought she had left her the house to keep it out of her father's hands and that might still be partly right, but it was mostly because it contained references to where they came from.

"We have some reading to do." Maybe she could find some answer about why they cast the spell in the first place. Maybe she could find out why their memories were all a jumble. Maybe she could find out what she had to do to put everything back into Pandora's Box.

CHAPTER 4 - AN UNNATURAL TRUCE

June 25 – 0630 EDT – Morristown, Tennessee

Nethliast flew through the early morning darkness enjoying the feeling of rebellion that pursued him. The feeling was a foreign, nagging sense that he was doing something wrong on his morning flight. He was a dragon. He was going to fly. He would not be trapped any longer, and he would show the humans what it meant to deal dishonestly with dragons. His father could wait for the guidance of his king. His mate could coddle her human lover. They could continue the acts that had doomed them to this insult if they chose too, but he would not be involved in throwing away the future he could see ahead of them if they were all willing to rise together!

How long had it been since dragons ruled this world? How long had they languished under the humans' thumb? Truthfully, he no longer cared. However long ago it had been, it had happened because dragons had lost their hunger for ruling. Nethliast did not share that with his draconic relatives. He was tired of trying to pry painful information out his memory to decide what to do. All he needed to know was self-evident. Humans had acted against dragons. They had to pay for their treachery. Nethliast could reconcile his actions with that.

The sun was rising in the east over fields that stretched between hills and through the valley below him. The green and golden glow of agriculture was interspersed between shopping malls and highways. Below him, he would find what he was looking for. He could feel this was where his quest would end. He could feel the presence he needed in the farm beneath him. It was calling to him and had been for nearly a day.

He dropped through the first rays of dawn toward the earth below him. As he approached the farmhouse, he leveled out and flew just above the trees and fields toward an old barn on the edge of an apple orchard. The large barn doors were open, and several people stood around a stone cistern in the floor. A woman, robed in an intricate cloak that predated the barn, stood in the center of the others and peered into the cistern. She was chanting something into the liquid in the shallow pool. Nethliast could see her lips moving in the distance, but her words were in his head.

Nethliast dug his claws into the moist soil just outside the barn and stopped his flight with his wings spread, filling the open doorway. The downdraft from his landing drove leaves, twigs, and dust into the circle. Several faces within the barn contorted with amazement and fear. Several lost their focus and cowered at his arrival. They should not doubt their high priestess who stood her ground as the detritus of his arrival swirled around her.

He said nothing but waited as they adjusted to his arrival. The high priestess lowered her arms, allowing the glistening, metallic robe to drop around her and encase her in a shimmering pattern of dragon scales. The look on her face was arrogant. Nethliast let a growl of disapproval escape his clenched jaw.

The high priestess dropped to the floor before him. The others who were not already cowering followed her example and prostrated themselves. The high priestess' cloak flowed out around her crouching form and reminded Nethliast of a dragon's wings. He looked closer and noted how the intricate needlework of the cloak knotted together in places to constrict and release the silken and translucent material. The article of clothing was ancient; probably handed down over the generations to this woman who lay before him. He did not take the time to see if it was magical.

He was not sure if she could hear his thoughts, but he reached out to the distant connection. She had appeared in his mind, and a longing he had struggled with suddenly felt relieved. He needed to find her. Here she was, a sad disappointment, really. She was human, pure human, not even partial dragon. His mind and desire felt soiled by her humanity.

"Why have you called me?"

"We have reached out to worship you, my lord. You have come here to find your devoted followers. We are yours to command."

Nethliast sat back and looked at the motley group of six humans. What did he need with a devoted band of humans?

"How did you find me? How can we talk?"

"I've sensed the confusion. I've sensed things are not right. I reached your mind and found what was missing in the others."

"Other dragons?"

"I am but your servant, lord. I assume the others are less than you. Their minds were pure chaos. When I touched them, they ran from me. You are the strong lord we need. Teach us to be your dragon kin."

He roared at the insult of humans being, somehow, related to him. The entire group shivered.

"Forgive me, lord. We are not worthy to be your kin. Let us be your worshipful followers. Command us and we will do what is your will."

"Show me these other minds you have contacted. I wish to see who among my kind may be in need of my guidance. You have reached out to the King of the Dragons. You shall be my loyal subjects. You will do as I instruct."

"As you command, lord. We are your humble servants."

Nethliast relished the worship of this group. It was a salve to his injured pride. Perhaps some humans would be allowed to live and serve him as his royal advisors.

"Show me."

The high priestess bowed to him and motioned toward the cistern and the water that filled it. As the rays of the sun finally fell upon the tops of the trees, Nethliast transformed. He shrank to the stature of a human form covered from shoulder to foot in enamel-black armor of interlocking scale plates that covered his form closely. The scales and plates made no noise as he crossed the dirt floor and joined the priestess by the pool. The other worshipers gaped at him as he walked past them.

"What do I call you?"

"I…" She stumbled on the words, suddenly losing confidence in what she was saying. She cleared her throat. "Please call me Ariela, my lord."

"Very well, Ariela. Show me what you can."

She blushed at him and motioned a hand over the cistern without looking away. The waters churned but showed nothing. He looked up at her with impatience and pointed to the pool. She shook her head, grinned apologetically, and stared into the waters until the image before them became clear. They were watching a young man, not much older than Nethliast's human form. He was calming and directing a collection of men and women who were covered with different levels of scales and tails. Each one he eventually secured into a stable stall before he returned to the door to address them all.

"He was not this calm yesterday, my lord. Something has changed here."

She focused, and the pool shifted to another scene. This one was disturbing. In the center of a dark room a reptilian man, covered in scales and with a long nosed dragon's head, sat laughing.

"He has not moved in two days."

Panic filled the laughter. Blood streaked the walls around him. Bodies, Nethliast counted four of them, laid around him.

Ariela focused several more times showing him similar scenes, some more disturbing and others as placid as the first one, before she waved her hand over the waters. They stopped churning.

"It's different today. Many are calmer than they have been. Several have moved to a new location. Many of the ones I just reached out to were in the same place. The first one has been collecting them together."

Nethliast turned from the pool and walked out into the morning sunlight. The fellowship reshaped around him and followed him out into the morning. He smiled.

"Ariela, can you locate these groups, the ones who are banding together?"

"Yes, my lord. They are near us here. I had to reach out further to find you."

"How far can you reach?"

"I've not found a limit yet."

"I want you to find them all." An idea was forming in Nethliast's mind, and this woman was going to help him. "Identify the most stable of them. Can you direct me to them? Can you communicate with them like you have me?"

"It's chaotic, my lord. They are not as stable as you are. I'm not sure they will hear me."

"Work with the best of them. I will have more to share with them soon."

"To what end?"

The question surprised him. He turned on Ariela with a caustic look. She shrank from him but held his gaze.

"Why do you question me?"

"To aide you better, my lord. If you have a goal in mind, I can help you reach it if I understand it."

"Find others who, like me, can sense you. Share my magnificence with them. Be my evangelist. The group that is mustering together is an example. I want to know where they are. I want to visit them. I want others like them."

"Yes, my lord. I understand."

Nethliast turned from her and looked at the others surrounding him. They were all showing the appropriate amount of deference. They were starting to make him think there were useful humans among the masses of uselessness. He sneered at the thought and one of the devout cringed away from him. Nethliast marked the man as weak and pointed at him. He fell away from the finger as if it were a sword. The cowering enraged Nethliast further. His followers could not be weak.

"Banish that one. He is not worthy of your league. I cannot use any who would cower at a finger, even mine." His order was indiscriminate, all of them were cowering and whimpering about his feet, but there was a cost to follow him as a human.

The circle around Nethliast acted very quickly. They closed ranks around him blocking out the weakling without looking back at him or speaking. The look on the man's face salved Nethliast's anger. Amongst the fear, there was anger on the man's face, but he said nothing and backed away. Pack animals were easy to manipulate, and these would understand the pain of being outcast from now on. Dragons had never suffered from that weakness. Those found unfit to be among dragons were killed; there was no reason to allow them to clutch. He shrugged and turned to look at his new Priestess.

"Show me where I can find this first brood."

June 25 – 0800 EDT – Morristown, Tennessee

Nethliast landed in the cornfield on the outskirts of Knoxville. His large black bulk settled heavily, shredding the high corn beneath outstretched wings. The crunch of the stalks under his feet felt funny. This was where Ariela had directed him. As he flew low over the trees, he had started to sense in his own mind the connection with *them*. He almost hated partials more than he hated humans. This hatred was instinctive. They were an abomination. The ever-present, painful irritation in the back of his mind told him dragons eradicated them ages ago. Why they had returned was as much a puzzle to him as how the humans had trapped dragons. Using them both to achieve his goals was poetic to Nethliast.

His namesake would be proud. No dragon in the history he could remember had done more to protect the race from humans. He deserved the honor. Everyone would again remember him for putting humans in their place. No dragon would stand against the message the name sent, but he had to be careful with partials.

Partials were not dragons. They weren't human either. They were a blend of human and dragon created by the magical interbreeding that happened when dragons spent time amongst humans in their form. Varying portions of each species over time created infinite versions ranging from a human who looked nothing like a dragon but manifested draconic powers to a human who could transform to a fully armored dragon form of their human body including small, still functional, wings that would allow some lift over a short distance. Nethliast laughed to himself at how much Melissa would like the idea of partials. It was the result of her human loving. Occasionally there were a few other things thrown in. With the right mix and the right magic, you got a crazy basilisk, and they were a problem for Nethliast. Basilisks were too close to real dragon form. It was not hard for the weak human mind to leap that giant gulf between the two and start looking for dragons. Nethliast didn't need them looking for dragons right now.

Partials were unfocused in their rioting. They were a wonderful distraction and a painful side effect of whatever magic the humans had used to build their snare. However, a smart investigator might be able to find an important lead if he looked hard enough. Therefore, they had to settle down, but that was the tricky part. Areila had given him the key without really knowing it. She had also reminded him that dragons could reach out to other dragons with their mind. Nethliast grinned at an odd human memory about humans and their pets; Humans had no idea how many creatures around them communicated telepathically.

"Do you know what you are?" He reached out to the partial who should be in the farmhouse.

"Not what I was a few days ago. Who are you and why are you talkin' to me like

this?"

"A friend."

"Friends don't hide and whisper. Where you at?"

"I'm in your field, friend."

Nethliast stood tall at the fence and made himself fully visible to the house. He sniffed the air. Livestock was penned here. The smell of animal fear filled the air, and they had been afraid for a long time. He tried to filter the exhilarating scent to see what else was there. In his next breath, he found the other smells. The mingled scent of human and dragon was vile. They were here just as she had shown him.

A door on the back porch opened. What looked mostly like a man walked out and stopped in the shadow of the roof. He was wearing overalls and a straw hat that hid his face. He was older. Nethliast tested the air again. He had seen this place in the cistern, but he could never be too careful.

"Come on up," the man called from the porch. Sleeves covered his arms, but Nethliast could see that scales covered his hands. Sunlight glinted off the black claws at the end of his hands. A passing glance would not reveal those signs, and this man would vanish into the scene of the farm. He was a smart old man.

Nethliast jumped the fence and walked on all fours to speed his approach. As he crossed the yard, he noted the old school bus in the back of the barn. Pages of The Knoxville News Sentinel obscured the windows. The smell of fresh blood filled his nostrils, and he shifted his gaze to the barn.

"Come on up here. I got nothin' but livestock out there. We need to talk. You can talk, can't ya?"

"I can, but why do I want to talk to you?"

"Ya came to me, didn' ya?"

"How have you dealt with the madness?"

"It ain't so hard when you live on a farm and raise livestock. Me'n my son, he's in college, figured it was just confusion, mostly. See, he thinks sumthin's missin' in ar heads."

Nethliast nodded, impressed. He wasn't sure if there were any others who had been able to overcome the madness this soon. Hunger was part of it, but the ready supply of cattle would have helped that. Even though a partial needed about the same amount of food as it had when it has human, the dragon in them would feel hunger upon emerging. They all had. Nethliast was sure that was the base of several of the newsworthy stories so far. The rest was because they didn't know who or what they were.

"Where's your son? I'd like to meet him."

"Who are ya? I see what ya are and figure ya got something to do with what happened here, or know sumthin 'bout it."

"I am Nethliast. As you can see, I'm a full dragon. You're a partial, or had you already figured that out?"

"A partial what? Dragon? 'ell, that makes sense. Why you here?"

"Just being friendly."

"Aint likely. I don' trust ya'. Neither would Alex. He's the one figured most o' this out. You need to be headin' on." The old man waved his clawed hands at Nethliast.

Nethliast transformed into his human form and made sure he was wearing clothes that were more casual. He appeared in blue jeans and a black shirt.

"Thought you'd surprise me, huh? Nothin' doin'. I already seen it."

"Your son? He can transform, then?"

"You're gonna need to go. I..."

"But, he can't teach you how, can he?"

The old man shifted on his porch, unwilling to say the words Nethliast knew were true.

"I want to help you. I know it's hard. I want to help all partials live, but I need some help. I can't reach all of you myself, and I want to help before the humans round you all up and, well you know. I'm sure you have heard of the hunt squads combing this area looking for your kind."

The old man looked at him out from under his hat. The eyes and draconic snout beneath the hat seemed interested in what he was saying.

"I know you're helping others. I know they're here. I can teach you how to transform. You can do business like you always have, or you can use it to make sure you and others aren't taken advantage of."

A barn door behind them opened, and a tall young man with blond hair and wearing overalls stepped out of the barn. Two larger boys stood behind him.

"Leave my dad alone."

Nethliast raised his hands and turned to face the young men. A grin briefly crossed his face as he took in the cluster. They were young, and they all looked very strong. It was apparent that they had learned, in their transition, how to keep some of their dragon strength. It was a good sign that they could learn others abilities as well. One of the flankers was staring at him over his phone.

"This here's a dragon, son." The old man introduced his visitor and Alex nodded patiently.

"I'm Alex. What do you want?" The cleaner youth in the middle stepped forward to confront Nethliast, but there was no denying that threat of the other two. "My father doesn't need your help, and we don't need you scaring us about what humans might do. Their hunt squads have already hurt a few of us."

"As I see you have discovered, we have the advantage of being able to take their form," Nethliast responded, playing his strong hand to keep control of the meeting. "It keeps them from hunting us down, but we can use it to our advantage in other ways as well."

The young man smiled. The conversation just got easier. Nethliast could see that he had found someone who shared some of his ideals.

"Alex, look. We don' need 'is help," the old man said.

"Pop's right. Why are you here?"

"Because, I can tell you where you came from. Because, I can help you understand where you belong."

"You caused this, didn't you? Dragons changed us somehow?" Alex asked, jumping quickly to answers. Nethliast would have to be careful how he worked with this one.

"Dragons are not your enemy." He lied carefully. Historically they had not been allies, but he didn't think they knew that. "Humans have caused this and hurt both dragons and partials alike."

"Partials? So, I'm right, we are part dragon. You returned and that has affected us because we are a mixed breed. Mongrels."

Alex chose to use the more derogatory term, and Nethliast could see he was not easily convinced.

"Yes, you are part dragon," The idea seemed to make the young men behind Alex grow taller, but the young leader held his ground.

"And that's something we should be proud of? It's currently the cause of our only torment."

"But it can be an advantage. You are quickly learning the simple advantages. We can show you the whole world of abilities at your command."

"And why would you do that?"

"Because, I want our brothers and sisters to stand beside us. I want to repay the humans for their treachery, which has led to your torment. Other partials are not adapting as well as you are."

"I'm working on it, where I can."

"We need to deliver this message to all of them. You have already started here. I want to help you. We need to teach them there is an option to the hunger and the doubt." Nethliast could feel Alex shifting. "Later when everything has calmed down we can pay the humans back." Nethliast tested the waters a little.

"Pay them back for what?" Alex looked at him with a curious look, but the hostility he had started out with was gone.

"They caused this. They entrapped all dragon kind, even you, and forced us to live in human form. Like this. They were playing around with magic and caused this." He smacked his chest. "Maybe they figured out we could take this form and wanted revenge or something. I don't know why they did it, but they did. Now we've broken free, and it caused others who were part dragon like yourselves to be released without any idea what they are. We can't reach them in ones and twos, though. We have to work together. We have to organize. I can help with that."

"I can use some help."

Nethliast felt the last remnant of resistance start to break.

"I have a lot of partials here. We need to feed them, and it's taken a toll on the livestock for sure," Alex said.

"Alex, no." His father still refused to believe they needed the dragon's help. "We don' need 'im."

"Pop, your pride is going to get you killed. What if he had been a hunt squad come to kill you?"

"Alex," Nethliast played his trump card. "If you'll help me gather the others I can help you with this. We can work together. How many of your group can't take human form?"

"Quite a few, there were some that we had to tranquilize to get here. They're hard to manage."

"Come down here." Nethliast motioned to the old man. He looked to his son who nodded and then walked out into the sunlit opening between the buildings.

Nethliast reached up and removed the straw hat from the man's dragon head.

"Never be ashamed of what you are. There will come a time when you can show your face with pride."

The young man with the phone walked closer to them and turned the phone sideways.

"Focus on your human form. Think of it here where we are speaking."

The old man nodded. *"Tell 'em all."*

"Think of your human form in your mind and focus on it."

The old man nodded again.

"With that image in mind you will focus your energy on taking that form."

"See it first, then think of changing." Nethliast used his mental connection to coax the old man to change, but the old man squeezed his eyes together and clenched his jaw, and nothing happened.

"You can't force it. It is a natural ability. It doesn't take magic words or even understanding. Just relax and see yourself the way you want to be."

The old man released the breath he was holding. When he relaxed his face and body, he suddenly changed into his human form. As the scales on his hands disappeared into his skin, he laughed.

"'ell, I be. Son, I can do it."

Alex laughed the laugh of a relieved man. He smiled at Nethliast and looked back and forth between his two friends.

"You can teach them that?" Nethliast asked.

"I think I can."

"Then let me teach you another mystery."

Alex looked puzzled.

"Can you speak to the others with your mind?"

"I thought something like that was possible, but I can't do it yet."

"Here, try this. Focus on my mind and think what you want me to hear. Your father can do it. He did with me."

Alex looked at his father. Nethliast could see the focus on his face and the amazement as the two talked.

"I have it now. Thanks to my father."

"That's a secret power of your dragon kin. You possess it. Use it to bring the others in." He could tell with those last gifts that he had won the boy. He transformed back into his dragon form and started walking back to the field.

"Alex, get them organized and communicating. Someone I trust will be coming to see you. Tell the others we're organizing to pay back the humans. Keep me informed. I have plans, and you can help me."

"What's in it for us and our kind, dragon?" the boy asked.

"The world, if you want it. It's a big place, and I need help with it. Once we were powerful. We ruled the world. We can again, with your help. Don't be trapped thinking within the fences of this farm."

The young man looked at his hands for a moment and then nodded back at Nethliast.

"Alex, I'll send someone to help you. Get it organized," he said over his shoulder as he leapt into the air and flapped toward the mountains. He had a few more places to get to before the end of this day. But, soon he would organize his own kind. These simple minded partials would follow him and with the help of the human worshipers he would return the dragon to the ruling houses of the world.

June 30 – 1030 EDT – Signal Mountain, Tennessee

Melissa had finally decided it was a good idea to talk to Nickliad's father. He had always been more like a friend to her, and what pieces of her dragon memories she could trust told her that he was faithful to her father. He was an old advisor and aide that was slow to anger, a calm voice among the excited. Nickliad's mother, killed in an accident on the "W" road the year before she and Nickliad had finished middle school, had been the one force that kept him from sinking into the familial quest. Her death had driven Nickliad deeper into the male bonds he had with her father and ultimately into the place he was now.

Melissa walked to the door from her Range Rover parked in the circular driveway. The stone and brick of the path to the door was surrounded by tiger lilies and hosta intermingled with monkey grass that reached out at her from the fringe. As she looked at everything now with both perspectives, she could see the draconic influence on the architecture and landscaping. It would be interesting to see if all dragons somehow expressed their inner being while trapped in their human form. She could not see what she had ever expressed in her life, but she also was not sure what kind of dragon she really was.

A gothic dragonhead held a knocker ring in its mouth on the door. She laughed a little at how ironic the symbol was and used the ring to attract someone to the door. After a few moments, the door opened and an elderly black man in a black suit answered.

"Miss Melissa, it's good to see you. I'm sure master Gerald will be glad to see you as well. How have you been?"

"I'm doing very well, Sedric. Is he busy? I didn't call, but I need to speak to him."

"I'm sure you know where he is. Go on back. He's not busy with anything important."

The grin on the man's face told her that at least some places were not that different. Did he even know that his employer was a dragon? Her father had to have visited. How could everything here seem so unchanged?

"Mel, you look amazing this morning. How are you child? I've seen your parents. Come in." The tall dark haired man standing in the door of his dark wood-and-leather study was as much a father to her as her own had been. He stepped back to let her in and closed the door behind him. The room was cave-like and comforting to her. There was no light from the outside entering the room.

"I don't know how to address you." Melissa realized suddenly that he deserved the honor of his position, but he was also someone she had called uncle for years as a human child. She really had no idea how to address him.

"Nonsense, child. I'm your Uncle Gerald. I've been that to you for many years before you called me that as a human child. There is nothing formal between us, at least I hope there isn't."

"You aren't upset with me about Nickliad?"

"Why, what did you do to Nickliad?" He grinned at her as he asked the question.

She smiled back at him and relaxed some.

"Uncle Gerald, what am I supposed to do? Nickliad is out to pay humans back for trapping us, but I'm not sure they really did. Father agrees with him. What can I do to keep them from starting a war?"

"Can you be sure of anything right now, Mel?"

"Yes. I'm sure humans didn't do what they think they did."

"Really, show me the proof you have. I'll take it to your father and tell him, Nickliad too. Just show me the proof you have."

Balanced, as he always was, Melissa could not be angry with him. He was right that all she had was some memories and a feeling, nothing worth acting on.

"Tell my father the same thing."

"I did."

Melissa looked up at his direct answer. There was a sadness in his voice.

"He is not in a place to be talked to."

That scared her. If Gerald, or Gerliast in his dragon form, could not calm her father then none could.

"You must convince him."

"I'm sorry, Mel. If there was any way I could show him proof, I could convince him."

"You don't believe it do you? You don't think we were really trapped by humans, do you?"

"I can't get a good enough hold of my thoughts to tell you what I believe. We have to figure out what has happened to our memories before we will really know, unless there's some kind of proof. What do you know?"

"Nothing certain." She frowned at her feet.

"What do you need from me?" He looked at her very seriously.

"Keep them from doing anything stupid. Protect my father and Nickliad, Gerliast."

"You have but to ask, and this request I provide without being asked. That is the root of my duty to your father."

"This conclave is dangerous business, uncle."

"Nothing more than we have done in the past. Situations like this have always ended up in conclave. The right decisions will come from the full meeting. Calmer minds will be heard in that room."

Melissa did not believe him. She trusted he would do what he promised, but would it be enough to sway her father and worse, could he really change Nickliad's mind? Melissa kept her thoughts to herself. This visit was not making her feel any better.

"If you had more, if you could show us who trapped us, if you could explain why, then we would have something to share at the conclave."

"Shouldn't the conclave require that before they act?"

"They should. That doesn't mean they will. There are a lot who agree with your father. There are many who do not want to wait to act. There are many who believe it is time to teach the humans a lesson about dealing with dragons."

"And, are they willing to deal with the results of this lesson? Do they not realize it is a different time now?"

"Some do, some don't care. Worse than that, something is missing that we had before we were trapped."

His words tickled a painful area in her mind that she had struggled with until she could not stand the pain. There was something missing, and she could not remember what it was.

"It feels like a madness has taken over our minds. I can't think like I should be able to."

"What should I do, Uncle? I can't let dragons fight humans."

"Your grandmother would know." He shook his head.

Melissa wondered if he knew how painful those words were. She was gone. Did he know she knew about all of this? "What do you mean?"

"Heliantra always knew how to advise us. She was a steadying force. I miss her now that we have emerged more than when I was only human."

"I miss her too, Uncle. I wish she was here to guide me."

"We will get through this, child. We will make it as we always have. Let the conclave deal with it. Find proof if you have it."

He put his arm around her shoulders. For the first time that she could remember it was not comforting.

CHAPTER 5 - PEACE OF SILENCE

July 2 – 1307 EDT – Washington, DC

Silas closed the folder and reached for the door to the small, glass-walled, meeting room on the main floor of the FBI offices. His own handwritten reminder from an early morning phone call with the White House urged him to break the stalemate caused by a sudden end to all "lizard man" activity, but the other note in his hand promised to help. Silas knew shutting him down didn't mean he would lose his job. On the contrary, he would likely be promoted to some other position where he could sit behind his desk and wait for a phone call, but he had a life sized puzzle in front of him that he wanted to solve, and now it was mocking him.

All of the lizard people, half-dragons, Naga, Melusines or whatever others wanted to call them—had escaped or died in the actions involving their appearance. Some had been more spectacular than the news services would ever know. Why? Because against all odds he had managed to keep most of the hard to explain events out of the news. His great-grandfather would be proud, but he was still worried. The more quiet things became the more likely they were to explode into an uncontrollable fire.

He focused on the second note as he held the knob and prepared to enter the conference room. It told him he was late for a meeting with a high-ranking officer in the Navy who had come to NCIS to clear up a situation surrounding the disappearance of his aide. Apparently, the lieutenant had failed to report twelve days before but had suddenly reappeared, in uniform, with a tale to tell. Because of that tale, NCIS had flagged the report and loaded both of them into a car to get them to this conference room where they were waiting.

The lieutenant, a rather attractive Asian woman who did the uniform a favor, had turned herself in. She refused to say anything about where her family was. They, a son, daughter, and husband, had lived on the outskirts of Annapolis until their home had burned down the morning of June 21. Officials had initially thought they had all been killed in the fire.

Silas could not help but find it interesting that all of these odd events started on the night of the summer solstice. He was further intrigued by the fact that the moon had been full that night. Neither of these facts necessarily had anything to do with those events, but he never ignored any clue when solving a puzzle. It was often the most insignificant item that later proved to be the most informative.

These were just a few of the bits and pieces he had been filing away over the last handful of days. Alone, they meant nothing, but something about the way they *could* fit together had these seemingly meaningless bits of trivia circling around in his head. The puzzle was there; he just had yet to click it into place.

Silas opened the door and walked into the room. The rear admiral stood as he entered, and the woman snapped to attention to match his show of courtesy. Silas extended his hand to each of them. The admiral's hand was sweaty; he was nervous because he knew, from any number of not so subtle clues, that the President was suddenly very interested in his otherwise unnoticed office. The lieutenant, on the other hand, had a firm, confident hand shake and showed no signs of fear at the meeting with the FBI. As a matter of fact, she seemed quite pleased to be exactly where she was, but Silas did sense an agitation just below the surface. He sat down opposite the pair with an internal grin and showed them a very serious frown.

"Good afternoon. Thanks for contacting us." Silas nodded to the admiral to help him relax, but it did no good. "So, what could the Navy possibly have that could help me with my investigation?"

The admiral shifted his feet and turned to look at the lieutenant who was sitting next to him. "I believe Lieutenant White has information for you. She has already admitted that she was in dereliction of her duty. We will be pursuing administrative punishment, but the reason she has provided is hard for me to believe. She has personally requested that we escalate this for some reason, and now we find ourselves here."

"Well, then. Let's let her tell me." Silas wanted to dismiss the political functionary completely, but he could not ignore the fact that the man felt inappropriately guilty about something. The evidence in the seat next to him told Silas it was not the traditional sex scandal in the office, so it had to be something else that was scaring the admiral. Silas flipped through his record mentally and found the notation that allowed him to discard the uptight man entirely and focus on the lieutenant. She was more radiant than the uniform should have allowed. She smelled of piquant Asian spices that reminded him of another woman who had recently been on his mind. He subdued a smile before it reached the surface and nodded for her to begin.

"Do you want the long version, or the short version? It will determine if I'm staying. I don't have time for people who will not listen to me or don't believe me. I knew this would take time, but I will not be patronized. I came back because of my sense of honor, and I feel what I have to say is important to our government and the world."

The admiral harrumphed in his seat and started to say something. Silas held up a finger to stop his protest.

"Why don't you tell me whatever it is you want me to know? Long, short, it doesn't matter to me. I have all day."

The lieutenant relaxed somewhat and placed her black clutch on the desk top, which indicated to Silas that he had at least convinced her to stay a little while longer.

"What do you know about dragons?"

To avoid giving away any information he didn't want to share, Silas marshaled any reaction to her direct question. Instead, he looked at her delicately angled eyes and marveled at the absence of any accent. Her file said she was first generation American. Just at the moment when the attention might seem inappropriate, just at the edge of offending the woman, he finally answered her.

"More than I knew two weeks ago, for sure."

"Do you know that they can take human form?"

"Rumors, legend mostly, I've not found any proof of it."

"You won't. What do you know about Partials?"

"Partials?"

"Part dragon, part human?"

"Wow, you're stacking legend on legend. Again, I don't have any proof that they exist."

She started to collect her things, and the admiral began to panic.

"Don't play games with me," she said. "You have hundreds of accounts of their existence. You have numerous reports that you are ignoring. I have serious information, and no one will listen to me. I'm trying to help."

"Okay, settle down." Silas did exactly what she had asked him not to do. "So these lizard people, snake people, whatever you want to call them are partial dragons?"

"Yes."

The admiral harrumphed again. Silas rounded on the mostly useless man. He vacillated between his two fears like the little white ball in a Pong game. Somewhere deep inside, Silas felt a little guilt for manipulating the man, but he could not stop now. He needed this win, and she needed to think he was on her side.

"Would you ignore her like this if she reported a cell of terrorists plotting to blow up a school in her neighborhood? You, sir, are letting personal fears color your perception. Either be quiet or get out."

The admiral shut down and sat back in his seat.

Silas looked back at the lieutenant, careful to hide his expectation, and caught her smiling before she became serious again.

"It's not his fault really. He is facing the impossible compared to just the difficult. Your example is something he can understand. He is trained to handle the difficult."

"I hope you don't say the same about me some day."

"You have listened far longer than I expected."

Silas had thrown out doubt about the strangeness of what was going on in the Texas dirt when a "Partial" had stopped a Humvee without a weapon of any kind, and independent of the evidence that was starting to dry up he believed there was more to come.

"Well, let's go on then. How do you know all of this?"

"Are you willing to go on if I don't answer that question?"

"I'm willing to listen. I may need to come back to that question, though. Tell me more about the partials."

She nodded. "The partials that were appearing in the news are suffering from suddenly realizing they're different. Many of them are so confused that they panic. They don't know what it means to be a partial."

"Why?"

"Because, they have no memory of ever being one."

"Why?"

"Because dragons have spent centuries in human form, and over those centuries they have unintentionally spawned partials. The dragons had no idea they were not human. Many of the families have maintained pure lines because they thought they were royalty and had to protect their bloodline. Others didn't have those controls, so they bred with other humans. When the dragons emerged, these partials realized what they were, but not why. You see, partials of any kind had been eradicated before dragons hid in human form."

Silas raised his hand to stop her, "Wait, what does any of this have to do with dragons? When did dragons show up? I've not seen any around."

"They emerged at the same time the partials started appearing. You will not see them because they have control of their forms and understand how to transform. The partials don't. Dragons are the root of this. Trust me, if you see a dragon, it's because they want you to see them."

Silas sat back in the chair. Her story was difficult to accept, but she really believed what she was saying. Nothing about her said she was crazy, no matter what the admiral's face was saying.

"Okay, lieutenant. I've been pretty open to what you're telling me here. I've been far more patient than anyone else you've told this to, I'm sure."

"But, you still want to know how I know all of this." She finished his thought for him.

"Well, honestly, yes. I'm a little afraid of what your answer will be, but yes." Although everything she was telling him agreed with his investigation so far, no one else had even suggested what she was adding. More than how she knew what she was saying, he wanted to know why she was telling him.

She didn't say anything else, but, as Silas looked at her, the skin on her face changed from almond to orange and then yellow. Her chin grew longer and yellow whiskers extended down to the top of the table. The transformation occurred in a flash and then she was back to her normal appearance. Silas questioned if he had actually seen it. The lieutenant had not moved. The admiral was not watching. She had been careful to only show Silas.

"Okay." He knocked his knuckles on the table and stood up. The Admiral, who had been studying the end of his sleeve, looked up. The lieutenant smiled and looked at both men. "I've got what I need." He tried to sound disinterested and failed. "Admiral, thank you for bringing this to me. You understand that everything we discussed is classified."

The admiral looked at him and realized that he was being dismissed. He looked at his aide with a puzzled look, as she did not rise from her chair.

"Great, lieutenant. If you will come with me, then."

She started to stand and collect her purse and folders.

"What's going on here?" the admiral asked.

"I think you're going to have to find a new aide."

The admiral started to protest, but Silas turned his back on him while directing the lieutenant toward the door. He was not overplaying his hand. The President had given him a lot of authority, more than he believed existed in Washington, and he didn't think this was going to hurt him. He had someone telling him things he had not heard anywhere else about what was going on. She had just proven to him, if she wasn't a dragon, she was capable of using magic he had not seen before two weeks ago.

She exited in front of him looking back for him to indicate which way to walk. He pointed deeper into the building toward a row of private offices where he planned to continue this conversation. He had more control of those offices and the people around them. If he took this story up the chain he would need proof, and, so far, he wasn't sure what he had. He didn't even look back at the admiral.

"Right here," he said as they reached his office. He opened the door for her and welcomed her in. The office had none of the character of his office at Langley, but he preferred to keep himself out of view when he was going to be meeting with people. He didn't want his guests to have that advantage. There was an old government surplus metal desk in the middle of the room and a line of file cabinets along the back wall. In front of the desk was an old steel chair with a green vinyl cushion. He pointed at it and walked around the desk to sit in his chair. Out of the left drawer, he pulled a video camera on a tripod and sat it on the desk.

"I'm not here to be a video diary or a documentary."

He looked up at her. She was not sitting down, so he released the camera haphazardly on the desk. It was a decoy to get the reaction out of the way. They were being videotaped from several directions since he had entered the room.

"Then why did you come here?" he asked, realizing she was ready to make her deal.

"I have children who are partials. I'm taking them to my parents' home where I can help them. Dragons in China are part of the nation's history. Other dragons, like my parents, are helping them learn how to fit in. What's happening in this country is bad for my children."

"Tell me, what is going on here?"

"You need to reach out to the dragons in this country. If you don't, things will soon get very, very bad."

"That sounds a lot like a threat."

"Not a threat, a warning, I'm in no place to threaten you, anyway."

"Okay, then what are you *warning* me about?"

"There's too much confusion right now. I'm not concerned about Asians; no matter how confused they are, they'll never disobey their leader. However, there is concern that other dragon families may remember their relationships with humans differently, particularly the European dragons."

"So you think they may be violent toward us?"

"It's hard not to find your arrogance offensive." The Lieutenant grinned at him sardonically. "The European breeds are not known for patience, and our memories are a little confused. It's possible that they may think you're a threat. The way you're reacting to the partials is not helping you."

"Why? Do they protect them? What are they, pets?"

"No. They usually kill them, but they may be watching how you react. It is rather revealing. It could be used against you."

Silas thought about that before responding.

"I see. So, if what you're saying is true, then these encounters and tales streaming in from all corners of the world can be attributed to what you call a *partial*. These partials, again according to you, are not the real threat. Dragons are the threat we have not yet seen. Your stance is that dragons are very much among us, and we must attempt to reach out to them, or the world as we know it could be in very real danger. Did I miss anything?"

"A great deal, but, as I expected, this is a waste of time. You should not assume partials are not dangerous. A leader will emerge among them. Who that leader is will be very important to you. The madness that overcame them when they emerged will make them controllable. Some can survive without help, but for the others, it will be most important who ends up leading them because they will have substantial power over them. The very fact that the partials are calming down indicates someone has already started organizing them."

"Are you saying—I want to get this completely clear—there is a group of dragons we should be monitoring, a group of them that are planning something?"

"I can't answer that question. I don't know."

"You mean you're not sure." Silas leaned back in his chair. "Why else would you be here? You feel a responsibility to us. This is how you clear your conscience before you disappear like others have."

Something happened on her face that told Silas he was right. He paused for a moment to think and looked up at the dragon standing in front of him. It was apparent he needed to know as much about dragons as he could, and he needed to learn it as quickly as he could. The lieutenant was planning to leave and take her partial children to China with her. He couldn't allow that. He needed her to stay.

He sat up again and placed his elbows on the desk.

"I'm going to need your help. I need to learn what I can about dragons and you're the only resource I have. If you can just give me a few more minutes…" He pressed a button on the old intercom system and a buzz emanated from it.

"Yes, sir." A female voice came through the speaker on his desk.

"Lieutenant Simmons, come in here and bring your pad." He looked up at her again and showed her an innocent grin of apology for the delay. "What do I call you besides lieutenant. It might get confusing here in a minute, and I'm much more comfortable using first names. I could call you Miss White, but that seems a touch formal and more than a little weird."

"You can call me Xue, if you must be informal, but I'm not comfortable with it." She turned to face the door as it opened. Silas watched as her grip on the clutch tightened until her knuckles whitened. She glanced around the room rapidly, obviously looking for a way out other than the door Simmons was coming in through. Silas expected he had only seconds before the real dragon emerged from the woman in front of him.

A blond in the gray mottled utility uniform of the National Guard tripped into the room carrying a yellow legal pad. As she kept herself from falling into the desk, she clutched her pad to her chest. With murmurs of apology the lieutenant turned to close the door, and Xue White exhaled a trapped breath and relaxed her shoulders.

"April is going to take notes as we discuss what you can tell me about dragons since you don't like the video. I want to get as much down as I can, and I can't take notes and ask questions."

Xue creased her eyebrows and began to protest when the bumbling lieutenant spun effortlessly around in place. The pad had dropped away in her left hand, and the barrel of a tranquilizer pistol was reaching out from her right hand. The soft wifft of the dart pistol made Xue White jump, but the dart was in and working before her mind could process that she had been shot. She collapsed onto the floor in front of April Simmons, who smiled at him for a show of approval.

"Good." Silas nodded, feeding her need. "Have them take her to the new base. I'll be there in a few days. Keep her sedated until we can find out how to keep her under control. Collect whatever samples can be collected without waking her. She'll not wake up in a good mood. See if we can find her family. We'll need them as leverage."

"Don't you think she was going to help us anyway?"

"No. I don't. I think she was saying goodbye and clearing her conscience at the same time."

Silas rubbed his chin as he looked at the quiet body of the woman who had voluntarily come to offer the truth. He shook his head, and hoped he had made the right decision. In his gut, he knew he needed more than information, and she was not going to volunteer what he needed.

July 4 – 0735 EDT – Kennesaw, Georgia

The house was beginning to close in on Adrian. It had been over two weeks since he had been outside, and it was the last summer before his senior year. It was the Fourth of July. He should have been out with his friends at the lake, not trapped in the house with his catatonic father. His mother should have come back. She was the one who abandoned him here exactly when he needed a parent.

Both of his parents, absent as they were, should be proud of what he had accomplished. He was fed, clothed and the house was clean—considering. But this was not the senior summer he had hoped for.

Stop feeling sorry for yourself!

He mentally castigated himself for the descent into self-pity and stabilized his thoughts before they kicked him into an emotional spiral that would leave him drooling next to his father. Appropriately chastised, he turned his chair back around to face the computer monitor and remembered what had thrown him into the mental spiral in the first place. The fifteen forums he had up in multiple browser tabs were waiting for him to return. They still held no more useful information than they had a few minutes before. No one had anything new to add.

He clicked back over to his new favorite online hangout, and his last hope, to wait for fallen1-87 to reply to the last post someone had just added.

She, he assumed she had listed her sex correctly, had started this new thread about her problem since the solstice. The whole site had turned into a cauldron of swirling comments about how things had changed since the solstice, but this particular thread had Adrian's attention because of the specifics. The young woman was terrified after changing into a horrifying creature in the middle of the Midsummer sabbat. Once Adrian had been able to find the definition of a sabbat on Wikipedia and had searched a few more pages to understand exactly what she had been doing, he understood why transforming into a scaled, lizard like creature in the middle of a neo-pagan rite might freak someone out.

There among the circle, she had transformed without warning or even much sensation. The wave of terror that had sent her coven running from her had left her confused and alone. Once she could see herself, she was terrified too. Initially panic filled her mind and she found it very difficult not to run, anywhere, but the more logical part of her mind fought back. It had taken her a few days of internal struggle to convince herself that the change was mostly physical. Once she had overcome most of the confusion in her mind over what had suddenly happened and the insatiable hunger, she realized she was the same person she had always been. That was when she turned to her friends for help and realized the depth of her solitude. So far, even her requests for guidance from the goddess were going unheeded, and she was beginning to fear she would never be normal again.

Adrian joined the moderated forum after several attempts to convince the gatekeeper he was really a Wiccan. Once he surrendered to the fact that he would not get past her pretending to be Wiccan, he told her he was a scale-covered, reptilian, human looking for help wherever he could find it. For some reason, that had worked.

Over the next few days, several people had posted suggestions on spells for fallen1-87 to try. Adrian had laughed at some of them. Now he wondered if anyone on the forum might have a solution for her, but at least they were still open minded about things. Other on-line groups were convinced anyone who had transformed was possessed. He knew because he had checked the website for the church his mother attended. Not the most open minded bunch. From there he had moved on to the most hilarious site he had found. It was the blog of a long time Satanist who swore anyone transformed at the solstice was the puppet of archangels sent by God on a desperate mission to finally destroy Lucifer for his supposed rebellion. Adrian read that raving lunatic's blog whenever he needed a heartfelt belly laugh.

He couldn't help thinking fallen1-87 was right that there was no solution and they would be trapped this way forever. Ironically, the world he had grown up in was supposed to accept differences in people. Apparently, these differences made him not human anymore. The sudden wave of negativity in her recent posts made him nervous. He was worried what she might do. The fear in her words was troubling, but underneath it all, he could hear the hunger gnawing at her. Adrian was convinced the hunger was what drove the others into frenzy. Had it not been for his mother's hoarding tendencies he probably would have broken into a panic already.

He checked fallen1-87's status on the forum again. She had still not signed in, but he could wait a few minutes more. He wanted to know she had not surrendered to her hunger. She was alone. She needed someone to look out for her.

"This is Lugh's friend with the books. Call me. I have your answer."

Adrian smacked the desk surface and sent a couple of paper clips skittering into the abyss between it and the wall. The new message had popped into the stream driving his hopes up that she was online, but, as he read it, it crushed his hopes of talking with her. If she did sign in, this thread would go offline for the solution. His one possible path to help was shutting down and a part of him would miss her.

After his flash of anger passed, he reminded himself he had work to do anyway and consigned fallen1-87 to the back of his mind. The breakfast exercise awaiting him had seemed slightly more futile than his web searching until that last post, now he only had the hopelessness of feeding his father to look forward to.

Adrian turned his attention to his dying father. He had not eaten since the night of the transformation. If he moved at all, it was because Adrian moved him. While he carried him from room to room, Adrian talked to his father. He told him everything was okay, that it would all be back to normal soon, that they would find a solution to their problem, but nothing seemed to be getting through. His father just stared at him as if he was the television droning on at the nursing home where his grandfather had died last summer.

His father's green and blue scales were dull in the morning light. Coated in a thin waxy film that flaked off when Adrian brushed against him, they looked altogether unhealthy. When Adrian had moved him into the living room that morning so he could watch the news, two scales had fallen off. He would not last many more days without eating or drinking.

Two days before, Adrian had broken down about his father's apathy and cried alone in the living room. That was the first time he realized that he could turn into his father. The icy fingers of catatonic panic had tickled his consciousness and threatened to pull him down into the pit with his father. To surrender would mean peace of a sort, but Adrian could not give up. His response had almost sent him scurrying out into the street where someone could see him, and he had to rein in that side as well. Some combination of his mother's flight response and his father's apathy kept Adrian in the middle of the emotional river. Overall, he was very unhappy with both of his parents, and he was not sure he would forgive either of them for surrendering to their base emotions.

Again, Adrian kicked himself mentally to get the day started. He would make a meal for both of them. After his father stared at the plate long enough, Adrian would eat his portion as well. Today, when breakfast was done, Adrian would make the decision he had been delaying. His mother had been a hoarder when it came to food, but even though his father refused to eat Adrian could not resist the incessant hunger he felt. He had eaten more in the last two weeks than he ever had before, and the pantry was getting low. It was time to do something about that and leaving the house was going to be difficult with the gargoyle across the street watching.

There was no way Miss Stonewise had missed the events of the twenty-first, and she would be waiting for the reprise. Sitting next to her on her porch pedestal would be her direct line to the Cobb County Sheriff's department and her father's double-barrel, but Adrian had to go to the market.

He shook his head and spun around in the chair to refocus his thoughts. The house was not as clean as his mother kept it, but he had done his best. Although he had fought with feelings of doubt and confusion after the transformation, his need to take care of the house and his father had carried him through what some online sights were calling *"the madness"*. He didn't think the description was all that accurate. He was not mad.

Jumping from the chair he walked back to his room. The door was now standing in the far corner at a broken angle. In his college footlocker there was a small collection of rings and necklaces from his mother's jewelry box. The compulsion to collect the little things disturbed him a little but he was still unable to resist picking up anything shiny and putting it into the box. As the collection had grown, so had his need to make sure it was still there. Later he would bury it in the back yard. Turning his back on his lair, he grinned and walked to the living room where his father was still sitting staring at the dark screen of the television.

"Morning, Dad. How'd you sleep?" He looked at the stationary form in the recliner. It didn't move. The eyes blinked but stared at the screen. Although he had moved him into the room earlier, the ritual didn't start until after he had checked the mail and surfed his forums. "You didn't, did you? You hungry?"

Adrian picked up the remote and turned on the morning news. Thankfully the number of stories about angry, possessed lizard people had died down. The meaningless droning of the morning show host followed him into the kitchen where he stared at the last of the canned meats he had brought up from the basement. The phone on the end table in the living room rang, drowning out the weatherman.

His father had kept the phone in the house even though everyone carried a cell phone and it was redundant. It had become the number they gave to relatives and companies they owed money. When it did ring, hardly anyone answered it, so Adrian let the answering machine take the call. His father's calm voice told them to leave a message.

"Uncle James, are you there? Pick up." The voice of Adrian's cousin, Karen, filled the room. "If you're there I need to talk to you. It's important. Adrian? Are you there? Anyone, pick up. Please be there. I know things are strange but pick up."

Adrian forgot about the food for a moment as a voice he recognized reached out to him. He crossed the living room quickly, upsetting a vase on the coffee table, and picked up the receiver.

"Hello." His voice rang out of the answering machine in a strange stereo effect, and he punched the button to turn off the recorder.

"Adrian?" Karen asked.

Adrian had not thought to call his Uncle Mike. He had not thought to call anyone in his family after the mess of the first night. He had just fallen into a kind of survival mode so the voice of a friendly relative was a little foreign to him.

"Adrian?" she asked again.

"Yeah, what's wrong?" He didn't know what else to say. Family calls had always meant something was wrong.

"You know what's wrong. You're part of this side of the family."

Her answer jarred him again. Adrian thought about it for a moment before answering. Karen was his cousin on his dad's side. Until that moment he had not considered that it might be hereditary. "You too, and Uncle Mike?" The sudden feeling that he had a real person to share his situation with overcame how odd the conversation was.

"Yeah, all of us. Both sides here, even Mom."

"So, why'd you call now? Mom's gone. Dad's catatonic. He tried to put a bullet in his skull."

"Ooh. How is he?"

"I don't know. The bullet bounced off but I'm not sure he didn't hurt himself. I'm a little stretched here Karen. It's getting desperate."

"I found a solution. We're back to normal—well as normal as looking human is."

"Where? How? I've been searching. I can't find anything."

"You never could Google, could you? It's some group called the Partials' Liberation Army."

"The what?"

"I can't explain it, Adrian, not over the phone. Their site says they can help us fix things. They said we need their help to survive. If the humans find out we're here, they'll kill us."

Adrian felt a sudden panic in his gut. In his mind he believed what she said, but it didn't make sense. "What are you talking about? We're human."

"Partly, that's why they call us partials. We're part human, part dragon. You haven't left the house because you're afraid they'll see you. You don't have to stay inside, but you don't want them to know. Ask yourself why."

"I don't know why, but no one is out to kill me."

"Do you really believe that?"

"No—I guess I don't." He thought about Miss Stonewise and realized she was right. Part of the panic he had felt was fear of what would happen if she saw him. He never thought of himself as anything other than human. He never considered that his own kind would hurt him. He suddenly realized why his father had wanted to kill himself and felt those icy fingers at the back of his eyes. Adrian still thought of himself as human, but his father had seen his wife react to him as if he was a monster. He looked at his father sitting across the room staring at the television screen and rotting into his chair no matter what Adrian tried. His cousin let him settle into his realization without speaking.

"Okay, so what do I have to do?"

"I'm e-mailing the link. I wanted to talk to you before I sent it though. There's a video of this awesome dragon that's helping us out. He explains how to transform. You have to join up to get permission to watch the video but it's a free registration, and they're quick."

Adrian stretched the phone cord over to the desk and sat down at the computer again. He punched a few keys to get back to his e-mail where the new message was waiting with the link to the site. With excited fingers he clicked on the link and ground his teeth as he waited for the site to load. It didn't take long, but he suddenly felt his mother's agitation and impatience eat at him. He wanted to get started on the required registration.

"Look, Adrian. We're leaving tonight to meet the others. If you figure out how to transform, you can come with us. We have to come right through there, well kinda."

"What do you mean, if?"

"I mean some people can't do it. They can't get it into their heads. Mostly older people. Mom can't do it."

Adrian cringed at her new information. If Aunt June couldn't do it his dad would never be able to. He looked up at his dad again. He wasn't able to feed himself, how could he hope to transform?

"So you're just leaving her? What about dad?" Adrian keyed in the required information to register while he listened to his cousin's answer.

"I'll bring mom over with me. They can live there together. Maybe she can help him. We can send supplies back. Dad and I were planning it all out before I called you. We weren't sure what to do about mom, but this works out."

A new e-mail popped up from the PLA site, and he clicked through it to gain access to the member only section. Adrian thought about Karen's plan for a minute and then made a decision. He had to do it. He had to get out of there. There had to be an answer to why they were this way. Maybe it did have something to do with the humans.

"Okay, but where are we going if we leave here? How will we survive?"

"Read their site. We're heading your way. There's a place in Virginia where they're training us. They can explain why this happened, and they have food." He could hear the same hunger in her voice that he felt. "There are others like us out there making a living. If we stay mixed in with the humans, someone will find out. We're not safe. We'll be there in about six hours. Be ready to leave."

Adrian nodded to what she was saying. It made sense. "Okay, I'm in." A sudden surge of relief filled him as one of his concerns about the future disappeared only to be replaced immediately by the specter of his father. He looked over at the catatonic form and frowned. Could he leave him behind? Anger bit at his indecision and, for a brief moment, his mother and father fought in his head. He turned back to the screen to watch the video he had queued up.

"See you in a few hours. Pack light."

He nodded again and grumbled an unintelligible response into the phone as the video started. A young man, probably five or six years older than him, was standing in a barnyard talking to an older man in coveralls. The old man was obviously nervous about the way he looked. Adrian listened as the young man coached him on how to transform.

"He's watching the video," Karen's voice said off in the distance on the phone. "Good luck, Adrian. See you in a little while."

The line clicked dead while he watched the video again and focused on his own human form. His tail was the first thing that disappeared. The scales on his arm vanished next, and he was suddenly very human. He looked at his hands and then turned to look at his father. He was staring at the screen, but his head was tilted a little to the left. Had he moved? Adrian couldn't remember. He reached over, started the video again, and then turned his father's chair to face the computer monitor. With his father positioned, Adrian went to gather his hoard and bury it before his cousin got there. Something told him more than fireworks were coming at the end of this Fourth of July. Between now and when they arrived, he needed to have made his best effort to get his father to transform. If he couldn't make it, Adrian was going to have to cut the cord and stand up on his own. His father would get him killed, and it was about survival now. That was what the site said. Now that he could transform, he could survive.

Just before he carried the box into the back yard, he queued the video up again for his father and switched back to the Wiccan forum where he dropped the link into fallen1-87's thread. Maybe he could help her, after all.

July 9 – 0745 CEST – Munich, Germany

Rebekka had learned her lesson. She now understood her Grandmother's warning. Playing with magic was dangerous. One had to be careful about how they cast spells. A smart witch would not cast spells unless they knew the effects, and then they would avoid spells that manipulated emotions like love and hate. She had learned. Over the past few weeks she had learned more than she had ever expected. Magic was not a toy. Magic was a weapon, and one should be very serious about how one used it.

She looked out over the crowd of executives heading to their meetings in the conference center. This was where she was going to turn her magic into business. Somewhere in this crowd was the man who would change her life. Why did it have to be a man? First, she enjoyed men; they were fun diversions. Second, they were the most common owners of multi-billion-dollar companies. And third, she was specially equipped to give him whatever he was unable to buy. She reviewed her plan as she waited.

Step one: find the target.

Step two: find out what he needs.

Step three: get it for him.

Simple plan, now she had to execute it.

Before she joined the flow of conference attendees heading back toward their rooms, she cast a complicated spell she had prepared before she left the house. With the last words of the incantation, she made the motion with the crystal magnifying glass that was described in the old text and waited. The book promised it would reveal the unseen and secret. Now, she wondered what that would look like and if anyone else would see it. She shivered the worry away and merged with the crowd. It was too late now.

She looked over the crowd moving around her and sighed. Everyone looked the same. Nothing looked different at all. When she reached the conference halls, she checked each doorplate looking for interesting companies or groups. Still nothing. Disappointed and alone after all of the rooms had filled, she turned towards the front of the conference center and walked with purpose back to where she started her search.

Back at the main entrance she reviewed her failure and sat down in a cluster of soft chairs to wait for the next break. With the schedules for the day memorized, she felt as prepared as she could be. A single failure early in the morning did not make the whole day bad. There was no way she could have seen everyone. Step one was like washing one's hair, there was always a repeat step.

With time on her hands she concentrated on reviewing the inventory of spells she had started a few days before. It had four columns; spells she knew and had cast, spells she knew but had not cast, spells she was afraid to cast and spells she needed to add to her list. The last column was a kind of wish list that she pursued when she had nothing else to do. After collecting all of the spell books she could find in her grandmother's things, she started looking for other sources of spells. Spell inventory, it turned out, was not a problem for her. Years of casting spells without seeing results was what was hurting her. She was too accustomed to nothing happening, but that was changing as she found interesting ways to practice. Once she ran out of bums in the park, she would find other lab rats in the raves and clubs unless she landed her catch today.

For an hour, she reworked her inventory while being interrupted by the clerks behind the hotel counter talking about what they had watched the night before on television. Each time she looked up at the giggling idiots, she had to resist the urge to curse each of them in some grotesque way. She overcame the desire by forcing herself to check the time with the clock on her phone. After three times of shoving it back into the pocket of her suit jacket instead of casting a spell, she stood up from the chair and prepared herself for the next break. She considered—for one last instant—testing a particularly nasty sounding spell that she had never cast before on one of the counter watchers, but decided it would unsettle the environment too much. If she failed to find a mark on this break, she would reconsider that as an option though.

She scanned herself for blemishes and straightened a few things before she turned to head back to the rooms. The light in the room suddenly dimmed around her.

A shadow, like a cloud hiding the sun, fell over her.

She looked up to find the shadow's source, and her heart skipped painfully in her chest. She choked back the scream that came with it.

An immaculately dressed man was walking toward her. Towering over him and walking in his footsteps was the menacing, shadowy figure of a dragon that filled the room.

The man was focused on an area over Rebekka's left shoulder and paying little attention to anyone else in the room.

The shadow of the dragon, however, was attentive and looking everywhere else. It paused to stare at each person in the lobby.

The lack of any reaction in the room drew her attention away from the shadow. She was the only person who could see it. Rebekka forced herself to relax, and she whispered a silent thanks to her grandmother and the goddess before she stepped out to follow him.

Her heart was still racing.

A fine sheen of sweat coated her palms.

A few steps later, the dragon shadow was staring at her.

Had she actually heard the growl or only imagined it?

Spooked, she stepped behind a pole next to a rack of attraction cards where the projection could not see her.

"I need to speak with the conference coordinator. I have a conference scheduled, and I'd like to check the facilities," he said to the first clerk near him as he walked up.

He spoke in very proper German, but he was not native, his accent was foreign. She guessed American, but he was having no problem communicating. When she looked around the pole to check for other indications of where he was from, the projection pinned her to her place with piercing eyes. It had no problem communicating either.

Slipping back behind the post again, she wondered what exactly it meant. She considered the news stories she had read since her spells had started working. The stories of lizard men and weird creatures had been interesting, but she had barely paid any mind to them after the first day. Now, standing a few feet away from her was a man who her spell that revealed the unseen or unknown was telling her was a dragon. She nearly jumped into the air and shouted. This might be exactly who she was looking for.

Her pulse raced again for a different reason, but she inhaled a slow breath, forcing herself to control her impulsive nature. Trying not to look out of place she snatched a brochure from the rack and stared at it without reading it. She didn't want him to see, but she needed to know who he was and how she could help him.

There had to be a way she could follow him without him knowing. She looked up and around the post as surreptitiously as she could into the eyes of the dragon, who was still staring at her. She sifted through the other spells she had cast recently or used before trying to remember her inventory, which had selected that moment to escape her memory. She reverted to the list she had used for years at work. She had never really believed she could be invisible, but she had often pretended the spell worked. It had become a joke to her and her coworkers over the years. It was how she told them she didn't want them around. As quietly as she could and with less flare than she used when she cast it at her colleagues, she chanted the old words and made the motions required to vanish. As the final phrase cleared her lips and the motions ended, she felt a jolt like static shock that had not happened on previous castings. She couldn't be sure that meant she was invisible, but she had little time to learn. Placing the card she was reading back into the rack and stepping boldly out from behind the pole, she walked directly up to the counter.

She was sure, if she had been visible, one of the clerks would have addressed her when she reached the counter. Then she reminded herself of the half-hour of inane discussion of some teen-dream's physical perfection, and she knew she had to be sure. She raised both hands and waived at the one she wanted to hex. The slightly plump young woman didn't react at all.

Convinced she was safe, she walked a few feet away from the man with the shadow of a dragon. He was paying her no attention. The dragon shadow, who seemed to find her interesting before now sniffed at the air. She was invisible.

This has its advantages, she thought.

An older woman, obviously convinced her dress would not affect her position at the conference center, walked from an office behind the counter and put out her hand to greet him.

"Yes. You must be Mr. Kellmunz from *The International Brotherhood of The Dragon*. Welcome, I've been expecting you. Please follow me." She walked to the end of the counter and out a door to meet him.

Rebekka turned and quickly caught up to them, mimicking the affected walk of the conference center manager. When she caught up to them, she drew up close behind the woman so she could see what she was carrying. The information on the file she held said his name was Nicklaus and that he was bringing nearly two hundred men to the conference center in four days. If they were all *Brothers,* then she was looking at a very powerful man indeed.

She smiled to herself while she ignored the way her closeness to the center's manager made the woman twitch uncomfortably. It was like she wanted to swat a large spider off her arm without revealing it was there. She was relieved when he suggested they check the rooms she had reserved for him, but seemed more distressed when she didn't escape the unexplained irritation. Rebekka wanted to laugh but needed to remain hidden. She bit her lip and continued to maintain her uncomfortable distance as she followed them back to the conference halls.

According to the form, Rebekka had seven days to learn what she needed to know about *The International Brotherhood of The Dragon*. He needed her. Why, she had to figure out. How, exactly, she would convince him was a third problem, but it was all part of the plan she would have ready in seven days.

CHAPTER 6 - THE CONCLAVE

July 16 – 0630 CEST - Munich, Germany

The Gulfstream with the king's delegation to the conclave, including Nethliast, landed in Munich after weeks of preparation. Nethliast was relaxed and ready for this meeting, looking forward to the conversation he expected to easily control. The head of every dragon breed would be there with his key male advisors, as was tradition.

Nethliast's confidence was based on the list of senior males that would support him when the voting started. There were a few wildcards left to manage, the most important being the Asian dragons, and that was why he still needed Valdiest. The good king still served a purpose.

Valdiest, King of the European Dragons, would oversee the first conclave of dragons since their emergence. Nethliast's father, Gerliast, aide-de-camp to the king, would be there beside them. He did not agree with their plans but, as was his job, he would keep his opinion to himself. However, Nethliast, the soon-to-be-crowned successor to the throne, would shine as the dragon that organized this monumental meeting, unafraid of human scrutiny. He would be known for leading all dragonkind to their historical place as rulers of this world.

Many who had chosen not to attend, and some who had finally agreed with pressure, worried that an open meeting was not safe. They wanted to meet in secret, in a cave somewhere. Nethliast would do his business out in the open, or as open as still hiding in human form would allow. The combination of convenience and some unnatural caution that he could not shake forced them to continue to remain in those damnable forms until he could get them all to agree to his plan. Then it would be the end of hiding in the shadows.

He stepped out of the plane into the comfortable Bavarian Summer. Pausing before slipping into the limousine, he inhaled a deep breath of the air he would soon rule. It had been too long since the ancient rulers of this land had come home. At the end of this conclave, he would take it back. No international body of humans would tell him he had no claim on the land his dragon kin had tamed. He could feel the edge of a nagging headache eating away at his consciousness but avoided it by focusing on his plan and not thinking about the past. Over the last few weeks, he had learned that it was a waste of effort to try and recover those fleeting memories. The pain was not worth the results, and what he had found beyond that veil of pain had not changed his mind about their history or the future he saw ahead.

He sat down into the leather seat of the limousine across from Valdiest. Melissa's father, at least, was no fan of humans and still believed in the plan that had grown from years of discussions over cognac and cigars in Valdiest's Tennessee manor. Those conversations had involved politically forcing the UN or the EU to respect their claims to ancient Swabia, claims supported by bloodlines protected and documented back to the days before the formation of Spain, Germany and France.

That was before they had emerged. Those bloodlines mattered because they were the pure bloodline of the dragons they were. Humans would not deny their sovereignty any longer. When they stood up and claimed it under the fiery force of dragon might, they would again reign over their birthright and beyond.

Nethliast pounded his fist into the armrest on the limousine door. Valdiest and Gerliast looked up from their repose in the seat near him and frowned. He simply smiled back at them with a childlike excitement while continuing to stir the cauldron of his plan privately in his mind.

The car pulled away from the tarmac and navigated the German streets toward the conference center and hotel. He despised his human form, but there were very few venues that could host dragons in their native form, and there were none that he was interested in meeting in. Since he could not remember where their ancient castles were, and he could not staff them and fill them with food, he had to settle for the best Munich had to offer them on this scale. Another spike of pain threatened, but he avoided it.

Valdiest, who had roused from his restful mode as they approached the hotel, looked troubled, like he wanted to talk. Nethliast had maintained a distance and a professional silence for the two weeks it had taken to organize the meeting, but, with everything falling into place, he could no longer avoid the conversation the old king had on his mind.

"Valdiest, your majesty, something on your mind?"

"Yes, Nethliast, I would like to beseech you to be lenient where my daughter is concerned. She is young and has much to work out. This has taken us all by surprise, and I think it has us a little on the unbalanced side."

Nethliast dropped his head and looked away from the older dragon. "There is no room for her type of compassion. She's a traitor. She's protecting those who enslaved us. She lives among them in the house you should possess. She continues to live her human life, as far as I can tell." He looked at the Armani suit he was wearing, the car he was in, and suddenly felt soiled.

"And, she kneed you in the eye," Valdiest reminded him.

Nethliast turned to look at his elder but kept his left eye out view. Any sign of injury had faded, but he could still feel the insult. How dare he bring that up? He had to control this meeting. There could be no sign of weakness, not even a subconscious irritation about some female on the other side of the ocean. He would not have that, not for himself. Let others worry and fret over their mates. He could feel his face burning from the anger.

"You need to be careful what fuel is feeding your anger. I want you to make peace with her." Valdiest continued to push him, this time making it a command.

"Does she want peace with me?"

"Remember your place, son," Gerliast growled from the opposite corner of the car. Nethliast bristled at the warning from his father, but said nothing. He was sure there was no way to rescue his reputation with his father but he would avoid damaging it any further.

"She will do what is right for us. We must think of what is best for the race. She will not forsake us for the humans," Valdiest responded.

"How can you be sure?"

"I'll not have you speak of her that way any longer. She is my daughter, and I will have you respect her."

"She is my mate, and I know her better than you." Nethliast continued to walk the knife's edge, but he felt he had a point to make.

The limousine pulled into the entrance of the conference center, and Nethliast saw no reason to continue the argument. He needed the older leader with him. He needed his knowledge and guidance. The younger dragons, like the African, Bida, looked up to him. It was important that Bida and the other young leaders see that the elder leaders wanted to move from their safe positions and act. The meeting of the key elder leaders and the new young leaders would set the tone for the conclave. If the elders took as long as they had in the past, they would never win the land back. Some of his supporters were impatient for results but none so much as the partials who were waiting daily for a sign of progress. Again, Nethliast felt a little soiled, but it was a partnership of convenience. He could easily forget it later. The door opened to allow him and Valdiest out, and Nethliast chose that moment to speak again.

"Sire, I will respect your wishes in this. I will do nothing more until after the conclave is settled. Then we will see where everyone stands. Perhaps you're right. She needs time to see our perspective." Nethliast smiled at the king and motioned for him to exit first. What his smile hid was his own opinion that Melissa deserved a giant metal spike through her heart for what she had done to him. He would not put up with her ways, and, at the end of this conclave, it would be resolved. He followed the king and his father out of the car and walked beside them into the conference center.

As he walked to the desk to check in, he left Valdiest and Gerliast to tend to their bags; he had work to do. The young woman behind the counter recognized his name, as he expected, and provided him with his key and the schedule for the room he had reserved for the meetings. He had already inspected everything the week before, so there should be no surprises and yet the woman still had one form him.

"Your assistant checked in this morning to make sure everything was ready. She is waiting for you in the conference room."

"Assistant?" he asked.

"Yes, she's waiting for you," the woman answered, a little disturbed by his question.

Nethliast smiled at her even though he had no assistant and had not sent anyone ahead. His pulse was racing. Who was messing with his plan? Was this Melissa causing problems? He turned away from her and faced Valdiest. He needed to see what was going on and needed the king somewhere else.

"I'm going straight to the meeting room. I want to make sure everything is set up before everyone arrives. Would you see him to the rooms and help him relax before we get started," Nethliast said to Gerliast before he took his own bag and turned toward the meeting rooms.

Valdiest reached out to stop him. "Nethliast, I know you were placating me back there. Think about what I said. Don't underestimate her and how she can help us... How she can help you."

He didn't need this distraction now while someone was pretending to be his assistant. This meeting was critical, and he had to make sure some human spies were not seeding his destruction. What could Melissa be up to? He had to get the old dragon out of his way so he could focus on the rooms. "Don't worry about it. I'm sure everything will be fine when we get back. If she's as interested in our welfare as you say, I have nothing to be concerned about, do I? Go with Gerliast. Freshen up in the room and relax a while before the meeting. It was a long flight. Stretch your legs and let me take care of everything down here."

He didn't wait for a response. His agitation was building, and he had to identify this *assistant*. If Melissa's father had anything to add, Nethliast had missed it as he walked away.

Down a hall that indicated it held the meeting rooms he was looking for, he found the double wooden doors with the place card in the slot that indicated there was a meeting of *The International Brotherhood of The Dragon*. He grinned at the card. Since he had succeeded in quieting the unrest of the partials and getting most of them behind him, the odd news about them had stopped. Humans had an amazing ability to ignore what they didn't think possible. So long as they believed dragons were mythical, he could act right under their noses. No matter how many centuries passed, they never changed. He grabbed the door handle roughly as he flirted with forgotten memories threatening the headaches he wanted to avoid.

With more force than he had really intended, the doors slammed open as he charged into the large ballroom. A noise, a gasp perhaps, at the back of the room drew his attention to a small woman in a tailored business suit. She was standing at the single large conference table in the center of the room. Her blonde hair dropped to her shoulder in simple waves. The style was last popular in the 40's, but it looked quite alluring on her. She looked like she had stepped out of a promotional video for Germany as the delicate but strong beauty for which the country was famous. She held his disapproving stare. He relaxed his face a little when she didn't react and prepared to address his *assistant*.

"Can I help you, Miss?"

"Probably." She appraised him quickly with a sweeping glance over his suited body, which made him suddenly feel very exposed and out of control of the conversation. "But, I think it is *I* who can help *you*."

"I do not recall needing any help."

Especially not from a human woman, he thought, but held back.

"You're obviously not my assistant, but you announced yourself at the desk as such. You knew I would know, and come to find you. What do you want?"

"You should watch your emotions. Contempt is not pretty." She smiled at him and whispered a word as her hands flashed in front of his eyes. "If any of your guests try anything, they'll know your secrets. Your face shows it clearly. Can you afford that? You need to control this meeting. Emotional outbursts will not help you."

She was a witch, and she had spied him out. He backed up a step and braced for her attack.

"I didn't come here to hurt you. I came here to help you. If you don't want my help, I'm sure I can find someone else here who can use my skills or what I have learned about you since last week." She turned away from him and headed for the maintenance entrance to the room.

"Wait!" he commanded. He couldn't let her get away. She could ruin his plans. He hated meddling humans who didn't know their place. "How long have you had these powers?"

"All my life," she answered as she stopped to look back at him.

Liar! his mind cried and he was sure his face showed it.

"I've been a witch from birth, but most of my more powerful abilities have only emerged in the last few weeks."

He smiled. She smiled back at him.

"You can't be here." He shook his head at her and looked at the door. "They'll not allow a female in the room and certainly not a female human."

She whispered another chain of words and vanished before him. An instant later, she was whispering in his ear.

"So, I won't be here."

"They can still smell you. I can."

"Maybe, but isn't the knowledge worth the chance?" she whispered. "I've been here all morning. My fragrance is all over this room, anyway. No one will know I'm here if you can control your emotions."

He considered her point and made a decision quickly, but kept it from her. He couldn't afford a mistake, but she did offer him a spy among them that he lacked. He sat down at the head of the table to wait. Her invisible hand settled on his shoulder, and a smile spread across his face.

"This will work," she whispered into his ear.

"Only if you are quiet and very careful. What's in this for you?"

"If I prove myself to you, and you succeed, how can it not be good for me?"

"How do you know I'll need you? How do you know I'll honor this deal?"

He could sense that she was smiling when she replied, "I expect you'll find several uses for me."

The double doors opened, and Valdiest followed by Gerliast, entered the giant hall. They walked to the table, and Valdiest looked at Nethliast as if he was in his seat. Gerliast looked away as if he was embarrassed by his son's actions. Nethliast slowly stood up and moved one seat to the right.

"Here you are. Everything is prepared, my liege." He motioned to the seat he had vacated. "The others will be arriving soon. We should greet them together."

Valdiest nodded and placed his briefcase on the table. He opened it and exposed the ragged edges of an old document laying on top of an ancient map of Swabia. Everyone had a handle. Some Nethliast had to search for, but others carried them around in their briefcases.

Gerliast bowed to his king and waited for his approval to leave the room. When the king nodded his approval, Nethliast watched as his father followed a protocol that Nethliast had no intention of following. Gerliast gave him a questioning look as he stepped backward out the door. A disapproving stare was the last view Nethliast had before the doors closed between them.

"It's good to be here, again, isn't it my king?" Nethliast asked once they were again alone.

"What?" Valdiest seemed to come out of some trance, "Yes, it's a nice conference center. I've never been here, though."

"No, sire. Here, back in our land. It's nice to be here again."

The older man's face danced with the truth, but he refused to submit to complacent belief that the fight was over. He had probably stood in the window of his room staring out at the landscape.

"Yes, I had forgotten how beautiful it was. I remember it differently, but those memories are a mess right now. I can't trust them." He winced. "We're going to get it back," he said and asked at the same time. Nethliast nodded to reassure him. The years of fighting for a cause settled into the lines of Valdiest's face and made him look older than he was. He brushed the old folder with his hand and stared down at it.

"Our dream is close, sire. If we can force the humans who've taken it from us to relinquish it, you will rule here again. I promise that." The ruling the old country as it had been before was symbolic to Nethliast, but his desire reached far beyond old lines on a musty map. His promise was not a lie, he really did intend to let Valdiest rule his legacy here when it was all over. It would keep the elder king out of his way.

"One step at a time." Valdiest smiled even though Nethliast could sense he was repositioning. "We have to be sure what we do is right. We cannot act with our memories of the facts so clouded. As the king of our kind, I can't act rashly, no matter what my heart says."

"Of course, sire," Nethliast chewed on his tongue, "That's why we're here. Don't fight with your heart. We know enough. We remember what is important. The conclave will act appropriately."

"I hope so."

They nodded together as the door opened again and a medium height Chinese man in a black silk suit with a yellow tie stepped into the room. He looked around and then stood very still in place. A moment later the door opened again, and a very old Chinese man in a ceremonial blue robe decorated with emperor dragons stepped into the room. He was carrying a small pearlescent orb in his left hand. A matching pair of black suited guards surrounded him, and a fourth closed the doors behind him staring at every corner as if something was going to jump out of the shadows. When the formation reached the vanguard, they all stopped. The older man's head was all that could be seen over the wall of black suits surrounding him.

"Wy Li," Valdiest said with respect and bowed to the formation of men.

The old man in the center bowed slightly in return before stepping out of the wall of guards. When he broke through the formation, each guard moved with serpentine grace to new positions around the room. One circled his master as if he was wrapping himself around him and then stayed exactly two steps behind Wy Li. The guard seemed to vanish into the shadows cast by the leader. The last Nethliast saw of the shadow guard was his head over Wy Li's left shoulder.

Valdiest observed Nethliast as the first greeting of the conclave began, and Nethliast bristled internally at the obvious sign of distrust. There was no reason for him to be concerned; Nethliast was prepared for this event. He waited for the ancient emperor dragon to reach his place before them. Although Lung Wy Li and Valdiest were peers, it was important to maintain the respect each dignitary deserved, and Nethliast would make sure they followed every protocol. Wy Li stopped at the end of the table and placed the small orb into a fold of his robes before he raised both hands together in an overlapping fist at his heart. Valdiest mirrored the honor, and they bowed the formal greeting. Nethliast mirrored his king even though the Asian emperor was ignoring his presence.

The magic of the Asian dragons was legendary, more so than even human myths could describe. Nethliast hoped to have that power aligned with his cause, but he would be lucky if Lung Wy Li didn't condemn their plans outright. Wy Li selected a place at the far end of the table nearest the door. Nethliast recognized that action for what it was; he did not plan to be here very long.

"Emperor Lung, we had hoped you would join us at the head of the table." Nethliast pointed at a chair beside Valdiest as Wy Li started to take his seat.

"The head of the table is often debatable, don't you find?" Wy Li answered, waving his hand over the opposite end. "Only once have I seen a table of true equality used in this form, and I miss the time I spent with that young king." The ancient Asian dragon grinned at something in his past, but Nethlist could only guess what humored him. He refused to tempt his memory to hurt him. "It is a shame that humans let their desire for control affect even the way they furnish their rooms." He sat down and looked up at Nethliast.

Nethliast smiled at him and nodded without really understanding his answer, but the message was clear. Wy Li had drawn a line. As the others arrived, they would know which side of the line they stood on as they picked their seats. Nethliast would have to trust that Valdiest could handle Wy Li and keep this conclave from falling apart.

Once he was in his place, Wy Li took out the sphere, sat it on the table in front of him and stared into it as if nothing around him was important. Nethliast felt a sudden urge to leap across the table and behead the insolent dragon. The disrespect he was showing the king and the conclave by watching whatever was so important in his scrying orb would have ended his life ages before. Nethliast was so angry that he could feel the non-existent spines on his back standing on end. Valdiest, apparently recognizing his agitation, placed a hand on Nethliast's arm. When Nethliast looked at him, he shook his head so slightly that even Nethliast wondered if he had actually seen it. Whether he saw the movement or not, the message was clear. There was no reason to react to the blatant insult.

A few moments later, the others began to arrive as if they had been waiting for the Asian delegation to enter. Nethliast and Valdiest suddenly became very busy greeting each new member. Nethliast continued to measure the arrivals as they took their places around the table.

Two South American representatives in very colorful robes sat next to Wy Li, making their stance very clear. The North American, a red-skinned man who looked uncomfortable in his ill-fitting basic brown suit, sat across from Nethliast, leaving the seat next to Valdiest open. He was oblivious to the conflict drawn out around the table. Nethliast had no idea how he would side.

An African in an immaculate white suit arrived and sat on Nethliast's left. They shared a nod of greeting before he showed his respects to any of the other dignitaries that were already seated. Bida's skin was nearly as black as his scales in dragon form. Nethliast had found the similarities between their dragon coloring and their opinions interesting when they had first met, but the camaraderie had blossomed into full-blown conspiracy before that meeting had ended. Bida's presence at the meeting and his position next to him at the table cemented Nethliast's resolve.

A rough looking man in a rougher looking brown suit entered the room. His air of relaxed confidence countered the rather stifling formality that filled it. Nethliast recognized the Australian by description even though they had never met. As far as Nethliast knew he could be in Wy Li's pocket; he was a wild card. When he sat down next to Bida, Nethliast looked over at his compatriot. Bida slanted him a quick, knowing nod and continued his conversation with one of the South American delegates. A short dark skinned man followed the Australian into the room. He looked Inuit and sat between the Asian and Australian. He seemed uncomfortable in the room as if it was a little too warm for him, and he spoke with no one else.

When all of the seats around the table were filled, Nethliast stood. He chose to make very small movements because of historical conflicts that had existed between some of those at the table. No need to start a fight immediately after everyone arrived. There would be plenty of time for that when the voting started.

"Greetings, I am Nethliast, Crown Prince of the European Dragons and, on behalf of the European dragon king, Valdiest, I welcome you all here. Thank you for the effort you made to come here. I know, for many of you, it has been a long journey." Nods from all of the other dragons told him they were at least not going to eat him. "You all know why we asked you here. We are concerned that we have all been badly abused, and I wish to end that abuse. We are suggesting that we all band together like never before in dragon history and exact retribution from the species that has chosen to attack us this way. We have all awakened from a slumber forced upon us. Now that we have emerged, we cannot allow that race to ever get the better of us again."

"And which race do you wish to condemn today?"

Wy Li was looking over his crystal ball. The whiskers of his mustache and beard wiggled about his mouth after he had finished his question. He looked to either side of him. Nethliast knew the old wyrm was weighing the audience. His question would unsettle anyone who was at all concerned with what he was suggesting; Nethliast had to be careful how he answered, but Wy Li did not give him a chance. "And, youngling, how could you possibly know that this is the only time in our long history that we have joined together to face an evil?"

"I have not come here to condemn any race. I am here for justice for our kind, yes, but that does not require the condemnation of another. Before we can open this conclave to our other brothers and discuss this in an open forum, we, the leaders, need to agree."

Nethliast ignored Wy Li's second question.

"But you come here with war in your eyes and heart, do you not? You come here with the fire of vengeance about you."

"I will admit that I harbor anger at those who enslaved us. But who here doesn't?"

"Who here was enslaved? Who here was tricked? And, who here can be sure of anything they represent?" Wy Li paused and looked at the other delegates. "How many of you have mastered your memories? I think, to take any action now, before we know enough, is unwise. Of course, I had an advantage of traveling directly here, so I could take more time to calm my charges and to review what we know, rather than acting on what we feel. I would recommend we all go back to those who look to us and find out what we really know before we venture into a pact and take actions from which we cannot return."

Nethliast felt the bile in his throat rise. He wanted to blast the arrogant wyrm out of his seat, but he needed him. He needed him to help sway the others. He looked at the Asian, wondering if there was any way to reach him before he teleported back to China. Just behind the Asian's head, a yellow tie bobbed, and the suddenly very visible guard's head followed Nethliast's movements exactly. Nethliast stood very still and looked around at the delegates, trying to ignore the threatening bodyguard.

The three representatives from the western hemisphere were agreeing with Lung. They seemed charmed by his words. Bida sat with his arms folded. The Australian watched with very little expression. The Greenland representative also watched but seemed to take no side. So, he had a split. How did he repair it? How did he bring them all together?

"Have you not noticed, my peers, the humans have not waited as our honored Asian delegate suggests we should? As soon as we appeared, they became aggressive. You all have seen the news and read of their aggressive stances they have taken with the partials who emerged with us. Hunt squads search even now for signs of partials. Where do they turn next? What keeps them from hunting us?"

The Asian dropped his head with a shake. Nethliast felt his anger rise. The old fool was so in love with the humans. He was possibly the exact opposite of Nethliast, reminding him of Melissa. He almost wanted to ask the ancient wyrm if he had already talked to her. He stole a glance at the North American who was listening still. It wasn't all lost. There had been more killings in Oregon where the North American dragons were mostly situated.

"If we were not as discrete as we have been, they would be hunting us to our lairs and killing our younglings. They are already killing anything that resembles a dragon," Nethliast continued.

"And yet, not a single *dragon* has been killed. You are misled and you mislead, Nethliast. The people of Asia are not attacking dragons. They have been beset by Naga, and those they have killed because they do nothing but evil. All of the other deaths recorded have been of abominations of dragon kind. There has not been a single dragon attacked since we emerged."

"I was attacked," Melissa's father responded. He had been silent until this. Nethliast was relieved he had chosen to speak, but he wished it had been one of the others. This was turning very one-sided. "As I have flown or as I have fed. Can any of you say that you have moved freely without being molested?"

Several of the others nodded at what he said.

"There is an expectation of respect we have, is there not?" Valdiest added. His previous silence made his words stronger. "Can we allow them to treat us like errant children? I understand that we want to live in peace with them. And, Lung, you have a history with the Asian humans that cannot be questioned. We should all be so lucky." The Asian nodded at Valdiest's words. "But, we are not. Our histories with the humans are spotted at best, and their lack of respect at this juncture is indicative of how they have treated us in the past."

Again, Lung dropped his head. "Do you not see, Valdiest, that our histories do not match our memories and some painful magic hides them from us? We should focus on discovering what magic wishes to obscure our memories and allows us to distrust humans so readily. We cannot act against humans based on those flawed memories, and you cannot hold this generation responsible for unproven slights to your honor from over a dragon's age ago. We have been absent from the land that long, and it has moved on without us. We must be patient and careful if we wish to reclaim the places of honor we held back then. We must work with those who now rule this world."

Valdiest did not respond to his comments but let the council think on them. It was clear to Nethliast that he was allowing them too much time to think. He needed them angry and reactive. He started to speak, but Bida spoke first.

"I have no use for humans, except as food. My young hunger because of how things have changed. I say we eliminate them. They are neither useful nor trustworthy, and they are the reason we find ourselves in this situation. I know enough of my history with them to know how to lead my kind."

The Australian was nodding approval. The North and South Americans were still not committed to either direction.

"I will not destroy centuries of good relations over this," one of the South Americans responded while the other nodded. Although they were of two different races of dragon, their situation was very similar. "My history is written in stone across the continent for all who look to see. All I must do is appear at one of their ancient cities, and I will have the respect you all crave." He nodded to Valdiest. "What course would you advise me? Should I destroy that by violently subjugating them?"

"I do not have that luxury, anymore, it seems," the North American spoke in response. "The people who once honored me are gone. I go to the ancient places, and they are empty. I listen for the crying voices that once filled the night, and they are silent. Those who occupy my lands now are not the ones I once knew." He looked down at his lap, shaking his head.

"You see," Nethliast took the opportunity to strike, "history is not all we have to consider. We must look at them now. Compare what we see to what we remember. Are they willing to let us back into their lives now that they have been rid of us for—for over a thousand years?" He didn't believe the number Lung Wy Li had provided, but he was not going to disrespect him openly. "They are arrogant, and they have no place for us. They are worse than our memories tell us they ever were. I do not have to delve into my memories to know that. The evidence is quite apparent on the very streets about us."

"They have no place for you." Lung answered. "My acceptance is written into the history of the Asian people. The current government may resist us because we scare them, but the people love us *because* of our absence and our legend. There have been no attacks on a single Asian dragon in Asia."

"But what of my kind in Asia? Have there not been attacks?" Nethliast was not going to surrender to this.

"Yes," the Asian answered flatly, "but your kind is not welcomed in Asia as peaceful and helpful. In fact, our legends draw you as the great invading evil, but I am not here today calling for your destruction as you are the humans. I have more evidence of how European dragons have dealt with humans in the past. Your kind is perceived as dangerous wherever you are, and from what I am seeing today, you have earned that."

Valdiest stood for the first time. "We are not here for that. I find your comments most insulting." Wy Li nodded and bowed his head to Valdiest in a sign of humility and apology. "We must be unified. We need to show a united front."

"You are not even united among yourselves." The Asian dragon waved his hand around the table and then pointed to Valdiest. "Which of you is really in charge, Valdiest? You speak wisely and when it is necessary, but this child among us speaks without control or wisdom. Is he your guard? Is he your child? Or, forgive me my friend, is he your superior? Of all of the delegations, yours is the only one with two representatives at the table. My followers know their place, as do my young." Lung nodded to the four men who watched the others from around the room. "You will note that they have held their tongues. I know their opinions, but they know their place as should your underling."

Nethliast hissed, a truly dragon characteristic that seemed odd coming from his human form.

"You must calm yourself," an invisible voice behind him whispered. "He's baiting you. He wants this conflict."

The closest guard appeared again at the side of his now standing leader. "I see that differing opinions are not welcome here. Valdiest, when you want to hold a true council, and when you have control of your young, contact me. I will gladly meet with you, my old friend." Wy Li bowed very deeply to him and started to turn away, but stopped. "One thing, before I go, have any of you considered that humans did not have the magic to do what you say they did? Not even amongst the most powerful of their wizards could they ever cast a spell to entrap us all. You are not thinking." The old man tapped his bald skull and vanished along with his guards.

July 16 – 1130 EDT – Kennesaw, Georgia

Elaine tossed her high school annual onto the stack of books she was *not* taking with her to college. She did not intend to remember any of the people she had spent four years avoiding. The jests and insults in gym and in the halls had never stopped. Her mother, who *should* have helped her deal with the situation, had told her that everything would be fine once she was on campus at Georgia Tech. Elaine never really wanted to go to Georgia Tech. She wanted to write. She wanted to be creative some other way. She didn't want to surrender and become the clone of her mother the engineer. Elaine looked at the stacks again. Neither of them really mattered as she walked down the gray path to her corporate prison; they both represented some level of surrender to her mother's master plan.

She had applied to MIT as a threat. She had never expected them to accept her, and the acceptance letter she had left on the kitchen table for a week had really tweaked her mother. She had immediately forbidden her to send in the completed application. Elaine hung it on the mirror in her room in protest as she contemplated her next move. Two days ago while staring at it and thinking over her situation the edges had burst into flame. She had barely been able to save the document, and she had cried for an hour from the shock of the event. She was still struggling to explain what had caused the fire. She hadn't hung it back up because she couldn't explain why it was charred, and her mother saw that as a victory in the career battle.

Her mother's graduation-gift-peace-offering, a new Apple-Android Typhoon was on her nightstand charging. The newest tablet had set her mom back a bit, but it represented everything her mother wanted her to be. It irritated Elaine that she actually liked it and used it. Her mother had not ignored the fact that she had downloaded every novel her favorite author had ever written to it either. Attempting to out-manipulate her mother with her own tricks continued to fail, and nothing she did made her listen. She didn't want to be an engineer, no matter what the tests said.

The temperature in the room suddenly dropped, and Elaine sighed loudly. To have to put on a sweater in the middle of the summer was ridiculous. She didn't understand why her mother had started messing with the thermostat this week or what was wrong with the air conditioner.

She had to come up with a plan. If she didn't figure out something, soon, she would be a freshman engineer on her way to becoming her mother. She felt a jolt at the back of her neck about that and swore sparks flashed around her head. She sat back and stared at the sleeve of the sweater. She could feel the anger about her situation pulsing in her head and looked up at herself in the mirror. She inhaled deeply while consciously calming herself and suddenly realized there was something about that pattern of events.

The drop in temperature, the sparks, the jolt; she looked around the room for wisps of smoke or something on fire and found it in the stack of things she planned on leaving. The edge of the junior engineering award she won last year was alight and threatening to ignite the entire stack. Tears filled her eyes as she grabbed the sheet of paper and flung it into the garbage can where it smoldered, mocking her.

A week ago she could have enjoyed the anger fest at her mother's expense, but now she had to be careful not to catch the room on fire. Avoiding further conflagration, she inhaled—held—and then released her breath slowly. Signs of her anger stood out to her around the room. The blackened hole in the pair of shorts her mother had found in the wash, the MIT application, the portrait of her absent father, the classic Macintosh in the corner and the banner her mother had bought her at Georgia Tech; the list was growing and her mother was oblivious to the real problem, as always. She thought her daughter was trying and failing to hide a smoking habit.

How did you explain the fact that you started fires like something out of an old Steven King thriller from the 80's to anyone, much less your engineer mother that never listened to you?

Elaine needed to think about something less irritating and glanced at her image in the mirror. She had abandoned the glasses just before graduation and decided she didn't look nearly so engineer once she could see her face. Now she only had to deal with the hair. Red was her color; there was nothing she could do about that, but she didn't have to keep it long. She had hidden behind it through high school, but college was a different story. In a flurry of hands and bobby-pins she rolled it up into a bun, out of her way. She would decide what else to do with it closer to September.

While she had been putting up her hair, the room had warmed again. She could take off the sweater, but her mother was coming up the stairs so she left it on. She hoped she could control herself enough that she didn't toast her mother in her own bedroom.

There was a knock at the door, and she turned to face it, controlling her breath.

"Come in." Her mother had been up every day since she had found the shorts and had seen the portrait with the charred hole where her father's head had been. It was a little creepy to suddenly have her attention even though she still wasn't listening. She would smell the burnt paper, there was no avoiding it, so Elaine tried to calm herself even more as the door swung open. When her mother appeared around the corner, Elaine knew exactly what she was not doing with her hair. She grabbed the bun and roughly ripped it away from the pins she had used to hold it in place. She shook her head to release the hair and it fell around her face like an unruly and completely disorganized mass. Her mother's neutral face quickly became a frown and with a sigh, she held out a book-sized express mail box.

"The mailman just delivered this. Were you expecting something?" She sniffed the air and looked around the room.

"No, maybe it's from MIT," her answer snapped her mother's head around to face her and obliterated any desire to find the odor in the room. Elaine was a little ashamed of herself for manipulating her mother. "Let's see." She took the box and opened the flaps with a fingernail file from her dresser.

Inside, lying on top of a leather-wrapped box was another envelope that was almost translucent. It looked like thin parchment paper, but it felt different. It felt *alive*. She turned the curious envelope over and inhaled sharply. The back flap, sealed with a dollop of black wax, had a dragon signet seal pressed into it. The seal was the same as the mark on every one of her favorite author's books. She sat down on the bed and stared at it.

"Oh, dear God, not that silliness again." Her mother turned a darker red than normal and left the room. The door banged closed as hard as she could slam it, but even that caused nothing more than a disturbance in the room's pressure and a loud thunk. Elaine smiled at how well her love of fantasy novels and her relationship with one particular author never failed to send her mother storming away from her. She turned her attention back to the letter and felt relaxed for the first time all day, even though the pain of Helena Schwendemann's recent death had not really numbed yet.

It had been months since she had last talked to her, and it had been tough when they had announced her death. There was no way she could have explained the trip to Chattanooga for the funeral, so she had not been able to go. She still blamed her mother for that, too. So it was with mixed feelings of sadness and anger that she looked at the envelope.

She never expected last year, when she was standing in the line at the local Fan Convention dressed in red satin and painted on scales, that she would become so close to the woman whose books had become her only refuge. She had sent Helena an e-mail at her fan-mail account the month before the convention and included some suggestions she had been thinking about based on some dreams she had been having, but she never expected the greeting she had received when she walked to the autograph table. Helena had recognized her name and brought her around to sit next to her as she completed the autograph session. The addictively energetic and fun woman had told Elaine she was not going to let her get away now that she had found her. They talked as if they had been friends for years while other fans filed past with stacks of books. After dinner and long conversations about her dreams, they had each left to go their own ways, agreeing to stay in touch.

That same night, excited by the meeting, Elaine had dreamed a disturbing and violent dream about a dragon ceremony at an icy, mountaintop castle. When she had calmed down from the excitement of the dream, she had written down the details and sent them to Helena. Who else could possibly appreciate it? That had sealed their friendship. Elaine had hidden it from her mother, who thought she was president of some fan club. Elaine's preoccupation with the silly fiction was bad enough, but had her mother known the truth she would have done something to stop her from talking with her hero.

Elaine closed her eyes to the tears and bunched up her shoulders before she looked at the letter again. What could it be?

Elaine pulled a ruler out of a box and slid it under the wax seal. With a little pressure, the seal released the parchment, but remained whole. She felt a trill of excitement and sadness. This was likely the last letter her friend had written her. It was such a fancy affair; it had to be a goodbye. Elaine was not sure she could stand that. They had seemed to grow as close as friends could be over e-mail and social networks. Helena lived a couple hours north of Atlanta, but Elaine had been finishing her senior year. There had been no time for them to meet. With all of the excitement of graduation, Elaine had not realized they had stopped talking until Helena's death. She had not even known she had been sick.

In the announcement, the publishers had also introduced a new book that Helena had never hinted she was working on. A selfish part of Elaine was thrilled about a new book and equally agitated that it wasn't finished. The publisher had announced a plan to find someone to help complete it so her last novel could be published. Looking at the envelope and the box, Elaine entertained a quick fantasy that it was an answer to her dream. What if it was an invitation from the publishers to help? She knew that was unlikely, but a young dreamer just out of high school could imagine such wonderful fantasies.

She opened the hand-folded envelope and removed the letter. The note was penned on the same material as the envelope. In the past, they had communicated online, and any time she had received a letter, it had been on a basic letterhead. Elaine could not suppress the feeling that this letter was very important. Had Helena left her something in her will? Elaine giggled at the silliness of that idea. The impossible ideas just wouldn't stop. She read the note several times as she allowed the meaning to settle in her head.

Dear Elaine,

As you receive this, some dire events have come about, and your assistance will be needed at my estate as soon as you can arrange to be there. My granddaughter, Melissa, needs your help and the contents of the box I have sent to you. I'm sorry that everything is in such a confused state. I was unable to organize this before I sent it to you. Be sure this is only delivered to my granddaughter at the enclosed address.

Please be discreet about this. I apologize that I will not be there to meet you as you have become a very faithful friend in a very short time. It is because of your faithful following of my writing, and something I sensed in you when we met, that you are needed. Please come as quickly as you can. Directions are enclosed. Always know that you are a special person and never doubt your abilities.

Thank You,

Helena.

What could she possibly mean? Did this have something to do with her next book or something else? What *dire event* was she speaking of? She considered herself an expert on the characters. Her friends considered her a true fan. Many of her conversations with Helena had not been about the books though. They had talked more about the dream she had after the convention. The image of the black dragon that had blasted her with fire just before she had awoken had terrified her and stayed with her even now.

Helena had told her it was just a dream, and then she had asked unending questions about who else was in it and where it happened. She had asked for descriptions of the colors and patterns of scales on the dragons. At first, Elaine couldn't answer her, but Helena had pushed her and soon the details she needed were there in her memory. It was like no other dream she had ever had. As she thought back through the dream later, she remembered three other men who had helped her. Even as she thought about the letter, she felt herself back in the dream. Elaine experienced it all again, including the final blast of fire that made her jump from the bed, and drop the letter.

She flopped back onto the bed shaking. She was shivering even in her sweater. She smelled smoke and looked at the cardboard express box. A small flame flickered in the edge of one flap. She brushed her hand across it to extinguish it and tried to relax on the bed. It took a little while for her heart to stop pounding, and she lay there thinking about everything.

It all felt so very adult, and she didn't feel all that old anymore. She thought about the recent stories in the news, and wondered how much of that was just a publicity stunt? There was no way dragons really existed. There was no way the magical beasts were walking the land of her engineer mother. She made up her mind and sat up on the bed.

She pulled an old backpack from her closet and started filling it with random stuff. Her mind was not on the packing. She had no idea how long she would be staying or what she would need, but she felt she had to get on the way. Her mother was downstairs working, and Elaine needed to be gone before she checked on her again. There was no way she could explain this trip away as part of the fan club. She couldn't explain it at all.

The heroes in Helena's books would never go into a situation unprepared; Elaine wouldn't either. She started paying more attention to what she was packing. She grabbed her tablet and charger from the nightstand and slipped it into a space in the bag. She pulled a small plastic bag from her desk, slipped the envelope into it, and slipped both the bag and the leather box in between a pair of pants and her favorite sweatshirt.

By the time she had finished packing, she had calmed down. The temperature was back to normal. Standing at the dresser looking into the mirror, she tried for the sixth time to pack an old teddy bear into the backpack. The old threadbare toy had been her only confidant through years of heartache and disappointment.

"Lancelot, how am I going to get there? What tale do I tell the guardian so I can pass?" She flopped on the bed again, somewhat disappointed at her fearfulness.

She reviewed the letter she had already memorized, and felt the imperative request in the words. It didn't matter what she told her mother, but she obviously couldn't tell her the truth. It was only a couple of hours north. She successfully stuffed Lancelot into the backpack and threw it over her shoulder. Why did she have to tell her mother anything? She scribbled a note on her bedside notepad telling her mother she was going on a trip and that she didn't know when she would be back. Unsure that the note would help she destroyed it then slipped out the door and ran down the stairs. At the front door, before she pulled it closed behind her, she casually shouted a destination to her mother.

"I'm going to the mall, be back in a while." That would buy her a couple of hours.

She didn't wait for the response, which she knew would be negative, but ran for the old Honda parked on the circular brick driveway, hoping it would make the two hour trip.

July 16 – 1500 EDT – Signal Mountain, Tennessee

Another spike of pain ripped through her head as Melissa struggled for the fourth time to read the first of her grandmother's novels. She stopped counting how many times she had tried to read the same paragraph and shut the book with a snap that echoed through the library's shroud of silence. With a gentle toss, she placed the irritating book onto the occasional table sitting between her and Charles.

He snickered at her and tried to keep his nose in his own book, but failed. She scowled over at him and then surrendered to her frustration and stared out into the back yard. Her mother had promised to be back that afternoon after she had spoken with Valdiest about the conclave. Kaliastrid was her only contact within the inner circle willing to share what she knew about what Nethliast was doing. Her mother was a willing spy, but a spy all the same.

"You're trying too hard. Why don't you concentrate on the here and now and I'll try to dig up the sordid secrets of your dragon ancestry." He patted the spine of the book he was completing.

She grinned at his comment without looking at him. It had been over two weeks since they had started researching together, and she knew as much now as she had when she started.

"Okay, let's try this again. Heliantra, my grandmother, dragon adviser to King Wilhelm of Swabia, has moved into the castle and is helping negotiate a mining treaty with a dwarven lord." Her mind protested, and she closed her eyes against the pain.

"Correct, and your mother is here. Why does she insist on flying between your estate and her own?"

Melissa watched her mother settle onto the back patio and then transform into her human form. Everything she did was graceful with a power that came with age and years of being the Queen of the Dragons.

"It's not safe for her or you."

Melissa rolled her eyes at him. "She's coming up to join us. I hope she has news of the conclave. They are trying to be discrete and stay in human form, but we need to fly occasionally, otherwise we will grow ill. I would prefer to be in my dragon form as well; I'm like this for you and to protect the rest of the world."

"Just like your grandmother?" He held up the book to her, and she shrugged. "I'm just used to, and prefer, this form."

"And, you're not as afraid of me in this form either."

"When's your father coming back?"

"Valdiest will be there until the conclave is over. By now, they've probably brought in the rest of the men. Kaliastrid will have news, like I said."

The doors to the library below them opened. Her mother walked in and started up the steps.

"Why do you insist on staying on the second floor? That's a long walk to have your mother make."

"I know you're ancient, mother, but I think you can make it." Melissa looked over her shoulder with a smile.

"My dear, have you told this young man how old you are?"

"Mother!"

Kaliastrid grinned at the win. "Anyway, what are you finding in those rotten novels?" She motioned at the stack of them on the table as she joined them.

"You still haven't read them have you?"

"And neither have you. No, I felt she was doing our families and all dragons a disservice by writing them. They make my head hurt anyway."

Kaliastrid bowed slightly as Melissa looked at her for the first time since she arrived. Melissa nodded an acceptance of the honor out of familiarity, still not sure why she deserved it. Out of the corner of her eye, she saw Charles note the deference. Kaliastrid wore a long green dress with black highlights that matched her shoulder length hair. Charles' attention moved from the formalities to her appearance, and he nodded approval and stared a little longer than professional or personal courtesy allowed. Melissa could understand why; her mother was beautiful. Since she had emerged as a dragon, many of the telltale signs of aging had vanished from her mother's face and hands. She was wearing a slightly modernized version of the courtly dress Melissa had seen in the paintings around the estate. Her skin glowed in the afternoon sun, and she looked even younger than she had the day after they had emerged.

I don't see you taking a form where you look older. Her own mind chided her. She ignored the gentle reminder that dragons controlled how they looked in their human form, to a point.

"She was writing our history," Melissa commented, "the true history."

"Really? How do you know it's all accurate and not just her own mangled memory, or what she pieced together from her favorite texts?"

"I don't, but everything I can remember matches. With Charles' help I've started a timeline, when I can stand it," she said reaching up to massage throbbing temples.

"So, what does she write about your father and me?"

"I have no idea. I can't get through the first one. As far as I can tell she hasn't written anything about you."

"How far along are you, then?"

"Three books are time-lined with rough dates, thanks to Charles. He's nice enough to tell me what he finds while I wince and whine. It's a slow process. I'm trying to match it with memories while someone's mining gold in my head." She pointed at the table of old books to their right. "There's nothing in the old texts to support this, but all we have are translations and supposition. I hate to say it, but the archeologists and historians are way off. There's a lost history they don't even see."

"Or... we're nuts,." Kaliastrid joked. "Humans were just beginning to understand what we and other magical races had known for years. I'm not surprised there's nothing in the history books. Historically, we vanished at the beginning of their dark ages."

"Along with everything else magical."

Kaliastrid nodded and uncrossed her arms. "Maybe I shouldn't judge those novels so harshly. My human ideas have mingled with my older ways, and I'm having a hard time separating them."

"Like you told me, you can't eliminate your human actions because they're still yours. You just don't have the hundreds of years of memories to go with them."

Kaliastrid grinned at her. "She picked her replacement well. You are young, but you will grow into the position."

"What are you talking about?" Charles asked.

"I'm not sure really. I know, somehow, that Heliantra was not the same as me. She had a position of power that required respect, but I can't remember what it was. I just remember how to treat her because it was bred into me."

"And Melissa has taken her place?"

"Yes. Of that I have no doubt."

"Why?" Charles asked before Melissa could.

"Her color. When she emerged it changed. She's metallic now." Her mother answered the question as if everyone should know the answer, yet Melissa had never thought about her own color. She had never caught the fact that in all of her memories she was red, not copper.

"She has always been red with that wonderful black striping. You got that from me, you know. Anyway, your color changed while we were trapped in human form to that beautiful bronze and copper color."

"So, I didn't cast the spell?"

Her mother paused and looked at her. Charles watched her as well. She could tell Kaliastrid wanted to tell her she hadn't. "I'm not sure. I don't remember anything about the end. No one I have talked to does, except you. You think you did, though." She paused and turned a queen's sad and gentle eyes on her. "I can't tell you any differently. I wish I could." Kalisatrid had learned long ago how to remain regal while suffering. The pain Melissa knew was ripping through her mind while she tried to tease a memory out of the tangle appeared as a tremor in her eye.

Charles looked down at his watch. "Would either of you like something to eat? I'm not used to your new schedules, so, I can't be sure when you're hungry. I need a snack. Can I get you something, a drink perhaps?"

"No, thank you, and you need to stop doing that," Melissa chided.

"That, Miss, is what you pay me for."

"I don't want a butler. I prefer it when you work with me not for me."

"Yes, but you're still paying me." He stood from the chair, set his book aside and turned toward the stairs. "I get paid the same for reading as I do for fetching, and I've done it since I was a small boy. Would you like anything, Ma'am?" He turned to look at Kaliastrid.

"Yes, I would love some wine."

Charles nodded and walked down the stairs. As he walked away her mother turned to look at her. "Your father is concerned about the conclave."

"What? Why? What's happened?"

"He won't tell me anything is wrong, but I can tell from his voice."

"You're not connected to his mind?"

"Not over this great a distance. He found some stones in the stuff passed down to us. He remembered using them from before, surprisingly. We're using them to talk—well, share thoughts—every night. I hate the way they eliminate my actual connection to his mind, though. I lose any sense of his emotions, but it is the most efficient way for us to speak."

"Mother, I need to know what's happening. I should be there. I need to know what's happening to other dragons. I can't answer what this is all about *and* keep Nethliast from taking on humanity from here."

"At one time you could."

Melissa looked at her mother, who looked like she had just stumbled onto a stack of gems hidden in a corner somewhere.

"What do you mean?"

"I mean there is something missing that gave you power to speak to the dragons, like the matched gems your father and I use only stronger, deeper." This time the attempt to recover the memory took its toll, and Kaliastrid slumped against the railing next to Melissa's chair.

Melissa stood up and guided her mother into her own chair.

"Enough of that for now. Tell me what Nethliast is up to. Why is father worried?"

"They're still in conclave, but Lung Wy Li has left."

"And that matters?"

"You *are* having problems with your memory." She grinned at the private joke that was becoming very common among dragons. "Wy Li is the highest ranking Emperor Dragon. He's the equivalent of your father in Asia. Truthfully his queen is the power, but he is the figurehead to the male fighters."

"Mother, I can't do this. I don't know what you do, and I'm too young."

"Listen, child. You can try that on your father, he'll probably agree and help you give up, but Heliantra believed in you. She passed this on to *you*. Any number of males would love to be where you stand, but they can't. I believe in you, because you've found a way to bridge what we don't know with what we do." She pointed at the books. "Make something of it. You'll gain their trust. You shouldn't have to work so hard at it, but that is what Heliantra saw in you. They will follow you. You just need answers. I wanted to bring the other females here to see you because they, like I, were trained to respect you on sight. They'd have no question if they saw you, but their fractured memories and human loyalty to their mates has clouded their dragon strength."

Melissa looked at her mother. The faith and advice had never been there as she grew up as a human child. Those most recent memories held the most power. A tear formed and rolled down her cheek.

"Stop that. You're letting those human emotions surface again. I remember you when you were just a hatchling." No matter what Kaliastrid was saying, she was standing up and reaching to hug the human daughter she had pushed away. Melissa felt the fear she couldn't explain pour out of her eyes. "Now, that's enough of that. We can figure this out." She stroked her hair gently. Melissa remembered a glimpse of her mother from her ancient memories. She had been more supportive then, but never emotional. Melissa controlled her emotions and stepped away from the shoulder she wanted to stay on. Her mother selected a copy of the first book on the stack and ran a thumb through it. She kept it and looked back at her daughter.

"Why don't the other females believe you when you tell them about my color?"

"It's instinctive. They won't react to me telling them. They'll have to see it, and, we can't talk about it without everyone getting raging migraines. Normally you would reach out to our minds."

"I can only do that with you."

"That's not true. All dragons can communicate over short distances through their minds."

"So how do I speak to them all the way you just described?"

"I don't know." Her hand was on her temple as she sat back into the chair with the book.

"How long will the conclave last?" Changing the subject to avoid the headaches, Melissa moved over to another chair and sat down.

"They've pulled in the lower ranks to talk about the details. If we hope to avoid conflict, we only have a few days."

Melissa pointed toward the stack of books and papers. "Then we will fail."

"They have a lot to talk about, and getting that many male dragons to agree is a task only Valdiest would undertake. Nethliast could never do it. So, there is time, but not much. Even after the decision is made, dragons do not move quickly against a foe. They plan and think before they strike."

Melissa shrugged. "Very comforting, mother, thank you." She looked back at the books and felt overwhelmed again.

Charles returned with a glass of wine for Kaliastrid and a bottle in case it was not enough. She accepted the glass, nodding to the bottle, and drank as if it contained a cure for the pain in her head. She held out the glass, and he filled it again and sat the bottle beside her.

"The gate buzzed. You have a visitor," Charles said with the frown that usually meant he was concerned.

Melissa frowned too.

"Who?"

"They don't know, but she has a letter with your grandmother's crest on it, and she says it's an invitation to come see you—by name."

"Where is she?"

"On her way up now. I wanted you to know before I went to greet her."

"Is the parlor repaired?"

Charles smiled at her and nodded.

Melissa looked around at the stack of things she had to read and looked at her mother and rolled her eyes. The new understanding between them felt more reassuring than the comforting squeeze of her hand.

"I'm going to sit here and enjoy my wine. I may even read a book or two to help you two out of your hole." Dismissed, they turned to deal with the new visitor.

Charles looked over his shoulder at Melissa as they left the books and their study for the first time in several days. They walked to the first floor together. In the foyer, she walked to the parlor to wait as he went to the front door.

"Can you tell if she's a dragon?"

"I don't sense one, but our human form conceals even very subtle signs."

She sniffed at the air and sensed nothing. A thought crossed her mind, and she tapped into the magic at her dragon core. Without an incantation or gesture, she simply focused on the her desire, and she felt the air around her turn warm. She walked to the front door, pulled back the small curtain that covered the windows on either side and looked out at an old car that had just stopped in the circular drive. The door opened, and a young woman stepped out of it. She was younger than Melissa by a couple of years. Her red hair was pulled back from her face in a cruel knot, and she was dressed in khaki pants that had not been pressed.

"She's no dragon."

Melissa answered his question and watched her walk toward them. Three steps from the car she put on her sunglasses, squared her shoulders and walked toward the porch as if she belonged there. Just before the steps, she tripped over the low brick border around the circular drive, defeating the feigned confidence. The barely visible aura around her, benefit of the spell Melissa had cast, told her more than she would ever know by watching her.

"There's something about her, though. She's enchanted somehow."

Melissa grinned as the visitor straightened up from her trip and looked around to see if anyone was watching. Four years ago, and a dragon's life now, she had been that age. Melissa abandoned her observations so the young woman wouldn't catch her staring at her through the side windows and stood up next to Charles.

He watched her walk up the steps and paused before he opened the door.

Hand placed to use the knocker on the door, the young woman stood in the open doorway with her mouth open trying to react to the sudden realization that someone had been watching her. Relaxing her hand, she adjusted the waist of her tan pants and tugged at the tucked in edges of her peach Henley. In her final attempts to recover, she smiled at them with a brief smile that vanished when she really took in Charles who was blocking her view of anything past the door.

She pulled the sunglasses off her face and backed up a couple of steps. Her fragile composure, momentarily recovered, collapsed. She looked back at her car and started to turn toward it.

"The gate indicated you had a letter?" Melissa asked.

Her words struck her, stopping her retreat. She looked at Charles again as if for permission and, when she moved, her eyes never left his. She pulled her backpack off, reached into the main chamber and pulled out a small letter in a plastic bag. Melissa recognized her grandmother's seal before the letter fully left the pack.

"Come in," she said.

The girl looked from Charles to Melissa and then back to Charles. He stepped aside and gave Melissa a long frown.

"I'm sorry, Miss, your name is?" he asked attempting to maintain some control of his responsibility.

"Oh, yes. I'm Elaine. Elaine Ambrosius."

Melissa recognized the antiquity of the last name. "Please join us in the parlor, Elaine."

Elaine followed Melissa into the parlor. Melissa motioned toward the facing set of wingback chairs that had hosted her conference with Nicklaus the night all of this had started. Elaine settled herself daintily into the offered seat across from the one Melissa was sitting in. The backpack slipped from her shoulder to her waist and then next to her feet, never far away and always touching. The furry head of a stuffed bear sticking out of the backpack looked up at Elaine, lending her strength by being near her.

"So, what brings you here, Miss Ambrosius?" Melissa jumped right to the point, skipping the entire introductory dance. The girl across from her either didn't notice or didn't mind.

"First, I was very sad to hear about Mrs. Schwendemann's death. She was an amazing author. She and I had become... kinda... pen pals over the last year, until she became sick and I was so busy with school."

Melissa could see that there was real pain in her eyes, and she was avoiding tears when she spoke of Helena. She nodded and straightened her pants. The girl apparently expected more and adjusted a little in the chair before going on.

"I received the letter today. I never expected to hear more from her, but there it was. I opened it and, I must admit, I'm confused." She lifted the letter again to show she had it and then laid it in her lap gently.

Melissa looked from the letter up to Elaine's face. "I'm sorry. I have no idea what that letter is about."

"Oh, I thought—I thought someone would be expecting me. I'm sorry. I should have called." She reached for her backpack and started putting the letter away while looking up at Charles, who was still towering behind Melissa.

"Wait." Melissa realized how difficult this had to be for the girl and tried to repair the awkwardness. "I'm not saying you can't stay. In fact, I want you to stay. I'd like to know more about why you're here. I just wasn't prepared for this. I'm Melissa, by the way. Helena was my grandmother. She told me nothing about you." She tried to remember if there was anything in the journal about Elaine, but could not recover anything specific. She had actually avoided reading the book ever since she had failed to cast the spell from it.

Elaine sat back in the chair and looked between Melissa and Charles again.

"Charles, why don't you relax a little and join us. I think you should hear this as well. Charles, is—was—my butler. He's a representative of the estate and is helping me with some research."

Elaine's eyes brightened at her comment about research. "Are you continuing Helena's work? Are you going to finish the last manuscript?" The mostly useless facade of a controlled professional vanished instantly, and the star-struck fan bubbled out of the young woman, but that did nothing to change the surprise Melissa felt upon hearing, for the first time, about a new manuscript.

Melissa sat back and looked at Charles, who was taking a seat next to her. He shrugged when he looked up at her.

"Last manuscript? What last manuscript?"

Elaine looked at both of them as if they were imposters. "The next novel she was working on. It was supposed to be the last one in the series. *Renard's Payment* is the expected title. At least that was what was leaked to the forums. We're all on edge about it because it's supposed to reveal Renard's plan and what he's done with Heliantra."

The names and memories that her words released exploded in Melissa's mind. She leaned forward and trapped her skull between her hands until the pain passed. When she had mastered her own mind again, she looked up through her fingers at the girl who was staring at her. Charles was on the edge of his seat, reaching for her. She raised a hand to him to indicate she was alright before continuing.

"Listen, Elaine, there is no last manuscript. She talked to me about them a lot, and in the last year, she hasn't worked on anything for a novel. I haven't found anything new that she wrote other than the journal she left me."

Elaine seemed confused. Again, her hand dove into the backpack that seemed to hold more than it really could and she pulled out a leather bound box. The tooling gave away its age. "Then, why am I here, and what is this?" She handed the letter and the box to Melissa and looked at her, waiting for an explanation.

Melissa opened the letter and read it. It was in her Grandmother's hand, and it had obviously been written in the weeks before she died. It was vague about what she had intended, but Helena had been so paranoid in the last weeks that she had not trusted anyone all that much. Melissa understood all about having something to do and not knowing how to get started.

She put the letter down on the table between them and started to open the box. As soon as the letter was on the table, Elaine recovered it and stored it in a small plastic bag in her backpack.

The leather box was filled with pristine white paper crowded with lines of text. The title on the first page was *Renard's Payment,* exactly as Elaine had said.

"Did you open this?"

"No," she answered nervously again, "not yet. Actually, I came straight here from home when I received the package. I took a moment to pack a few things." She looked down at the comforting eyes of the little bear in the backpack and then back up at Melissa. "I hoped it was her manuscript and you needed my help to finish it. I'd love to be a writer instead of an engineer like my mother wants, and I was just so afraid it was something else and not the manuscript that I couldn't open it. So what is it? Why am I here?"

"It's the manuscript you were just talking about."

Elaine's eyes widened. The temperature in the room dropped a few degrees, and instantly she jumped up from her chair. The backpack was at her hip, and her eyes were searching the room.

"Excuse me. I need to—Um... I, Uh left something in the car... I need—Uh..."

Melissa nodded and the girl left the room and nearly ran out the door into the front drive of the house. Melissa set the book on the table and watched the young woman stand next to her car. She never opened the door or even tried to get into it. She simply stood in the driveway looking around wringing her hands.

"She's enchanted." Kaliastrid's voice came from the top of the stairs where the upstairs hall joined the library to the foyer.

"I thought you were drinking your wine," Melissa answered.

"I was, until she made the house uncomfortable."

"You felt it?"

"Of course. Like I said, she's enchanted. Worse, I don't think she knows it."

"What does that mean?"

"She's an enchantress," she said as she entered the foyer and watched the girl through the small window beside the door. "How do you not know?"

"I think I do."

"Well, that sounds confident."

Suddenly Melissa understood. "The temperature drop! She was excited—agitated even—and made the temperature drop. She emerged when we did, just like the half-dragons. She has to be terrified."

"If she even knows. She may not have any idea."

"What are you saying? She's a witch?" Charles asked.

"In the simplest terms you can accept, yes," Kaliastrid answered. "That's not what we would call her, but that's the most common term you will know, inaccurate as it is."

Charles frowned at her and seemed hurt by the way Kaliastrid answered him.

"So what do we do with her?" Melissa asked the room

"Keep her from getting excited until someone can help her."

Melissa tilted her head toward her mother and gave her a be-helpful look.

"I can help her with the magic when it's time. But, why is she here?"

"Heliantra invited her here to help us and sent this with her."

"What is it?"

"Her last book."

Kaliastrid instinctively put her hand to her head and looked away from the book on the table. After a moment's thought she looked out the window again.

"Then I suggest we let her help us. Neither of us is going to be able to read it and make any sense of it."

Melissa had no idea what to do, but she was not going to argue with her dead grandmother. She needed to find out why she had cast the spell centuries before, while keeping her dragon mate from starting a war with the entire world. The only answers she had found were in her grandmother's novels. Books that she couldn't read without severe pain. Now she had a new novel no one had ever seen before that her grandmother had mailed to a fan who was enchanted.

"Charles, would you please go get her? Don't scare her any more than she already is, for your own sake. Find her a room. Let her know we need her help with the timeline and the new novel. Maybe we can make some progress in finding a few answers."

"Maybe she can help us find the talisman," Kaliastrid said as if everyone would understand.

"What?"

"That's what's missing," she answered as if she had just realized it was the truth.

"Mother, you're not making sense."

"The talisman is missing. It's how you can speak to all of the dragons. It may be why we can't think and remember. Maybe she can help us find it."

Melissa wanted to sink further into the chair.

"You're sharing this for the first time now, because?"

"Your mind is as messed up as mine, and you ask that question. It just came to me. Maybe it was the wine. I don't know."

Melissa shook her head at the deepening challenge her grandmother had left them. Now she had to find a talisman she never knew she needed. She wished that her grandmother was still around. Melissa dropped her face into her hands and, not for the first time, wished she had just finished the spell.

July 16 – 2100 CEST – Munich, Germany

Nethliast disengaged from the conversation that was circling around him by leaning back into his chair and shifting himself around to get the blood flowing again. He rubbed at his tired eyes and looked at his watch. The day was ending, and they were no further along than when they started. After Wy Li left and the other males had joined them, the conversation had become a tedious exercise, but it had kept the South American delegation at the tables. He had surrendered control to Valdiest, and had fed him occasional hints from the invisible witch that still floated about the room gathering intelligence for him. They still had the delegations in place, but Nethliast was beginning to wonder how they ever accomplished anything with this ancient exercise in futility.

Without Lung, the South Americans had been harder and harder to convince, but they didn't matter to Nethliast anymore. He had decided, as the day had grown longer, that he could not rely on cooperation alone. It would never work, as this conclave proved. Coercion was the only way to get the commitment he needed.

Nethliast looked over at Bida, who shook his head and nodded at his watch. All he needed was Nethliast's approval and larger, more complex wheels would start rolling, but once those were set in motion, there was no turning back. There was too much to do, and this prattle was a waste of time.

Nethliast looked at Valdiest. He looked like he was enjoying the talks. He really believed this was getting them somewhere. No wonder they had lost their land. No wonder humans were able to trap them. The old man would have to be handled; it was time to move on. The old ways were not working.

It was time to discuss how they were going to make the humans submit to their new rule. He was sitting in the middle of his legacy pretending to be a human executive. Some day he would shed the embarrassing disguise and expose himself to the world as the dragon he was. They would regret what they had done to dragons. He bent the hotel pen in his hands as he thought about how, a month after he had emerged from his captivity, the humans were still trapping him. Bida raised his hands to either side with a questioning look.

"They're lost." A whisper at the back of his head brought him back to the table and made up his mind.

He lunged to his feet, sending the uncomfortable chair sliding across the floor into the wall behind him with a crash. The room became suddenly silent.

"Choose!" He shouted and slammed his fist into the conference table splintering the veneer.

"You either stand with, or you are against us. Make your choice. I will wait no longer. We must take action."

He didn't pause to see what happened at the table around him. He could see Valdiest shaking his head out of the corner of his eye.

"Tomorrow is a different day. Tomorrow we discuss how we will deal with the humans. I will see where you all stand in the morning."

He threw the mangled pen onto the table and looked at a young male sitting at the table next to him. They shared a prearranged signal no one else witnessed before he turned away from the table and walked the length of the room without looking back. As he yanked the door open and burst into the cooler air of the hallway, the room exploded in emotional arguments. He could hear Valdiest struggling to manage what he had created. That was the right chore for the old king. Everything would look different in the morning.

The space next to him suddenly filled with the blonde witch. She was smiling at him and working hard to keep pace. He found himself sharing her contagious grin. He didn't slow his pace.

"You have a plan they don't know about," she said.

"You're a dangerous woman."

Her smile deepened. She enjoyed danger, too. He could see the flush running down her chest where her blouse opened.

"Why are you following me?"

"Have I not proven that you need me? I know I need you."

"I don't need a human. You know what I am. You know what I plan. Why do you want to help me?"

"I see what you can be. I see what you can make me. I want to be there with you."

He had no idea if she was telling him the truth, but the blood was pounding in his ears. His anger; the lack of action; the difficulty to get the other dragons to agree were all driving him. They were just like Melissa, paralyzed by years of being human. It was pollution. He would purge the human pollution from his dragon blood.

They were at the front of the conference center before he realized where he was going. The smell of the city and its human occupiers was not the refreshing smell he needed. A valet was next to him in a moment opening the door on one of several limousines that were on station. The young boy motioned toward the door, and Nethliast made his decision.

He stepped into the limousine and gave the driver directions to take him out of the city. He needed to see the countryside. He needed to see his legacy. It was dark now, but he would still enjoy the drive. The blonde was in the door behind him. He looked at her and held up his hand.

"I'm not in the mood for company."

She pushed herself into his hand and climbed in beside him.

"Take us to the Perlacher Forst," she ordered as she closed the door, and the limousine pulled away from the curb.

"You're lying to yourself." She took over the conversation. "You've been alone too long. You've forgotten that, at times like this, it's important to share your emotions. You're angry. You need to break something. Why else would you be out here? You've had to hold back those emotions too long. I want you to let them out." She was next to him on the seat, and he could feel her emotions. She pressed herself into his chest and kissed him before he could move back.

The passion in the kiss ignited his own desire, and his anger flared. How dare she? He thought of Melissa and how she had spurned him, how she had driven him to do this alone. He grabbed the woman and pulled her head back roughly. Before she could act, he transitioned into his scaled partial dragon form and was upon her. In a moment, he was taking his anger at the conclave and his irreparable hatred of Melissa out on her. He had no idea he was so angry. She was exactly where he wanted all humanity. They would pay. They would be subjugated, just like this woman.

He pushed her frail form away from him. His anger and lust dissipated, he relaxed into the drive and savored his conquest. She stared at him for a moment. Nethliast didn't care if she cried or screamed, but her reaction surprised him. She laughed. He could feel a twinge of his anger ignite again at the base of his neck.

She pressed the intercom button near her head and instructed the driver to drive to an address in the suburbs of Munich. She sat on the far side of the seat and displayed his conquest to him. He looked at her a moment and then turned his attention to the darkness and the receding city.

When the limousine reached the address, Nethliast transformed back into his human form and handed her his suit coat.

"Cover yourself."

"Pick us up here in the morning," she told the driver, who nodded and left them there.

She walked to the door of the modest house and invited him in with a gesture. Inside, the lie that she was a normal woman continued. Everything looked quaint.

"So, this is not you. This is a show for your neighbors and friends. Who are you? What's your name?"

"Rebekka Kluge." She thrust her hand out to him as if they had just met. "Until a month ago this was me, quiet, suburban witch, who presented nothing to the world and practiced dark arts on evenings and weekends with friends. It's far easier to be invisible, but you know all about that."

She shrugged off his jacket, handed it off to him and walked to the stairs where she looked at him over her bare shoulder. It was not as challenging or exciting this way. He was not as angry, but he could not deny his interest so he followed her up into her inner sanctum.

—

As the late evening swallowed the neighborhood and he released Rebekka to the black sheets of her bed, Nethliast was thinking of the other conquest he had set into motion when he walked out of the conclave. He had told them that in the morning things would be different. Things were already different. He looked over at the resting woman who had swept him into her web. She was dangerous. Fully relaxed, he lay back against the satin to think about dangerous women and the changes dawn would bring.

CHAPTER 7 - BETRAYAL

July 16 – 2145 EDT - Signal Mountain, Tennessee

Sneaking into a house to capture a full-blood dragon queen had never been on his bucket list, but these days it seemed like everyone was a soldier. Carlos Sanchez was not special anymore; he was Private First Class Sanchez, and he was part of a team. His drill sergeant had taught him that much in the first few weeks of training at the old military school in Virginia. Now, as he slipped across the manicured lawn and hid in the shadows of the house, he wished he had been able to complete all of his training.

Based on the schedule, Carlos' class was several weeks away from graduation and had only started their combined training. His squad had just formed under him when they were rushed onto the buses, assigned real ranks and told they had a special mission to complete. Carlos had no idea where the rest of his class was now, but he and his squad were crawling toward a stone mansion with the simplest of instructions: Capture the dragon inside.

It wasn't like they didn't know what they were doing. There had been specific instructions for his squad after they were away from the camp, and Carlos replayed those instructions through his mind while he waited for the order to go. Between quick capture drills on the way to Tennessee and waiting for instructions, they had been able to gather some information on their target. That was how he knew it was the dragon queen.

That realization came with mixed feelings. The fact that his squad was selected to capture the queen made Carlos proud and nervous at the same time. He was so nervous about it that he kept it to himself. His squad didn't need to know or be worried about *whom* they were capturing.

Inside, behind the blinds and fancy curtains, was the dragon queen; Carlos was fine keeping that information to himself while they moved into position.

He didn't know the scale of the operation beyond this target, but, from conversation with the officers he knew the rest of his class was assigned locations just like this one. Operation Talon was designed to capture key dragon hostages. Why capturing dragons would help pay the humans back for their treachery escaped Carlos, but that was something else his drill sergeant taught him: It didn't matter if he understood.

Carlos inhaled the damp summer air, shoved the negative thoughts into the back of his head where they belonged and walked around the wall until he was at the back door. It was time to complete this mission. Carlos reviewed the plan in his head before committing to action. He and Petros were breaching the house to make the capture, Petros would breach from the front, and he had the rear entrance. Cowart, White and Gordon were backup in the van if they needed them and to make sure they could get out clean. Satisfied with the plan Carlos exhaled the tension out of his body. It was time to test their training.

"Petros, set to move?"

"Set."

The house was one of several large mansions on top of the mountain. It was secluded, which meant neighbors weren't watching what was going on. That was good for the privacy-minded, but it also made this type of operation easier on the assault team. All they had to worry about was whoever was in the house. The guard at the gate was dead, Petros had taken care of that while Carlos was scaling the back wall. All they had to do now was surprise the target, subdue her and then call in the rest of the team with the van to take her to the warehouse.

He reached up, touched the handle to the back door, and carefully turned it to see if they were trusting people who believed their neighborhood was safe. The knob resisted his turn. No, they were going to make him work for it. He hadn't been trained to pick locks. Anything he did would make noise, but he was already too far down this path to turn back now.

"Go!"

Carlos focused on the spot on the door just beside the lock and cast the first spell they had taught him for this mission. The invisible force hit the door. Splinters of wood flew from the doorframe around the deadbolt and a loud pop filled the air. He cringed at the noise but continued to move. They could not delay at this point without aborting the mission.

It was just a matter of time now. Once they had breached, the faster they found her the easier this would be. If she was asleep, they had a chance. He pushed the door open, and stepped into a laundry room. Beyond the doorway was a small kitchen, probably used by the staff. There was no one in the room as he passed through it. A thin door with a small circular window in it led into the main house's kitchen.

He hated not knowing where she would be in the house, but they had not had the time to gather any better intelligence. They had watched her fly back into the yard while they were waiting for the sun to set. The car in the garage hadn't left, and she hadn't flown away while they were waiting for clearance to move, so she should be here.

He walked through the kitchen and into the dining room. There were three entrances to the large room with the antique table and matching buffet: the kitchen, the living room and a foyer leading to the front door and staircase. He could see the front door standing open, announcing to anyone outside that something was not right in the house.

The foyer was empty. He had entered through the kitchen, leaving only the living room on that floor. It was mostly dark. A single lamp lit the immediate area around a high-back chair in the middle of the room. Another chair sat next to it and had its own table and lamp. There were several fine rugs hanging on the wall, and dark wood filled the room. He stepped through the open doorway into the room focusing his power to trap his target sitting in the chair.

Without warning, his head exploded in a flash of pain. He was suddenly blind, gripping his head and kneeling on the floor. He had lost any contact with the magic he had been preparing and was forced to roll away from the next strike of the fire poker aimed directly at his now throbbing head. The cast iron, hooked end whistled just above his skin as he rolled forward. He didn't have enough room to complete the roll, and his feet smashed into the small table. The lamp tipped to the floor and shattered, showering him and the rug with chunks of stained glass. Panic and pain finally overcame his human side, and, instinctively, scales flashed out across his body to protect him. His head became more draconic and his fingernails changed to black claws. Energy surged through him as the transition reminded him that he was more than human. He jumped up, turning to find his attacker while his enhanced vision scanned the room for life. He had to find the threat and neutralize it as soon as possible. In the heartbeat he had gained as he jumped to his feet and turned toward his attacker, he cursed at being caught in his human form and wondered why he had not transitioned before.

As he completed his turn, he saw her. His target was standing in front of the doorway into the kitchen. Emerald scales covered her from head to toe, and a wicked pointed tail thrashed at the air behind as if it was looking for a target. Lightning was erupting from the black talons at the end of her fingertips, and his body was already reacting. He could feel his muscles contracting, and he could do nothing to avoid the highly charged bolt that bounded toward him. It struck him in the chest and vaporized the center of his shirt. His armored chest protected him from the searing heat as it threw him off his feet. His muscles were trembling as he was hurled over the chair and against the wall. Unimaginable power coursed through his body, destroying vital organs as they reacted to the overstimulation. Landing on the couch beyond the chairs Carlos watched the dragon queen release another bolt into Petros, who had entered the room just as she had attacked. Her movements were smooth compared to his novice reactions. He was quickly neutralized and flopping against the wall. As she spun around to face any other opponents who might be in the room, her tail drove into his stomach pinning him to the wall. Petros' body slumped against her tail before she extracted it and left him crumpled on the floor. The queen moved toward him with her tail poised over her shoulder to strike if he moved.

Carlos could not get his muscles to stop twitching. What breath he could command into his lungs smelled of burning fabric and some other odor he could not describe. He could barely move his head, but he looked down at the smoking circle on his chest. His muscles seized one last time, and everything went black.

July 17 – 0625 CEST – Munich, Germany

Nethliast looked across the pillow at the halo of blonde hair that encircled Rebekka's head. Bile rose in his throat as he thought back over the events of the night. He had fallen to Melissa's level. The witch had soiled him. She had drug him into her human pit. She would not drag him any deeper. He was nearly out of the bed when he looked back at her. What type of woman would track him down as she had? At the same instant, he struggled with a desire to stay with the woman and a drive to leave and never look back.

"Don't even think about leaving me behind."

The seductive German accent whispered up from the pillow. The one eye he could see over its satin top blinked at him accusingly. He said nothing in response to what he convinced himself was a joke. There was no way she could know what he was thinking. He continued his exit from the bed and collected his erratically discarded clothes for something to do. He didn't care about this woman. He wouldn't care about any female, especially a human female. Perhaps, after he had taught the humans a lesson, he would find a female who deserved his seed, but this woman was not her.

He had made up his mind. This woman was not going to affect him. He transformed himself and covered his naked body with a new suit. He left the bedroom and promised himself he was not returning to it.

He reached the door and had almost left Rebekka behind when her voice stopped him.

"Wait." She was standing at the top of the stairs. Her eyes drooped a little, and her small frown chilled him. "You need me."

"I don't need you," he shouted.

"Right, you have all of this under control and don't need any help. Yesterday is an excellent example of how much you don't need me." She walked down the stairs and into the kitchen. He remained at the door and didn't answer her. She suddenly reminded him, again, of Melissa. Anger flared at the back of his neck. He didn't need this. Today everything would be different. Even Melissa wouldn't stand against him anymore. He held all of the cards.

Rebekka rattled a few dishes in the delicate pink kitchen to start a pot of coffee and then returned to the living room. Her nakedness, and her absolute ease with it, tickled another region of his brain and wanted to merge with the trickle of anger he had just felt.

"You may come if you wish, but I don't need you."

"Fine, coffee's on if you want any. I'll be down in a few minutes. The limousine will be here shortly." She turned her back on him and walked away. As he wondered why he was still waiting and why he wasn't on his way out the door, he heard the water in the bathroom upstairs. While she showered and dressed, he wrestled with the argument, and still refused to admit any

Legacy of Dragons: Emergence

understanding of why he had not left. Was it because she was powerful? Did she really know what he was thinking? He finally settled on the reason he was happy with, the limousine was not there yet. He was not afraid of any human. He looked over his shoulder as if she might be watching him in her antonymous lair.

Before he could decide if she was watching him, she returned, dressed in another attractive business suit. The lavender skirt and jacket brought out purple flecks in her eyes. She filled a travel mug with coffee and looked over at him.

"Can you be a little more careful with my clothes? I can't just change my form and throw on another Armani like that."

Her chiding joke stung, and he suddenly felt like a little boy who had soiled his pants. The flame of anger prickled again at the back of his skull, and he wanted to rip the suit off her to teach her to respect him. He moved toward her, still thinking to punish, and she turned to the door without a flicker of fear. His anger flared with nowhere to go.

"Limo's here." She walked out the door without a backward glance.

All the way to the conference center, she sat in one corner of the back seat and stared out the window over her mug of coffee. Nethliast settled into his own thoughts and put her out of his mind. Soon he would take his place at the head of his empire. He didn't need her.

When they arrived, Nethliast left the limousine alone, though he knew she was beside him as he walked through the doors and headed to the meeting room. Valdiest crossed the lobby to intercept him. His face was a sour snarl.

"You left me there with them after that. You need to learn your place. That's twice you made me look like a suckling. I will not be disrespected like that. It is hard enough to keep them all in the same room and to move them to your ideals without outbreaks like that."

Nethliast noted the sudden change in pronoun the old king had applied. The ideals obviously were no longer theirs, but his alone.

"You can't let him treat you like that." A whisper to his right poked at the anger in his head and, like oxygen rushing into a firebox, it flared and threatened to consume him. He controlled his anger before speaking.

"Yes, sire. I expect you handled that much better than I did. I was frustrated, and I don't have the experience of your years."

The response mollified the old king. Apparently, the news had not yet reached everyone. He needed to check the progress of his agents around the world to see whom he could expect to reconsider his plan this morning.

"Sire, please excuse me. I need to check my messages. I'll try to be more patient today."

"Unless you want this all to be for nothing, I would recommend you remember your place. I will not look like a fool in front of them again. I'll be repairing the relationship with Wy Li for years."

Nethliast bowed his head in response. The elder dragon dismissed him with a nod, and he walked toward the front desk.

"Interesting," the voice beside him whispered.

"I'm not unaware of politics or diplomacy. I still need him, as you may observe today, unlike you."

At the desk, he pulled out his cell phone and checked the last minute reports from each of his partial leaders. Each report contained a single name. He scanned them and then deleted all of the messages. A tickle of anger returned at the base of his neck. There was no report from the most important team. The queen had not fallen.

"I want you to stay close to Valdiest today."

"Oh, you need me *now?*"

"No, but I will use you. Stay with him. I want to know where he goes and what he does."

There was no response from the invisible witch. He assumed that meant she understood, and he walked to the meeting room.

When he entered the room, there were several males standing around talking. The room felt different. The conversations ended or became subdued as he walked to the front and sat down next to Valdiest.

After a few moments, the old man stood and addressed the room. "Brothers, please. Let's get started. We have a lot to cover."

Everyone moved to their seats and filled in the ranks. It was quickly obvious that they had lost the Mexican and South American contingents. That was a hit, but they would pay, in the end, along with the Asians. The rest had held and, for most of them, he knew why. As the seats filled, Valdiest looked at him as if to say, 'See, this is what happens when you lose your temper.' Nethliast simply nodded acquiescence.

"I think we all know what recommendation has been put before the conclave. I would like to open the floor for discussion at this time."

The room acquired a sudden rumble that died again, and a single man stood. He was a member of the African contingent.

"I move that we vote. I don't think there's any reason to discuss this further."

Valdiest speared Nethliast with another stare before he straightened the papers before him and answered the motion on the floor. "Well, I think there may be some need to continue the debate."

Another dragon stood. "I second the motion. We should vote."

Valdiest looked again, angry this time. Nethliast simply shrugged.

"Very well, we will vote and put this recommendation to its test. All in favor of the recommendation on the floor?" Nethliast found the situation humorous. They were about to vote on the future of human kind. They were about to decide if there was a future to their race. "All in favor, a show of hands, please." The air filled with hands. Only a small cluster had chosen to take a chance that Nethliast was not vengeful, or wouldn't remember. They had even made it easier by clustering together around his father, who stared at him as he sat silently watching his plan unfold. Valdiest seemed surprised at the outcome. He stumbled a moment before going on, but he covered the slip by noting the count on his pad. "Alright, and those opposed, again by show of hands." The truly brave thrust their hands into the air and stared at him. Nethliast nodded to each of them in turn. He would not hurt their families, yet, but they would not like where he would use them.

Valdiest sat back in his chair and looked around the room. He looked at Nethliast and then back at the counts on his pad. "Very well, the resolution passes. We agree and will act according to the decision of this conclave. I would..." A standing dragon in the middle of the floor stopped Valdiest. "Yes, you would like to add something?"

The young dragon seemed very nervous in the middle of the room, but he spoke. "Yes, I would like to move..." He swallowed and tugged at the tail of his jacket, "uhm... that we appoint Nethliast our leader. It's his resolution, and he should be allowed to lead it."

Valdiest's face turned red. He suddenly realized what was happening. Nethliast inhaled slowly as he enjoyed the old wyrm's reaction to his abscision. The old man started to speak, but another voice in the crowd spoke first. "Second."

The man who had been king looked to Nethliast and then the room. Nethliast had to be proud of the old wyrm. He took it like the very king that he was. "Very well, in favor?" An obvious majority of hands filled the air. "Opposed?" The outnumbered did still vote. Among them, with his hand thrust higher into the air than any other, was the king's Aide-de-camp continuing to stand by his king. Nethliast was proud of them all. He was very proud of any dragon that stood with his beliefs in the face of odds like this. He shrugged and stood to take his place at the head of the table.

As he and Valdiest switched places, he measured the crowd. Most of them were looking at him with scowls not smiles. He could deal with open hatred better than he could deal with subterfuge. This was the way he liked it, straightforward. He might have to make an example or two to keep the more defiant from acting.

"Thank you all, but I must ask that Valdiest remain at my side. I am a young dragon, and I will make mistakes. I need his wise guidance to make it through this." He looked at Valdiest who nodded as protocol required. "There are tough decisions ahead. I want to divide into geographic and functional groups to deal with each area of my plan. I will spend the next few moments outlining it for you, and then we will split up to start moving on the details."

After several hours, when he had finished presenting his plan to the group, he was a little worried there was more indigestion than he wanted. He didn't care anymore though. He wanted to celebrate. They had acted exactly as he had expected. He could deal with the dissenters later.

"Valdiest, will you please see to the room divisions. I will be back. I need to check on some other things."

Valdiest nodded and swallowed whatever he was thinking. He had no choice but accept the bloodless coup. Nethliast turned away from him and walked out of the room as each of the groups he had laid out started to form around a personally selected leader.

As the door closed behind him, a lavender blur appeared next to him.

"How did you do that? That was your plan all along."

"Magic."

"Right—not that crowd. What do you have over them?"

He smiled. She was quick.

"You started this yesterday. No, you started this long ago; you just gave the order yesterday."

"Why are you here?"

"What?"

"I thought I told you to stay with Valdiest?"

"You did, but he's..."

He turned on her and stopped their progress toward the door. He was not ready for a repeat of the day before.

"Do not underestimate a dragon. I hurt him. I want to know how he takes it. I want to know if he turns on me. I don't have him in my pocket. Plans like this are never completely successful. If you wish to help me, then help me. Do what I need for you to do."

She stopped and looked at him like an abashed young girl. The tickle of pleasure her submission caused rushed in behind his anger. He could see that the role switch pleased her as well as they continued this little game, and he immediately grumbled at himself for caring.

"Of course... I was caught up in your excitement. I'm sorry." She started to turn away, and he caught her arm. He slipped his room key into her hand and turned toward the lobby.

Instead of leaving out the front doors, Nethliast walked out the back and down a walkway toward the road behind the hotel. People going to and from their meetings surrounded him. He hated them. They went about their normal day, mostly unaware that anything was different. The news had reported dragon emergence poorly because they had not understood what was really happening. In the month since, he had successfully kept the truth in the tabloids where it was safe, but he was tired of hiding. Today they would see a real dragon emerge.

At the end of the walkway, he walked into the middle of the crosswalk next to a turning circle and transformed into his full form. His sudden growth among the crowd threw people onto the hoods of cars and sent them tumbling into the turning circle. Cars swerved and crashed to avoid the people suddenly in front of them.

Throwing back his head, Nethliast roared out a challenge to any who dared come near him. All around cars and people froze in terror as they tried to make sense of the giant beast now standing where just seconds before there was nothing more than a small group of people crossing the street. They would not ignore him now.

He flapped into the air, leaving the chaos behind him. As he lifted from the ground he watched several phones snap to life as one by one the people around him attempted to capture the impossible image of a dragon taking flight before their eyes. With these shaky videos, along with the traffic and safety cameras, there would be no way to deny what had caused the pileup of humans and vehicles. Nethliast felt no concern for those he left behind. They should have thought before they raised their fists at dragons.

He flapped vigorously, pushing for altitude, filling each stroke with anger and excitement about how well things had gone. He spared a moment of thought about Rebekka and the celebration he would enjoy when he was done, but decided this was his moment. He would not foul it with positive thoughts of any human. At altitude, the refreshing flow of cold air over his wings thrilled him. He spread them out to lazily spiral down toward the city unafraid of anyone seeing him. Finally the freedom was his again. He knew he was breaking some rule, but he was now in a position to make those rules. He would no longer be bound by rules designed to protect humans.

The familiarity of this place filled his mind and reminded him of a time when he had been like a king in this land. Humans had been a small race that had been weak and completely dependent on dragons for their safety in the magical land. Soon, Nethliast would have that again. He would reclaim the land and drive the humans from it. When their presence was completely wiped from its surface, he would repopulate the hills with livestock to feed dragons and return the land to its long lost magnificence. He could hunt again in peace in the hills of his childhood. He stroked at the air once more, gained altitude, and turned south. The home of his memories was somewhere to the south. Painful barriers hid the place from him, but he would start his kingdom there and someday he would find the place he had once lived with his mate. When he found it he would have her brought there to see what they had once shared.

And he would kill her there before he took a new mate and raised his offspring to rule the land forever.

Below him, the city turned to fields. In the distance, he could see the mountains. He longed to soar over them as he had before the humans had somehow fooled them. Dipping his head, he plunged into an exhilarating dive. Because of the discretion forced on him, he had kept his own flights low and short to avoid unneeded attention. He no longer cared if the humans knew he existed. The world needed to know and fear his return. He would enjoy flying again. The air whistled past him, and he looked around at the nothingness beneath him. He opened his mouth and took the air through his nose and mouth. The odor of humans even reached these heights. It would take years to clear that smell out of the land and get it back to something like he remembered.

He closed his eyes and allowed himself a moment of doubt where he wondered if he would ever see the land back the way it had been. He inhaled the tainted air again and purged his mind of doubt. He would eliminate the blight of man on this land if he had to burn it down around them to do it. It would heal as it had in the past, and dragons would again reign.

The air pressure around him changed, alerting him that he was not alone. He opened his eyes and scanned for what had drawn his attention. Ahead of him, a pair of dots approached. They were small because they were far away, but they were closing quickly. He focused on them, and his vision drew them closer. They were airplanes from one of the human governments. He had expected this; in fact, he had been inviting it. The aircraft were small, fighters with wings loaded with missiles. Nethliast grinned. The hunt was on.

How would they react? They were intercepting him. Would they attack first? Would they try to destroy him? If they did, he only had to let them. Then no one would say he had attacked them first. Others would use their own actions to make his actions valid.

He considered this as they flew past him, answering his question. Since they chose to be cautious, he did not intend to become a martyr in his yet undeclared war. He watched both planes turn to come back around. They were slowing down to get a look. They wanted to see him. He had the advantage; they would doubt what they saw. Their radar would only show him as a contact. The ground stations would be unable to help with an identification so the pilots would be required to identify the contact and ask for permission to engage him. As they completed their turns, he stopped to hover and climbed above them.

Both planes adjusted and climbed toward him. He stopped to hover again. They climbed toward him but they could not slow down enough to hold position with him. They would have to fly past him or orbit him to complete their identification. They were lining up to pass by him again.

The lead plane turned into a slow circle to orbit him. Nethliast expected the pilot was reporting everything he saw back to the ground and was wrestling with what he was seeing. One of the planes would have him on video by now. Nethliast inhaled a deep breath and waited. He was holding his distance as both planes continued to circle. When they completed their next circle and they came out from behind him, he bolted toward where they would be. The lead pilot sensed the move, and started to turn away as Nethliast closed. He hovered as the plane turned to the right. He could hear the engine's pitch change as the pilot was pouring fuel into it too late to escape Nethliast's attack. He expelled the gas in his glands into the air around the plane and ignited it into a long stream that crossed the path of the plane. The heat ignited the paint on the surface of the plane's skin and crazed the cockpit canopy. The engines ingested fire through the air intakes and immediately shut down from lack of oxygen, but the rich fuel left in the combustion chamber ignited as the flames entered through the air path in uncontrolled bursts that ripped fan blades from the impellers. The jet engines consumed themselves, expelling debris, fuel, and fire from the back of the plane as it exited the stream. The nose pitched down as the pilot struggled to control the suddenly unpowered and damaged aircraft. Smoke and debris chased the plane as it descended in an oscillating half roll that threatened to turn into an uncontrollable spin that would ultimately end badly.

With a single exhale of remaining gas, Nethliast ignited the fuel pouring from the ruptured lines in the plane, and its descent continued from the expanding explosion in large smoking chunks. The other plane had been following its wingman down as the pilots struggled to figure out what happened. As the explosion shook the second plane, the wingman broke right and accelerated out of Nethliast's range. The scream of the twin engines turned into a banshee wail as the pilot pushed the plane to combat speed and turned in a wide circle toward him.

Not waiting to close this time, a missile fell from the wing and ignited. The sudden glow as the engine came to life was brilliant, and the missile shot away from the wing faster than Nethliast could fly and nearly faster than Nethliast could react. Not sure if it would work, Nethlist exhaled again directly in the flight path of the missile and dropped from the sky at the same moment. Assaulted by the fiery gasses, something inside the missile failed, and it exploded above Nethliast's head. The pilot had continued his path and adjusted to Nethliast's maneuver to line up in a strafing run. Flashes burst out at him from the point where the wing joined the fuselage. The air near him whistled with rounds, and bright streaks from tracers flashed past him as the pilot adjusted his flight to bring the cannon on target. Nethliast drew his entire form into a tight ball, collapsing his wings in around him to eliminate any flight. Two rounds caught his shoulder and ripped through his scales before he could drop below the plane and the line of angry hornets. The force of the impact rolled him over onto his back. He took advantage of the position to exhale a stream of acid from another gland onto the bottom of the aircraft as it passed over him. It was not as effective as the flame, which he could not prime fast enough to use against the plane, but it would act quickly against the delicate connections and components beneath the plane. It might even cause some of the ordinance to explode in time, but Nethliast was not waiting to continue the fight. He had destroyed one of his attackers. The other one was more likely to crash than land. Nethliasts was already falling away from the combat zone toward the farmland below. He extended his wings and returned to flying. Now he would see how the world reacted to the first appearance of a real dragon.

July 17 – 0530 EDT - Signal Mountain, Tennessee

Melissa leapt into the air with a growl. The cave below the estate disappeared below her quickly. The morning dew had settled, and the light of the moon cast an eerie glow over the land. Something in the night, a dream that would not end, had made it difficult for Melissa to sleep. The agitation in her mind eventually drove her to this flight to find her mother. She attacked the air, propelling herself toward her parents' estate in the hour just before dawn.

The river below her was a shimmering ribbon where the water reflected the silver light. Her eyes adjusted quickly to the night, making it easy for her to see the terrain around her and the wildlife that filled it as easily as if the sun were high in the sky.

Each stroke made her feel better. She could feel the agitation ease as she worked out the neglected muscles. Charles was just worried about her safety, but his preference that she not fly around the estate was hurting her. An adult dragon had to fly to keep fluid from building up in their lungs. There was a cost to being a large flying creature, but she would pay that cost any day. She stroked her wings to climb higher into the cool morning air.

That is more like home.

Melissa instinctively flinched but there was no pain from the thought. *Home* was not here, and wherever *home* was it was cooler. The odd memory without pain made her think that there might be a way around the pain.

So where is home?

In an attempt to tease the answer from her mind, she asked herself a question, and her head protested as it had in the past. She whimpered softly to the air in frustration.

At a thousand feet above the ground, she leveled. There was no need to fly any higher for the trip across the top of the mountain to the estate that looked into the valley on the other side. The view on that side was urban and would have more traffic at this hour, but none of them would be looking up for dragons. Her mother often talked about how she loved to look out from her back patio into the lights of the quiet city below her. The streets were visible below her as she circled around the mountain peak and turned toward the house sitting out on the edge. As she circled to align her approach with the estate's sloping back yard, the city lights were replaced with the darkness of the forested mountaintop of Walden's Ridge, where all types of people looking for a secluded place to live bought property. Some kept farms because they loved the lifestyle and wanted nothing to do with the city below them. Others used the relative seclusion of their farms to hide what they didn't want their neighbors to know about. Charles had organized, at a high cost, a supply of livestock to feed them from several of the farms on this ridge and the pastoral Sequatchie Valley beyond it.

Nickliad liked to hunt too.

"Yes, he did, but he is not Nickliad anymore. He's something far worse."

Perhaps.

Melissa felt the trickle of sadness in the voice in her head. She could not distinguish if it was at their inability to hunt without attracting too much attention or if it was for her one time mate who now hated her. She chose to believe it was for the lost hunting. It was another of the instinctive needs of a dragon that had to be set aside, for the moment.

Believe what you like.

Melissa smiled at the comforting agitation her internal thought caused. She was not sure if it was keeping her sane or making her mad. Either way, if she could figure out what she was supposed to do, she might be able to get dragons back some of their ancient freedoms, but first she had to discover what had really happened.

All of the lights were on at her parents' estate. Her mother, who liked to sleep late, was pacing back and forth on the brick and stone back patio. That alone validated her morning flight, but the erratic pattern her wings made as they twitched on her back made Melissa consider turning around.

Before she could change her mind, she folded her wings back to release air and sacrifice all lift, committing herself to the visit. She needed to get down. Twenty feet above the house, she flared and stopped her descent. With powerful backstrokes, she settled onto the edge of the patio where her mother made room for her.

Kaliastrid's spines were up and rigid, and her foreclaws were cycling like scissors.

"What's wrong?" Melissa asked as she landed. "Something felt off, and I came here. Why?"

"The females and children have disappeared. They're gone without telling me or anyone. I've tried to contact them, and I get fearful returns and images of imprisonment. There are two dead half-dragons on the floor of my living room."

"Why? Why would they attack us overtly? There's no way for them to know who's a dragon and who isn't, is there?"

We can sense them, but they can't sense us without training.

Kaliastrid roared into the brightening morning light. The pain of her mental search dulled her eyes, and she shook her head. "This is not right. I knew last night that something was wrong, something in how Valdiest was talking."

Melissa turned her head to look at her mother and raised her tail into the air.

"No. I don't think he had anything to do with this; not directly. Perhaps by inaction, but he would never act against other dragons this way."

"You think Nethliast is involved?"

She shook her head violently. "I don't know. As soon as I killed those things," she pointed into the house, "I knew my concern was warranted, but I never expected they would attack the others. I'm his mate. I'm always a target. But the others are innocents in all of this. What gain does it bring to take them hostage?"

"None of this makes sense. We're dragons. We don't take hostages. We kill anyone who threatens us, our clutches, or our hoards," Melissa answered.

"That's how we used to be, true, but generations of being human, the crazy overlapping memories, and jigsaw-puzzle history has us confused about what we are," Kaliastrid said as she shifted across the stones again. "I've already contacted Valdiest this morning. It's been a busy morning over there."

Her look struck Melissa. There was fear in her eyes, and that was most terrifying on the face of a dragon.

"Nethliast removed him as head of the conclave. He overthrew your father."

"What? That's not like him. He's always worshiped father. I know he saw the throne as his someday, but he wouldn't usurp the throne. He respects the royal lineage too much."

"It seems we really can't trust what we remember about ourselves."

Melissa dropped her head toward her chest and sat back onto her tail. She thought through all of the events since they had emerged before she spoke again.

"Do you think the half-dragons are connected, or is it just a coincidence? Is Nethliast aligned with the abominations?"

You can't believe that!

Melissa shook her head at the conflict from her own mind.

"I don't know."

Her mother's answer silenced the conflict.

"It all seems too curious," she continued. "Valdiest said the meeting changed this morning. He said the South Americans didn't come back, and groups that had been on the fence yesterday, after Nethliast's rant, came back ready to vote for his proposal without further conversation."

What? Unlikely. Melissa's inner voice cried with incredulity.

Someone less familiar with dragon politics would think very little of that comment, but male dragons never abandoned the opportunity to analyze something to the bone before deciding something. An individual dragon would act out of anger or spite instinctively. As dragon civilization had developed from their angry, greedy history that much human legend was based on, the males had learned how to debate, and rarely did two males come to a decision quickly without some external motivation.

"Power has shifted somehow. Nethliast did not have enough support from other dragons to accomplish this."

"So, Nethliast used half-dragons to take hostages and shifted power among the dragons."

"Perceived power, yes. True dragon power is never invested in the male, but this has perverted that somehow. Something has allowed him to wrest control not only from the civilized government we respect but also from a far more ancient and underlying structure... Ahhh!"

Melissa turned to look at Kaliastrid. Her foreclaws were on either side of her head, and her eyes looked tortured with pain. The memory had cost her mother a lot.

"The males will never stand for this. They'll kill him."

"A thousand years ago, this would never have happened. The talisman is missing." Kaliastrid turned to look at Melissa with a dawning realization showing on her face. "Yes, that's it. There's no power to control the males, and they don't recognize the power when they see it."

Kaliastrid nodded at Melissa, who was confused and trying to follow her mother's line of thinking, which had suddenly changed directions.

"They, like us, have memories of human lives. That has changed the way they look at things. Where before, they would have frenzied and killed Nethliast immediately, independent of the danger to their young or mate; now they might wait to see if they can save them. Valdiest warned me that Nethliast was up to something. Valdiest doesn't know what, but he was out all night last night and he's having private meetings."

"So he's made a deal with the half-dragons."

"Maybe."

"He hates humans. Why would he?"

"Because he's more like a dragon than any of us."

"Is he? Really? Is that what you think, mother? Where we really that bad before?"

"I don't know." Her claws clashed in front of her eyes and she shook her head. "I know that the one thing that keeps us together is missing. I know that, any time I try to figure out what's happened, my head feels like someone's stoking a fire in it. This is not the way we were, but it's the way we can be."

"Is that why we cast the spell? Was it because we couldn't live alongside humans?" Melissa shook her head to try to relieve the sudden pressure that filled it with her attempt to remember.

"I can't answer that, but Nethliast makes me wonder."

"Is father going to stay there?" The question she wanted to ask was, 'is father still helping Nethliast?' Kaliastrid's eyes told her the answer; he wasn't coming home yet.

"Come home with me. It's not safe here."

"It's as safe here as it is anywhere."

"I know, but I would rather know you were safe with me. Power in numbers and all."

"I'll be over later. I need to get rid of those things."

"Don't be long. I don't like the way this feels. No matter how much my honorable and ancient dragon mind cares about Nethliast, I don't trust his motivation. If he was behind this, we're his enemy."

This is not like Nickliad at all. Perhaps you are right about his being different.

The concession surprised Melissa, and she nearly missed her mother's next comment.

"You're worse. He sees you as a sympathizer."

"What...? Yes. In a way, I am. The humans don't deserve this, they have done nothing to us. We don't attack humans without cause. I know that in my bones without thinking about it. He's reacting to his human emotions, and now he's using human tactics that normally would not work against dragons." She swished her tail across the tile patio.

"But now he has cause to rally the males behind him even without their captured families."

Melissa thought about that. What had happened? Kaliastrid had another surprise for her in this morning of surprises. She was not ready for another. She waited for the answer.

"He was attacked over Germany," Kaliastrid answered. "He says it was unprovoked. He says they attacked him. The news only reports the incident. The video is horrible quality, but it is clear to anyone who can see what it shows. Humans will believe what they're told, much like dragon males. The surviving pilot reported what he saw. Added to the sightings since we emerged and the news has no problem saying it was a dragon"

"And he survived?"

Kaliastrid nodded

"So, what does this mean?"

"You know what it means. He has everything he needs now—Doubt about the human's intentions; leverage to get control; and an attack that he can say was unprovoked." She paused. "When he came back to the conclave he was glowing and telling them that he was attacked. Two holes in his shoulder and the news going crazy was all he needed. Most of the dragons were convinced immediately, whether he was holding hostages or not."

Melissa growled. He was going to get them all hunted to extinction. He had ripped the veil. What had been assumptions and possibilities was now known.

"Enough of that." Kaliastrid yanked her out of her reverie. "Nothing we can do about it here. How's Elaine?"

"I'm not sure, really. Heliantra invited her to visit and told her we needed her help. She didn't tell her anything specific. She has those pages of a novel and she's reading them, but it is too soon to know what all of this means. Charles and I believe she may be the only way we can figure out what happened."

Kaliastrid looked at Melissa closely.

"You know she's enchanted, somehow, and she really understands all of Heliantra's stories. I think we should tell her the truth and see if she can help us."

Kaliastrid nodded but her tail was rigid behind her head. "You need to solve this soon, before it gets out of hand. Based on this morning's events, we're running out of time, and we've made very little progress. Things are going to get worse and rapidly. We have no allies. Trust Heliantra."

"You've stopped wondering, then?"

The change in Kaliastrid was dynamic. She moved toward the door to the house and transformed.

"We're out of time," she said in answer to Melissa's question. "Time to act. You need to get that girl started, now. I need to get this cleaned up. We have to marshal what we have. Mel, have her focus on finding the talisman. We need it to solve this problem." Kaliastrid stopped and looked back at her. The look on her face asked why Melissa was still standing there.

"Why didn't she pick you?"

"Who, Heliantra?"

A smile formed on Kaliastrid's face. She laughed.

"She never trusted me. I was too reckless, and, as soon as you were born, any hope for me was lost in her eyes. She loved you from the first crack of your shell."

Melissa felt sorry for her mother for a moment and then realized it was her human emotions playing with her.

"A wise leader must know how to use her assets, however they're best applied. Think of me as an adviser, if you must, but I've always been better at breaking than fixing."

Melissa nodded and accepted that her mother was not hurt by the place she held and was, in fact quite comfortable with it.

"Then you'll be over as soon as you're done?"

"Yes, I can't deny the wisdom of closing ranks. We need to find our answer now more than ever."

Melissa smiled.

"I'll see you then. Be careful."

Melissa flapped into a hover and turned toward home. Nethliast was underestimating the humans. Even she knew they had weapons a dragon could never resist. The picture of the basilisk lying in a pool of blood in a London street came back to her, and she suddenly saw her mother laying there. Her agitation made her speed up to get home, but, as she dropped toward the estate a few minutes later, the ominous sound of a helicopter rushed up behind her. The sound alone was not troubling as there were enough of them around during the day, but in her rush and excitement to leave she had broken her own rule. She was out and exposed during the day.

She dropped toward the ground to hide among the ground clutter and hope they had not seen her. After a few moments of hope that she had not been seen, the speed and location of the helicopter told her she was wrong.

She turned to look. Maybe it was a TVA chopper running the river power lines, she hoped. The military markings on the side of the olive-drab body told her it was trouble. Her actions were predestined. She had no intentions of fighting them and becoming the next dragon on the news. She was almost home. The cave was her only option, and with effort she could reach it before they saw her. Dipping her wings and aiming directly for the dark hole in the cliff side, she flapped harder for the ledge.

In an instant, she was plunging from the air toward the hole and drawing her wings back. She stretched her body out and arrowed straight at the hole, but it had not been soon enough. The change in the air told her they were coming after her. No chance they hadn't seen her. How long would they wait before firing on her? The cave was not far away, but she could not outrun their machine guns if they chose to attack. She had no idea what Nethliast's flight had caused, but the presence of a military helicopter in the valley was unusual. Just before she slammed into the stone landing, she threw out her wings and flapped back to try to hover. She failed but was able to slow down enough that she only slid across the floor inside rather than slamming into the rock wall.

She hopped on into the cave and settled onto the floor with her forelegs spread out at wide angles to stop her forward slide. They could have killed her. She panted at the exertion and trembled. What were they going to do now?

Apparently Nethliast's actions had more than hunt squads out looking for dragons, and her morning flight had attracted their attention. With one action, dragons were hunted again and this time with more than metal swords and lances. Modern men had never hunted dragons. Dragons had never stood against modern weapons. They could resist magic because they were magical, but the powerful weapons of the modern world would rip through the armor that had protected them from older weapons. Rifles and pistols would not hurt them, but there were weapons that were more powerful in the human arsenal.

"Mother, you can't fly here. The humans are looking for us. I attracted their attention by flying out to meet you this morning. If you fly, they'll kill you. We can't outrun them, and there are more of them than there are of us."

She hadn't been able to keep the panic from her message.

"Understood."

Again Kaliastrid proved that she was the calm one. Melissa needed her alive, not risking her neck flying around.

The helicopter was circling. She could hear them outside the cave, but she didn't dare look out. Charles would know how long they would search. If she could get up to the house without them seeing her, she could figure out what to do. Transforming into her human form, she charged up the stairs. At the top, she paused to breathe. She knew there was no way to avoid being seen when she opened the secret door, but she couldn't stay hidden down here either.

You're a magical being.

The thought caused her to pause, and she realized slowly what her mind was trying to tell her. With the slightest movement of her hand and a breath of concentration, she disappeared. The door would open and close—she couldn't help that—but they wouldn't see anything come out. Maybe they wouldn't be looking. Maybe they were focused on the cave entrance below.

She took another breath and spun the wheel that sealed the door and pushed. Daylight poured into the entrance. As soon as she could slip through, she was laying on the stone of the overlook, letting the door close behind her. She didn't move immediately. She could still hear the rotors and the whine of the jet turbine, but she couldn't see the helicopter. So far her plan was working. She giggled to herself that she even considered this a plan and then remembered it came from her ancient memories where this must have been much more common.

Yes, you have but to listen.

Melissa laughed at the timing of her arguments with herself.

She stood up and walked toward the house. She was not used to the cover of invisibility so she hunched her shoulders a little and ran up the long yard. She grabbed the handle to the French doors and was in the library before she stopped. She stood there, invisible and breathing hard.

Charles came through the entrance to the library with his rifle at his shoulder looking through the sight. His shoulder was pressed into the stock and he was crouched with his legs bent moving with cautious steps. His eyes darted from place to place, evaluating potential threats.

"Who's in here? Show yourself, now, before I open fire. Nothing in this room will protect you."

"Charles, it's me." She couldn't keep the fear out of her voice. She needed his help, and there he was with his gun again. Everybody was at war, and he was suddenly, truly terrifying. She couldn't control the instinctive transition to her armored form.

"Mel, where are you?" His body and rifle turned toward her voice. He crouched lower dropping to one knee behind the desk. His hands clutched tighter on the forward stock.

"I'm here." With a thought, she appeared in front of him. Fear ran through her like ice. As soon as she appeared, his fingers tightened for an instant on the trigger before he relaxed and brought the rifle down to his knee and across his chest in broad movements.

He did take a moment to glance at her up-armored form.

"What's going on out there? Who's in the chopper?"

"I don't know. They chased me here. I didn't know what else to do. I don't want to fight them but—they're—it's—I don't want to fight them. I don't want him to win."

He crossed the room quickly and drew her into his chest ignoring the spines and scales. He held her for a moment and then stepped back to look into her eyes. "Go up and sit down. What were you doing out there anyway?" He asked less harshly than she expected. "You need to rest, and I have to change. They'll come in before they leave. Did they see you exit the cave?"

"No, at least I didn't see them when I came out. I tried to make sure. Oh, Charles, they're not giving us a choice. I can't keep them from killing us, or worse, us killing them."

"You can, but it means you have to beat Nick... I mean, you know. You have to beat him to the punch. You have to give him up. You have to expose yourself." He walked her up the stairs together as he was talking to her.

"What? They came after me. If I show them where I am, and that they're right, they'll never let me alone."

"That's not what Helena says. She went to them, exposed herself to them. She was honest about what she was."

"Charles, she had a king who was ready to accept dragons. He was open minded."

"Was he? Or did she manipulate him a little?"

Melissa closed her mouth. Why did everyone else so easily consider using magic to solve problems, and why did she have such a hard time with it? She was still acting like the twenty-year-old human.

Who refuses to listen. Melissa smiled at her own deprecation as Charles guided her into the seat.

"Charles, Can you contact the pilot? We need to get them to go away."

"Maybe, but I expect he'll contact us. He needs to get into that cave and hovering out there is expensive. He'll want to go down the wall. He won't ask, but we can push back a little. It depends on how hard-assed he is. I'll see what I can do. I need to change though." He turned and left the library.

Melissa turned to the stack of books that they had collected. She looked at the time line they had started. She needed time to finish it. She needed to stop Nethliast. She needed to make sure he didn't live up to that name. It all took time, and he wasn't going to wait. She needed Elaine's help.

"Mother, I need you to tell father what's happening. I need for you to get through to him. Nethliast is going to get us all killed, and I can't handle him and the soldiers on my lawn."

"I'll see what I can do."

"I don't want to fight with them, but they know where I am."

"What are you going to do?"

"I'm not sure yet."

"I'm sure you'll make the right decision when the time comes."

Melissa swallowed the different ball of fear that welled up from the thought of everything that could go wrong.

"I'll have to. Otherwise we'll be hunted to extinction. We can't stand against them, mother. Never mind their weapons. We didn't in the past. There had to be a reason we didn't destroy them when they were easy to destroy. That's what Nethliast is forgetting."

"I will speak to Valdiest if I can."

Melissa was feeling a little better and a lot worse. The physical fear of what had happened was going away, but the emotional doubt about what she was about to do was taking over. The helicopter had climbed to the top of the overlook and was hovering over the open space. They were going to land. Melissa turned away from the window to look for Charles when her eyes crossed Elaine's. The young girl was quietly standing at the doorway across the library staring at Melissa.

Charles was back and walking toward her in his best suit. He quickly took in the scene and handled it the best he could.

"They can't see you like that," he said as he walked past and she realized she was still armored. She transformed and grinned at him and looked at Elaine with a sheepish admission of what could not be denied.

Charles nodded and walked smartly down the stairs and out the back door. He had to deal with that. He was probably the best to deal with it. Kaliastrid had told her the truth, it was about using your resources. She needed to talk to Elaine.

"Elaine, listen." The girl backed up a step but didn't run. "I have to tell you something. Things are going to get strange… okay, things are already strange. I need your help. I trust Helena to send me what I need." She paused and took a breath to settle herself while Elaine did the same. "Helena, was a dragon. I'm a dragon. We have been trapped in our human form for generations until the spell broke on the solstice because I didn't recast it. I don't know why I'm supposed to recast it. In fact, I don't know what I'm supposed to do. I have my grandmother's journal that she left me. I've read it. She says I have to recast it, and I'll know what to do if I failed and we emerge. I don't. Our memories are scrambled and don't make sense all the time. We often find our human emotions and memories driving us more than our history. If we try to figure this out ourselves, we get violent headaches, so we're not making good progress. I need you to help me understand what I'm supposed to do and how I'm supposed to do it. My mother says there is a talisman missing and that we need to find it, but we have no idea where it is and I'm not even sure what it looks like. I know this is a lot but I need your help with this. Helena was right. I need your help."

Elaine swallowed and then smiled. Her eyes were huge and filled with questions. Melissa paused to let her get it all under control.

"There is more. Helena's judgment of you is based on the fact that you have a magical aura about you."

"Wait." Fear welled up in her eyes. "You're saying I'm magical somehow?"

"Not exactly, I'm saying there's something magical about you and I don't know what it is, but I expect Helena had an idea. My mother and I can see it in you and expect you have seen signs of it yourself. Either way, we think this is why Helena asked you here."

She pushed her bangs out of her eyes and swallowed again. "That's why I came... well not exactly. I came because I thought Helena wanted me to help her—you—finish her manuscript. I never expected this. But, I'll do what I can."

"Good. I'll make sure you have anything you need. I have nothing else to hide, I don't think. Is there anything you can tell me right away that might help me keep the world from going to war with dragons?"

Her eyes widened behind her glasses as she took in the question and chewed on it. "You need to focus on men. Your charms will work better on men. Women never trust female dragons, so they'll be harder to overcome."

Melissa smiled. Women didn't trust other women, so that wasn't all that different.

"Oh, and you should be fine anyway." Elaine brushed away any concern as if some information made it all unimportant.

"Why do you say that?"

"Because, you're the dragon ambassador?" the girl said after a pause.

"I'm the what?"

"You're metallic colored."

"Yeah. So?"

"You're the only one."

It was a statement not a question, but Melissa answered it anyway. "As far as I know I am, yes. There could be others. We haven't actually had a class reunion."

"No," Elaine shifted some in her place and giggled at the confusion. "There can't be another. There's only ever one. Helena wrote about it. Her heroine is the ambassador. She is a metallic dragon. You say Helena was a dragon. It seems these books may be autobiographical, so she was the old one. She was a metallic dragon, right? You took her place. She picked you."

"What are you talking about?"

"I could be wrong, I never saw her in dragon form, but it makes sense. It fits the story."

The girl is right, Heliantra was metallic.

"What story?"

"It's something very old I found last year at the library at Georgia Tech." A frown crossed her face as she remembered something, "It was a neat little dragon drama. It was a lot like Helena's stuff; that was why I liked it. But, see, it talked about the Great Wyrm, which was a council of ancient dragons that never left a cave somewhere. It never said where, but the ambassador knew because she had to go before them. She was the voice of the Great Wyrm and helped to tell the other dragon kings what the council wanted."

Melissa looked over her shoulder at the meeting happening on her back lawn and then impatiently back at Elaine.

"I'm sorry, it's just a story I read. It may not mean anything. Sometimes I forget the difference and get lost in the stories. You have more important things to deal with." Elaine dropped her head and started to leave the room.

"Wait." Melissa suddenly realized what Heliantra had seen in the girl. "Don't apologize. That's what I want you to do. I need for you to think like that. I need for you and Charles to find how the fiction and fact come together. That's an interesting idea." Melissa thought about what Elaine had said. Her mother said she had been raised to respect the color. She said she just reacted instinctively to it. Maybe this was why. "Tell Charles about it when he gets back. I'm not sure what's about to happen."

"Where are you going?"

Melissa jumped at Charles' question. Elaine blushed a little at his voice and when she looked up at him. He was standing half way up the spiral staircase. A sweet aroma filled the air around them. Melissa would have sworn Elaine had sprayed the air with perfume, but she hadn't moved.

Elaine looked over at Melissa. "Is Charles—a—you know?"

"Dragon? No, he's not a dragon."

The relief flushed over her young face. Melissa wanted to smile, but this was the oddest time she could think of for romance to blossom.

"Are they coming in?"

"Not yet, they're looking around. I wouldn't let them repel into the cave. They're not happy, but they aren't willing to push it yet."

"Please bring them inside. I need to speak to their commander."

"What's the plan?"

"Right now, I'm making them go away. After that, I'm not sure. It depends on what you and this young woman find. Remember what you said about going to them when I came in. Talk to her. She has an interesting tale I want you to hear. Maybe you can go find the book she's talking about if it's not here."

Elaine blushed and nearly hopped in place at the idea of going somewhere with Charles. Their ages where not that far apart, but Melissa was going to have to talk to her about being discreet.

There was a knock at the back door. Apparently, they had decided to come to her. Melissa nodded to Charles, and then smiled at Elaine. Some things were coming together, now all she had to do was get through this moment.

"The library's yours. See if you can find that story here. I'll check back in after this is—well, whenever I can." Melissa turned away from her and headed down stairs to greet the man at the door. She felt confident that Helena had made a good choice, and that confidence suddenly strengthened her decision.

Just before she reached the door, she thought about what she was wearing and checked her appearance. Whatever it was she would have to deal with it. There was no way she could change the way she looked in front of the soldier standing at the glass door. She was wearing a day length white skirt with a red short-sleeved sweater top and a scarf. It would have to do.

She swept the door open. The soldier smelled of stress. His flight suit was dark in places from the effort of searching. His tactical vest bristled with antenna, knives and all manner of gear which, combined with his direct manner, made him look like a porcupine. He glanced from Charles to her, and he visibly relaxed his spines a little.

"I'm sorry to disturb you, ma'am, we're looking for..."

"A dragon? Yes, I expected that."

Her answer threw him off balance. "Uh, yes, well. It seems it flew into the cave beneath this property, and we intend to repel down there."

"You *intend* to repel..." She paused for him to provide the name.

"Hollis ma'am. Captain Hollis."

"So you, *intend* to repel down there, Captain Hollis?"

"Ah, yes, we need to and..."

"And, when you get down there, what do you *intend* to do?"

"We intend to capture it, ma'am."

"If it's really a dragon that you followed into my cave—don't you think that might be dangerous?"

He paused as if she questioned his manhood, stood up taller and continued. "Really, I think we can capture it. I'm..."

"You've not really thought about what might happen? What if it breathes fire?"

"What? Oh, that's just nonsense."

"That it might breathe fire or that it might be a dragon?"

He slumped a little; he clenched his jaw and closed his eyes. "Ma'am I just need to search that cave." He opened his eyes and looked at her again.

"If you do search it, what happens if you find nothing down there at all?"

"Well, they'll call me back, I'll take a few eye tests, spend all night figuring out what I saw with several close psychiatrist friends, and then I'll fill out my weight in paper work."

"Very well, Captain, you can repel down and search my cave."

The Captain exhaled like she had removed a stone from his chest. He nodded to her and then Charles before turning and walking toward the door. Charles twisted around and looked at her. He had not expected her to give in. She waited until the captain was down the stairs and calling his men back to the helicopter.

"Work with Elaine. I've got this."

"What happens when he gets down there and sees the chests and that pentagram?"

"Nothing. He's looking for a dragon. Neither of those are what he's looking for. But, I need to get down there to make sure he sees what I want him to see."

Charles looked at her.

"I need for you to work with Elaine." She smiled over her shoulder as she walked after the captain. For just an instant she felt that this might be fun.

It will be.

—

Melissa stepped into the open chamber beyond the staircase just as the men were reaching the ledge beyond. She had run most of the way because their ropes would allow them to move faster even if they were cautious. Before they entered the chamber, she made a quick motion and disappeared. When she was invisible, she touched the magic around her and transformed the chamber. Each of the chests on the floor became stalagmites and what had been the polished mosaic floor was now gray, mottled and dark. The fireplace transformed into an alcove in the cave wall. Sleeping bats covered the ceiling and guano covered the now uneven floor. The staircase entrance disappeared into the wall. The illusion was complex, and she would have to maintain her concentration to keep it up and be responsive to their actions.

With all of her preparation done, she backed against the wall to avoid bumping into anyone who came that far into the room. Noise from the entrance, lost to human hearing but enhanced by her semi-dragon form, told her that they were coming. She settled against the wall to watch.

Although she could hear them moving across the floor in the outer landing and knew they were coming, she was unprepared for what happened next. Two flashes and amazingly loud explosions on the left and right side of the cave stunned her for a moment. Her eyes reacted instantly, and protective lenses fell into place saving her from being blinded; but her hearing was stunned. She struggled to keep the illusion up and barely remembered to drive the bats out of the cave past the approaching men. She could barely see the shapes of two men slipping in and moving around the wall toward her intent on killing anything that threatened them. They had been slowed some by the bats but continued into the cave. As her eyes cleared a little, she could see the way their weapons led them into the room, covering every position in which an enemy could be standing.

Fear leapt into her throat as she realized her dragon arrogance and faith in magic may not have taken into account human technology. Each man was wearing goggles that obscured most of their face but allowed them to see in the dark. She could not be sure her invisibility would help her against their goggles. Two more men moved into the room. Before their scans crossed her location against the wall, she ducked down and slipped around the corner into the landing for the stairwell where the wall obscured her along with the illusion.

Peering around the corner, trembling from the fear of having everything fall apart around her, Melissa watched each soldier advance to a point where they had full command of the room. A fifth soldier entered down the center in a crouch and stopped before he crossed anyone's line of vision. Only seconds had passed since the first explosions had distracted her, and the illusion held even though her senses were overloaded.

The five soldiers reached covering points in the room at about the same time and stopped to assess the room. No shots were fired. The chamber returned to silence.

Each soldier relaxed but only slightly as they took a final look around the cave to make sure they had not missed anything. The soldier that entered last looked directly at her and took two steps toward her before she stepped back where she could not see him anymore. Every muscle in her body tightened, and she focused on the illusion to refocus the magic to protect her from whatever he thought he detected.

"Carver. Check that space directly across the cave."

If they found the doorway her illusion would be defeated, and they would have reason to stay and search more. Her ears were starting to recover from the ringing, but not enough for her to hear the diligent steps of the soldier approaching her hiding place. All she could do was hope that her illusion was good enough. A metal thunk against the wall next to the entrance rang through the chamber.

"Nothing here Chief, just more wall."

Melissa wanted to relax and sigh, but she held onto the breath until she knew they were leaving.

"Valkyrie, this is Dagger, we're clear. All we have down here is an old cave. No-Joy on anything else."

Melissa couldn't hear how the soldier on the other end replied, but now she could hear the men in the cave moving away from her. She looked out the hidden opening again to watch them walk back toward the entrance and released a long-held breath. Once she had marshaled her emotions and stopped her hands from shaking, she rushed back up the steps to the entrance. Cautious, quiet and invisible—she slipped out the entrance. Charles had managed to convince them, somehow, to set up their ropes on the far right side of the overhang away from the door, and the idling engine noise covered any noise the door made. Convinced she had exited unseen, she slipped past the helicopter and across the lawn before she joined Charles on the back patio. She transformed into her human appearance before becoming visible and stepping out from behind him on the stairs. He jumped visibly as she appeared next to him.

Shaken by the many ways everything could have gone wrong, she could hear the wavering in her voice as she courageously made everything sound fine.

"I think I'm starting to get the hang of this." She smiled.

Charles shook his head as she wiggled her index finger in her left ear that was still ringing. The Captain left his helicopter and walked toward them with his head down. Melissa dropped her hand from her ear and returned a very placid and somewhat concerned look to her face. When he reached them, he looked up.

"Sorry to have wasted your time, ma'am. We'll be out of here as soon as we've recovered the men."

"Did you find it? Am I safe here?" She pushed her magical aura out to buffet against his weakened confidence, and she could almost feel him surrender to her charm.

"Nothing to worry about, Ma'am. There's nothing down there." He waved his hands and turned to walk back.

"Don't ever do that to me," Charles said as he watched the very confused man walk away.

"How do you know I haven't already?"

He turned and looked at her with real fear in his eyes. She smiled and shook her head to indicate she was joking.

When they returned to the library, her mother was standing next to Elaine. They were both looking over a set of older books Melissa remembered from her mother's bookshelf. Kaliastrid turned as they entered.

Melissa was glad she was here. Everything she needed to protect was in this room, and the threat that had descended on them was leaving.

"Whew, what a morning," Kaliastrid said to welcome her daughter.

"Yeah, but I think we have a new plan."

"Oh, do tell."

"Elaine can explain it better than I can."

Kaliastrid turned to look at the young girl standing beside her.

"Well, go ahead child. Explain." The motherly smile on her face made Elaine glow with pride.

She looked from one to the other and opened the book she was holding. "Well, if I'm explaining what I think I am, she's the ambassador of the dragons. A position passed down from her grandmother by right, not ancestry."

"That's right!" Kaliastrid exclaimed as if she suddenly remembered something. "It doesn't hurt as much when someone else reminds you."

She grinned at the interrupted young girl and motioned her to go on.

"As I was saying, as the ambassador, she is going to reach out to the government to set up a dialog before this gets any more out of hand. Perhaps that way she can short-circuit Nethliast's plan before he can complete it."

They all chewed over that idea for a moment while Melissa wondered how she was going to make it work.

July 19 – 1335 CEST - Bavaria, Germany

Valdiest awakened in a dark cave with a headache, a dry mouth and a feeling that he was surrounded by magic. His last memory was the blonde he had seen exit Nethliast's limousine and walk toward his car when he had followed them from the hotel in Munich to the farmhouse in the Bavarian countryside. He had never met the woman before and had been surprised to see anyone in the car with Nethliast. So surprised that when she started waiving her hands about in front of her and chanting he had not realized she was casting a spell until it was too late. And that was why he was where he was.

He never expected Nethliast to be associated with a witch. She had looked so harmless in her yellow suit and calm expression as the spell had woven around him. Now he was in trouble, trapped in a cave, under her control.

The cave was silent except for the sounds of water, perhaps from thawing ice. He was sure they were in the nearby Alps and not too far from the farm he had followed them to. At some point she had somehow forced him to transform fully, which meant Nethliast had been involved. Only a dragon could force a dragon to show his true form. Nethliast's betrayal was complete.

The hush in the cave was probably caused because he had stirred. Lesser creatures in the cave were trying to avoid his notice. They had no idea that he was worse off than they were. As he lifted his sore head from the ground, the rattle of metal chains echoed through the silence and made him cringe. He became suddenly aware that they were attached to a large ring around his neck.

He shifted his feet and found similar rings around them. Binding a dragon was futile because of their ability to take any form. All Valdiest would have to do was change forms and slip his chains, and soon he would challenge those bonds but not until he knew more about where he was, who has holding him and what challenges he faced once he was free.

He sniffed at the air and was immediately assaulted with an overpowering flowery perfume. The heavy scent seemed to coat everything and attacked his sinuses. He squinted and sneezed the foul air from his nose before trying again with a lighter sniff. With effort, he could tease other scents from the air and over time he did find traces of Nethliast on the air. After recovering from how strong it was in the cave he remembered the scent. He had smelled it on Nethliast when he had returned to the hotel the morning of his treachery. He had ignored it because he quickly had more to be concerned with.

Was she behind his treachery? Was she the cause of all of this?

If she had enchanted him with her magic it could explain his change in mood and even his actions in the conclave. The thought of a dragon such as Nethliast under the control of a human woman troubled Valdiest. Sadness and understanding warred in the old wyrm's head until his wisdom returned.

He grinned and dropped his head to the stone floor. Charms didn't succeed long on dragons. Nethliast would soon realize what she was up to, if he didn't know already, and when he did realize he was manipulated the witch would not be safe anywhere. Why were humans still trying to manipulate them?

Valdiest opened his eyes to search the cave visually. The darkness made no difference to him, and he could see a form standing around the corner to the entrance to his cave. The form moved; it knew that he was awake.

A ball of light appeared above his head, causing searing pain in his rapidly adjusting eyes. When the flash-blindness cleared, he continued the scan of his surroundings. The cave was not much taller than he would be standing on his hind legs, but the chains would never allow him to stand that tall. The chain at his neck kept him limited to the height of most humans. The witch who had attacked him, the source of the perfume, stepped out of the shadows. She was dressed in a new, plum business suit. Apparently, he had been unconscious more than a few hours.

She smiled at him with a possessive grin.

"Valdiest, right?" Standing directly in front of him, she was either brave or very confident.

He concentrated for just an instant and formed a lightning bolt that leapt between them. What he had imagined as an enormous bolt of energy had manifested as a simple static spark that she seemed to catch in her hand.

"Now, now," she shook her finger back and forth at him, "there's no reason for us to get off on the wrong foot. Nethliast has left me here to watch you until he can finish what he's working on. It was not very nice of you to follow us. Why did you do that, anyway?"

Valdiest yanked at the chain in the floor that held his head low and lunged against them with all of his might. He felt the ring on his neck slide between the ridges and then catch. The loop, driven into the floor, held and would not give. The other chains jerked his legs back and dropped him on his belly. There was no fighting these chains; he could not get a physical advantage against them. He flapped his wings to gain height to try again to force the chains free. She mumbled ancient words and made intricate gestures before him, pointing her fingers at his wings. Invisible forces left her fingers and slammed into the leading edges of his wings near his shoulder. The loud crack of bone scared him more than the pain that rippled through his back as the bones shattered. His useless wings settled on his back in odd angles, and he fell to the floor again with a thump. He struggled to get his feet under him and stood up. He was not going to cower in front of the witch controlling Nethliast.

"I hope you understand now. I am serious and don't want to have to deal with your attempts to escape. This cave has been protected against most magic. I happen to know the spells that will and will not work. There is a very short list, and most will not help you." Her voice sharpened as she chastised him like a child.

Valdiest exhaled quickly into the cave with a blast of fire that filled it and swirled around him. The heat was intense, but somehow it did not pass the entrance to the small cave. She stood beyond it with her arms crossed.

"You see, your attempts to harm me are not going to work. I am the superior here, and you will submit to me. Nethliast expects answers to some questions. He expects me to help him extract those answers."

Valdiest watched the witch walk in front of the barrier. She could not cross it, but her spells could. He settled quietly onto the floor and chose to ignore her. He was not going to answer her questions. She had said Nethliast wanted answers, but that could not be true. She had to be manipulating him. Valdiest refused to believe the dragon he had thought of as a son had turned him over to a human like a plaything. She must know he would never submit to a human. Valdiest laughed at her.

"What's funny? I'm surprised you find anything humorous right now."

He thought of a protected human form and brought to mind the steps to take it. The chains would fall away from the smaller form, and he would still be protected. In the instant he expected to change, he found he was still in his dragon form. Nothing had happened. Somehow she had overcome his ability to transform. He was trapped. Panic threatened to struggle up into his mind, and he refused to submit to it. He gave no sign to her that he had failed but remained still.

"Now, are you done? There's no sense in resisting me. I'm well protected, and you're trapped. A very interesting priestess and my dead grandmother were quite helpful in keeping you right where you are. I'm the only way you'll leave this cave. What shape you're in when you do leave is dependent on your answers."

Valdiest closed his eyes and said nothing.

The familiar words filled the cave and were followed by a massive blow to his ribs that filled his chest with pain. His body jerked in reflex against the chains, but he said nothing. Valdiest opened his eyes and looked at her again. The glimmer in her eyes, her open-mouthed laughter, the flush on her cheeks; all of these things told him this was going to last and she was going to enjoy it. He closed his eyes and settled his head on the floor looking for a way he could protect himself from the punishing torture he was about to endure.

"Were you reporting everything that happened at the conclave to Meliastrid? Were you a spy all along? Did you ever believe in Nethliast's plan?"

She mumbled her spell again and this time slammed her powerful strike into his head. His ear rang with the force, and his head swam as he fought to maintain consciousness. Had she just been lucky to strike the sensitive ear region of his head, or had she studied dragons to know how to hurt them? Who is this priestess she was talking about? He focused his mind on his mate and his memories of his family before they had been forced to be human. The headache that filled his head was nothing like the pain she was inflicting, but if he could focus on something else it might make the pain more bearable. He latched onto memories he wanted back, and the searing pain in his head overwhelmed the pain in his body. He dove deeper into his memories against the pain. It didn't stop the pounding or the questions, but it allowed him to ignore her.

He had no way of knowing how long she had questioned him. The whirlpool of pain seemed to stretch on to the edge of his life. At the very corner of his mind Nethliast stood calling to him. His voice and memory came without pain and soothed him. He followed it for the depths and settled on rampart walls to listen. Silence washed over him like a cooling rain. The questions had stopped. He was not sure how long she had not been beating him but that had stopped as well.

Nethliast's call was not a memory. He was calling his name. He was in the cave with the witch. Nethliast called to him again. Had he broken her charm? Had Nethliast come to rescue him from her torture?

The hope drew him from his pain-faceted sanctuary. He released the excruciating memory of his ancient castle which he now knew was not far from where they had captured him to ascend back to reality. Pain, different from the blinding pain in his head that he had hidden in, rippled through his body as he lay chained in the cave where he had fallen. So much was broken. Valdiest was not sure he would survive.

Nethliast was there standing in his human form beyond the point where her barrier had been. She was still standing there, and he could see the anger ripple down her cheek and her fists clench. A surge of pride rippled through his broken body and bolstered his beaten resolve. She had failed, and she knew it. But, why was she still alive if Nethliast had come to save him?

"My king, why have you betrayed me like this? Were you always my enemy? Did you intentionally run off Wy Li when I needed him? How deep does your treachery go? Are all of my plans known to the human-lover?"

The words seemed out of place coming from Nethliast. Was he aware of what she had done to him? Was he still under her spell?

"What? I fought for our goals. I was faithful to the plan. You betrayed me. You had me removed from my rightful position. This witch has you charmed. Can't you see it?"

"It's you who is charmed. Your old age has made you weak. You can't control your offspring. You should have killed Meliastrid the moment we emerged for her insolence. She protects the humans who have made fools of us."

"And you do not? Are you not here with a human now? What is the beast standing with you? Is she at least part dragon so I can say you have not lowered yourself by associating with her?"

Nethliast's eyes flashed at the attack.

"This is not about me. You are the one who has shared my plans with Meliastrid. You are the one who poisoned my relations with many of the male leaders. What have you done? What have you shared with Meliastrid?"

"I have shared nothing with anyone, you disloyal brat, but I should have. I should have stomped your egg before you could hatch."

Valdiest's heart ached as he surrendered to the nagging worry that Nethliast was in full control of himself and not charmed by the witch. From his journey into his own memories, he had the benefit of understanding who Meliastrid really was. It was clear that they had both been disloyal in even holding the conclave. He had failed to lead his kind through this challenge.

"Why do you dishonor your king this way? Why have you turned me over to this witch? You're as guilty in this as I. You are no better than the human who did this to me."

Nethliast transformed and stepped into the small cave passing through the barrier. Valdiest released a blast of fire that engulfed Nethliast and rushed back into the narrower cave beyond. Nethliast stood, and Valdiest laid facing him in the swirling flames that consumed the lichen and turned the moisture into steam. He hoped the human witch had been caught up in the conflagration as punishment for her actions, but as the flames subsided and she returned from around the corner he was disappointed. Her fists were clenched, and her jaw was set. He could smell the vengeance on her. Her plum outfit was charred in several places. Smoke rose from the very edges of her hair, proving she had barely escaped the scorching he had wished on her. With a comforting inhale he enjoyed the aroma of his fire, free from her sickening scent.

Nethliast struck Valdiest's head with both of his forelegs in a powerful downward strike that drove his head and chin into the cave floor.

"You will control yourself, Valdiest, or I will destroy you here. You are only alive because I need you. When I tire of you, I will kill you for your treason." As Nethliast withdrew his forelegs and released him, Valdiest could smell the burnt aroma of the witch's perfume that still wafted off Nethliast's scales.

Nethliast stepped back out of the cave but waited to transform completely until the witch had cast another spell, probably resetting the barrier.

"Kill me then. You've already made up your mind about my loyalty, but let me clear up any doubt, Nickliad." The change of name was noticed. "I will not follow you when it includes using hatchlings as tools to control their parents. I will never support your alliance with half-bloods and certainly not this unnatural partnership you have with this rotting carrion."

He exhaled and laid himself before the male he had once considered his son, the future king to replace him and stand with his daughter. He had been so proud of Nickliad's desires to help restore the kingdom to the way it had been.

"Nickliad," Valdiest said quietly without raising his head from the floor or even opening his eyes. "Meliastrid will defeat you. She has already defeated you. She has the power of the Great Wyrm on her side. You will never stand against that." This knowledge had come from his painful retreat. Valdiest knew it now like he knew his own name. He knew that Nickliad would never have her as a mate because she served a higher purpose and commanded a purer power than Nickliad could ever hope to know. Valdiest smiled as he thought of the day when the child standing before him would bow to her.

"The what?" Nickliad walked to the edge of the barrier. "What are you going on about? What is the Great Wyrm?"

"Search your memories, child. Realize the truth like I have in the last few hours and end this path before it devours you and every dragon who follows you. I don't want to see you destroyed, but I'm afraid you're already on your way there. When she realizes what she is, and she may already know, she'll come for you with all of her rightful power and with her slightest wish you will cease to exist. You are truly confused and need to stop before you destroy us all." Valdiest now understood Kaliastrid's deference to Meliastrid. He had learned so much as he had taken his beating from the witch. There was hope for dragons in Meliastrid.

That ancient curse of pride and greed that dragons had overcome ages before, when they had come to understand their magical ability, had returned in Nickliad when he had emerged. Why else would he pick that name instead of his hatching name? Valdiest could not suppress the incredulous laugh at Nickliad thinking he had even a portion of the majesty of that ancient gold dragon. That arrogance was even more of a sign that Nethliast was lost to his own pride.

Nickliad struck the barrier and roared at him but couldn't reach him through it.

"Don't play with me, old wyrm. I'm going to repay the humans and return them to where they belong on this world without you, and Meliastrid can't stop me. She is too far away and lost in her care for the weaker race to stop me, but your words may give me what I need to complete my plans. There is something to your rambling, isn't there? She is missing something she needs to exercise her powers. I'm here where dragons were the most powerful race for ages. I'll find her secret and rule the dragons."

Valdiest laughed at the young dragon to cover his mistake. He might be able to find what Valdiest now understood gave her the power to control dragons. He didn't know where it was, and he didn't think any other dragons did, but there was a chance the arrogant hatchling could stumble on it. Valdiest had only just realized what it was when Nickliad had called him out of his memories.

"Even you see it, don't you?" Nickliad asked. "I've won with the diligence

I've put in. I have proven myself the true dragon king. They will bow to me and I will rule the humans."

Valdiest laughed again at the mania that filled his speech. "Take your whore-queen then and go. I'm tired of this and you. I have nothing more for the spoiled Crown Prince of Dragons, Nicklaus," Valdiest chose his human name to deepen the insult, "who doesn't know his name. I have no more patience for you and this strumpet you stink of. Her stench dilutes your strength, great child king Nicklaus." He taunted him now to force his hand. He had fallen deeper into the control of humans than Melissa ever had. Valdiest understood her love of them now. He could see it was her oath to protect them, not some unnatural bond like the one forming between Nicklaus and the witch.

Nicklaus roared again, and Valdiest heard him walking away. At the end of the hall, he heard the last orders he left the witch and cringed.

"Punish him how you see fit, but do not kill him. I need him alive. I need to know what he knows. Once I have destroyed Meliastrid and have Kaliastrid in my control, he will tell me where the root of her power lies. When you're done, meet me at the farm. Do not kill him."

He left after that and the witch's somewhat weakened and singed aroma returned to the barrier. Valdiest retreated into his mind again to wander among his broken memories in the peaceful pain of the search. Maybe he would learn something that might help before it was too late. Perhaps he could find the Talisman of the Great Wyrm.

CHAPTER 8 – AMBASSADOR OF THE DRAGONS

July 23 – 1447 EDT – Signal Mountain, Tennessee

"This book was written by your grandmother!"

Elaine had extracted herself from the 15th century book she had found in a chest along with the corset and peasant blouse she was wearing. She had just looked up for the first time in hours and realized someone else, other than Charles, was in the room.

"All this time I thought it was a different author with a similar style but it's not. The writing style is exact, even though the language is a little different. But, how is that possible? She wasn't born then. How could she write this?"

"It seems that we may have lived many lives to reach this point in time. She would have been a different person then."

See, you can contribute.

Melissa grinned at the voice that was becoming more a part of her.

"Our line was carefully preserved. How does that book help us though? Does it shed any light on the spell? Why I cast it? Where the talisman is? Anything?"

Elaine withered a little under the questioning, and Melissa realized again that she did not have Charles' way with showing her appreciation for the efforts even when she wanted more results. Elaine would talk for hours about something with Charles, and he would just listen. Afterward he would still leave the room less aware of how Elaine felt than when he entered, but that was an entirely different frustration.

"I'm sorry, Elaine. Go on. You're the only one of us able to make any sense of this."

She looked up from her tablet where she was making notes either on the book or how Melissa had exploded again to continue her revelation.

"So far I haven't found anything about the reason the spell was cast. I'm not sure anyone ever wrote that down. Maybe, since it seems she wrote something in this previous incarnation, she wrote stories further back. Maybe she wrote about the spell somewhere else. Are there any books older than these?"

"You and Charles have found more in a few days in this house than I knew existed." Melissa stared out at the small grave where they had buried Helena and let the useless response trail away.

"Still no response from anyone at The State Department?"

"No," Melissa answered without hearing the question.

Elaine turned her attention back to the pages.

Am I doing the right thing? Is this what you wanted from me?

Not for the first time, Melissa wished Helena had not died. She wished her mentor from two worlds was sitting at her desk waiting for Melissa to give up on the new puzzle she had given her to ask for help. But she wasn't. She was gone. She had known how important this was. She was the one who understood what had happened and why. *She* was the ambassador.

Melissa clutched the small claw beneath her blouse as if it could tell her what to do. She knew there was something special about it. She had already used its power once, but not intentionally. The gem encrusted claw, as always, felt warm in her hand. She took it out and held it up to the afternoon sun. Before her eyes it seemed as if each individual sun beam danced and flickered through the gems, creating red flares on the ceiling. Melissa followed the shimmering dots as they ran across the old mural of two ancient dragons and the giant mountain castle their tails enclosed.

She had always loved that mural. It seemed so much like a home she would like to live in. The castle had tall towers with pointed circular roofs that sprouted from both the main keep and all of the walls. There was no road to it up the side of what appeared to be a snow-covered mountain. She always wondered how the people got to the castle. As a child she had been convinced that it had to be an artist's mistake.

Not if you fly there.

Melissa nodded.

The female dragon's tail wrapped to the right side of the castle and crossed over the curtain wall behind the forward wall tower. The sharp point of her tail pointed into what looked like the mosaic pentagram in the cave below them. In the center of the courtyard and at the heart of the pentagram was a gem-encrusted egg sitting on two legs and a tail that broke through the gem covered shell.

Elaine's face suddenly appeared over her head looking at the claw with odd interest. Melissa jumped at how close she was.

"I'm sorry. Did I surprise you?"

Melissa grinned but didn't answer as she tried to marshal her heartbeat.

"What's that?"

"It's a pendant my grandmother always wore. Well, it's more than that really, but I'm not sure how much more."

"May I see it?"

Melissa mindlessly removed the chain from her neck and handed it over to her. Elaine took the chain and held it up to the light. With her forefinger, still covered in a cotton glove, she touched it to turn it in the light. A sizzling sound drew Melissa's attention. Elaine's hands never moved. She still stood with her finger pointed as if to stroke the pendant but the very end of the glove on her finger was charred and the pendant had landed in Melissa's lap.

"Ouch," she cried and shook her hand while staring at the amulet resting in Melissa's lap. "It burned me. I can't touch it."

"It never burned me." Melissa thought about the heat that pulsed through her arm after it had thrown Nethliast off her. She lifted it by the chain and replaced it around her neck. Elaine turned briskly while removing and discarding the now useless glove. In her excitement she attacked the delicate pages of the book with less care than she had been using before. When she found the spot she was looking for, she jabbed the page with her middle finger and ran down the page guiding her eyes quickly through the text. Melissa thought about asking her what she was looking for, but found she didn't really care. Instead, she sat back in the chair and stared, again, at the view of the valley.

This was taking too long. Nethliast could have an army prepared to attack by now. Her father was missing so they were not getting any information, even the passive kind he was providing to Kaliastrid. The silence from both sides was painful. Neither dragons nor humans were talking to her. Charles had added guards since the encounter with the helicopter, in case the paperwork drew some attention, but not even her enemies seemed to be looking for her.

Charles walked quietly up the spiral staircase and paused behind Elaine while calculating the best way to pass between her and the window without contact. Melissa paused to watch the often repeated dance which had started to fascinate her. Convinced he had room he began to gingerly make his way through the pass when inevitable she would shift just enough to force him to touch her.

Charles mumbled, "Excuse me," and squeezed out of the contact as if touching her burned him. His face was red, and he was mentally castigating himself when he reached the chair on the other side and sat down. As he passed Melissa, she could see Elaine's blush and swore she was giggling. Just to be fair to Charles, Melissa considered telling her ill-equipped close friend that the young woman was playing with him, but decided it was too fun to watch their sad dance. Once Charles was seated, Elaine returned her attention to the book, where she quickly found what she had been searching for.

"It may be. It just may be," Elaine mumbled aloud.

"What's she on about?" he asked.

"This." She pulled the pendant out again to show him.

Charles ducked a little in his seat and put his hands out as if to ward off an attack. "Watch that thing. I saw what it did to Nicklaus, and I don't see a safety."

"What did it do?" Elaine asked without looking away from the text.

"He was attacking Melissa the night of the emergence. She pointed it at him, and it threw him across the yard. I don't know how he wasn't crippled when he bounced off the wall and smacked the ground."

"He was partly overcome by his dragon side…" Her defense tailed off as Elaine pursued her idea.

"Did it act on its own or did she…you command it?"

Charles didn't answer. Melissa thought about it and answered, "It acted on its own."

"Then it is." Elaine turned around and sat down on the table. She crossed her legs and pulled the old book into her lap.

"It is what?" Melissa asked.

"This." She pointed at a page that she had been reading. Melissa didn't move to read the text; she didn't feel like fighting off the pain.

"I think it's what this story calls the Scepter of The Great Wyrm. It's the symbol of your power, or at least half of it, the half you can never lose. It was passed to you on the death of the old ambassador according to this text. It should be impossible for anyone else to possess it without your specific instructions while you live, and it should protect you from attack."

Melissa looked down at the small claw and jewels. It seemed to fit. "So what's the other half and how does it help us?"

"I don't know. This text only talks about the scepter."

Melissa shook her head and looked back out at the small grave. Something Elaine said struggled with pain in the back of her head, and she chose not to ask her more about the Great Wyrm, at the moment. Since her inner dragon chose not to share anything with her either, she knew that quest would probably hurt a lot. She allowed a little complacency to sweep the thought away and thought about her grandmother.

"I miss her. She left me with this, and I need her guidance. I'm not ready for any this." She looked over at Charles, smacked the arm of his chair and continued. "What do I do if we ever find someone that will listen to us? None of the dragons I should have standing beside me are here, and the humans seem oblivious to what's going on around them."

"You'll do what you have to, just like you have from the beginning," Charles answered. He had pulled a random book from the stack and leafed through the pages as if it might answer her question.

She shook her head, unconvinced.

At the moment she wanted to continue feeling sorry for herself, but her mother came up the stairs with a frown on her face forcing her to put away her self-pity. Kaliastrid paused behind Elaine and pulled the unruly hair that was falling around the young girl's face back, wrapped it in a quick elegant knot that caused her hair to cradle her face in sweeping wings but forced the rest down her back and out of the way. She secured it all with an ancient pin. Satisfied with her work and rewarded with a smile over the shoulder from Elaine, Kaliastrid turned to look at Melissa.

Melissa tilted her head at her, and she could feel her own eyes grow wider as she pulled her head back at an angle. Kaliastrid shrugged the unspoken question away and leaned against the table beside Elaine.

"Nethliast is here."

Melissa stood up and looked around the library suddenly concerned that he might learn something he didn't need to know.

"Sorry, not here," Kaliastrid added and Melissa sat back down, "but he is in town. Gerliast is trying to keep me informed about his movements and plans, but he is basically a prisoner of the new king."

"How is father?"

"Still no word. I've not heard from him since last week. Gerliast has not seen him, and he doesn't dare ask about him. Your father was not convinced that forcing Nethliast to recognize him as king was the right move. He said he still needed to check something out. He wanted to give him a chance to defend against my theory about the half breeds. I'm sure Nethliast is recruiting them to fight the humans. He used them to collect the hatchlings and the females to maintain control of the dragons. He has to be promising them something to keep them in line. I know that's why they have settled down and disappeared. We have to tell someone about it. They have to be prepared. There's no question Nethliast's going to attack. If Valdiest could just let me know what he had found, I would know what steps to take."

Melissa grabbed the pendant to ignore the knot in her stomach. Fire raced up her arm, and the room around her vanished into a dark silent cave. Initially she sensed more than saw the form on the floor, but her vision adjusted and she could make out the what looked like her father. She reeled in her mind away from the image of broken wings, battered scales and chains holding him to the cold stone. She found her eyes were closed and opened them to see both Kaliastrid and Elaine looking at her.

Elaine had set the book aside and was pale. She mouthed, "What the...?"

Kaliastrid who seemed calm after fixing Elaine's hair, suddenly looked terrified. Like Elaine, she was pale and her fingers clutched the edge of the table. She released the table and brought her hand to her mouth as a tear slipped down her cheek.

The phone on the desk below them rang, ripping the silence that had settled on the group. The new assault on Melissa's nerves rattled her, and she looked at the other two women who had not moved.

"Get it back?" Kaliastrid cried as tears ran down her cheek.

"I don't know how I got it in the first place."

Anger rippled through her mother's eyes like she had never seen before, and Melissa felt a desire to vanish into the wallpaper rather than face her. Kaliastrid turned to look at Elaine, who still wanted an answer to her unspoken question. Kaliastrid put her arms around the young girl, pulled her to her chest and stroked her hair. Melissa watched the motherly exchange.

The irritating jangle from the ground floor continued. Oblivious to what just happened, Charles stepped through them as it continued to ring.

"Don't everyone move at once. Don't worry though, the butler will get it. Wait, that's me." He rushed down the stairs to answer the phone.

Reaching it on the fourth ring, he lifted the receiver to his ear. Melissa reserved one ear for the phone call while watching her mother seek and share comfort with Elaine, who was confused by everything that had happened. Melissa could not explain it and was happy that it was over. Convinced there was nothing she could do to help her mother at the moment she turned her full focus to Charles and the phone.

"... Yes, this is her residence." There was a pause while the voice on the other end rattled in the small speaker.

"No. I'm her butler."

"Yes, she will be here today."

"I'll be glad to check."

He rattled the calendar back and forth randomly and then spoke again.

"I don't see a conflict."

"Yes, I think that will be fine. I'll let her know that you called, and we will see you then."

He hung up the receiver and looked up at her. "I don't like it."

"What?" Melissa asked, excited.

"An Agent Loxley with the FBI. He wanted to know if you were going to be in tonight. He wants to come by in around an hour to talk to you."

"And you agreed?"

"I figured you could handle him, and you wanted a connection in the government. He may be as high as you can get to start."

"So what don't you like about it?"

"I don't know. He reminds me of someone I knew in the Gulf."

Melissa exhaled a sigh.

The call and the quick vision of her father were bothering her. Her pulse was up, and the amulet at her neck was warm. Charles' comment about the man on the phone reminding him of someone had made Melissa think of Nethliast.

None of it made sense. It didn't belong together, but there it was.

She could see his draconic face just as it had been the night of their emergence when he wanted to kill Charles. The angry desire to kill etched in his eyes. His jaw fixed tightly with his teeth bared. His animal rage and lust for blood filled her mind and made her shiver.

Kaliastrid had released Elaine and was pushing her toward Charles, who was reaching the top of the stairs when the pressure in her head exploded in a hot wash of anger and rage. More images of her father were mixed in the rage. Then the chaotic feelings cleared, and she had the vivid impression that Nethliast was coming to kill her.

This I have seen before. He is dangerous when he is like this and he's…

"…Coming." Melissa finished her thought out loud and leapt from her chair. Kaliastrid was leading her out onto the balcony and into the air. Melissa was quickly behind her. They both transitioned in the air and flapped steadily for altitude as soon as their wings were fully formed.

The presence in her mind was near. Its lust was sharp in her mind. He wanted her. She wrestled with the overwhelming emotions he was projecting and forced his presence into a deeper part of her mind where she did not have to focus on it. At the moment she had to focus on fighting. It was apparent Nethliast was on his way, and he was not coming to talk.

"How do I know he is near? How do I know he is coming to kill me?"

"I have no idea, but I know it too," Kaliastrid answered and her rage came across as clearly to Melissa as Nethliast's blood lust. Her mother wanted to kill Nethliast. She believed he had hurt Valdiest. She believed those images were his memories. Melissa suddenly understood where the images of her father had come from, and she had to force her own rush of anger out of her mind to remain focused on everything that was happening.

That's right, her own mind told her, *don't let your anger make you an easy target.*

Melissa focused on getting higher over the valley while she could. Altitude was life. She stroked the air forcing herself higher and watching around her for the threat. She had no idea where he would come from.

Something in her mind made her look to the east toward the city. Air traffic was light at the local airports at three in the afternoon, but it would be difficult to see Nethliast's black body against the busy background. She scanned the horizon, doubting she would see anything; but again something guided her to the approaching dot of her mate-cum-assassin.

"There, he's following the river. He doesn't know we are in the air. He's heading for the estate."

"Then we have him."

Melissa could feel her mother's excitement as she was preparing for a fight. As soon as she had pointed him out, Kaliastrid had cut toward him. She was keeping herself between them.

"You will not sacrifice yourself for me! That will not help father."

"*Back off, Meliastrid!*" The order came with such force Melissa had dropped a stroke and fallen further behind her mother. She stroked to catch up. "*You have your duty, and I have mine. So, don't make me do my duty in opposition to your orders. I can control my passions better than a male.*"

Melissa chewed on her mother's words while they both turned toward the black dot that was steadily approaching the estate. She would assume her mother knew her abilities. She would trust her to fight smart. Kaliastrid clawed at the air for more altitude. Melissa waited. He should see them by now, but his anger and arrogance convinced him that they were not aware he was coming. With all rights, they shouldn't know. They waited as he passed below them then turned to follow him. Melissa looked around for any other air traffic wondering how long it would take them to get aircraft to the location once they had appeared on radar. She would just have to deal with that if it happened; one threat at a time. Kaliastrid was not paying attention to anything other than Nethliast.

She folded in half at the top of her climb and drew her wings back. Her body formed an arrowhead shape pointing to the location where Nethliast would be when she finished her dive. Melissa folded her own wings back and started her own dive to support her mother's attack. They were both silent missiles streaking out of the sky at Nethliast. They had the advantage in this fight. His assumptions had set him up for the kill.

As they approached Nethliast's undefended back, Melissa watched the way her mother angled toward him. Her forward claws thrust out, ready to dig into and around his armor plates to find vital organs. Her rear claws angled to grab whatever she could hold. They were closing so fast and he was so low that there was no way they could avoid crashing into the trees on the side of the mountain when she struck him. Kaliastrid had to know this, but she did not flinch and she did not hesitate. When she was less than one dragon's length from him, she opened her mouth and aimed for the back of his neck where she could control his head and separate the brain from the rest of his spine if she could get her teeth through the thick armor, spines, and muscle on the back of his neck. Most predators were equipped to take their prey but also to kill their competition, which quite often is one of their own. There was no denying that dragons had fought each other in the past, before they had built a civilization around their magic and ages of shared knowledge. Melissa was a little ashamed that Nethliast had reduced them to the basest of animal instincts and returned them to their violent past.

Nethliast remained focused on his revenge and surprising them at the estate. His plan would have worked if there had been no warning of his approach. He had used this approach before when he snuck up on Charles the morning after their emergence.

Kaliastrid was within her own length of him before he realized she was there. It was a deadly mistake and Melissa was not sure, as she watched him drop out from beneath Kasliasrtid, how he was able to avert the well prepared attack.

The only thing that saved him from her deadly grasp was his last second plunge away from her. She expected the move even though it was a dangerous choice, and she reached out at him as he slipped below her by the slimmest margin. Her claws raked the back of his neck. Sparks flew between the steel talons and his flinty scales. Melissa adjusted her own path as Kaliastrid maintained her pressure on him even though he was turning within her own arch.

They were turning in on Melissa's path and still descending. Kaliastrid had successfully forced him there, so she had the advantage, but to capitalize on it she would need to drop in front of him, which was a dangerous place to be. They were not really flying anymore but falling with the aerodynamics of a rock.

She made little adjustments with her wings to put her into the position she needed to grab him. His late dive made him slower, and she was able to close with him before he could accelerate.

Kaliastrid was now below him, and they were both falling backward toward the ground. Nethliast was focused on Kaliastrid's teeth that were snapping at his neck as he maintained as much distance as he could without slowing down and surrendering to her grasp.

It was a dance of delicate adjustments. Nethliast shifted to avoid capture, and Kaliastrid shifted to trap him and drive him into Melissa's approaching grasp.

Melissa struck him like a boulder, and grabbed with all of her claws. His claws instinctively raked her chest armor with little affect. Her left foreclaw found purchase in his recently injured shoulder, and she drove the talon deep under the damaged scale. His growl of pain was lost to the air currents, but their bodies were touching so she could feel the vibrations between them.

Kaliastrid took advantage of Melissa's strike to slow her fall a little and finally grab Nethliast's neck and back.

The fatal ball of dragons plunged into their last hundred feet when Melissa realized the claw amulet was glowing and hot against her chest. It was going to act to protect her from the fall, and she had no idea what it was going to do. Last time, it had thrown Nethliast away from her, but this situation was different. What would it do now? What would it do to Kaliastrid?

As they raced toward the trees below them and the amulet grew hotter, Melissa thought that they needed to get out of the air. She thought about the threat of humans getting involved. The image of the cave beneath her estate filled her mind. She braced for the impact and held onto Nethliast. The fire in her chest near the amulet flared to cover her whole body and engulfed the entire cluster just before they slammed into the first trees.

In an instant, all three of them vanished above the trees as if they fell into a hole in the sky. They fell out of the hole in the air at the very top of the cavern beneath the estate. Melissa only had seconds to realize what happened before all three of them slammed into the floor of the cavern. The amulet continued to glow and cushioned her impact but it threw everyone away from her in different directions. She could not maintain her grasp on Nethliast.

They all tumbled away from the center and gained their feet to face each other. Kaliastrid was the first to reach her feet, followed by Nethliast, but he was not interested in her. He turned toward Melissa, and she could see the intent in his eyes.

"Why are you here again, Nethliast? I thought I told you never to return here."

"When have you ever had power over me? I want the secret to this power your father believes will save you from me. He believes you can stop me."

"My father? What have you done to him?" She felt the anger in her body flow out from her, and he reacted by grinning back at her.

He jumped across the floor toward her. His eyes crossed over her chest and the amulet that hung there. Realization and resolve filled his eyes. He extended his neck at her chest and bit at the amulet. She smacked her forclaws together on either side of his head at the soft ear holes, and he backed away shaking his head.

She considered his attack and the way he had reacted when he saw the amulet. There was no way he could be allowed to win. He would destroy them all. He was after her power, and that could not happen. She wanted him gone. Suddenly, all of her agreed that Nethliast was a threat to dragons and to her. She would no longer resist what she knew. He frightened her, and the whole world would be safer if Nethliast was gone.

He had recovered and was coming at her again. Kaliastrid was angling toward his back. Melissa could see the finality in his eyes. He was going to kill her and take the amulet. Fire engulfed the talisman on her chest. Nethliast could see it and the magical show enthralled him, drove him deeper into the frenzy. He abandoned care and leapt at her with all of his claws extended and his tail pointed to strike.

"No!" she cried and the fire leapt across the chamber to surround Nethliast. Kaliastrid leapt at the same moment, and Melissa stepped away from his attack. In a flash, the fire consumed him before her eyes.

Kaliastrid plunged through the fire and air he once occupied. When her charge failed to make contact with him, she turned to defend an attack that never came. Her teeth gnashed at the air where he might have been.

"Where did he go?"

"I don't know."

"Did you destroy him?"

"I don't know."

Kaliastrid tilted her head and stared at her without a response. Melissa could tell she was upset about something.

"What?"

"Nothing."

"Say it, don't start holding back on me now, mother."

"I'm not angry if you destroyed him, but you're letting magic control you. You must control it or chaos reigns. That is very human of you."

"I don't know what caused it."

"Are you sure?" Kaliastrid shook her head and turned toward the outside entrance to the cave. Her wings vibrated with the excitement, exertion, and anger that flowed off her.

Melissa could not deny that at the last moment she had not cared if Nethliast was destroyed or not. She had not given any guidance to the magic that had consumed him. She had simply decided it had to end. She would not feel sorry for defending herself from his murderous rage no matter how she had stopped it.

Melissa transformed into her human form and cringed at the thought of stopping her mother as she walked toward the ledge.

"We should walk up the stairs. If they sent planes to investigate our fight, they may be here soon. We should avoid that conflict."

Kaliastrid stopped in mid-stride and spun toward Melissa with her tail pointed menacingly at her face. After a moment's pause, she transformed. Her emerald silk blouse and blue jeans made her look much less menacing but the fire of her anger still smoldered in her eyes. She walked past Melissa and up the stairs without a word. Melissa could still feel the anger and excitement emanating from her. She had committed herself to the fight, and now she was burning through the cool down. Melissa let her lead the way to the top and all the way to the house in silence.

At the stairs leading up to the patio, Charles and Elaine stood watching them walk up. He had his rifle over his shoulder, and Elaine was staring at both of them with amazement.

"You do realize that rifle will do you little good against a dragon, right?" Kaliastrid's mood continued to poison the atmosphere as she walked past the greeting party and into the library. "You would be just as well off with a fire iron."

Charles watched her walk by and looked at Melissa with a worried question on his face. He could not maintain his normal professional detachment any longer. "What was that all about?"

Melissa took a step back at the harsh tone to his voice. "What do you mean?"

"I mean, you took off—literally—without telling us anything. I had no idea what was going on." Although he was angry and she could tell it, he maintained a calm, but sharp tone. "You can't keep me in the dark. I can't help you that way as your butler, your bodyguard, or your friend. Not to mention that you never gave any thought to the others that are now involved in this adventure."

Melissa looked at Elaine, who was excited over what she had seen and agitated that Charles was upset. She really didn't have anything to add but static crackled around her from the excitement. Charles was right. She had not thought about how Nethliast's attack might affect him. She also realized this was what she wanted from Charles. She wanted the soldier more than she wanted the friend.

"You're right. I should have told you. I know you want to help. I'm sorry I didn't tell you what was going on, but it just happened."

"I—We can help you down here if you tell us what's going on."

"I'm not used to this Charles, none of it. Maybe we are a little closer now than we were, but I still don't know what I'm supposed to do. I'll try to remember that in the future."

He backed off a little when she made it clear to him that she was overwhelmed.

"But, I need for you to help me. Be the warrior that you are. Don't wait for me to ask anymore. Trust your training and skill."

He nodded. With that point resolved, he moved on. "So, why is Kaliastrid so mad?"

"I'm not sure. I think she's upset because I may have destroyed Nethliast before she could, but it is more likely because I did it by letting magic control me. I have no idea what happened."

"He's gone? You destroyed him? Then this is over?" Elaine asked bouncing and crackling beside Charles.

Melissa grinned at her joy over her mate's death, but she knew now that this was about more than one dragon. He had started a movement and she would have to get to the bottom of the problem before she could say it was over. To get to the bottom she would probably need the talisman.

"No, there are others who share his ideal. We still need to solve the problem with our memories and why we were trapped in the first place."

Melissa wanted to celebrate their victory but she knew this was not it.

"One less threat is a plus." Charles grinned an authentic grin and then looked at Melissa with an apologetic wink. "Why don't we go up and get everything calmed down before your appointment gets here. I expect he'll be early."

Melissa carefully put her arm around Elaine to guide the young girl back to the house. Three powerful arcs of magical electricity jumped from her shoulders, numbing the skin on Melissa's arm. Elaine shrank a little but then settled into the friendly gesture. The air around her still crackled and sparked. Melissa could smell ozone on the air. She was a powder keg of magical power, and Melissa suddenly realized they were very similar. Their magic was controlling them and Kaliastrid could sense the chaos of it.

"I think we can get some control of this mess if you trust me."

Elaine looked at her with pleading eyes.

They walked into the library. Kaliastrid was pacing in front of the wooden desk. She stopped when they walked through the doors.

"You do realize what could have happened don't you? You could have destroyed us all."

Melissa stopped as another of her supporters needed to vent. She did deserve the chastisement, however.

"Yes, Mother. I realize. It was not intentional. It happened too fast, and he was gone before I truly knew what was going on."

"The amulet did it," Elaine suggested.

"Well, that would explain why I didn't really know what was going on."

"That's no excuse," Kaliastrid shouted.

With a little more control, Kaliastrid continued, "You can't let magic control you, Mel."

"I know, Mother. I'm not used to having a protective talisman that will not let me be threatened. I had to act to keep it from hurting you as we were falling to the ground."

"And you thought a closed-in cave with one exit was the best place to fight an angry dragon?"

"Yes... No... I thought it was the best place for everyone. I needed to get the fight out of the air before it attracted attention."

"Too late."

The voice came from the second floor library. A strange man in a casual business suit stood next to the timeline and stack of books.

Charles sidestepped away from Melissa and Elaine while dropping to one knee. As part of the same movement, he pointed the rifle at the stranger above them. Melissa heard a loud click as he thumbed off the safety.

"Okay, you've got me outgunned, and I'm not really supposed to be here. Why don't we start this uncomfortable meeting at the top?" His empty hands rose from the rail, and he grinned at them.

Melissa released Elaine and stepped out into the center of the opening where he could see her better. As she crossed in front of Charles, he shifted to keep the intruder covered with his rifle.

"Who are you, and why are you in my home?"

"Loxley, Silas Loxley. FBI. I have an appointment with you in about fifteen minutes."

Melissa looked over at Charles, who nodded slightly but kept his rifle centered on his left eye.

"Where did you call from, the driveway?" Charles asked.

"Close," he answered.

A quiet whimper reached Melissa's ear as the temperature in the room dropped noticeably.

"Okay, Mr. Loxley, why don't you stay where you are for a moment?

Mother, would you please take Elaine to the parlor and continue the conversation we were having about control when we were interrupted."

Kaliastrid paused to process what she was saying. She noted the static cloud covering Elaine and the temperature drop, then nodded.

"I'd rather everyone stay in this room if you don't mind," the agent suggested from the top of the stairs.

"What you want doesn't really matter. You really have no idea how bad this situation can get. I suggest you trust me. It will be safer for us all if I decide where everyone goes, and you're an intruder in my home, anyway."

He shrugged assent and watched from the balcony.

"Charles, put down the rifle. Mother, take Elaine. Mr. Loxley, we're coming up to you."

Kaliastrid did not wait for anyone. She walked toward Elaine, collected her by the arm as several sparks zapped her, and passed behind Charles to walk the dangerously charged young woman away from further stimulation.

"Why don't you call me Silas?"

"I don't trust him," Charles said without dropping his aim. "I told you, he reminds me of a guy I worked with in Iraq. I learned I couldn't trust him if I wanted to live. I'm not dropping this until he's dead or walking out the way he came in."

"Ouch. That's not fair. You've just met me," Silas replied.

"I've met the type. You think the rules are for everyone else because you're protected by your position. By law, I could drop you now and never have to explain why."

"True, you could, and I took a chance exposing myself like I did. You should ask yourself why I did that."

"Mel, he's not what he says he is. He's a spook. Half of everything he says is a lie."

"So you can trust half of what I say."

"Only if you want to die."

"I see," Melissa said.

She looked at Charles and could see the intensity of his focus on the man on the upper level. Charles saw him as a real threat, and she had just asked him to be this very person. She could not overlook his concern.

"So who are you, Silas?"

"I'm the federal agent following up on the report of a local helicopter crew that reported seeing a dragon fly toward this estate before disappearing into a cave beneath it."

"I see. This is a particularly interesting meeting then, for you. I imagine the conversation you overheard while illegally entering my home has you intrigued."

"To say the least, but I'm not your average uninformed agent. I already know dragons are real. I just want to know what's going on. Why is all of this happening? Why did the weirdoes that came out last month just stop? I'm not the only one asking, either."

"That is an interesting tale. If I told you I might be able to help with that, and that I was looking for a chance to speak with someone higher in the government, what would you say?"

"I would say that I might be the exact person you were looking for. I can make that meeting happen. There is a particular woman I know who is interested. I think she might be high enough in the government for you?" The look in his eyes seemed playful as if he was having fun with this.

"Okay. I think we need to arrange that meeting."

"Mel," Charles growled from his position.

"Charles, I have to reach out. I can't let this happen without trying to warn them. Silas is offering to help."

"That's right, Marine. She has a duty."

She shot Silas a warning look. Charles would kill him if he didn't walk a careful line, and she needed him alive. Silas got the full meaning of her look and raised his hands from the rail again to emphasize that they were empty and in the air.

"Sorry, didn't realize he was so sensitive."

"Silas, let's focus on this meeting and stop irritating my butler."

He grinned and nodded with a mildly apologetic look and a surrendering shrug. "As you suggest. Charles, I'm going to reach into my outside jacket pocket very slowly for a card. I'm not interested in ending this very interesting conversation with a shot to the eye, I'm kinda fond of that eye. I'm impressed that you can keep that bore so squarely pointed at it like that. Your instructor should be proud. You ever do any sniper training?"

"We trained for a lot of things in Iraq. Some of it was not on the books."

Silas nodded as his hand reached the pocket and slowly extracted the business card. He showed it to them both.

"Now, I need a pen. I'm not going to take a chance with pulling one out of my pocket. I'll just borrow one of these up here on the table next to this very interesting chart. I'm writing a tail number, time and name onto this card and leaving it up here for you."

Charles adjusted his aim as Silas moved slowly around to the table and leaned down to write on the card.

"And this information is for?" Melissa asked.

"This is your flight information for tomorrow."

"I'm flying somewhere?"

"Washington."

"I see."

"I'll make sure the appointments are all handled. If you will allow me to leave the way I came, I'll see you tomorrow in Washington." Silas backed away from the table and turned his back on Charles.

As he walked through the hall, down the stairs and out the front door, Charles relaxed his hold on the rifle and stood up. When the door closed behind him, Kaliastrid walked back into the library to stand next to Charles. Melissa backed up to the large desk and sat down on its edge. She was shaking from the confrontation and felt very tired.

"That's not exactly how you wanted to make your connections was it?" Charles asked her.

"No." She shook her head and dropped her face into her hands.

"I'm not letting you go to Washington alone."

"Thank you. I would appreciate your company. I think you scared him a little."

"I hope I did. He was nearly dead and didn't know it."

"I think he knew it. How's Elaine?"

"Powerful," Kaliastrid answered calmly "I sent her up to her room to take a break. She was over-stimulated. I've never heard of an innate human. If we don't help her, she's going to hurt herself or someone else. Humans were never meant to be magical creatures." Kaliastrid grimaced and shook her head at something in her painful memory. "I think we'll start training her on that in the morning. When are you two off on your trip to Washington."

"Tomorrow. Mother, are you sure about this?"

"No, but there's no choice." Kaliastrid gave her a look that told her to change subjects. "Are you sure about this trip?"

Melissa shared a concerned but committed look that told her exactly how she felt. "I asked for it."

They both nodded.

"What about Nethliast's plan?" Charles asked.

"Yeah, what about Nethliast?" Melissa parroted.

"You are going to have to learn what that talisman is doing," Kaliastrid said, closing the circle on the interrupted conversation while ignoring the new question.

"Yes, Mother. I will pay more attention to it. Now we have to see what Nethliast has set in motion. I can't believe it will all fall apart without him. We don't even know what he's planning."

"We should assume whatever he is planning it will be very big and very far reaching and most likely centered in the old country."

Melissa nodded at the wisdom.

"I wish Valdiest would contact me."

Melissa let her mother's sorrow punctuate the conversation, but she was not convinced their suffering was over. Although this was the end of another long day, tomorrow promised to be just as long.

July 24 – 1130 EDT – Washington D.C.

Charles and Melissa stepped out of the chartered Cessna Citation and walked across the tarmac into the midfield, commercial terminal at Dulles International Airport. Charles felt naked in the open field of the airport without his pistol but knew it would be impossible to get through security into the nation's capital with it. He shook off the feeling that someone was watching them by admitting Silas would most certainly have someone watching them and there was nothing he could do about it. A few steps ahead of Melissa, so he could keep an eye on the crowd, he scanned for signs of the watchers.

The commercial terminal was not busy, so he didn't have as much to work with. He scanned the converging hallways and forced himself to relax as the crowd thickened where the concourses merged. Soon they were on their way out the front doors leading to the limousine loading area where the pilot had told them their car would be waiting. Charles refused to relax his scan even as they reached the doors. He didn't trust Silas.

The automatic doors swept open. The midday sun temporarily blinded him, but he still caught a glimpse of the threat. He threw on his sunglasses and looked back toward the two men he had seen. A pair of completely exposed agent types, wearing matching suits that said "Federal Marshal" in the stitching and sporting obvious bulges under their arms, were standing next to a black Escalade. Charles tensed into combat readiness dulled somewhat by the years away from constant training and actual combat. He stopped where he was and put his body between Melissa and the two men.

"If I say run, do it. Don't hesitate."

The marshals stepped away from the black Escalade and moved to encircle them. Charles looked at the closest and shifted his feet to prepare for the attack. The agent smiled, stepped back into a relaxed but ready stance to avoid any physical contact with him. He raised his hands in front of his chest with his palms out and shook his head. Once he had indicated he was not there to fight he pointed to the black Escalade sitting in the white zone. The other agents took a similar stance on his other side and nodded politely to Melissa. She looked to Charles for directions and waited calmly for the men to work out what was next.

"I suggest you load up, Marine. The TSA around here is serious about their rules," the agent next to Charles said with a practiced military air.

"So you're our ride?"

The agent pointed to the open door of the Escalade. Charles knew they had walked into dangerous territory but it was nothing less than he expected since he had met Silas Loxley. There was no winning this conflict. The agents would have backup. They were on their home field. He knew that as soon as they had stepped on the chartered jet and expected as much. He nodded, showing his hands in a sign that he was not there to fight and headed toward the open door. In the darker corners of his mind he knew some of the show was payback for last night. As they walked toward the car and the agents fell in behind them, he shifted Melissa in front of him.

When they reached the dark vehicle, he held her back as he stuck his head in to see what they were getting into. The back of the SUV held a U-shaped seating area that circled the cabin of the vehicle like a stretch limousine. It allowed everyone to look at each other as they traveled. There was a socket in the floor for a table if it was needed, and a wet bar was open over the passenger side wheel well. The windows in the back were tinted far beyond legal. The midday sun fought to penetrate them. LED lights in the ceiling cast circles of light onto the black seats. Silas was sitting all the way in the back staring at a metal cube in his lap. When Charles looked in, the agent barely glanced up and then returned immediately to staring at the cube. A curious pair of lenses was sitting on his nose.

Charles handed Melissa up into the seat and followed her in. They sat opposite Silas and waited. The agents closed the doors behind them, and he felt more trapped than he had on the sidewalk.

Silas carefully set the cube into a battered shipping box and removed the lenses from his face. Slipping the lenses into a protective cloth case and placing the case into his breast pocket, Silas glanced down at Melissa's legs, exposed to the knee by her skirt. He paused at her calves and then slowly scanned back up her body. Charles discreetly cleared his throat and scowled at the man when he looked over at him. Silas held up his hand in an unspoken apology and grinned at them both.

"Welcome." He held out his hand. "I hope you had a good flight."

Charles ignored it, but Melissa placed her hand in his. He bowed his head to her hand to place his lips just above it. If he had been standing, the full motion of his kiss would have put him into a kneeling position before her. Instead of kissing her hand, he touched it to his forehead and then looked up at her.

"It is good to meet under less stressful circumstances," Melissa said.

"So, Charles, about that. When did the Marine Corps add butler as an MOS?"

Charles grinned at the playful jest and, for a moment, the atmosphere relaxed. He still didn't trust the man.

"I have the President's ear in this situation. I'm not your enemy... unless you're ours."

The car pulled away from the terminal, and Loxley motioned for them to scoot on around toward him. "Come on and get a little closer. We've got one more passenger. She will join us in a few minutes if I like what I hear."

Melissa scooted a little closer to the agent, and Charles followed. There was no easy escape from the moving vehicle. They were trapped.

"So, what's this all about? Why do you want to talk to the President, and what do you want to warn us about?" he asked.

Melissa smiled at him and started to speak. Charles put his hand on hers to keep her from answering. She didn't want to wait, but she allowed him to go on.

"We came here to speak to someone who can do something. We have important news that you don't want us revealing just anywhere. You're CIA, so there's nothing you can do here. Much like yesterday, you're breaking several laws right now."

"I'm here for the President of the United States. I have so many official titles that I lose track of them. The term '*official*' is no lie, so, if I say I'm FBI, you can believe it. Independent of my actual job title, I represent the President. Would you please let the lady talk? If she wants an audience with the President, she talks to me. That's how this has to work."

Melissa patted Charles' hand and answered.

"I'm the dragons' selected ambassador, and I'm here to speak to those in charge so that we can set up friendly diplomatic relations."

"So you consider those weird events a month ago and all the attacks on police and the military friendly diplomatic relations, do you? You think hiding dragons and magic, and who knows what else, is diplomacy?"

Charles started to respond, and Melissa squeezed his hand. She was going to take this on without any help, and that bothered Charles.

"I'll assure you, there were no attacks on police by dragons. You know that or you wouldn't be here. The only attack on the Military I am aware of was a dreadful mistake."

"Excuse me? Those lizard men weren't human. They looked like dragons to me. What were they if they aren't dragons?"

Charles could see that the accusations were bothering Melissa who was not trained as an ambassador, and that Silas was a trained agent doing his job. Charles wanted to help her but had no idea how. Silas did have a point, although he was being rather hard about it.

"Would you consider yourself an expert on dragons Agent Loxley? Are you the foremost expert in this field? I happen to be an expert on dragons. It is my responsibility to help explain these differences to avoid the mistakes common to dragons and their lore. I can see how one could mistake a basilisk, for example, for a dragon, but not the lizard men as you call them. I'm here today to see that there are no more *mistakes*."

"Well, let's see. The scales, the forked tongues, the teeth, the real bad attitudes. Yeah, I can see how I made that mistake too."

"So, you're prejudiced by your own history, and you're unable to accept that there may be a story other than the one widely accepted. If that's the case, I'm inclined to accept Charles' characterization of you as a useless, deceptive, unreliable lackey that is working only to draw a government pension. But, I don't really know any other people who work for the CIA, and I've chosen to judge you based on the seasoned experience of my former-Marine friend and the last action movie I saw. Is this how you want this conversation to go? I can stereotype as well as you can, and there are far more skeletons in the human closet."

Loxley smiled at her, and Charles sat back in his seat. The temperature dropped a little making his collar a little more comfortable.

"So, you don't like it if I stereotype dragons. That means you believe in who you represent, at least a little. Why did they pick you? No one knows you. You came out of nowhere. Your family can be found easily enough and has some interesting connections in other countries, but no real hints of anything concerning dragons. In fact, you basically don't exist, even though your family goes back to very old German stock. Who are you?"

"My grandmother was the previous ambassador. Now it's my job. Does every ambassador you work with have a criminal record?"

"Your grandmother? She had an easy job then, and you should too, since there are no dragons."

"I'll assure you, there are. But, I don't have to, you have already admitted to me that you know there are dragons. Why else would I be in this car driving all over Washington, D.C.?"

"So you admit those things that were attacking police were dragons."

"Those two statements are not the same. Dragons exist. Those examples were not dragons."

"What about the long Asian style dragon they killed in Africa?" He pulled a picture from his right breast pocket and held it out in front of her. She had seen the same picture the morning after they had emerged in Charles' stack of papers.

She looked at the picture and smiled at Silas. "You know what my answer should be on this. You're testing me to see if I'm for real. Everyone knows that's no dragon. Anyone who can read a book knows that's a basilisk, as I said before."

"Semantics, he's a dragon."

"She, actually, and don't let a real dragon hear you say that. They'd be very insulted. To insult a real dragon by comparing them to that abomination could get you killed." Silas looked at the picture again as he pocketed it and nodded.

Charles looked away from Silas and stared at the back of the driver's head through the partition to keep the agent from reading his joy at her handling of him.

"But, they're related," he continued.

"In a very awkward way."

"In the same way they're related to the mostly human ones?"

"Somewhat."

"That's like saying my sister's kid isn't related to me because his father's Chinese."

"With the basilisk, it's more like saying your nephew is not related to you because his father is a dog. Basilisks normally take strong magic to create. They don't occur naturally. I have no idea how this one would have come about."

Silas' eyebrows raised when she mentioned magic but he said nothing about it.

"But the mixed humans are cousins, right?"

"Ours and theirs," she answered very carefully.

"So they're half-breeds."

"Most of them are far less than half. They're more human than dragon."

"Okay. So, why are you the ambassador to the dragons? Why did they pick you?"

"They didn't pick me, the former ambassador did."

"Your grandmother, who just died?"

"She was my grandmother and she recently passed, that is correct."

"You're an ambassador alright, never a straight answer."

"Just like all the spooks I've ever known." Charles could not avoid the jab, and everyone in the car seemed to accept the stability of universal distrust.

Silas pressed a button on a small console in the seat next to him, and the driver changed lanes and slowed to make a left turn.

"Where are we going now?" Charles asked, watching the driver and looking for signs he could see out the front window. He couldn't tell where they were.

"We have to pick up our other passenger. She wanted to meet you at the airport, but I convinced her that it could send the wrong message and would cause her some trouble with her base. Dragons and magic don't set well with the more conservative in her party. She is very excited to meet you, though."

Melissa nodded. "I have very important news to share with her. Thank you for organizing this meeting."

"Really, what is it?"

"I think you should save it for her," Charles advised.

She smiled at him and shook her head. "I need to tell someone, in case the President is not interested in listening, and who better than her paranoid friend."

Silas smiled at her and looked at Charles. "That's right, let the lady talk. You keep interrupting her. I thought butlers were supposed to be silent and supportive." He looked back at her and asked, "You really think I'm paranoid?"

"I think you're paranoid," Charles answered for her, "and I think you're a nut-job spook who never grew up after the Cold War. I don't trust you as far as you can throw me, and tonight I'm not a butler I'm her body guard—the pay is better."

"Don't you mean...no, I guess you don't. Well, it doesn't matter anyway. Hazard pay, I get that. If we weren't on opposite teams right now, I could grow to like you. Anyway, I'm just glad you don't have a vote in this. Tell me your ground-breaking news, Miss Schwendeman."

The Escalade pulled to a stop before Melissa could continue, and the door opened. Sunlight filled the interior of the car, blinding everyone. When the flash blindness had cleared and the vehicle was moving again, a rather young looking woman Charles recognized as the President of The United States was sitting next to him on the only available seat. Beside the President was a quiet statue of a man. Years of training brought Charles to a seated attention. The President noticed the movement, waved her hand and smiled a disarming "at ease."

Charles watched as Loxley and the President greeted each other. There was no physical contact, but there was no denying the familiarity.

"Anyway," Loxley said. "You were saying, Miss Schwandeman?"

"Good afternoon Madame President, I am Melissa Helena Schwandeman, and I am here as a human representative of the dragons who have most recently returned from an extended exile. I was explaining to Agent Loxley," she continued after glance at Charles, "there is a large faction of dragons who want to start a war with humans in retribution for allegedly trapping them over a millennium ago. A smaller faction believes a show of force will be enough to remind you where we belong in the world, but they are a losing minority. I want to assure you that neither stance is the formal position of the dragons. I can explain the problem, but I cannot change the fact that there is a risk I have been fighting to reduce. Yesterday we made a major step in ending the standoff, but it is too soon to say we have won."

Charles watched the exchange between the President and Loxley as Melissa delivered her message. The President was not spooked or excited. She reacted with practiced caution in every action. Loxley affirmed what he could and shrugged at items he could not confirm. He was not afraid for Melissa to know what he felt.

"I see. I'm not sure how to react to this sudden notification that humankind is being judged for an alleged millennium-old slight to dragons. How could we even hope to defend against such an offense?"

Melissa continued, noting the President's question. "If you will bear with me, I will explain. During their return, the dragons' memories were affected somehow. Those who wish to avoid conflict are still trying to discover how they were trapped, and they are working against any plans to act rashly. If their memories were clear, the factions would not exist and there would be no threat. However, one individual among the dragons, Nethliast, had a strong following. We expect they are planning to take action. Although Nethliast has been dealt with, there are others who are more than willing to continue in his footsteps."

"The dragons wanted you to share this with us?" Loxley asked.

"I am responsible for the relationship between human and dragon kind. I felt it was important for the relationship that I share this information."

"Okay, semantics. Whatever. Until today you had no relationship with human kind. It looks like dragons have a problem. You thought sharing this with us would help our relationship?"

"In the spirit of cooperation, I felt I should make you aware of everything. I don't want a war."

"But this one dragon and his followers, they want war?"

She nodded.

"So, where is he so we can get him off the streets or out of the cave, so to speak?"

"As I said, we have dealt with him. He was in Germany. I expect that is the root of his plan, but I cannot be sure. He has supporters around the world. He's the dragon who fought with the German aircraft which empowered him more because it proved humans indiscriminately attack dragons when they can. Germany is symbolic to him and will be the root of his plan, but his followers will likely touch every country when they act."

"How does he have that much support? How was he funded? We need information about this." The President was interested now.

"If any of this is even true," Loxley countered and looked at Melissa with narrow eyes, "Do you offer any proof of this? How do you expect us to believe you?"

"I don't," she stated flatly. "In fact, I expect you to ignore what I'm saying completely. I'm surprised I was even allowed to speak to the President. Even that was a fluke, don't you agree?"

The unflappable agent's eyes narrowed but he didn't speak.

"No, I expect the realization that my words are important will come when Nethliast's followers complete his plan and attack. You will wonder how they did it. I'll be pretty busy, much like I have been trying to stop them by then, so I'm not going to be available to talk."

The President sat back in the seat and looked at the girl who was predicting the future. She was not convinced, but she was concerned.

The SUV stopped at the curb again.

"Silas, I think you need to get to the bottom of this. You need to define the threat." With those last words to them, the President and her statue were gone as quickly as they had arrived.

"Busy woman, country to run." Loxley smiled at both of them as the door closed and the vehicle pulled into traffic again. "I need more. How is, what did you call him—Nethliast—or his followers, going to accomplish it? What's he planning?"

"I don't know."

The look on the agent's face called her a liar.

"Really, I don't. We think he was working with groups of half-breeds. That's why they've stopped acting out. They have someone to follow. I'm afraid his absence will only strengthen their resolve."

"You're not helping me here. I need details."

"I don't have any. I came here to warn you. I'm trying to stop it from my side, but I'm not sure I can before it's too late. You have more resources than I do."

"Yeah, forewarned, forearmed, so to speak."

The SUV stopped again.

"Thanks, if I have any questions, I know how to get in touch with you."

Melissa's eyes widened, and she sunk into the seat.

"Wait." Charles put his hand out. "You can't doubt her. I've seen Nethliast. He's real. He's serious. His plan and his followers are serious. This is not a hoax."

"Thank you."

The two agents were back at the door, waiting to hand them out of the SUV. The noise of the airport verified they were back where they started. Charles stepped out backward using his own body to block the agent at the door. The agent couldn't stop the body check and stumbled backward. His partner stepped toward the door and Charles gave him a look that communicated his interest in slamming him into the window of the Escalade. The agent stepped back. They wouldn't want a public conflict. Charles was counting on that.

Melissa stepped out and looked at the scene. She smiled at the discomfited agents and took Charles' offered arm to walk into the terminal. When they were as clear of their agent followers as they could be, Charles whispered to her.

"You knew he wouldn't believe you?"

"As soon as we got in the SUV."

"How?"

"Something about him and puzzles, he doesn't have all the pieces yet, but he's collecting them. He won't believe me until he finds corroboration. That will come too late."

"Why didn't you give them to him?"

"What?"

"The pieces he needs."

"Like?"

"You could have told him that dragons can take human form." Charles couldn't help getting a little louder.

"I felt that was a secret I needed to keep to myself for now, and I don't think those pieces will help him."

Charles didn't know what to say. She had asked for the meeting just to hold back key pieces of information.

"Charles, don't look at me that way. If I told him, they would turn their search internal trying to find all dragons and seeing ghosts at every corner. It would be such a mess. It would limit my ability to move and act. They probably would have taken us both into custody to try to prove we were dragons. How would that help?"

Charles had to admit that her point was correct. He didn't have to like it. There had to be a way to share what they needed to know without risking her. He stewed on that as they walked back to the plane where their adventure had started.

July 24 – About the same time – Dulles International Airport, Washington D.C.

"Listen, I did this as a favor because, when you try, you do good science, but we had an understanding. I told you, none of the elves and dwarves stuff. I'm even okay with all the Odin stuff, it makes the digs more interesting, but I can't have you undermining the science of this dig with theories about fictional creatures. I'm going to have to cut you loose, Aldrich. I hate it, but we had an understanding, and you broke it," the tall blonde man with very large forearms and biceps for an archeologist had said to Aldrich six hours earlier.

They had both been standing on the site of a dig on the Southwestern shore of Lake Superior. Aldrich had been about a foot deep in the mud looking up from his four foot height into the towering face of his old friend, Olaf Sigurdsson. The scene had to remind Olaf's friends of a father scolding his children even though Aldrich was a couple of years older than his friend.

"What have I done? I followed your rules."

"Did you? Then why are the students asking me questions about that damned piece of wood you wear around your neck?"

Aldrich's hand moved to his neck and the smoothly turned piece of wood with gold-leaf filled runes carved on it.

"They heard the stories and asked if I was wearing it. I always wear it, you know that, they know that. You can't hold me responsible for that."

"You're as much of a pollutant to my sites as that piece of wood was."

"You're as wrong now as you were then. I can prove my position. All you and those other scientists can prove is that they are hiding behind unreliable texts written in a weak time in our development as a race. You know you can't trust texts that came out of the dark ages. Show me how they align with texts before they were written."

"Aldrich, we're not arguing that again. Not here. We had a deal. You broke it. You know what that means."

"I did not break our agreement."

"They're asking me questions about elves and dwarves. How did you not break our agreement?" Olaf's anger nearly tipped him into the mud with Aldrich.

"Then there is hope for our future."

"Get off my dig!" Olaf turned and plowed into his tent, where Aldrich would never go.

Now, sitting where Wodin had sent him when he had consulted the flight schedule, he rolled the two-inch dowel of polished wood on the end of a leather thong between his fingers. It had damned his career since that fateful day in Viborg when he had found it among a collection of broken implements at the foot of a posthole.

The truth that the piece of wood had actually been found at that dig didn't matter to Olaf. It hadn't mattered to any of the other scientists, either. They had all dismissed it as modern pollution to the site.

Aldrich remembered that moment clearly. It was his one chance to save his career by being quiet. Wodin wouldn't allow it then much like he had not allowed it earlier that day. But, unlike a few years before, now he had proof, proof in his own hands.

Aldrich always found it amusing that Olaf could believe, with absolute devotion, that his ancestors had not only made it to the mainland of North America, but had traveled inland and even set up communities, but he could not believe elves, dwarves, and magic ever existed. There was more written and physical evidence of magic around the world than anyone had ever found in Minnesota to support Olaf's Viking migration theory. Aldrich harrumphed in his seat at the Cinnabon in the Dulles International concourse and continued rolling the two-inch long piece of alder between his fingers. The fine carved runes on it flashed as it rolled over the top. It glowed today, unlike the first day he had found it. If it had glowed that day, he might have kept that job.

Aldrich laughed at the thought that a *glowing* piece of wood with unidentified carvings on it would have changed the outcome. Those very glowing runes had sparked the questions that led to his early morning departure from Minnesota. Wodin had no plans for him to have a comfortable career where he knew where his rent was coming from month to month.

He sat back in his seat at the table and crossed his arms to stew over his most recent termination. Wodin was certainly treating him harshly for his indiscretions. He had not quite figured out what the nascent dreams of dragons had to do with it, but it would become clear soon.

If he had been paying attention to the dreams, he would have known he was going to lose another job. The date and place had been clear enough in the dream. If he had kept the job, there would be no reason for him to be in this concourse on this day waiting out an incredible layover at the Cinnabon. Now all that was missing was the most beautiful dragon he had ever seen walking down the concourse. Although dragons had disappeared over a thousand years ago, he refused to believe that they had not existed. He had too much evidence to the contrary, but it seemed unlikely he would see one walking through an airport. Either way, he was here, as the dream had predicted. The glowing elvish text was telling him a magical creature was nearby, not an everyday event.

The crowd was starting to build, and the cart had just passed with the angry woman in the inflatable splint. She was coming. He slipped out of the chair, walked to the edge of the seating area and looked at the passing passengers.

"Well, Wodin. Is this where you want me? Think we can work out the rent now?" he said to no one in the crowd.

Aldrich pulled the earbuds out of his ears and the Viking metal he had been listening to became a whisper on his shoulder. The moment was approaching. The dream had very clear time indicators, and Aldrich could feel everything falling into place.

The cart with the five golfers drove by, and the last guy dropped his bag. Golf clubs, balls, and tees spread across the concourse floor. The cart stopped. The initial chaos disturbed the flow of people and created an opening.

Aldrich prepared for the smiling nun. She had smiled at him in the dream. Maybe she liked short men. As she walked by, she ignored the bag, clubs, and the guy scrambling about to collect everything and looked at Aldrich. Somehow, as if someone had flipped a switch, she looked up and smiled at him. It had happened all through his life. Anyone devout in their belief recognized it in him and smiled or showed him some sign of solidarity. In some cases, like this one, Wodin sent them to tell him he was in the right place and right time. A small offering would have helped but the smile was nice. It didn't bother Aldrich that they had a different name for Wodin. The Allfather was not too fussy about who he used. That was one of his best features, and there were too few of those to count.

Aldrich looked up the concourse for the dragon, and his heart dropped. A couple appeared in the place where his dragon should be. He stared at the them trying to figure out what his deity had in mind while knowing the very thought was arrogance.

There had to be an explanation. The tall man had been in the dream too. He had stood beside the dragon in brightly gilded armor. Once he made the connection the scene changed. A giant shadow covered the crowd, and the image of a glistening bronze and copper dragon hovered all around the woman dressed in a very attractive red business suit. The aroma of hot cinnamon filled his nostrils, and the image shimmered in his mind. As he had in the dream, he stood there and watched her walk by.

Meliastrid. A voice in his head whispered the name as she walked by. The tall man next to her, dressed in full plate armor and carrying a sword, turned slightly to look at him as they passed. The shadowy suit of armor surrounding the man in Aldrich's vision saluted him when the man in the concourse smiled at him.

By the time they had walked by, the golfers were gone, and the crowd was back to its normal flow. Aldrich sat back down in his seat and let his pulse settle.

"Where to next, Wodin? I've been faithful, sorta. I came here and watched your movie. Did Leif float about the ocean like this as you guided him? Did he wonder where lunch was coming from?" He asked the noisy room around him. As always Wodin didn't answer, but he would. It would come in a vision, a dream, or some other interesting sign. In the past month, the visions had been clearer and more common, but that was all that had changed about following Wodin. The pay had not increased any. For a moment, he hoped Wodin needed him in Germany. It would be nice to go home for a while, and that was where his current ticket was taking him, in six more hours. If Wodin didn't like his path, he would change it, in the most inconvenient way possible.

"Aldrich Handleman," a booming male voice from the sky called to him. He jumped from his seat as a cold sweat broke out all over his body. Wodin had never addressed him directly and never out in the open. It took a few seconds for him to realize it was just the public address system. The first announcement was over, and he had to wait for him to repeat the call to catch the end of the page. "Please report to the ticketing desk."

Wodin was working fast on this one.

He was already through security so he would get to enjoy that process again, but he was sure it would be worth it. It was time to find out where Wodin really wanted him. The tickets provided by his employer would be non-refundable, non-transferable so this would probably come out of his very shallow pockets, but one suffered for his faith if one did it right.

He stuck the ear buds back into his ears and walked back toward the ticketing desk, braced to accept whatever the changes were. Maybe he would get to see the south pole on his way this time. Aldrich grinned and flipped off his deity, in his mind.

July 25 – 1034 EDT – Signal Mountain, Tennessee

The knock on her door thrust Melissa out of a very peaceful rest. She could tell that she had overslept again, which she had been doing a lot since becoming a dragon.

Don't blame that on me. I'm an early riser; you just stay up too late.

Melissa grinned at her inner conflict and rolled her feet off the bed.

"Yes, what is it?"

"You have a visitor." Charles called back through the door. Something was bothering him, and she wondered if it was yesterday's trip or today's visitor.

"Who is it this early? I'm not expecting a guest."

"I could describe him for you. I could tell you what he told me. None of that would reduce the questions or increase the answers. I suggest you just come down."

Melissa started to press him for more but realized it was useless.

We could eat him, you know?

"He would be tough and gristly."

She shared a laugh with herself and changed her appearance to a relaxed but dressy pant and blouse combination of crimson and copper highlighted with black.

In a few moments she was downstairs entering the parlor to greet her new guest. Whether Charles had anticipated that she needed to be prepared for a surprise or he was playing with her, she had no reaction to the short bearded man standing in the middle of the parlor when she arrived. He was probably the most bedraggled man she had seen in a while. Mud still clung to the seams of his boots, and the cable-knit cardigan that he wore over a faded Korpiklanni T-Shirt was long enough to look like a robe. His beard and hair were unkempt, like he had just woke from a long sleep to meet her. He looked, for all the world, like one of the seven dwarves, but she couldn't place which one. He dropped to one knee and looked up to greet her.

"Good morning, Meliastrid. Wodin sends his greetings and warnings through his servant Aldrich Handleman."

She resisted stepping back when he used her dragon name.

"Wodin? The Norse god, Wodin?"

The smile on the small man's face was contagious and answered her without words. She realized she had probably been rude with her response and quickly adjusted.

"Thank you, good man for delivering his greetings. What warnings do you bring?"

"I've traveled here at his direction, at some pain to myself, to tell you that you must be cautious how you travel from here and that your path is not safe."

It will do you no good to ask him to explain it.

Melissa nodded to her own inner voice and resisted asking searching questions.

"I thank you again. Is there anything more you have for me?"

"Nothing more than my personal desire to tell you that I am so pleased to be in the presence of *the* Dragon Ambassador, and that I look forward to the day that I can see you in your most regal form."

Melissa heard a nearly silent intake of breath from Charles and looked at Aldrich a little harder.

"What do you know of my forms? First you use my name, and I ignored it, but now you go too far."

"I'm sorry madam, I meant no disrespect, and if it is your desire to keep that to yourself, I shall not divulge it to anyone. I did not realize you wished to remain hidden, but I needed for you to know I am very serious."

"How do you know all of this?"

"I am guided by Wodin, as I said, and he provides me more insight than most. I offer my vision, knowledge of history both contemporary and arcane, and what support Wodin will bring to your quest. I expect you have a need, which will be greater soon. It would only be honest to warn you that Wodin may guide me to assist you even if you choose to send me away. He is not concerned with what pain and expense that will take to accomplish. If you choose to send me away, please do not take my appearance later as an insult, just understand Wodin is not accepting of my disobeying his direction."

"Are you saying Wodin has sent you to help me?"

The small man stood and walked forward. "My lady, He has sent me here through dreams and some hard corrections to warn you and help guide you."

I like him.

Again she nodded because she agreed.

"Then there are others here that you need to meet."

Placing her hand on his shoulder they turned to leave the parlor. Charles was standing at the door with his arms crossed and his face saying no.

"First, this is my butler, my friend, and most recently my body guard, Charles."

"You, Honorable Knight, I have seen twice before, but only once in person. I am sure you will not remember me from the dream, but perhaps you will remember me among the crowd yesterday at the airport when Wodin put me in your path."

Charles nodded and smiled to the small man, indicating he did remember the meeting and looked up to Melissa with a warning look that was milder than before.

She shook her head to tell him there was no threat in this man. Melissa remembered the scene from the day before. There was no way he could know what he did without help. She focused on him to see what magic she could see and immediately accepted his story. Whether he was there for good or ill was still to be seen.

Charles shook his head and turned to lead them up the stairs. Together they walked to the second level of the library where the others were supposed to be working on new information Elaine had found while they were in Washington.

Elaine was not standing over the books as she had been for weeks. She was sitting cross-legged on the floor in front of the window watching the morning shadow creep up the back lawn. It was apparent to Melissa that unfinished business was boiling beneath that surface.

Melissa looked over at Charles as they entered, expecting some answer about why she was moping, but he shrugged that he didn't know what was going on. Kaliastrid was seated in Melissa's favorite seat with one of Helena's novels resting open in her lap. From the placid look on her face and the fact that the book was upside down, Melissa knew she was not reading it.

"How was the …" She started to ask her question as she looked up into Aldrich's eyes. "…trip?"

Elaine also turned around at the disturbance and looked at the new visitor. Her mood shifted a little, but she was still agitated about something. Melissa could now see a small black book in her lap that may have been the cause, but she could not be sure. She would need to defuse the situation, either way. It was positive that the young woman was not surrounded by a cloud of static energy.

"The trip was interesting. Mother, Elaine, may I introduce Aldrich Handleman? He has offered to aid in our research."

He dropped to one knee again in front of Kaliastrid's chair and bowed his head before her. "Your Majesty, I also bring you greetings from Wodin and wish to tell you how much I have looked forward to meeting you. It is not every day one is in the court of the Queen of Dragons."

"How is it that you know me, sir?" Kaliastrid asked.

"I know you all. I have met you all through dreams and visions that have guided me here. I was, most recently, working at a dig in Minnesota when Wodin moved to place me in your daughter's path in Washington yesterday. He then changed my travel plans and sent me here."

"Wodin, sent you?" Elaine asked from her spot in the floor as she turned fully around to face the visitor.

With a look to Kaliastrid to be sure he was polite, Aldrich stood again and looked down slightly toward Elaine. "It is a pleasure to meet you as well, Elaine Ambrosius, human child of magic. You have no idea at this time what gift you have been born with. The gods have smiled upon you." A tear ran down her cheek as his words released the flood of emotion the young woman was fighting. He reached out to place a hand on her cheek. As his hand touched the tear, fire engulfed his hand. Elaine flinched as the fire seemed to cover his entire hand, but instead of jerking his hand away he pulled it slowly from her face and turned it over in front of her. The flames danced around his small fingers and then rose from his palm as he completed turning his hand over before her.

He smiled at her, and her face relaxed as the fear that she had hurt him vanished.

"Let me take that pain from you for a while. There is no need for you to suffer so with it. There is nothing unnatural about you, child. Let the knowledge of Wodin assure you that you are highly respected and your gift highly prized. You have something sought after for the ages. It was, from what I have read, a bone of contention amongst other races."

Kaliastrid inhaled a little this time, and Melissa looked at her. She waved her away and continued to listen to their visitor.

Aldrich reached back out to her with the fire still dancing on his hand. Elaine, unsure of what to do, fumbled with the book in her lap before she abandoned it and rose to her knees in front of him. She lifted her hand to his and their palms touched. He turned their hands together to face each other. "Take this back from me. It has not harmed me, and it will not harm you. Be at peace with this gift. You will not fail at this."

The flame that had disappeared between their hands engulfed their joined hands and then vanished between them as if she had doused it like a candle.

Aldrich smiled at her.

"You see, you did not hurt me. You can control this." The contagion of his smile jumped to Elaine, and she relaxed back onto the floor looking at her hand.

Aldrich turned away from Elaine and stepped around the room to a point where he could face everyone.

"As I have been guided to see, all is as it should be here. There is a sixth on his way, but that story is unwritten yet and will surely involve more pain before Wodin is done. There is much happening now that no one knows about, and it is focused here with you and the dragons. Wodin sent me to help you in your quest."

"So, I was right," Kaliastrid said to Aldrich, "Elaine is a sorceress. She's an innate human."

"Yes. Once a rarity. In fact, from what I have read, it never existed." Aldrich answered.

"I think our return has..." She looked at each of them and hesitated, "I think others are starting to show signs of magical ability. Innate ability, not trained or learned."

"It seems so. It would appear that some of us are half-breeds of long-lost magical creatures." Aldrich nodded.

Melissa shook her head and looked out the window. "How can that be, mother? Humans never had innate magic ability." She turned back and looked at Aldrich. She could see that her question had disturbed Elaine a little, and Kaliastrid was looking at her with concern.

"I can't stop it. When I get angry or upset, something catches fire or flies across the room."

Elaine stood up from the floor and stood next to Aldrich.

"I'll show you how to control it, dear," Kaliastrid said reassuringly.

"You will master it soon," Aldrich added in support.

"What? What am I mastering? What are you going to teach me to control?" Her voice sounded panicked even though Aldrich had calmed her a great deal.

Elaine looked at Charles with real fear in her eyes, and Melissa suddenly understood. She expected Charles to reject her because she was different. Melissa turned slightly to look at Charles. She needed to find a way to tell him what she had just figured out.

Charles looked directly at Elaine and added, "Magic, Elaine. You're an enchantress, a sorceress. Powers like these have not existed in centuries. There is no way you could have known until now. This must be very hard to deal with. I'm sorry you've had to face this alone, but we're all here to help."

Aldrich nodded.

Kaliastrid grinned at her and added, "I don't know if Helena knew or not. I didn't know what it meant when we first met, but it makes sense. Dragons are magical. We can direct magic to do what we want with just a thought. Humans could never use magic that way. They wanted our help becoming magical, and they even researched for many generations how to make magic happen. That is where tales of wizards come from. But you are something else entirely. It seems that the problem of innately magical humans has been resolved. We can only guide you. How it works for you is personal. You'll have to experiment to find out."

"So, what? I'm a witch?"

Melissa smiled at her. "A witch? No. Witches and wizards study magic. They learn how to capture magic into forms and rituals. They can never hope to be as powerful as you will be. Sorcerers and the enchanted live in magic. It is part of them. It is part of you. You channel it into what you want to happen."

"I don't want to burn holes in my clothes and books."

"All innates go through this as adolescents when the magic becomes more powerful. They usually have parents who know how it works for them that can explain it," Kaliastrid said.

"Someday you may even be able to create powerful magical talismans like this one." Melissa pointed to the pendant around her neck. "Human wizards never matched the magical abilities of the magical races. They turned it into science because they couldn't sense it. You may be the first of your kind."

"Not the last, though," Aldrich's voice added warning.

Melissa continued, "Like I said, You will be very powerful if you give yourself to the powers you're experiencing. Ultimately, that is the only way you will learn to control them. Right now, it's difficult because you're afraid of them."

"And, like I told you yesterday," Kaliastrid added, "it is critical that you control it. If it controls you, it can be catastrophic."

Elaine nodded at the warning again with her eyes wide. She was trying to understand what was happening to her. Melissa really looked at the girl for the first time in a few weeks. She had changed some since coming there. She was growing into something more than any human had ever been. Melissa could see that she was struggling with the new problem. The conflict in her head drove her to look around the room as if she was looking for something from each person.

When she looked at Melissa and their eyes met, Melissa felt a warm comforting acceptance in her mind. For an instant the pain that had been lurking beneath the surface vanished. When the contact broke, the pain flowed back in like a tide.

Elaine looked at Kaliastrid and Aldrich next, holding the connection for a moment before moving on to Charles. He smiled at her, and she lingered there for a little longer. Her face showed a moment of concern and then she smiled at him as well. When the young girl completed her circuit, Melissa could feel the emotional turmoil subsiding, and the room relaxed with a universal emotional sigh.

"I think I know what happened. I think I know why the dragons disappeared," Elaine announced.

Melissa said nothing, but looked at Kaliastrid and Charles for some indication they knew what she was reporting. When no one responded, Melissa rolled with the next surprise of the day.

"Okay. I'm listening. What happened?"

Elaine walked over to the table and leaned forward over the books and timeline. She seemed to struggle again for a moment, as if afraid of what she was about to say.

"How bad can it be? I'm nervous now. Charles, can you help her with this?"

"I've no idea what she's about to tell you. I'd like to hear it, though."

Melissa noticed the smile that passed between them as he moved over to stand next to her. It was a mix of pride and reassurance. She stood up a little straighter and turned to look Melissa in the eyes. Aldrich moved beside Elaine as well and looked up at her. Although he had just arrived, he seemed to know where she was going.

"First, I'm not positive. I've had this idea for about a week, but I needed more proof. I seem to be a part of that puzzle, or at least a hint."

Melissa nodded, and Elaine seemed to gain more confidence.

"All of the books, even the oldest ones we've found, tell stories of how the dragons, apparently you guys, were helping the humans in Swabia and most of Europe at the time. Swabia was the center of your power and would have remained so if you had not disappeared. I believe this is when the first cycle of human-dragons took over. This is also the point in history where all magic vanished from this world, religion took over, and man descended into a dark age. It was almost like someone turned off a switch and humans were alone. In the midst of this turmoil, Swabia lost all control and was swallowed into the countries that formed around it, Human countries that came out of the dark ages far more powerful than it."

"You're suggesting this happened just prior to the European Dark Ages, then?" Aldrich asked.

"That seems to fit with the timeline. I pieced that together from legends and tales hidden in this library. None of this is in any history books. Some groups, mostly the Church, demonized magic and dragons during the Dark Ages. But, I found one book, written after the Renaissance, that talked about wizards who fought dragons."

"Don't you mean knights who fought dragons?" Charles asked.

"You would think that, based on your European education about dragon mythology, but that was why it was such an interesting book. Humans have been meticulously taught that mortal men, knights in shining armor, went out to do battle with dragons and slay them. I hadn't really thought about how insane it was to believe that a knight with a lance and a sword could slay a dragon, not until I read this book. Not until I saw an actual dragon."

Charles nodded agreement. Aldrich stroked his beard and chewed on what she was saying.

"You see, that was what everyone accepted, Saint George and the dragon and all. After hundreds of years of no dragons, no magic, and literature and the Church drawing both in rather negative ways, the world started to accept the notion that neither ever existed. They started to be glad they were just fiction. But, this one book put it into perspective. Witches and wizards, the few human ones that ever existed, disappeared at the same time as dragons because magic disappeared with them."

"Some—outside of the mainstream—archeologists believe that the reason Europe descended into the Dark Ages was because of a technological blackout caused by the disappearance of magic," Aldrich added.

"I read that, in here." Elaine nodded excitedly at Aldrich's point and smiled to have him support her story. "Just before the disappearance, according to some historians writing after the Renaissance, there was a push for humans to acquire magical powers however they could. There was a hint in these articles that humans had been striving for that goal for generations. You all just verified that, so we can continue under that assumption." She paused again.

"Acquire, by what means?" Charles asked.

"They never explained that. To write something like that during that time was dangerous. I expect that the copies in this library may be the only surviving ones. So, why is that important?" Elaine was starting to enjoy the role of teacher. "According to the book about wizards who fought dragons, there was no way a warrior or knight could fight a dragon without magic because they were magical creatures. The author proposed that all of the *fighters* who ever faced a dragon were either wizards or they were fighters with magical help, like magical weapons. Once magic was gone and the magic of dragons forgotten—well, as much as it could be—it was easy for the authors to do two things: make heroes who fought dragons without magic and to make dragons evil."

"Wait," Melissa interrupted, "you're saying that dragons and magic disappeared together?"

"Yes, and most of the positive stories about dragons were never told again, at least in Europe. The conspiracy doesn't seem to spread to Asia and the Americas. Helena's stories were always hidden in a niche. Her current stories were romances about dragons. That was why they sold so well. They were different. Every generation, she wrote positive tales of dragons who helped humans instead of subjugating them. Every generation, they were wildly popular. This was something that people wanted to believe. It seemed to be part of a shared consciousness, an archetype; and as you move farther and farther away from the point in history where dragons disappear it gets easier for people to accept that dragons could be intelligent and good."

"So why do dragons always end up evil?" Charles asked.

"Because, for generations there have been more people writing or continuing the bad tales, until recently."

"So, maybe that's why the spell failed this time." Kaliastrid joined the conversation, rubbing her temples. Aldrich stepped over to her and placed his hand on her shoulder. She looked over at him with a relieved look on her face.

Elaine nodded, picked up her point and explained it to everyone else. "Right, because humans, even humans who were really dragons, were able to see dragons in a positive way, so the pressure to keep them locked away relaxed on a subconscious level. Sooner or later the spell was going to fail."

"Heliantra…" Kaliastrid added and then shifted to her human name, "Helena knew that was going to happen. She expected the spell to fail."

Aldrich winced at the pain he was sharing with Kaliastrid. He reached his hand up and snapped his fingers at the sky as if he was frustrated, then opened his hand as if to let the pain he was feeling out of his hand. He grinned at Kaliastrid, and she nodded back to him.

"How do you know that Heliantra expected the spell to fail?" Melissa asked.

Kaliastrid shook her head and looked at her daughter with relief in her eyes. "I don't know I just do. Memories of Heliantra are coming back to me as Elaine is explaining."

"What does that mean?"

"I don't know," she answered.

Everyone watched them for a moment, waiting for an answer or another question. Neither of them continued, and finally Melissa looked back at Elaine to continue.

"The author of the book about wizards who fought dragons was Asian. He was the only one who would or could write something like that at the time. The Asians, you see, loved their dragons and hated to see them run down in literature. As soon as the West met the East and the cultures started to blend more, he wrote his book about how Europeans couldn't possibly be right about knights killing dragons. You can imagine it was not well received in Europe. The version of his book we have is a translation, and a good one from what I can tell. In the forward, the editor, who is never identified, indicated the text was actually banned by the Church. But, what's important is that he studied some interesting European folk tales that existed through the Dark Ages and used them to support his theories. One he referenced specifically was called *Heliantra's Ransom*."

Melissa, Kaliastrid and Charles all reacted to the title. "Right," Elaine said, smiling. "We all know that name from the more modern of Helena's novels. Helena and Heliantra are the same person, which makes my story even more likely. The old folk tale said..."

"You have it? You've read *Heliantra's Ransom*?"

"No. See, I don't think it ever really existed. If it did, it's not in this library. It's possible the author made it up as a reference to support his point. As I read his writing, it feels like he *lived* the events instead of just reading about them hundreds of years later. I thought that was impossible, but I've had to rethink possible since I've been reading books that Helena wrote over two hundred years ago. I expect the author was, like Helena, a dragon in human form. The lines between reality and fiction in these tales are very blurred. I couldn't really prove any of this."

Melissa shook her head in disappointment. "Go on."

"Anyway, the tale said that Heliantra was a popular, silvery-black dragon that lived in Europe and was considered good luck for the rulers of the regions around where France and Germany are now, Swabia. She had brought blessings to their land for generations, and she had helped humans in many ways until a new ruler appeared. The author highlighted the term 'ruler.' It is clear from the way everyone writes about him that he was not a king. He was not a fair man. The author argued that Heliantra knew the true source of his power, an ancient cult of dark wizard magic passed from one master wizard to the next but never shared beyond that. You see how all of this could be ignored as fairy tales if you discount the existence of magic? The cleansing of history was very complete."

Elaine paused and took a breath as if what she was about to say was harder than what she had revealed already. Aldrich nodded agreement with her and seemed ready to take in more of the tale. He stood with his hand still raised and monitored Kaliastrid and Melissa. Elaine looked to Charles for support as she prepared to go on, and he smiled at her and nodded.

"The author argued, well more than argued, he *stated* that Heliantra was helping this evil wizard."

Melissa and Kaliastrid growled at her words, but she bravely held up her hand to indicate there was more.

"In order to expose him for what he was and to end some kind of plot that he was part of, she was working with him, but in the end she was unable to stop him. The author suggests that she couldn't do what she should have done because she was in love with the wizard ruler."

Melissa and Kaliastrid inhaled sharply. Melissa shook her head in denial of the accusation about her grandmother.

"Before you get too excited, I can tell you that Helena as much as admits that she had affairs with humans in some of her earlier books," Elaine continued. "Based on what I now understand—Helena was Heliantra—her modern books actually talk about it openly. Her older books were more cautious with the talk of relationships with dragons, but those were the most telling because she could write her true feelings about the kings without admitting anything. So, it is possible that she fell in love with the wizard ruler who was acting like he needed her help. It is even possible that she was charmed."

"I'd believe that before I believe that she..." Melissa started but couldn't finish.

"I think you're closer than we want to admit." Kaliastrid nodded. Her eyes seemed to be telling something more. Aldrich grimaced and wiggled his fingers in the air.

"What, mother? What are you saying?"

"Just, there were times, before I was human and forgot all of this, that Heliantra shared things with me. She was ashamed of how she felt about someone. I never realized what she was saying. I never realized it was him. Melissa, I've only just remembered. Forgive me; I had no intention of deceiving you. Thank you, Aldrich."

He planted his feet into a slightly wider stance and nodded back at her.

Melissa couldn't be mad at her. Her memories were as fractured as anyone's. It was clear she was fighting pain to pull these memories out, and Aldrich was somehow enabling her deep dive into her mind. Melissa's own spikes were suddenly subdued, but she could not find any memories to corroborate what Kasliastrid was saying. A flash of pain nearly knocked her out of her chair then subsided as Aldrich looked at her meekly and seemed to transport the pain from her directly into the air. When the pain receded, she saw a courtyard of a smaller castle. She saw the late evening sun falling over its walls. It looked deserted, but she knew it was not. It was the same castle from her flying dream. She knew someone was there waiting for her.

"Mother. She realized what was happening didn't she? She realized he was using her." She looked into her mother's eyes as they shared a vision.

"Too late, I think, she realized that he was dangerous and she had to react to fix what she had allowed to happen."

"He trapped her," Elaine said. "According to Wy Li, the wizard trapped her and requested a ransom for her release. He requested the heart of the dragons. I thought he was just being metaphorical, but he literally meant something very important to the dragons, didn't he?"

"Who? Who did you say?"

Elaine looked at Kaliastrid eyes, wide, unsure of what she was asking as she was working through her own question.

"What name did you say?" Kaliastrid had a surprised look on her face as well.

"Wy Li? Lung Wy Li. He's the author of the book I was talking about."

Kaliastrid laughed. "Lung Wy Li is most certainly a dragon. In fact, he's the oldest Emperor Dragon. He would have some idea of what he's saying. What else does Wy Li have to say?"

Melissa had a vision of a long blue dragon standing in the outer courtyard of the castle depicted in the mural above their heads. He was delivering a long scroll to Heliantra and Kaliasrtid. She looked up for a moment and stared at her grandmother's dragon face. Her tail was wrapped around the castle and the very tip was either touching or hovering just above an egg encrusted with gems and sitting on a tripod that looked like a tail and two claws emerging from it.

When she looked back down, Kaliastrid was looking at her and then together they looked up at the ceiling mural. When their eyes met again, there was realization in them. Melissa released her mother's gaze but could feel the shared emptiness that had haunted her right after the emergence. She had been able to ignore it over time, but with the pain in her mind relaxed, she could feel the deep emptiness return. Where was the talisman? She looked to Elaine to continue her tale.

"What else?"

"What are you two thinking?" Charles asked.

Melissa kept the secret to herself and shook her head. She knew they were close to an answer. She knew they were close to figuring out why the spell had been cast.

"Nothing yet, keep going, Elaine."

"Right, that's the thing. I can't. The story ends there, or at least all I've been able to find so far. Wy Li just says that the ruler asked for the ransom, but he disappears and the story ends. Either no one wrote an end to the story or the ending was intentionally obscured. I think the ending was hidden for some reason that no one has ever explained. I think Helena was about to tell it. That was where her next book was going. It was turning out to be the tell-all on what happened. As you know, its title is *Renard's Payment*, but it's an incomplete manuscript. It's filled with errors, misspellings and ramblings that make it nearly impossible to read. I've not been able to make any sense of it. Quite disappointing, too."

Everyone sighed with Elaine's revelation about the manuscript, but she continued.

"The wizard ruler Wy Li was talking about was named Reynard. Too close to ignore, right? He was powerful, and he was in her last book as the dark brother to a prince who was in line to be king, if his brother died. The dark brother, Renard, was into something sinister, but she never revealed what it was in that book. In the end of Helena's last book Herald disappeared, and the king believed Renard had something to do with it. The king asked Heliantra for help finding his son. She agreed to help before she realized it meant she had to find out if Renard was involved. She was interested in the darker brother if not involved with him. In fact, she implied that Heliantra might have been involved with the plot Renard had crafted to remove his brother from the line of succession."

"Oh. My." Kaliastrid stood up and walked over to the window.

"What?" Charles asked.

"He wasn't dead. Renard had captured him and locked him away in the dungeon of his castle. Heliantra was going to rescue him. She told me that Renard was going to kill him and that it was her fault. Renard planned to ransom him, but he would not hesitate to kill him. That was the night before she went to rescue him. I never saw her again."

"Why didn't she tell me that? I had no idea," Melissa asked her mother's back and got no answer.

"So, what happened?" Charles asked, looking at Elaine.

She raised her hands to indicate she had no idea where the story went from there.

Aldrich shifted from speaker to speaker, trying not to miss any critical detail and continued to siphon pain from the dragons.

Kaliastrid answered for her. "Renard caught Heliantra trying to release his brother. She was captured. The brother was a trap to see if Heliantra really loved him. He had figured out she was a dragon, or he had known all along because his father knew. She was the key to the Great Wyrm because she was the ambassador. This was not common knowledge. The king knew nothing about the Great Wyrm, so how Renard knew surprised us all. But he knew and he also knew she was his key to the power of dragons, the Heart of the

Dragon. With her, her scepter and the Heart of the Dragon he could control us all. He could control magic."

"This scepter?" Melissa held up the pendant.

"Yes." Kaliastrid looked back from the window with tears flowing down her cheeks. Melissa felt a little jealous for a moment. Why did her mother know this and she had no idea? She looked up at her with the question on her face. "I don't know why you don't know. I don't know why I've spent centuries in my human form hating Helena. I was her friend, apparently her very close friend, and you were her choice to be ambassador. I only know now that she trusted this story to me before she went to save Herald. She was ashamed of what she had done, and she couldn't disappoint you with her failure. She said knowing the truth would make your task harder. I never understood what she meant, not until just now."

Melissa looked down at her hands. She couldn't look at her mother, who was obviously suffering with the pain of betraying her daughter. Aldrich had freed them to wander in memories blocked before, but he would not be able to funnel their pain away much longer. He was turning pale.

"Meliastrid, you were her selected replacement. She was teaching you and you couldn't be corrupted by her shortcomings. That's why you cast the spell, but she had to recast it each time it expired." Kaliastrid turned to look out the window again.

Elaine, who had been the storyteller sat down to listen to this part.

"There was no choice, his ransom was something dragons couldn't surrender. It took all the magic we knew or could call on to cast the spell. Heliantra had worked on the spell with the Great Wyrm as she maneuvered to stop Renard. He wanted the talisman. If he had it and Heliantra, he had unimaginable power. We couldn't let him have it. As a race and at the instruction of the Great Wyrm, we cast the spell." Kaliastrid turned to look at Melissa with the look of consolation in her eyes. "You were just the voice of the spell. We all had to agree to the entrapment in order for the magic to work." She turned back to look out at the grave as she continued her tale. "We, dragons, had to trap Renard with the one thing he would be blind to. He had to think he was getting his ransom. He had to think he had won. He had to believe it. Heliantra knew that. She knew he had to think he had dragons trapped in an unwinnable situation. We trapped him with his own greed and our sacrifice. Now, oh what have we released on this land?"

Kaliastrid covered her eyes and sobbed. Melissa realized suddenly what she meant. With the dragons emerged, it meant that something far worse than a few half-dragons was loose now. The spell and the dragon sacrifice that was meant to trap him was broken. That was why it was critical for Melissa to cast the spell again as the first act as she took over as ambassador. That was why it was critical that she not fail. Melissa had not only released the worst evil dragons had ever faced onto the world, she had dumped the dragons into a world they were not prepared for with a broken memory of the past and a burning desire to fix what was wrong. The one fact that redeemed her for casting the spell was lost in fractured dragon memories.

She stood up from her chair and turned to leave the room. Both Charles and Aldrich started to follow her, and she waved them both away. She needed to be alone. She now knew the answer, and she was more afraid than she had ever been. It was not about dragons. It was not as simple as why had they been trapped in human form. Where was the Talisman? Where was the last human, the only human, to ever possess it? It was not in her control like it should be. Now she understood what was missing. Now she understood what she and other dragons were longing for but could not reach. There had to be an answer. Heliantra had to have a plan. She always had a plan. What had her mentor planned to do when the spell failed. Kaliastrid said she expected it to fail. What was the backup plan?

At the foot of the stairs, Melissa opened the door and walked down the yard to Heliantra's grave.

"Why didn't you trust me? Would it have mattered if I had known? Did I know it all and just can't remember it? You had to carry all of this alone for so long."

Melissa sat down on the grass next to the headstone and waited for another sunset. She needed to be alone for a while to figure out what to do about her failure.

ABOUT THE AUTHOR

T.D. Raufson spent his childhood as a software engineer and project manager. Once he finally figured out what he wanted to do when he grew up, he focused on writing his favorite kind of stories and sharing them with the world. He currently lives in Tennessee with his wife and three cats while searching for time to write all of the other stories he has never been able to write.

Made in the USA
Columbia, SC
14 January 2022